THE
COURAGEOUS
PRINCESS ™

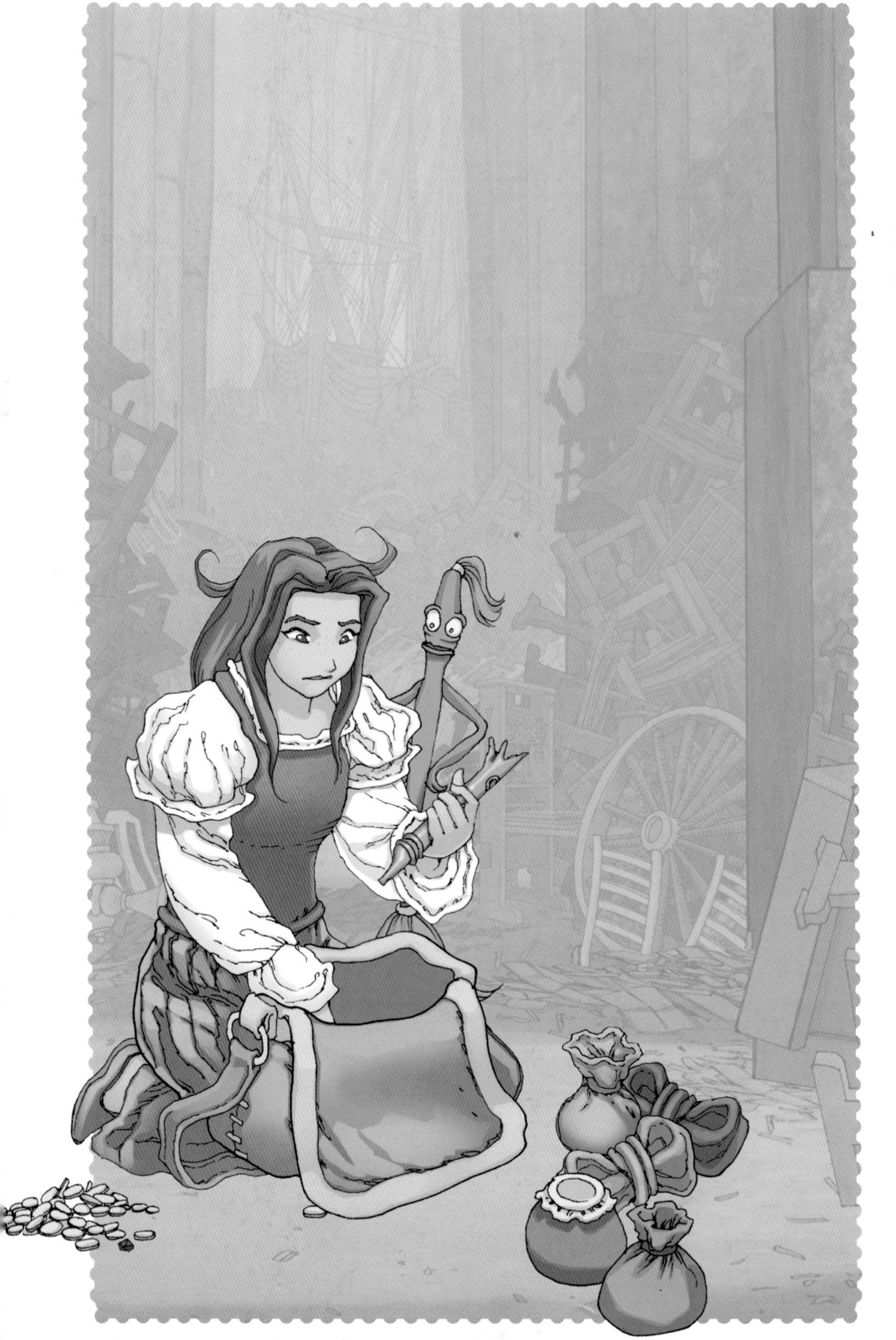

THE
COURAGEOUS
PRINCESS™

VOLUME 3

THE DRAGON QUEEN

BY
ROD ESPINOSA

DARK HORSE BOOKS

president and publisher
MIKE RICHARDSON

editor
RANDY STRADLEY

assistant editor
FREDDYE LINS

collection designer
TINA ALESSI

NEIL HANKERSON Executive Vice President TOM WEDDLE Chief Financial Officer RANDY STRADLEY
Vice President of Publishing MICHAEL MARTENS Vice President of Book Trade Sales SCOTT ALLIE Editor
in Chief MATT PARKINSON Vice President of Marketing DAVID SCROGGY Vice President of Product
Development DALE LAFOUNTAIN Vice President of Information Technology DARLENE VOGEL Senior
Director of Print, Design, and Production KEN LIZZI General Counsel DAVEY ESTRADA Editorial Director
CHRIS WARNER Senior Books Editor CARY GRAZZINI Director of Print and Development LIA RIBACCHI
Art Director CARA NIECE Director of Scheduling MARK BERNARDI Director of Digital Publishing

THE COURAGEOUS PRINCESS VOLUME 3: The Dragon Queen

Published by Dark Horse Books
A division of Dark Horse Comics, Inc.
10956 SE Main Street | Milwaukie, OR 97222

DarkHorse.com
International Licensing: 503-905-2377
To find a comics shop in your area, call the Comic Shop Locator Service toll-free at 1-888-266-4226.

Library of Congress Cataloging-in-Publication Data

Espinosa, Rod.
 Courageous princess / by Rod Espinosa.
   volumes cm
  Summary: "The plucky Princess Mabelrose uses brains and bravery when she is
kidnapped from her home by a greedy dragon. Rather than wait to be rescued,
Mabelrose finds the courage to save herself"--Provided by publisher
 Contents: v. 1: Beyond the Hundred Kingdoms -- v. 2 The Unremembered
Lands -- v. 3 The Dragon Queen.
  ISBN 978-1-61655-722-5 (volume 1) -- ISBN 978-1-61655-723-2 (volume 2)
-- ISBN 978-1-61655-724-9 (volume 3)
 1. Graphic novels. [1. Graphic novels. 2. Princesses--Fiction.] I. Title.

PZ7.7.E87Co 2015
741.5'973--dc23

2014037517

First edition: September 2015
ISBN 978-1-61655-724-9
1 3 5 7 9 10 8 6 4 2
Printed in China

*To you who delight in telling,
sharing, listening to, and reading stories,
and who love happy, joyful endings.
Till we meet again.*

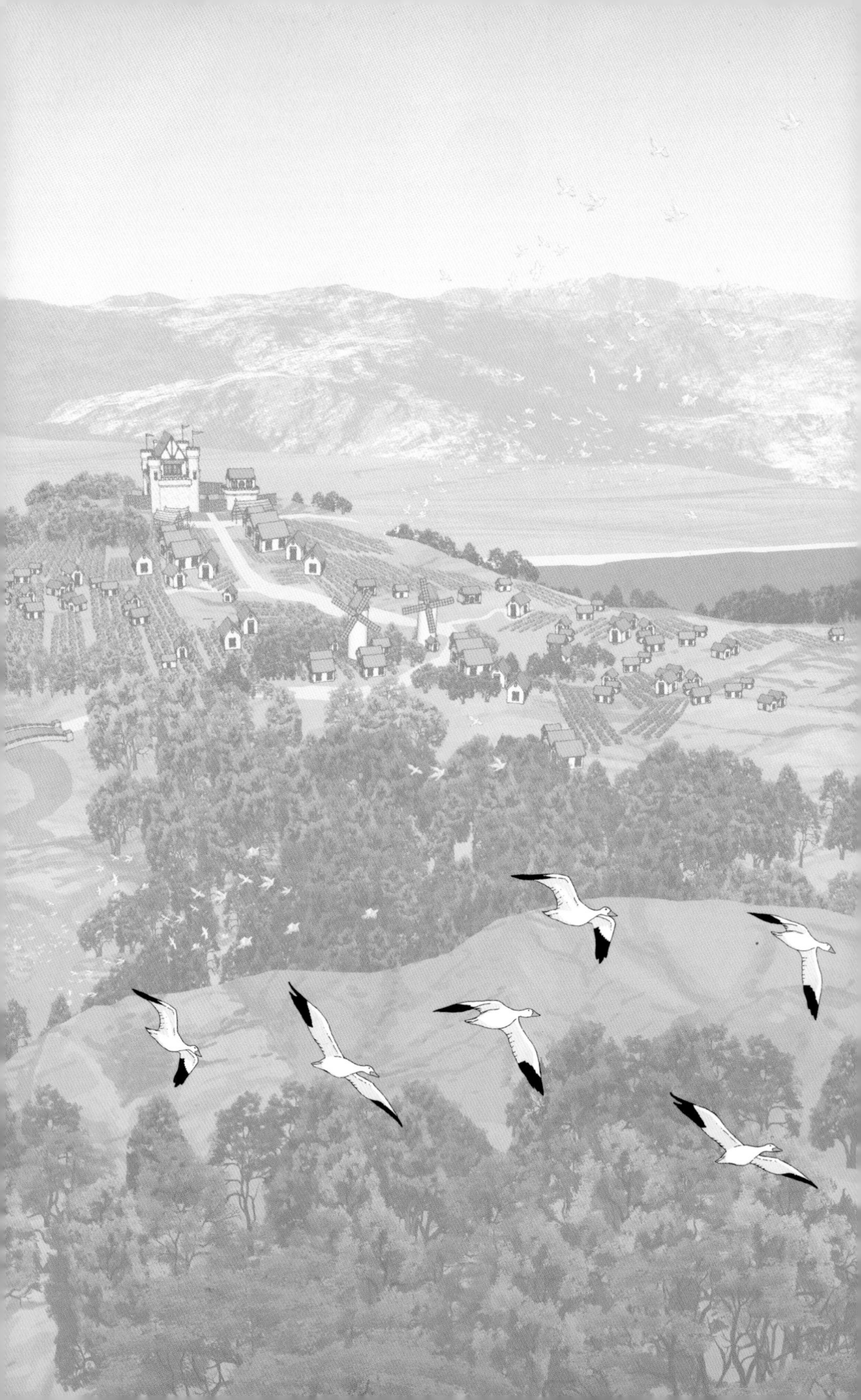

THE STORY THUS FAR . . .

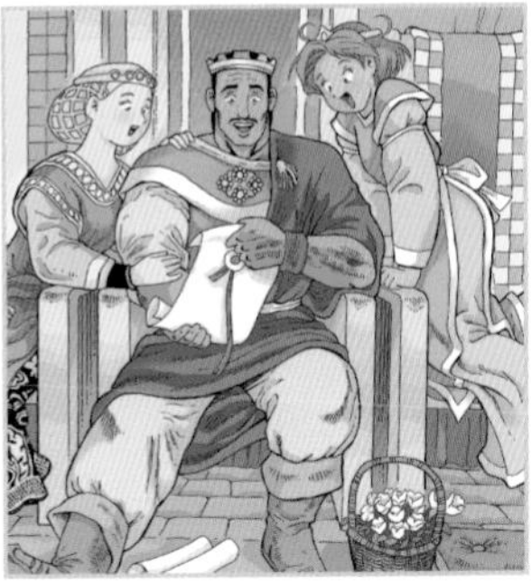

Once upon a time, at the northwestern edge of the land known as the Hundred Kingdoms, there was the tiny kingdom of New Tinsley. In this kingdom there lived a princess, Mabelrose, loved for her good heart and charitable nature. For, though she was not as beautiful, or as talented, or as rich as the princesses from other kingdoms, King Jeryk and Queen Helena had always made sure that Mabelrose was taught that courage, wisdom, and love were more important than any circumstance of birth.

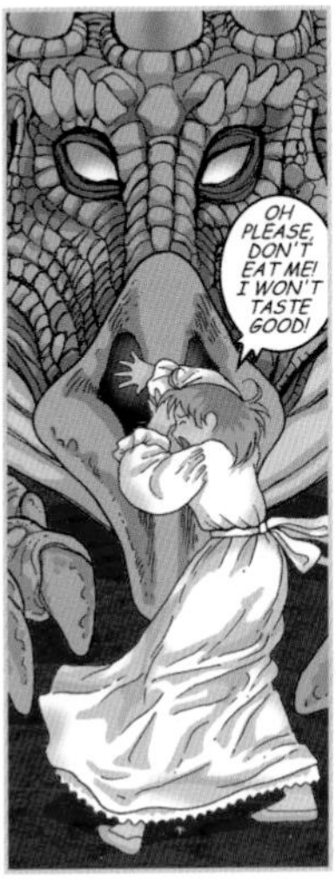
OH PLEASE, DON'T EAT ME! I WON'T TASTE GOOD!

These lessons served Mabelrose well when she was kidnapped by the dragon Shalathrumnostrium and carried far away to the south, to the ruins of the Briar Kingdom.

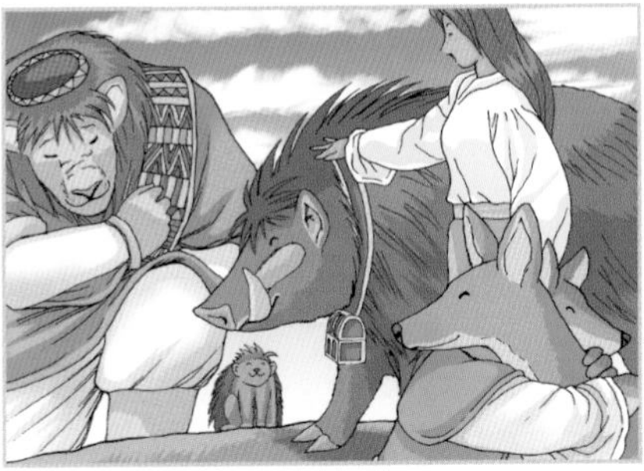

Mabelrose knew her parents would search for her, but she was also aware that they had no idea where to look for her. So she decided to rescue herself!

With the help of a hedgehog named Spiky and a magical rope, Princess Mabelrose was able to escape the dragon's realm and begin making her way home. Along the way she had many adventures and helped and inspired many new friends with her intelligence and bravery.

Meanwhile, King Jeryk had assembled a team of brave and talented companions to aid him in his quest to find his daughter.

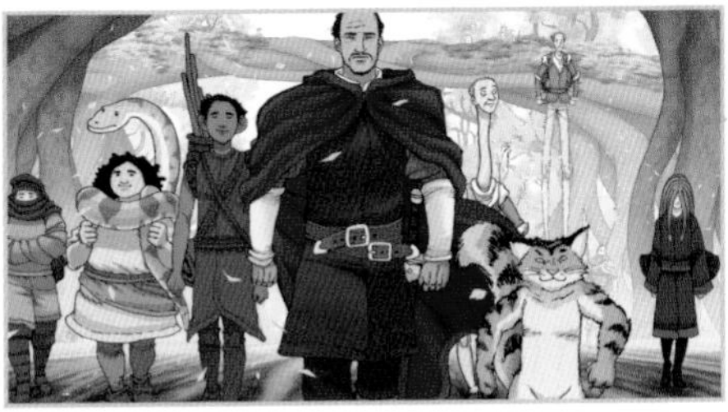

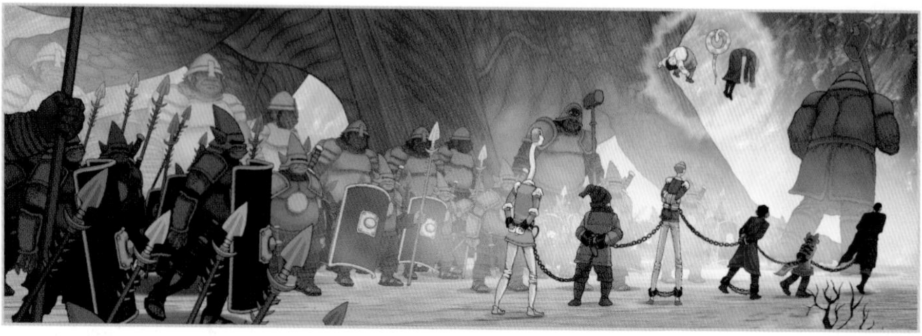

They crossed into the Land of the Giants—where they battled giants, were ultimately defeated, and were taken prisoner by the mighty dragon Orogigantum,

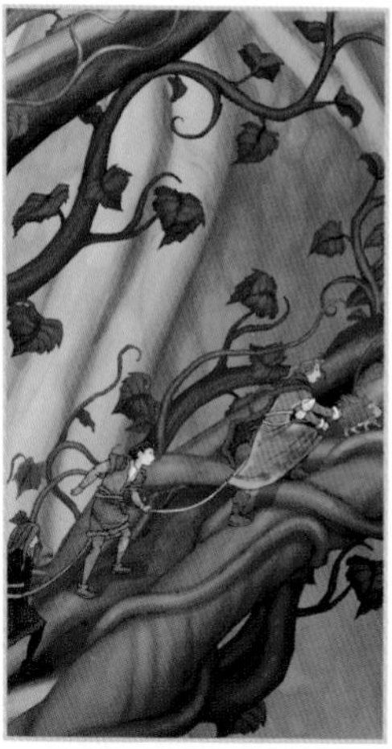

who escorted them to Cloud Castle, floating high above the Unremembered Lands.

When Mabelrose learned of her father's plight, she and her companions climbed a giant beanstalk to Cloud Castle and battled the castle's defenders.

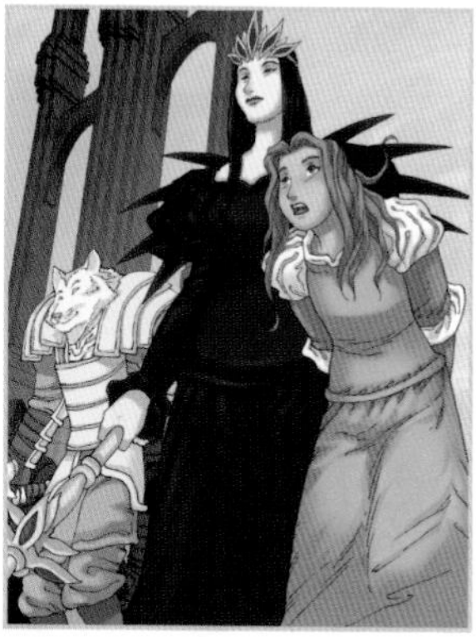

But just when she was reunited with her father, they were both astounded to discover that the person behind all of their troubles was Mabelrose's aunt Ursula!

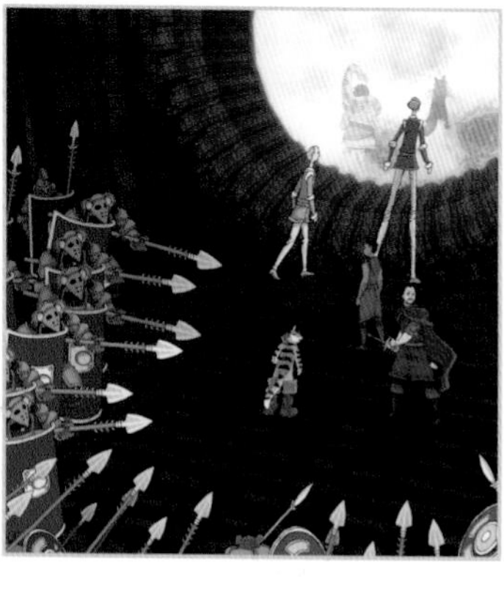

To save his daughter's life, King Jeryk and his friends laid down their weapons and were forced to enter a magical portal to the Lands of No Return.

Mabelrose was now alone with her Aunt and trapped in Cloud Castle . . .

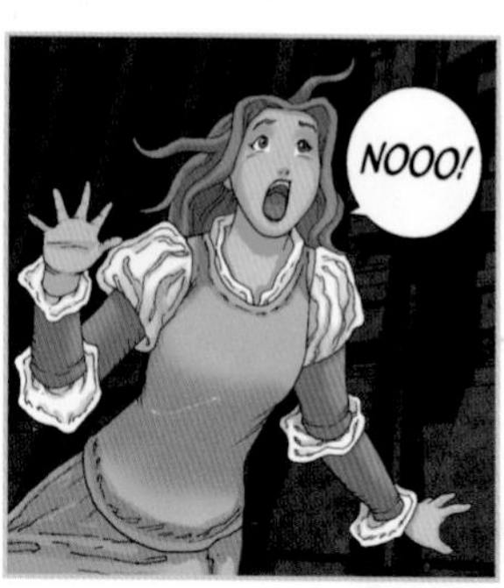
NOOO!

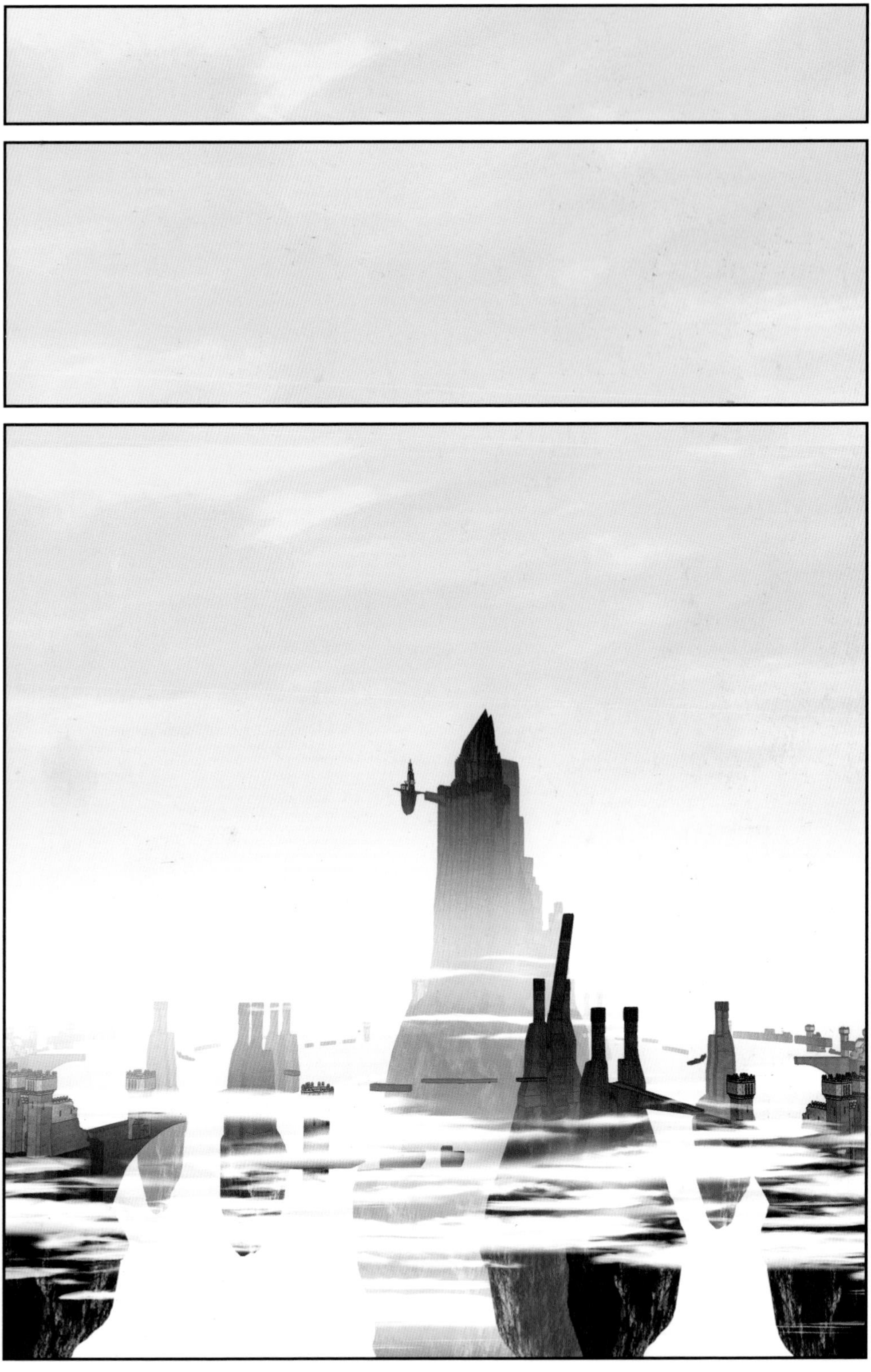

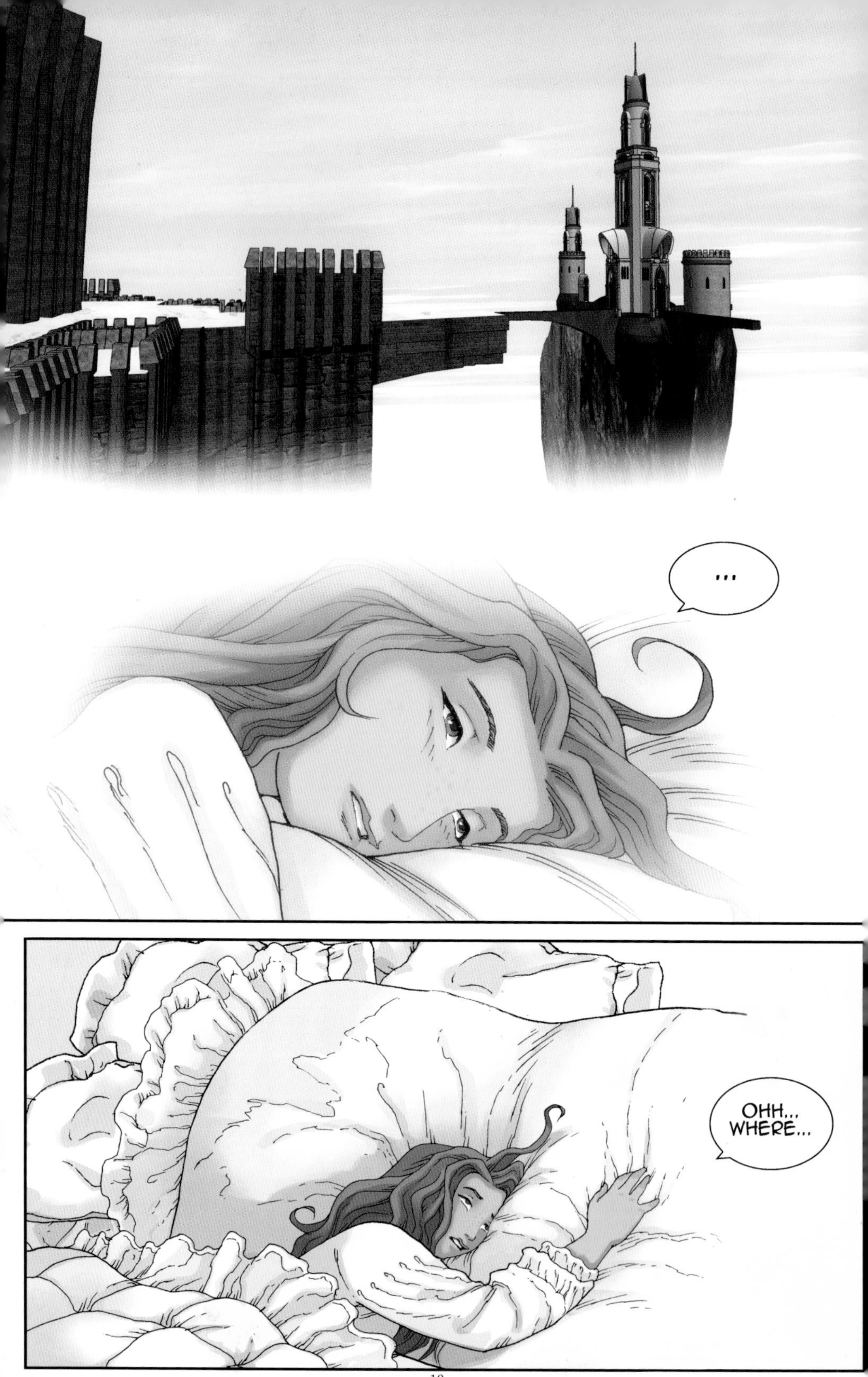
...
OHH... WHERE...

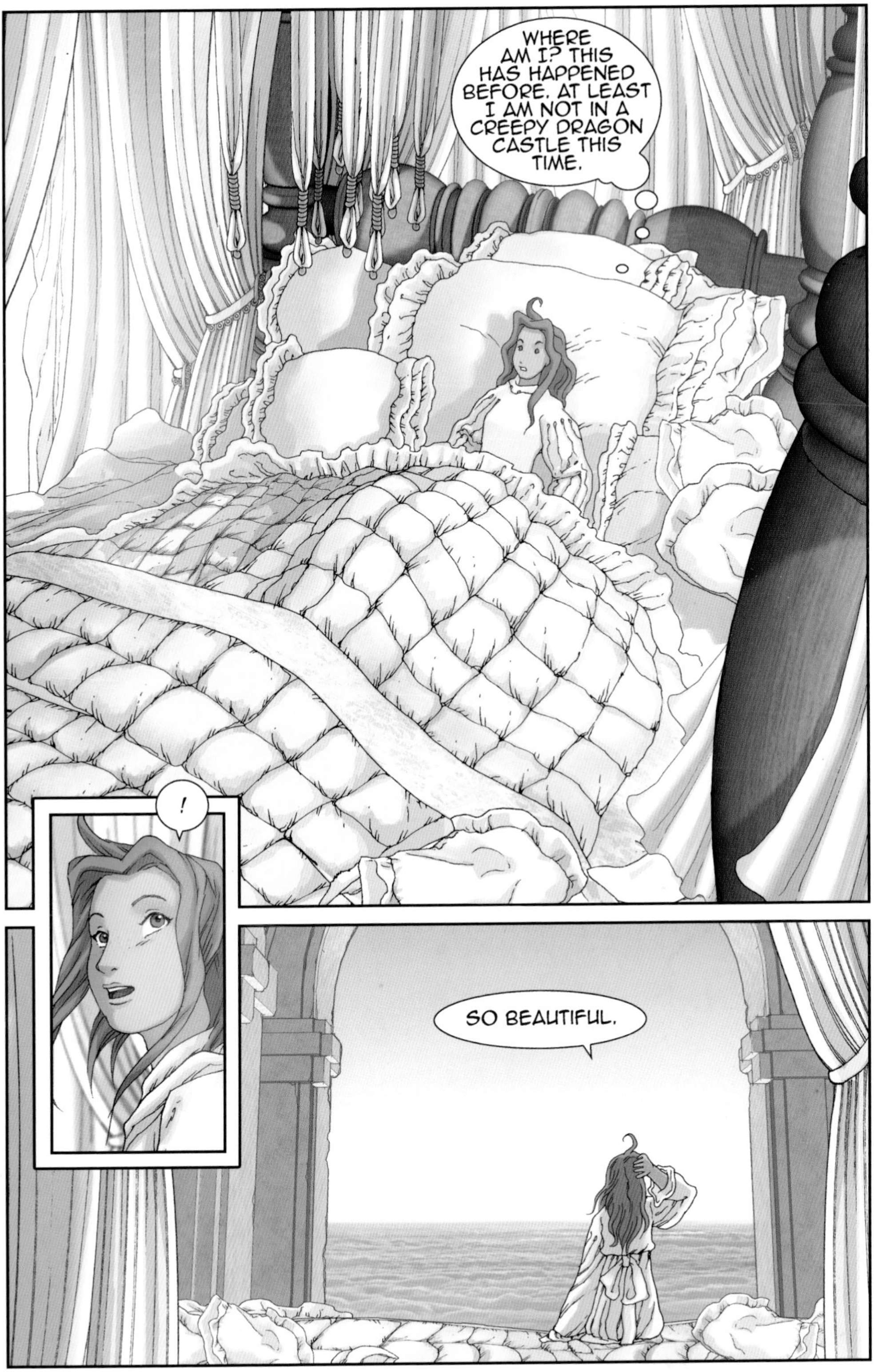
WHERE AM I? THIS HAS HAPPENED BEFORE. AT LEAST I AM NOT IN A CREEPY DRAGON CASTLE THIS TIME.
!
SO BEAUTIFUL.

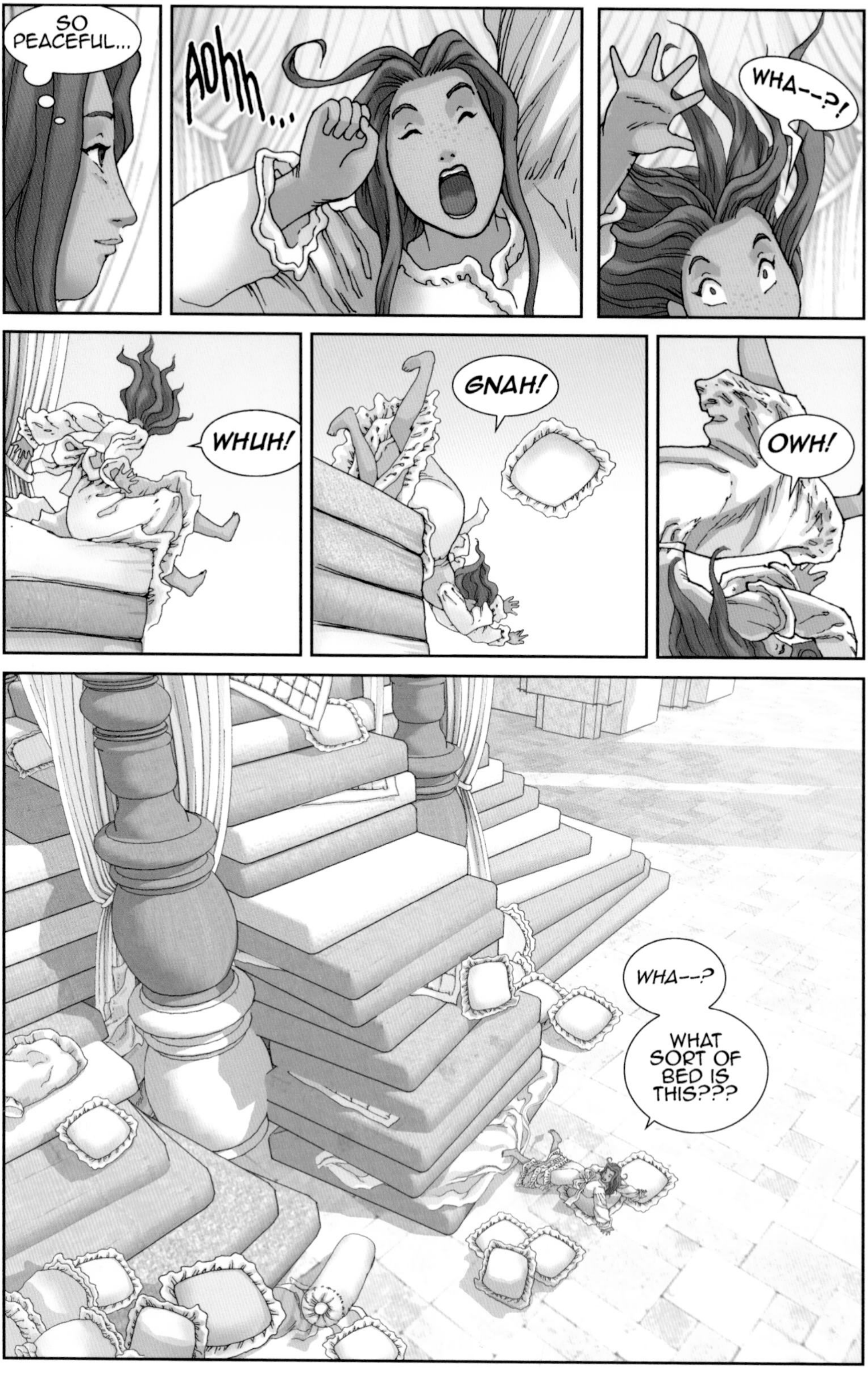
SO PEACEFUL...
AOHH...
WHA--?!
WHUH!
GNAH!
OWH!
WHA--?
WHAT SORT OF BED IS THIS???

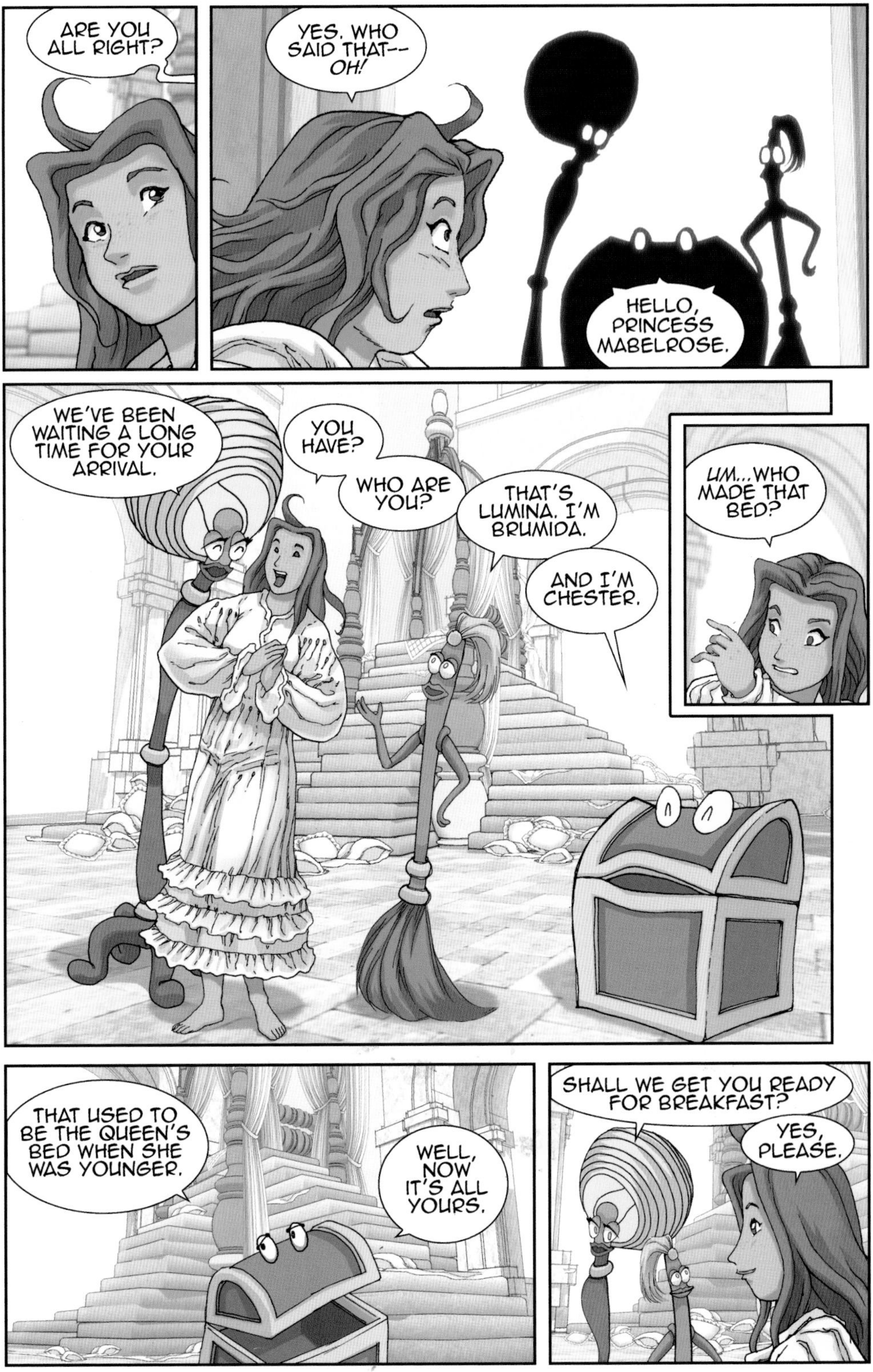
ARE YOU ALL RIGHT?
YES. WHO SAID THAT-- OH!
HELLO, PRINCESS MABELROSE.
WE'VE BEEN WAITING A LONG TIME FOR YOUR ARRIVAL.
YOU HAVE?
WHO ARE YOU?
THAT'S LUMINA. I'M BRUMIDA.
AND I'M CHESTER.
UM...WHO MADE THAT BED?
THAT USED TO BE THE QUEEN'S BED WHEN SHE WAS YOUNGER.
WELL, NOW IT'S ALL YOURS.
SHALL WE GET YOU READY FOR BREAKFAST?
YES, PLEASE.

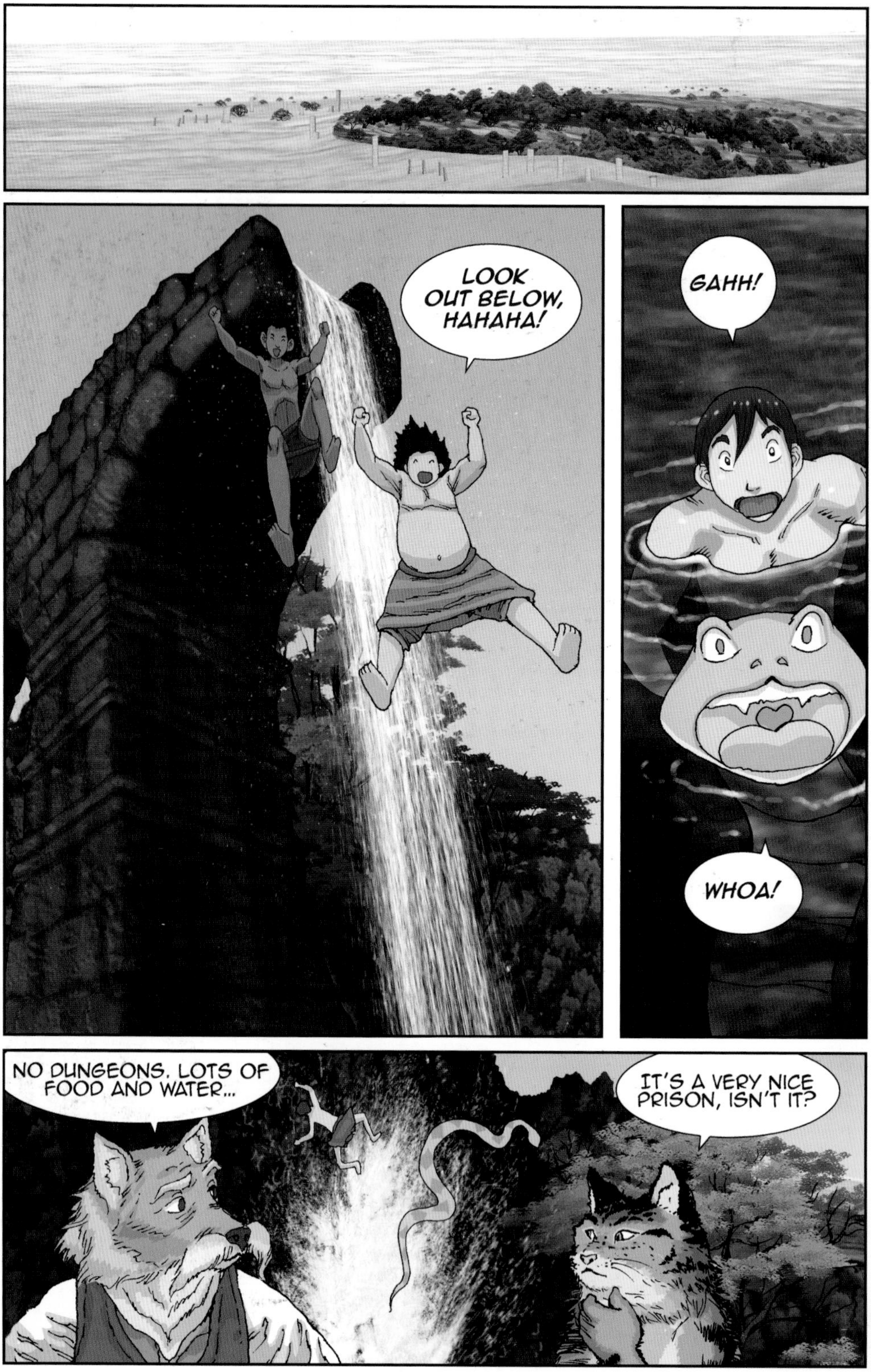
LOOK OUT BELOW, HAHAHA!
GAHH!
WHOA!
NO DUNGEONS. LOTS OF FOOD AND WATER...
IT'S A VERY NICE PRISON, ISN'T IT?

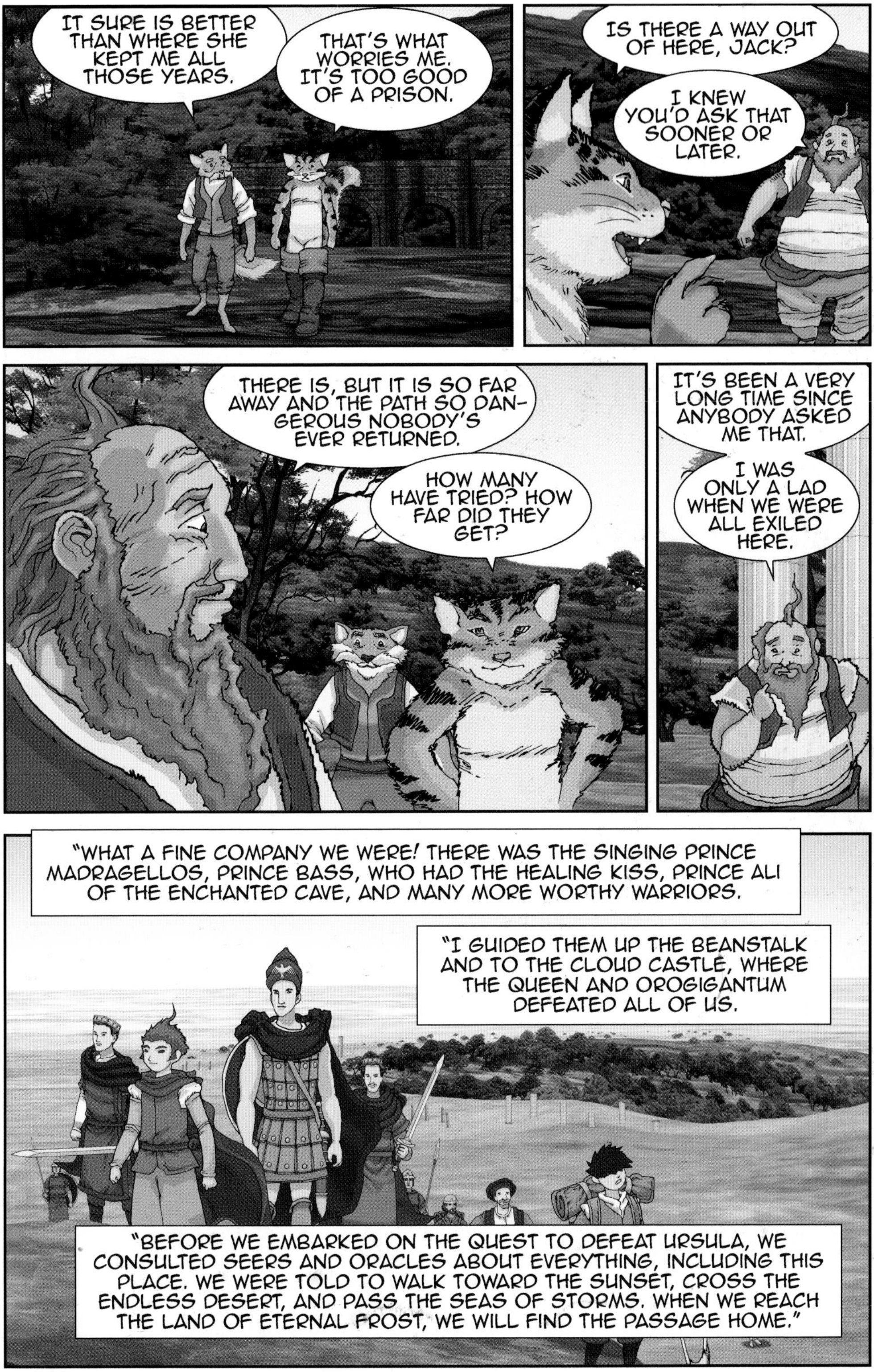

IT SURE IS BETTER THAN WHERE SHE KEPT ME ALL THOSE YEARS.
THAT'S WHAT WORRIES ME. IT'S TOO GOOD OF A PRISON.
IS THERE A WAY OUT OF HERE, JACK?
I KNEW YOU'D ASK THAT SOONER OR LATER.
THERE IS, BUT IT IS SO FAR AWAY AND THE PATH SO DANGEROUS NOBODY'S EVER RETURNED.
HOW MANY HAVE TRIED? HOW FAR DID THEY GET?
IT'S BEEN A VERY LONG TIME SINCE ANYBODY ASKED ME THAT.
I WAS ONLY A LAD WHEN WE WERE ALL EXILED HERE.
"WHAT A FINE COMPANY WE WERE! THERE WAS THE SINGING PRINCE MADRAGELLOS, PRINCE BASS, WHO HAD THE HEALING KISS, PRINCE ALI OF THE ENCHANTED CAVE, AND MANY MORE WORTHY WARRIORS.
"I GUIDED THEM UP THE BEANSTALK AND TO THE CLOUD CASTLE, WHERE THE QUEEN AND OROGIGANTUM DEFEATED ALL OF US.
"BEFORE WE EMBARKED ON THE QUEST TO DEFEAT URSULA, WE CONSULTED SEERS AND ORACLES ABOUT EVERYTHING, INCLUDING THIS PLACE. WE WERE TOLD TO WALK TOWARD THE SUNSET, CROSS THE ENDLESS DESERT, AND PASS THE SEAS OF STORMS. WHEN WE REACH THE LAND OF ETERNAL FROST, WE WILL FIND THE PASSAGE HOME."

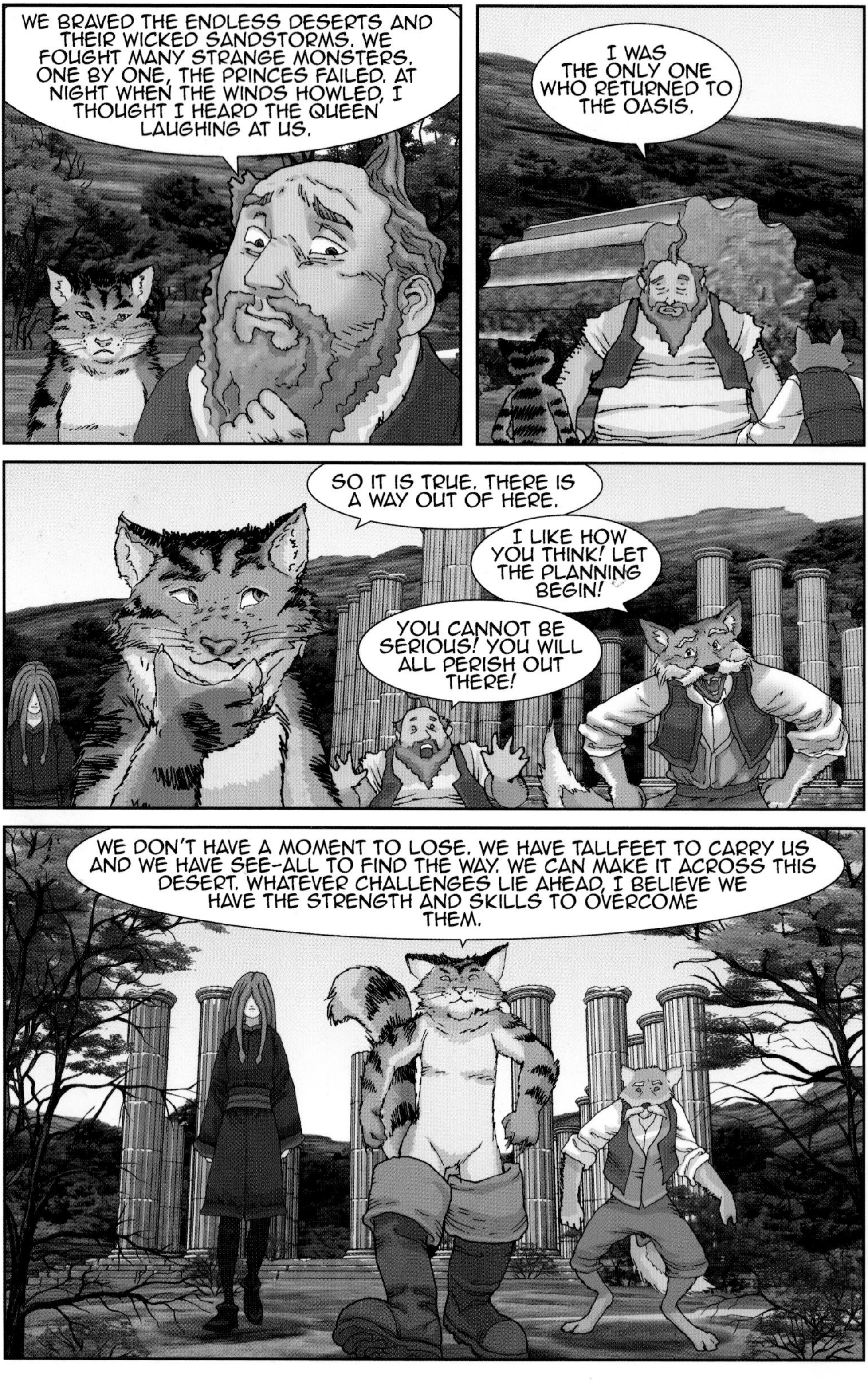
WE BRAVED THE ENDLESS DESERTS AND THEIR WICKED SANDSTORMS. WE FOUGHT MANY STRANGE MONSTERS. ONE BY ONE, THE PRINCES FAILED. AT NIGHT WHEN THE WINDS HOWLED, I THOUGHT I HEARD THE QUEEN LAUGHING AT US.
I WAS THE ONLY ONE WHO RETURNED TO THE OASIS.
SO IT IS TRUE. THERE IS A WAY OUT OF HERE.
I LIKE HOW YOU THINK! LET THE PLANNING BEGIN!
YOU CANNOT BE SERIOUS! YOU WILL ALL PERISH OUT THERE!
WE DON'T HAVE A MOMENT TO LOSE. WE HAVE TALLFEET TO CARRY US AND WE HAVE SEE-ALL TO FIND THE WAY. WE CAN MAKE IT ACROSS THIS DESERT. WHATEVER CHALLENGES LIE AHEAD, I BELIEVE WE HAVE THE STRENGTH AND SKILLS TO OVERCOME THEM.

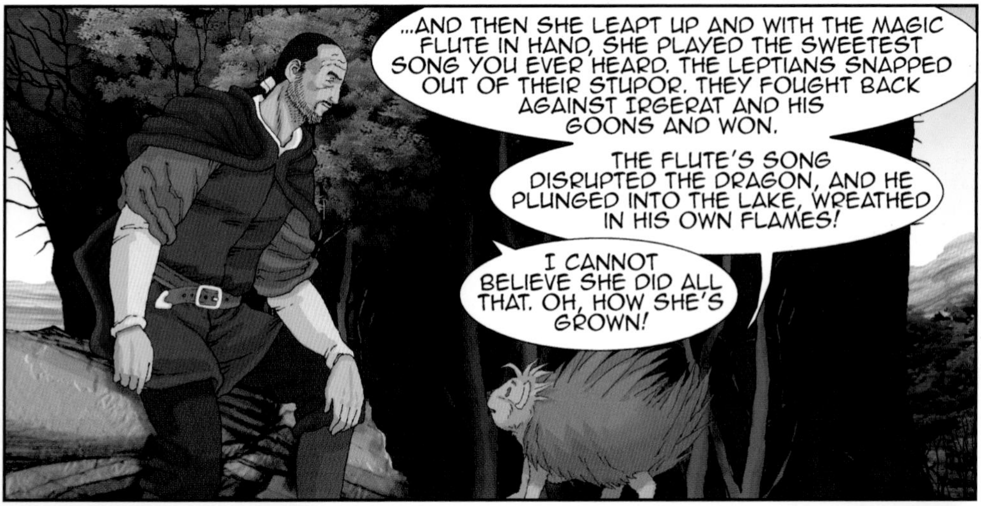
...AND THEN SHE LEAPT UP AND WITH THE MAGIC FLUTE IN HAND, SHE PLAYED THE SWEETEST SONG YOU EVER HEARD. THE LEPTIANS SNAPPED OUT OF THEIR STUPOR. THEY FOUGHT BACK AGAINST IRGERAT AND HIS GOONS AND WON.
THE FLUTE'S SONG DISRUPTED THE DRAGON, AND HE PLUNGED INTO THE LAKE, WREATHED IN HIS OWN FLAMES!
I CANNOT BELIEVE SHE DID ALL THAT. OH, HOW SHE'S GROWN!

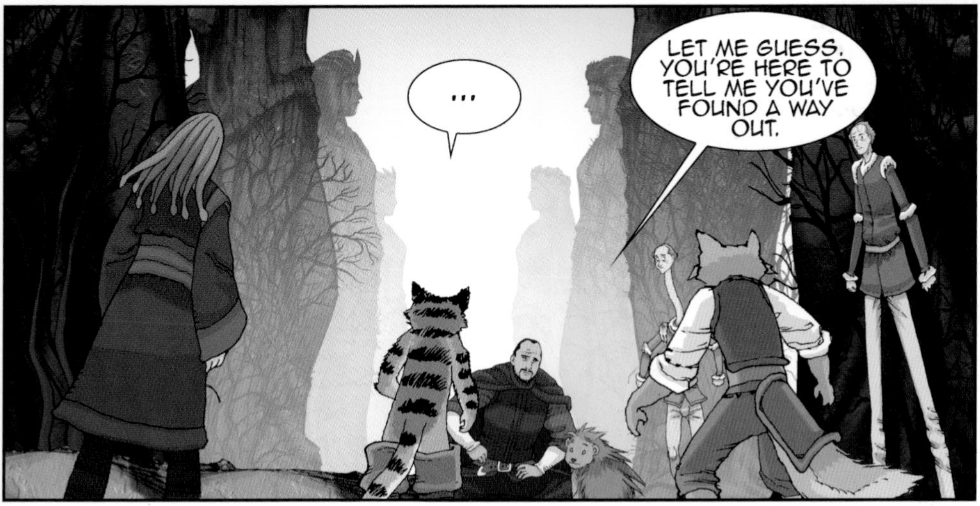
...
LET ME GUESS. YOU'RE HERE TO TELL ME YOU'VE FOUND A WAY OUT.

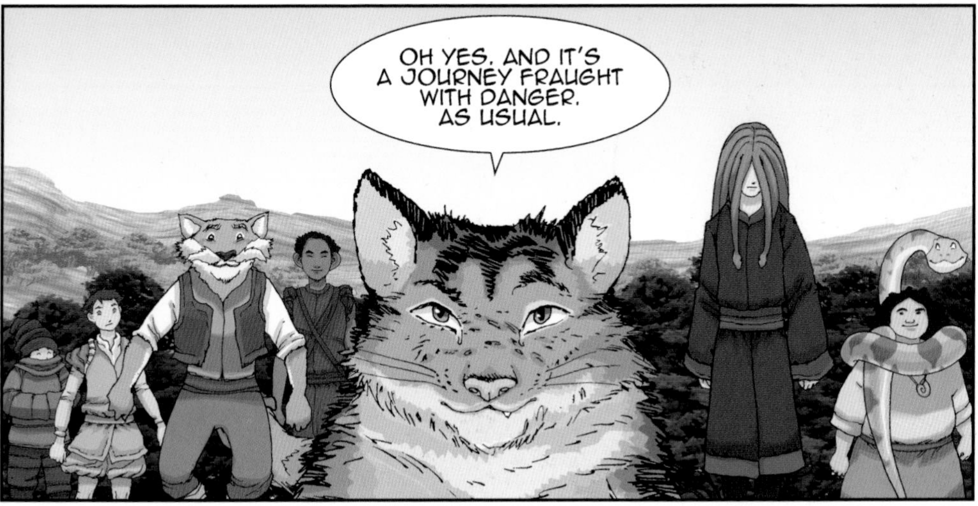
OH YES. AND IT'S A JOURNEY FRAUGHT WITH DANGER. AS USUAL.

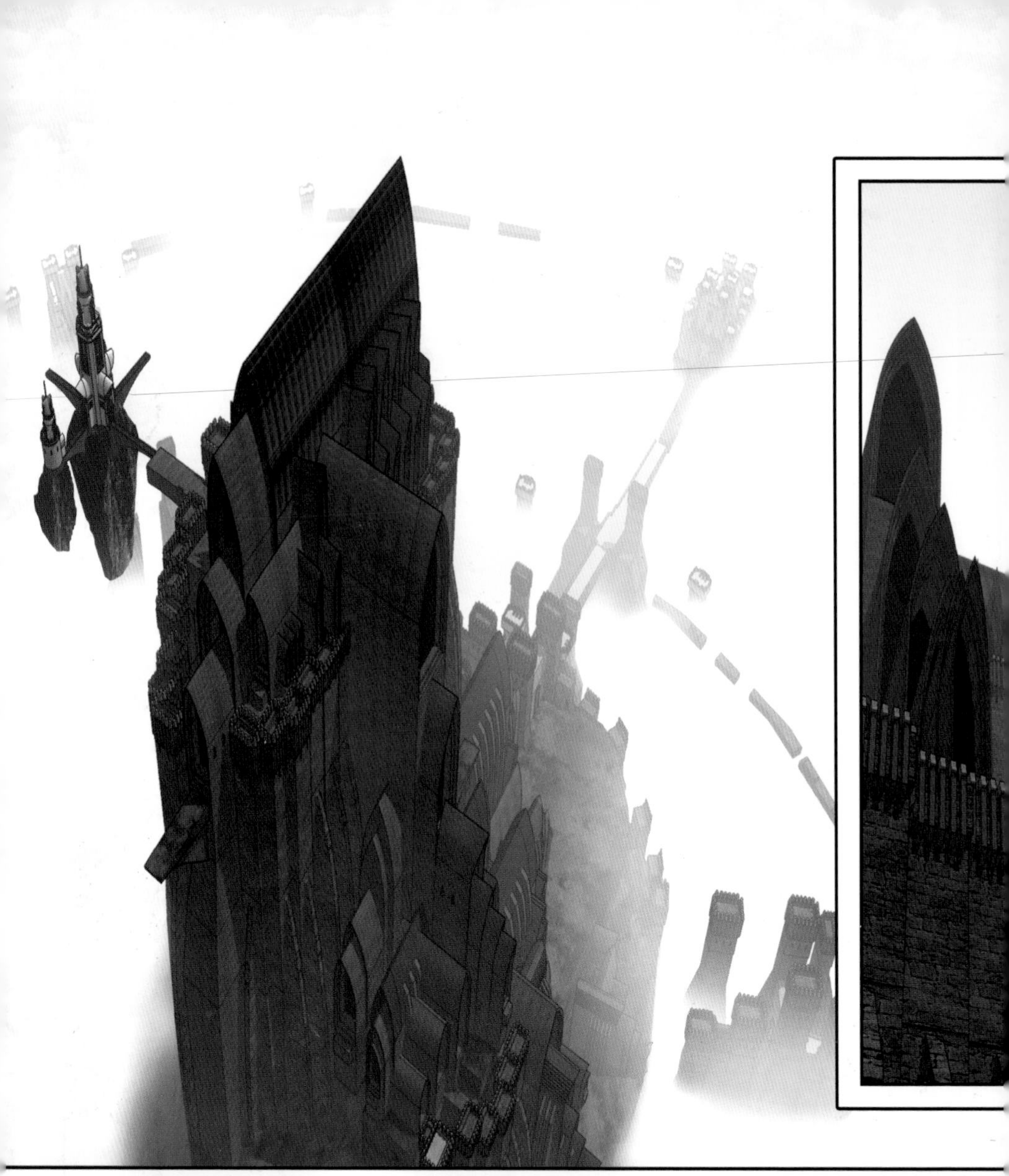

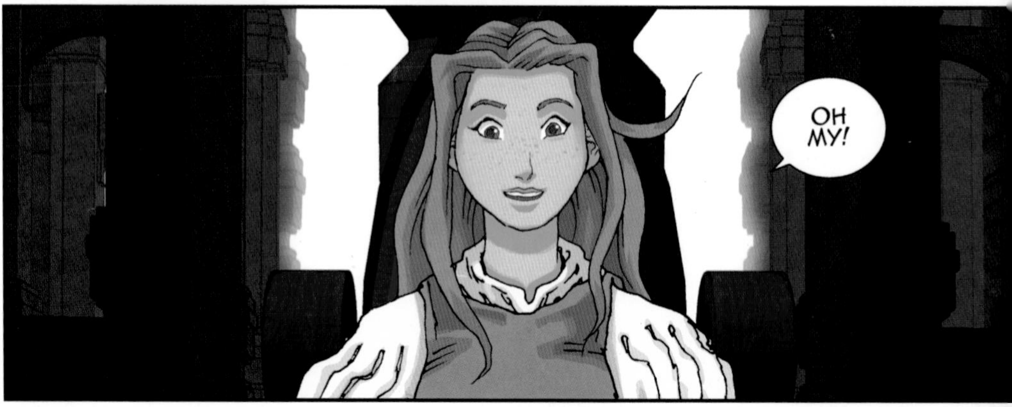
OH MY!

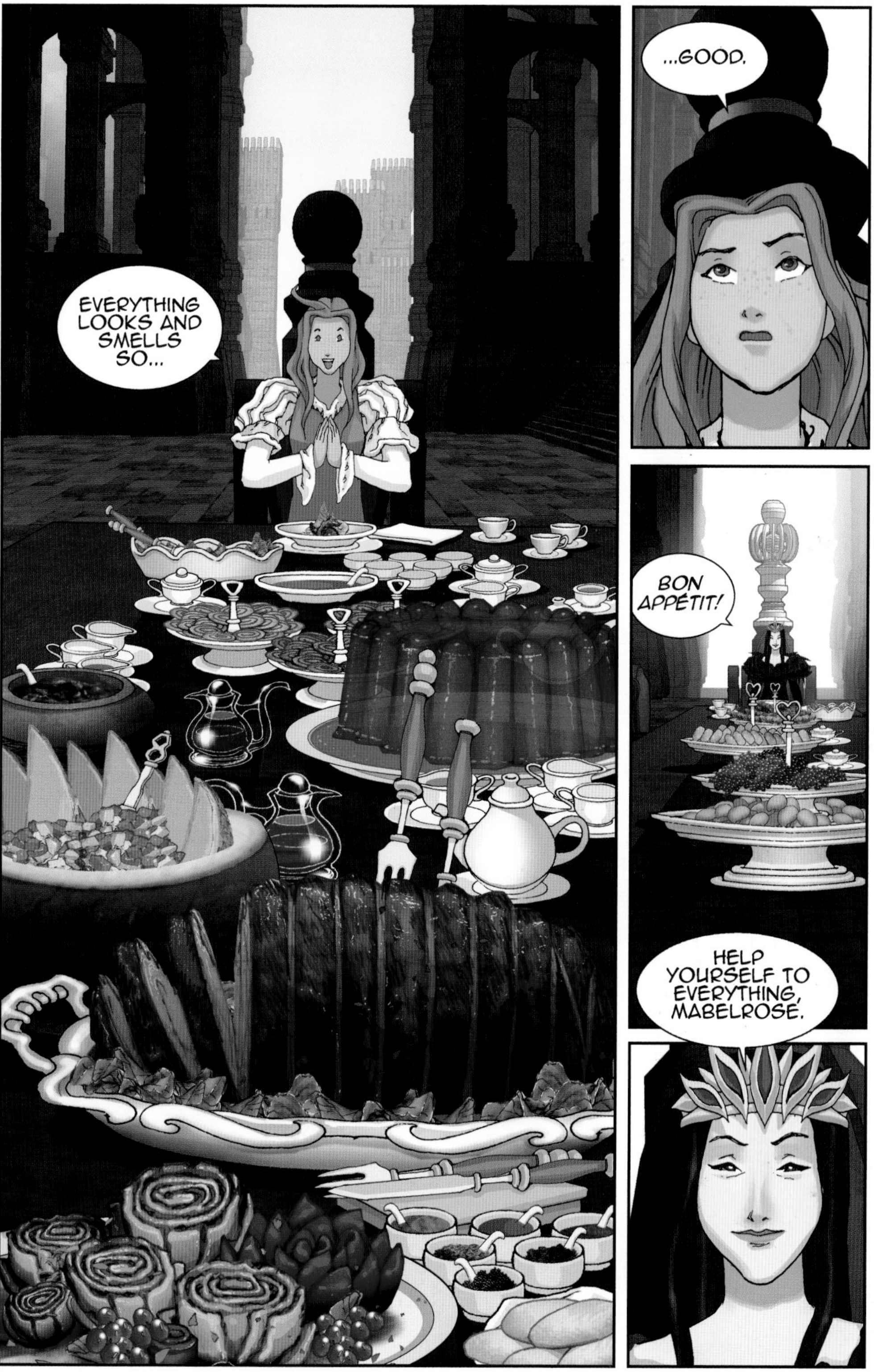
EVERYTHING LOOKS AND SMELLS SO...
...GOOD.
BON APPÉTIT!
HELP YOURSELF TO EVERYTHING, MABELROSE.

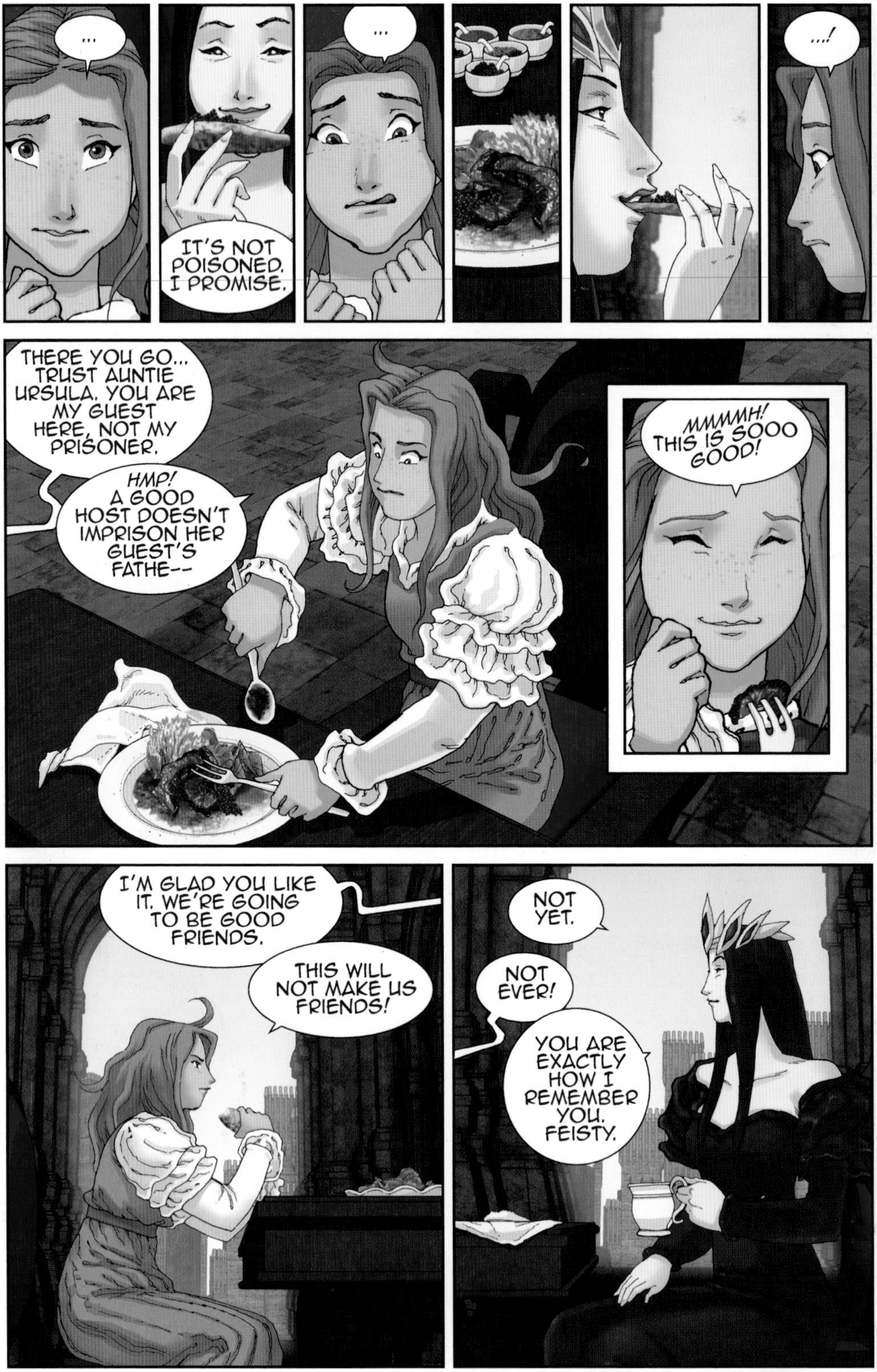
...
IT'S NOT POISONED. I PROMISE.
...
...!
THERE YOU GO... TRUST AUNTIE URSULA. YOU ARE MY GUEST HERE, NOT MY PRISONER.
HMP! A GOOD HOST DOESN'T IMPRISON HER GUEST'S FATHE--
MMMMH! THIS IS SOOO GOOD!
I'M GLAD YOU LIKE IT. WE'RE GOING TO BE GOOD FRIENDS.
THIS WILL NOT MAKE US FRIENDS!
NOT YET.
NOT EVER!
YOU ARE EXACTLY HOW I REMEMBER YOU. FEISTY.

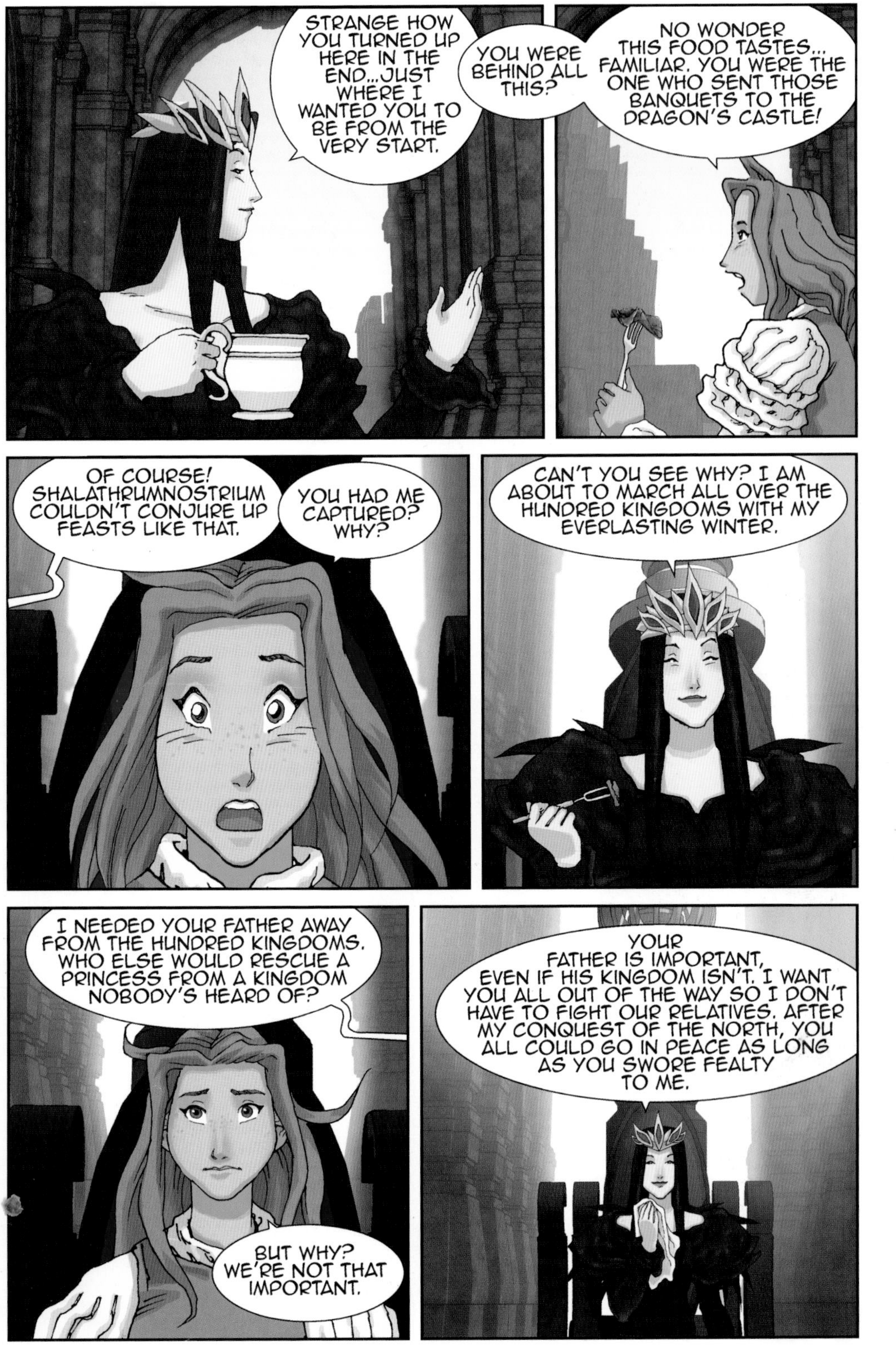
STRANGE HOW YOU TURNED UP HERE IN THE END...JUST WHERE I WANTED YOU TO BE FROM THE VERY START.
YOU WERE BEHIND ALL THIS?
NO WONDER THIS FOOD TASTES... FAMILIAR. YOU WERE THE ONE WHO SENT THOSE BANQUETS TO THE DRAGON'S CASTLE!
OF COURSE! SHALATHRUMNOSTRIUM COULDN'T CONJURE UP FEASTS LIKE THAT.
YOU HAD ME CAPTURED? WHY?
CAN'T YOU SEE WHY? I AM ABOUT TO MARCH ALL OVER THE HUNDRED KINGDOMS WITH MY EVERLASTING WINTER.
I NEEDED YOUR FATHER AWAY FROM THE HUNDRED KINGDOMS. WHO ELSE WOULD RESCUE A PRINCESS FROM A KINGDOM NOBODY'S HEARD OF?
BUT WHY? WE'RE NOT THAT IMPORTANT.
YOUR FATHER IS IMPORTANT, EVEN IF HIS KINGDOM ISN'T. I WANT YOU ALL OUT OF THE WAY SO I DON'T HAVE TO FIGHT OUR RELATIVES. AFTER MY CONQUEST OF THE NORTH, YOU ALL COULD GO IN PEACE AS LONG AS YOU SWORE FEALTY TO ME.

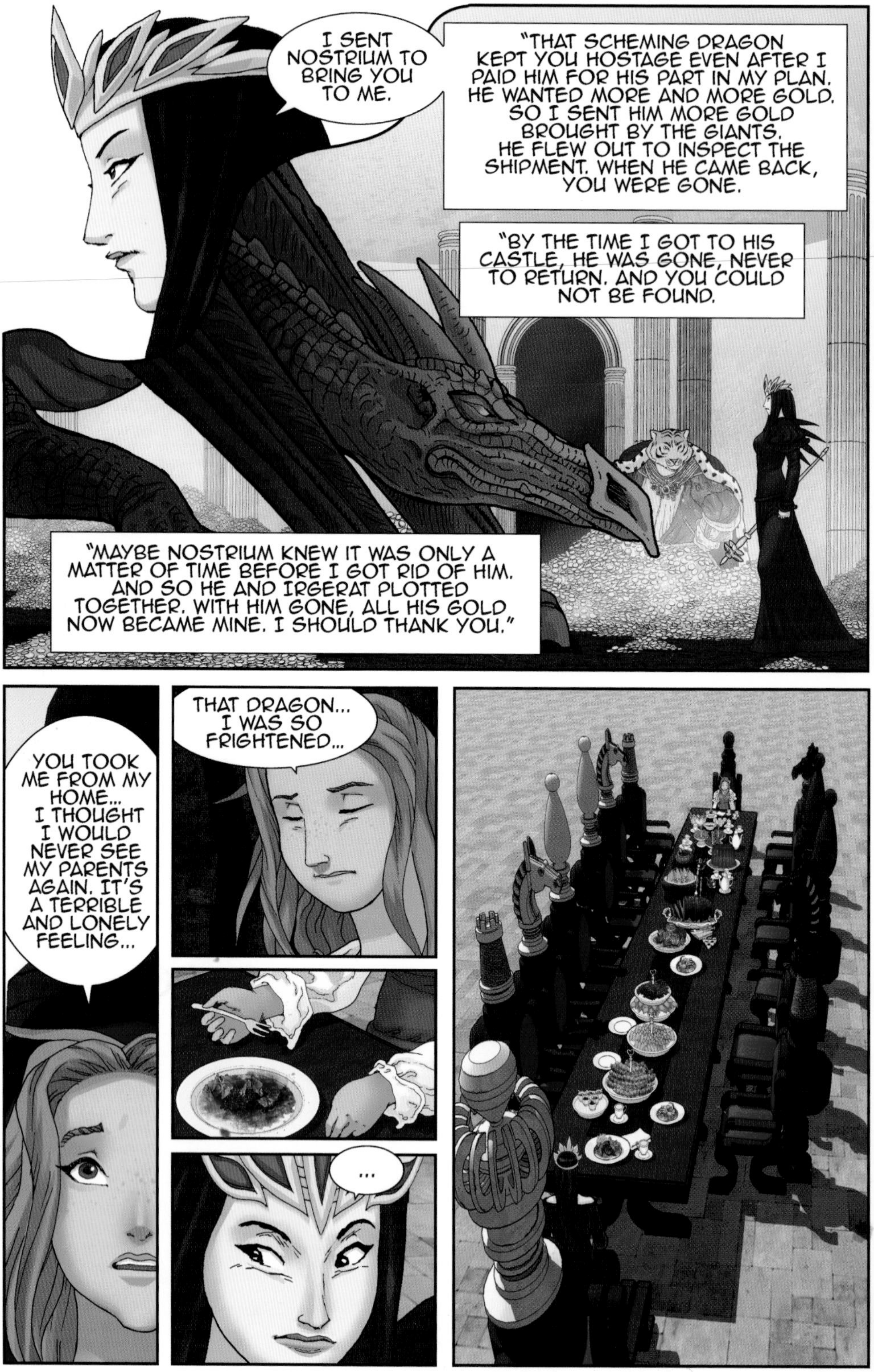
I SENT NOSTRIUM TO BRING YOU TO ME.
"THAT SCHEMING DRAGON KEPT YOU HOSTAGE EVEN AFTER I PAID HIM FOR HIS PART IN MY PLAN. HE WANTED MORE AND MORE GOLD. SO I SENT HIM MORE GOLD BROUGHT BY THE GIANTS. HE FLEW OUT TO INSPECT THE SHIPMENT. WHEN HE CAME BACK, YOU WERE GONE.
"BY THE TIME I GOT TO HIS CASTLE, HE WAS GONE, NEVER TO RETURN. AND YOU COULD NOT BE FOUND.
"MAYBE NOSTRIUM KNEW IT WAS ONLY A MATTER OF TIME BEFORE I GOT RID OF HIM. AND SO HE AND IRGERAT PLOTTED TOGETHER. WITH HIM GONE, ALL HIS GOLD NOW BECAME MINE. I SHOULD THANK YOU."
YOU TOOK ME FROM MY HOME... I THOUGHT I WOULD NEVER SEE MY PARENTS AGAIN. IT'S A TERRIBLE AND LONELY FEELING...
THAT DRAGON... I WAS SO FRIGHTENED...
...

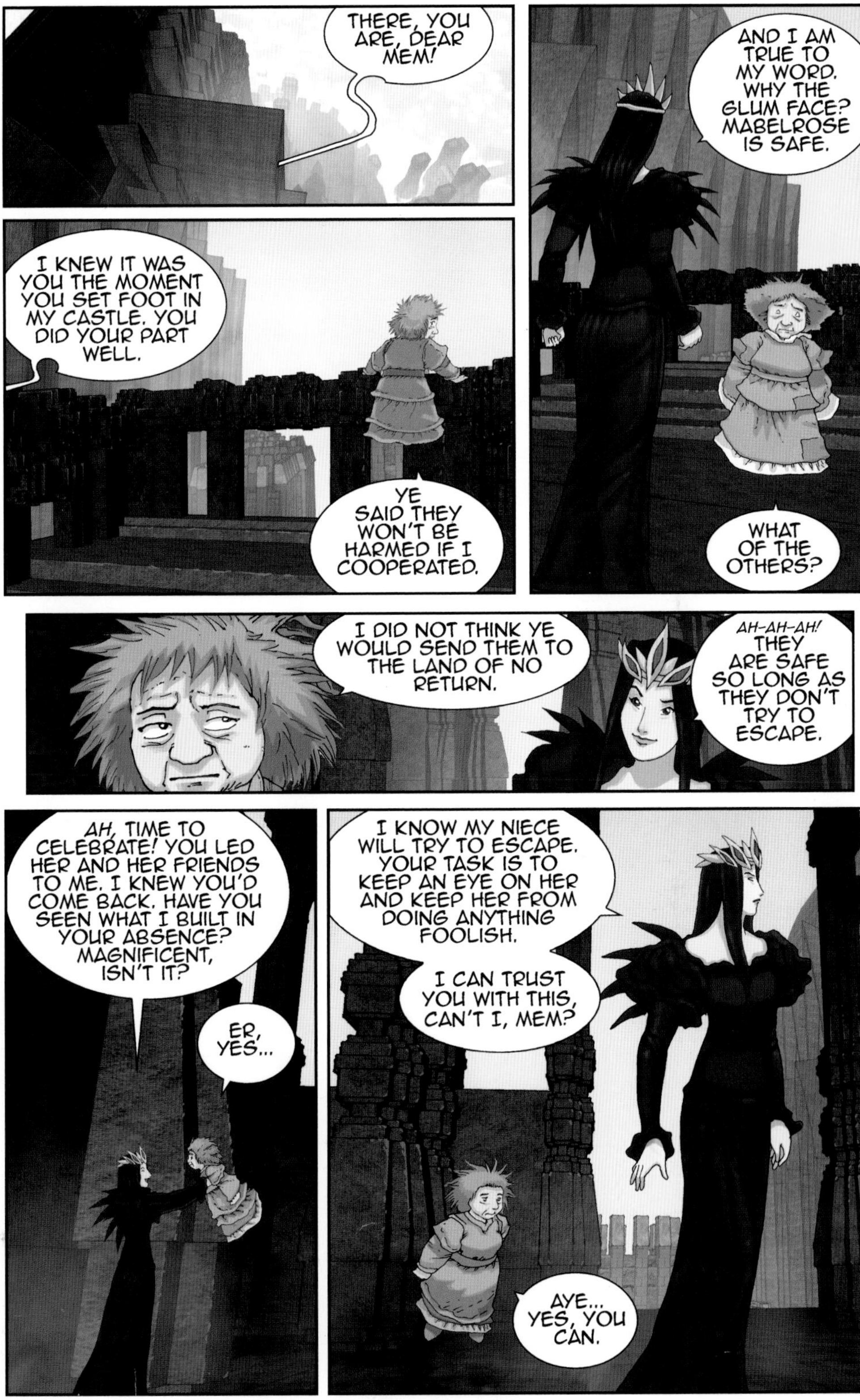
THERE, YOU ARE, DEAR MEM!
I KNEW IT WAS YOU THE MOMENT YOU SET FOOT IN MY CASTLE. YOU DID YOUR PART WELL.
YE SAID THEY WON'T BE HARMED IF I COOPERATED.
AND I AM TRUE TO MY WORD. WHY THE GLUM FACE? MABELROSE IS SAFE.
WHAT OF THE OTHERS?
I DID NOT THINK YE WOULD SEND THEM TO THE LAND OF NO RETURN.
AH-AH-AH! THEY ARE SAFE SO LONG AS THEY DON'T TRY TO ESCAPE.
AH, TIME TO CELEBRATE! YOU LED HER AND HER FRIENDS TO ME. I KNEW YOU'D COME BACK. HAVE YOU SEEN WHAT I BUILT IN YOUR ABSENCE? MAGNIFICENT, ISN'T IT?
ER, YES...
I KNOW MY NIECE WILL TRY TO ESCAPE. YOUR TASK IS TO KEEP AN EYE ON HER AND KEEP HER FROM DOING ANYTHING FOOLISH.
I CAN TRUST YOU WITH THIS, CAN'T I, MEM?
AYE... YES, YOU CAN.

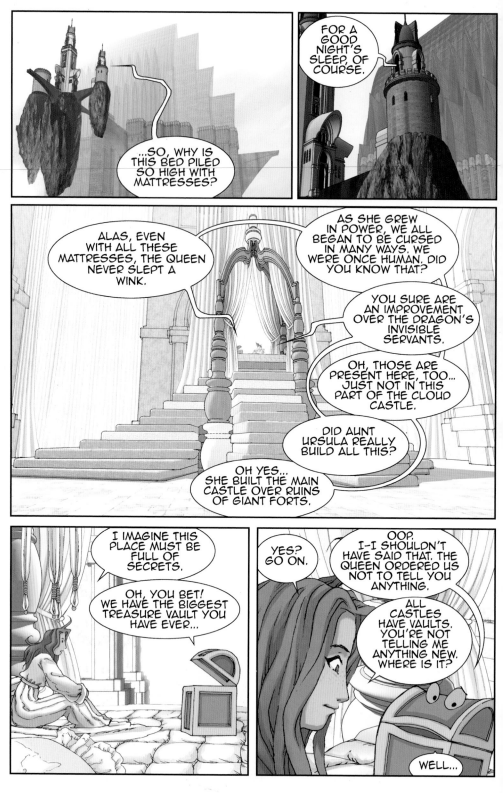

FOR A GOOD NIGHT'S SLEEP, OF COURSE.

...SO, WHY IS THIS BED PILED SO HIGH WITH MATTRESSES?

ALAS, EVEN WITH ALL THESE MATTRESSES, THE QUEEN NEVER SLEPT A WINK.

AS SHE GREW IN POWER, WE ALL BEGAN TO BE CURSED IN MANY WAYS. WE WERE ONCE HUMAN. DID YOU KNOW THAT?

YOU SURE ARE AN IMPROVEMENT OVER THE DRAGON'S INVISIBLE SERVANTS.

OH, THOSE ARE PRESENT HERE, TOO... JUST NOT IN THIS PART OF THE CLOUD CASTLE.

DID AUNT URSULA REALLY BUILD ALL THIS?

OH YES... SHE BUILT THE MAIN CASTLE OVER RUINS OF GIANT FORTS.

I IMAGINE THIS PLACE MUST BE FULL OF SECRETS.

OH, YOU BET! WE HAVE THE BIGGEST TREASURE VAULT YOU HAVE EVER...

YES? GO ON.

OOP. I-I SHOULDN'T HAVE SAID THAT. THE QUEEN ORDERED US NOT TO TELL YOU ANYTHING.

ALL CASTLES HAVE VAULTS. YOU'RE NOT TELLING ME ANYTHING NEW. WHERE IS IT?

WELL...

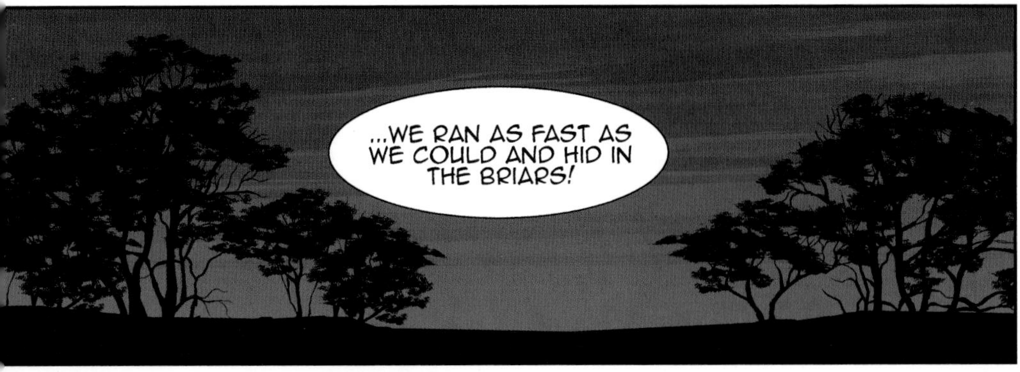
...WE RAN AS FAST AS WE COULD AND HID IN THE BRIARS!

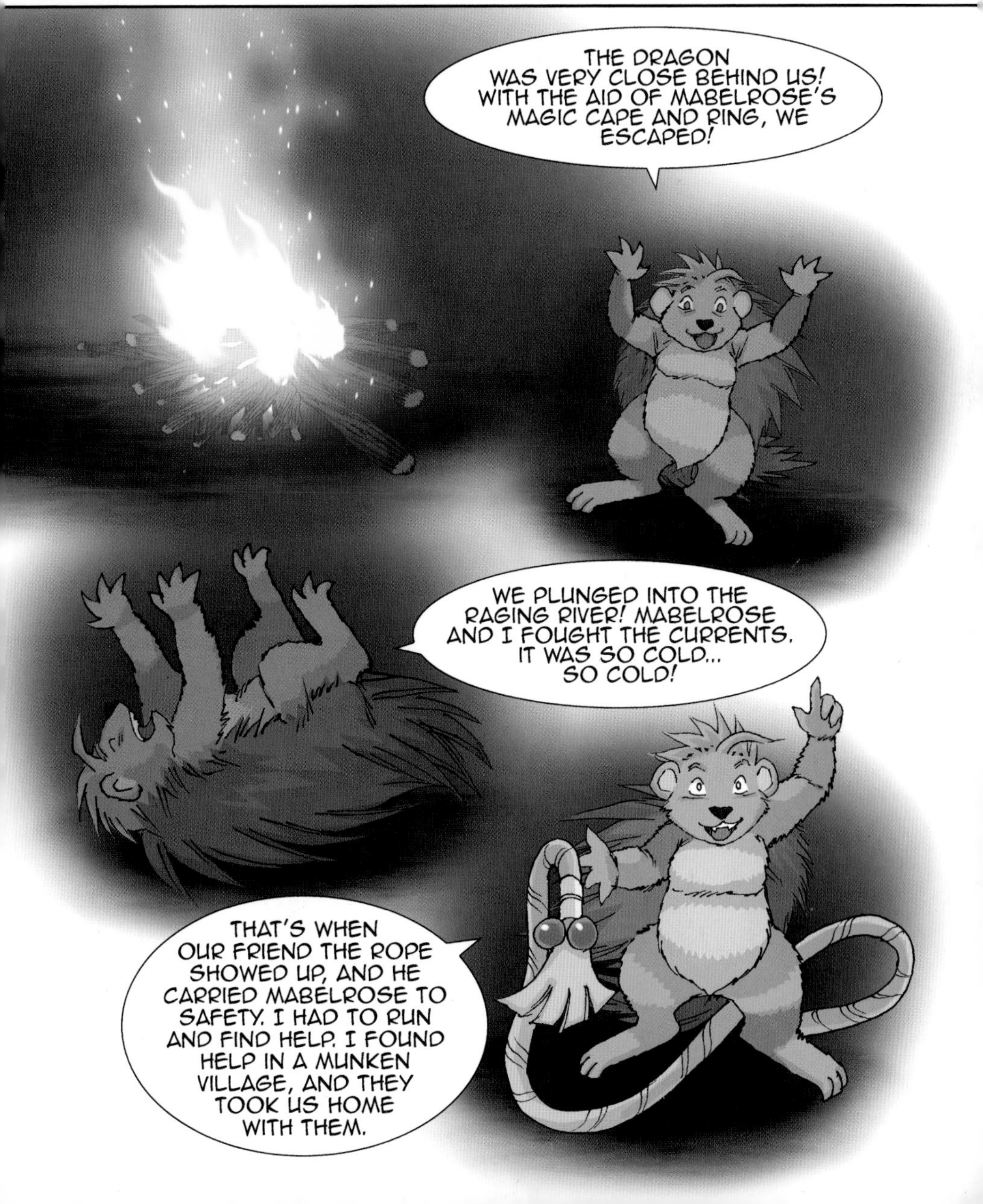
THE DRAGON WAS VERY CLOSE BEHIND US! WITH THE AID OF MABELROSE'S MAGIC CAPE AND RING, WE ESCAPED!
WE PLUNGED INTO THE RAGING RIVER! MABELROSE AND I FOUGHT THE CURRENTS. IT WAS SO COLD... SO COLD!
THAT'S WHEN OUR FRIEND THE ROPE SHOWED UP, AND HE CARRIED MABELROSE TO SAFETY. I HAD TO RUN AND FIND HELP. I FOUND HELP IN A MUNKEN VILLAGE, AND THEY TOOK US HOME WITH THEM.

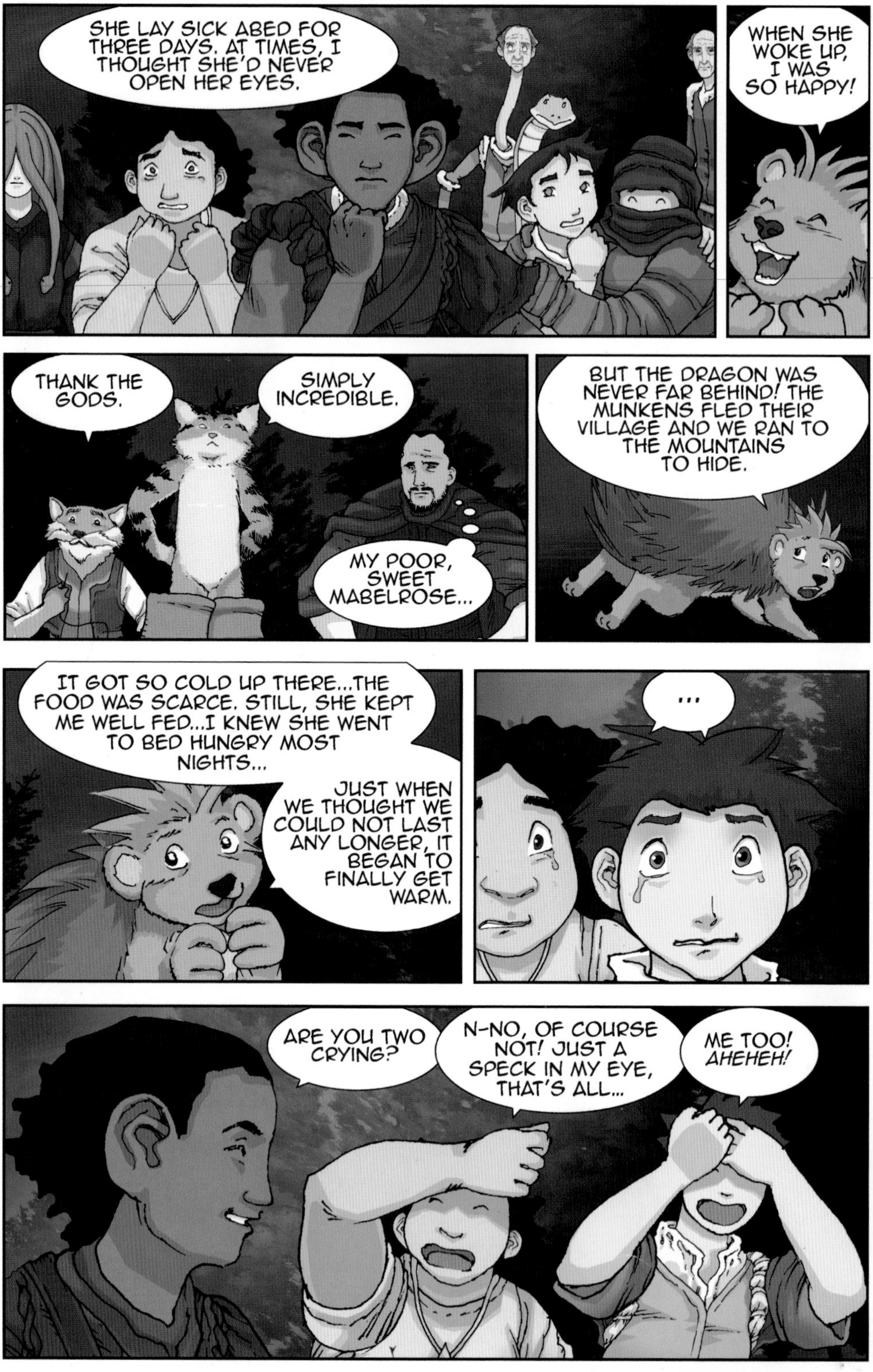
SHE LAY SICK ABED FOR THREE DAYS. AT TIMES, I THOUGHT SHE'D NEVER OPEN HER EYES.
WHEN SHE WOKE UP, I WAS SO HAPPY!
THANK THE GODS.
SIMPLY INCREDIBLE.
MY POOR, SWEET MABELROSE...
BUT THE DRAGON WAS NEVER FAR BEHIND! THE MUNKENS FLED THEIR VILLAGE AND WE RAN TO THE MOUNTAINS TO HIDE.
IT GOT SO COLD UP THERE...THE FOOD WAS SCARCE. STILL, SHE KEPT ME WELL FED...I KNEW SHE WENT TO BED HUNGRY MOST NIGHTS...
JUST WHEN WE THOUGHT WE COULD NOT LAST ANY LONGER, IT BEGAN TO FINALLY GET WARM.
...
ARE YOU TWO CRYING?
N-NO, OF COURSE NOT! JUST A SPECK IN MY EYE, THAT'S ALL...
ME TOO! AHEHEH!

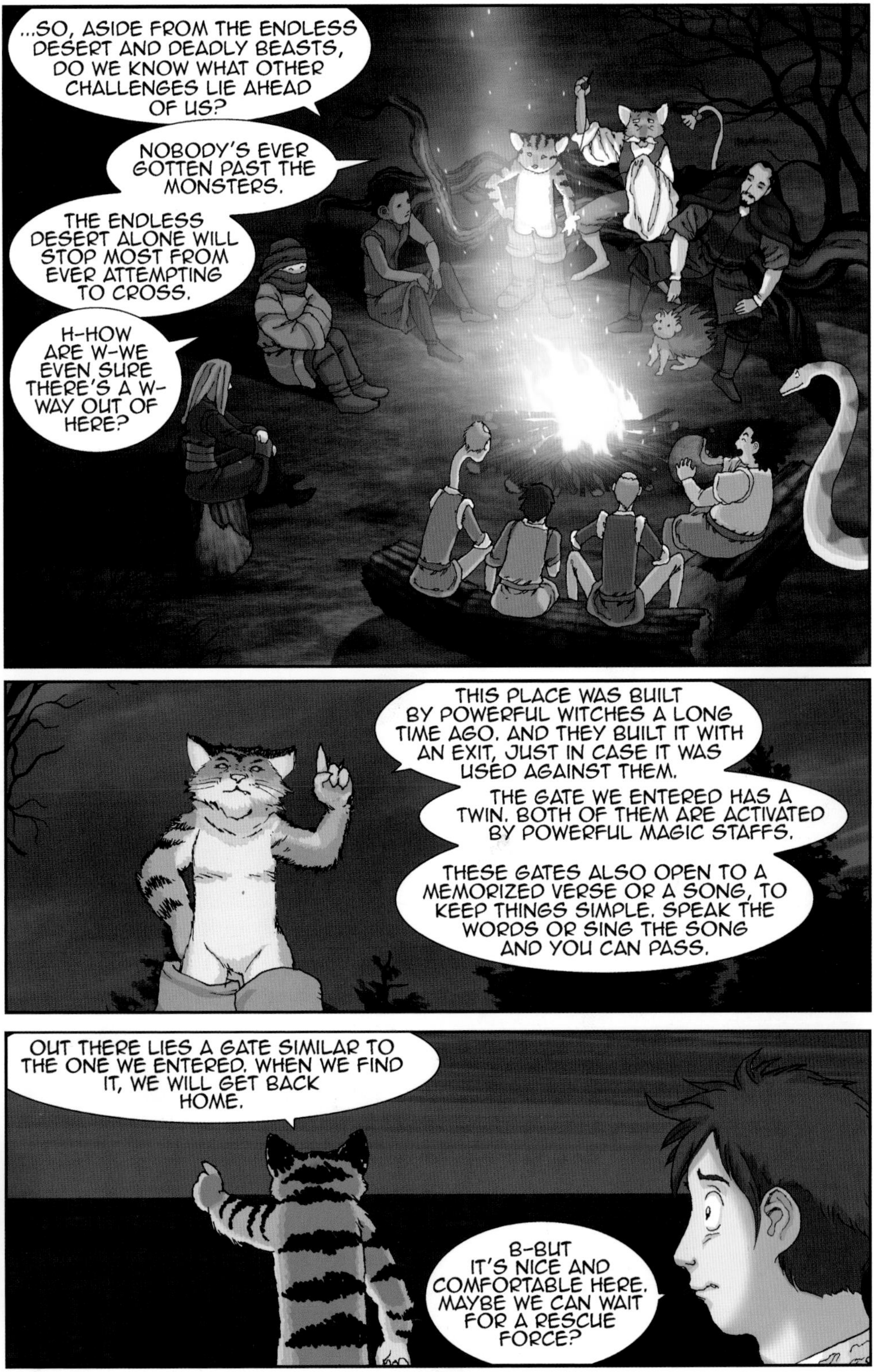
...SO, ASIDE FROM THE ENDLESS DESERT AND DEADLY BEASTS, DO WE KNOW WHAT OTHER CHALLENGES LIE AHEAD OF US?
NOBODY'S EVER GOTTEN PAST THE MONSTERS.
THE ENDLESS DESERT ALONE WILL STOP MOST FROM EVER ATTEMPTING TO CROSS.
H-HOW ARE W-WE EVEN SURE THERE'S A W-WAY OUT OF HERE?
THIS PLACE WAS BUILT BY POWERFUL WITCHES A LONG TIME AGO. AND THEY BUILT IT WITH AN EXIT, JUST IN CASE IT WAS USED AGAINST THEM.
THE GATE WE ENTERED HAS A TWIN. BOTH OF THEM ARE ACTIVATED BY POWERFUL MAGIC STAFFS.
THESE GATES ALSO OPEN TO A MEMORIZED VERSE OR A SONG, TO KEEP THINGS SIMPLE. SPEAK THE WORDS OR SING THE SONG AND YOU CAN PASS.
OUT THERE LIES A GATE SIMILAR TO THE ONE WE ENTERED. WHEN WE FIND IT, WE WILL GET BACK HOME.
B-BUT IT'S NICE AND COMFORTABLE HERE. MAYBE WE CAN WAIT FOR A RESCUE FORCE?

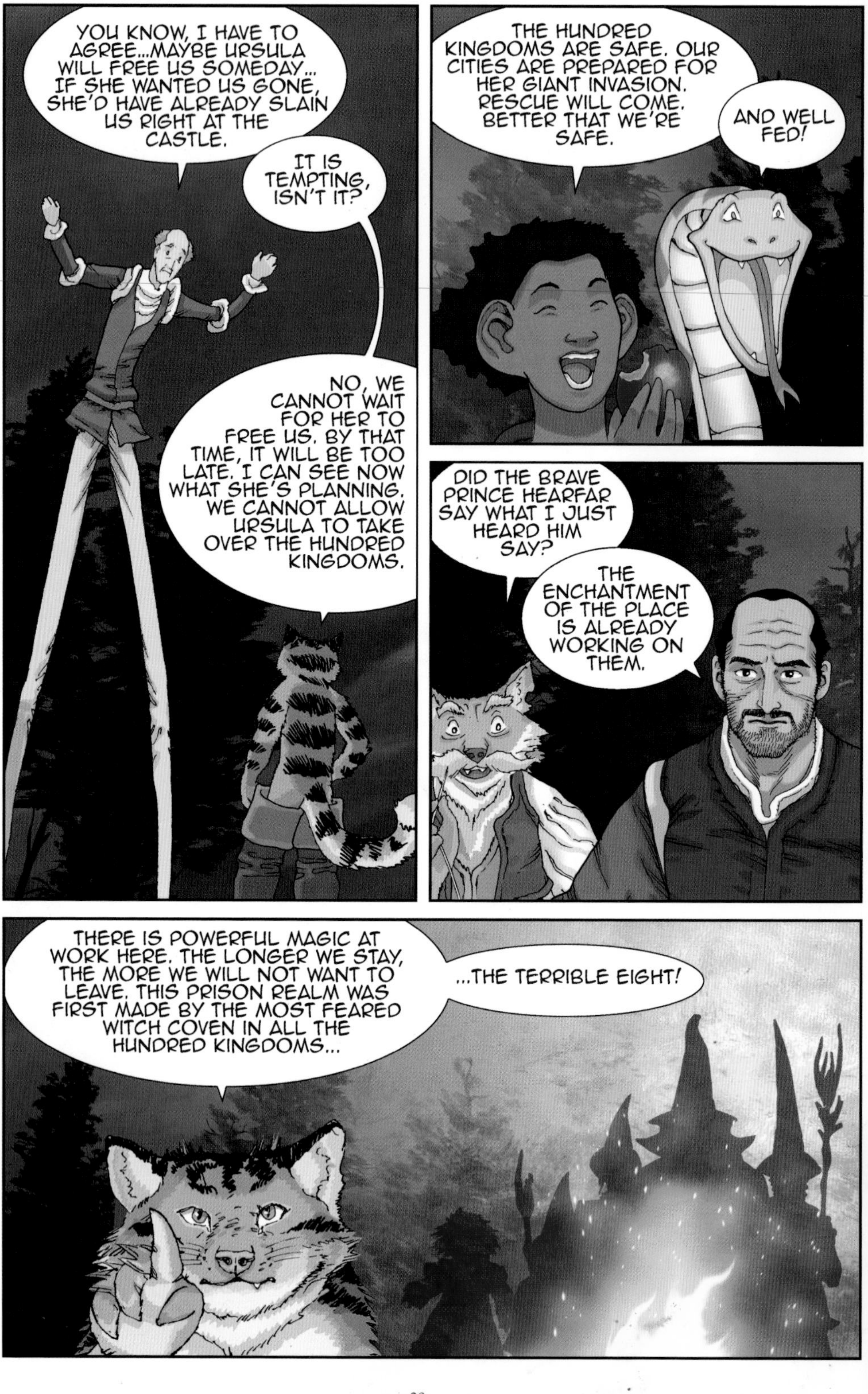
YOU KNOW, I HAVE TO AGREE...MAYBE URSULA WILL FREE US SOMEDAY... IF SHE WANTED US GONE, SHE'D HAVE ALREADY SLAIN US RIGHT AT THE CASTLE.
IT IS TEMPTING, ISN'T IT?
NO, WE CANNOT WAIT FOR HER TO FREE US. BY THAT TIME, IT WILL BE TOO LATE. I CAN SEE NOW WHAT SHE'S PLANNING. WE CANNOT ALLOW URSULA TO TAKE OVER THE HUNDRED KINGDOMS.
THE HUNDRED KINGDOMS ARE SAFE. OUR CITIES ARE PREPARED FOR HER GIANT INVASION. RESCUE WILL COME. BETTER THAT WE'RE SAFE.
AND WELL FED!
DID THE BRAVE PRINCE HEARFAR SAY WHAT I JUST HEARD HIM SAY?
THE ENCHANTMENT OF THE PLACE IS ALREADY WORKING ON THEM.
THERE IS POWERFUL MAGIC AT WORK HERE. THE LONGER WE STAY, THE MORE WE WILL NOT WANT TO LEAVE. THIS PRISON REALM WAS FIRST MADE BY THE MOST FEARED WITCH COVEN IN ALL THE HUNDRED KINGDOMS...
...THE TERRIBLE EIGHT!

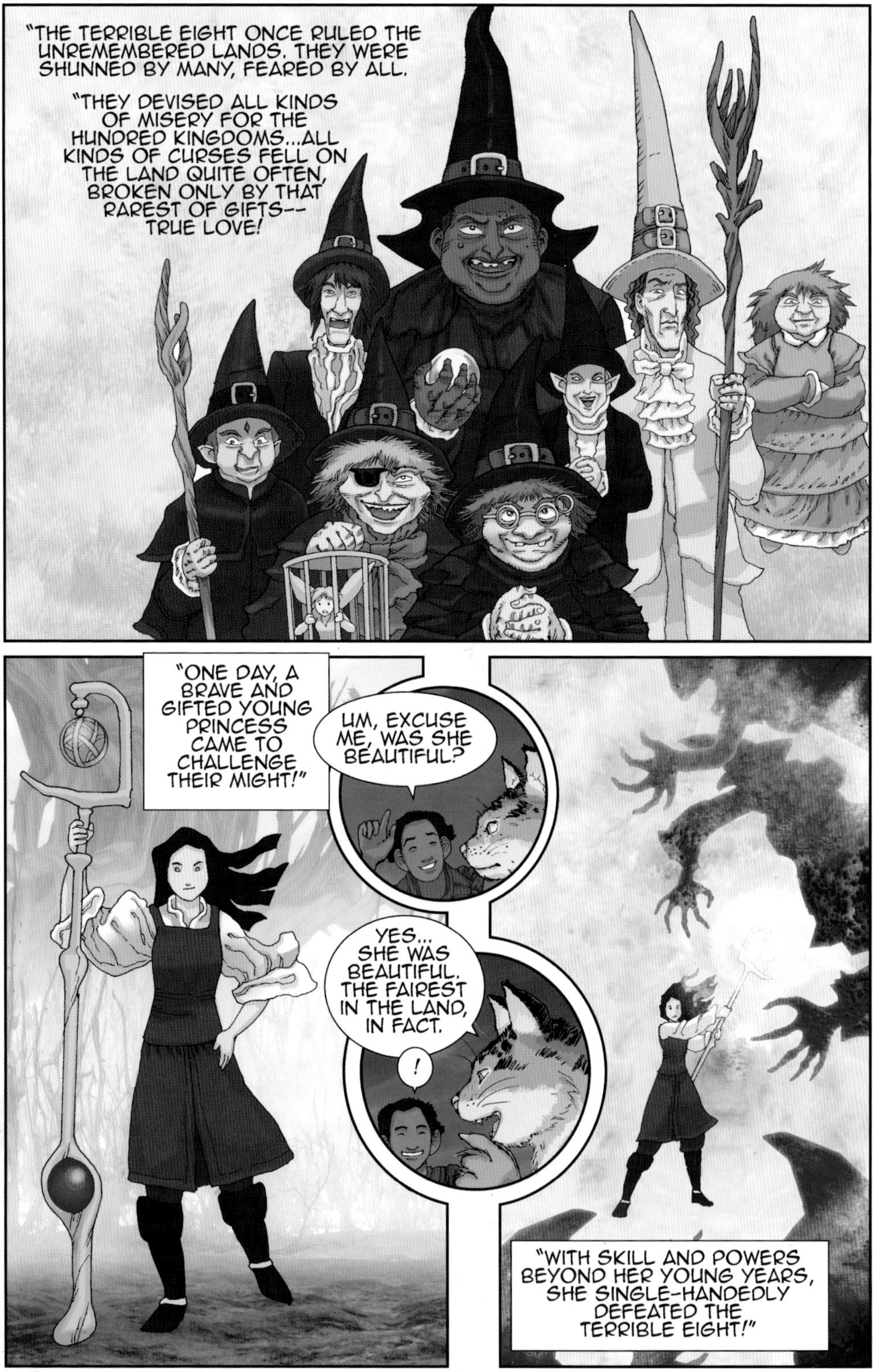
"THE TERRIBLE EIGHT ONCE RULED THE UNREMEMBERED LANDS. THEY WERE SHUNNED BY MANY, FEARED BY ALL.
"THEY DEVISED ALL KINDS OF MISERY FOR THE HUNDRED KINGDOMS...ALL KINDS OF CURSES FELL ON THE LAND QUITE OFTEN, BROKEN ONLY BY THAT RAREST OF GIFTS-- TRUE LOVE!
"ONE DAY, A BRAVE AND GIFTED YOUNG PRINCESS CAME TO CHALLENGE THEIR MIGHT!"
UM, EXCUSE ME, WAS SHE BEAUTIFUL?
YES... SHE WAS BEAUTIFUL. THE FAIREST IN THE LAND, IN FACT.
!
"WITH SKILL AND POWERS BEYOND HER YOUNG YEARS, SHE SINGLE-HANDEDLY DEFEATED THE TERRIBLE EIGHT!"

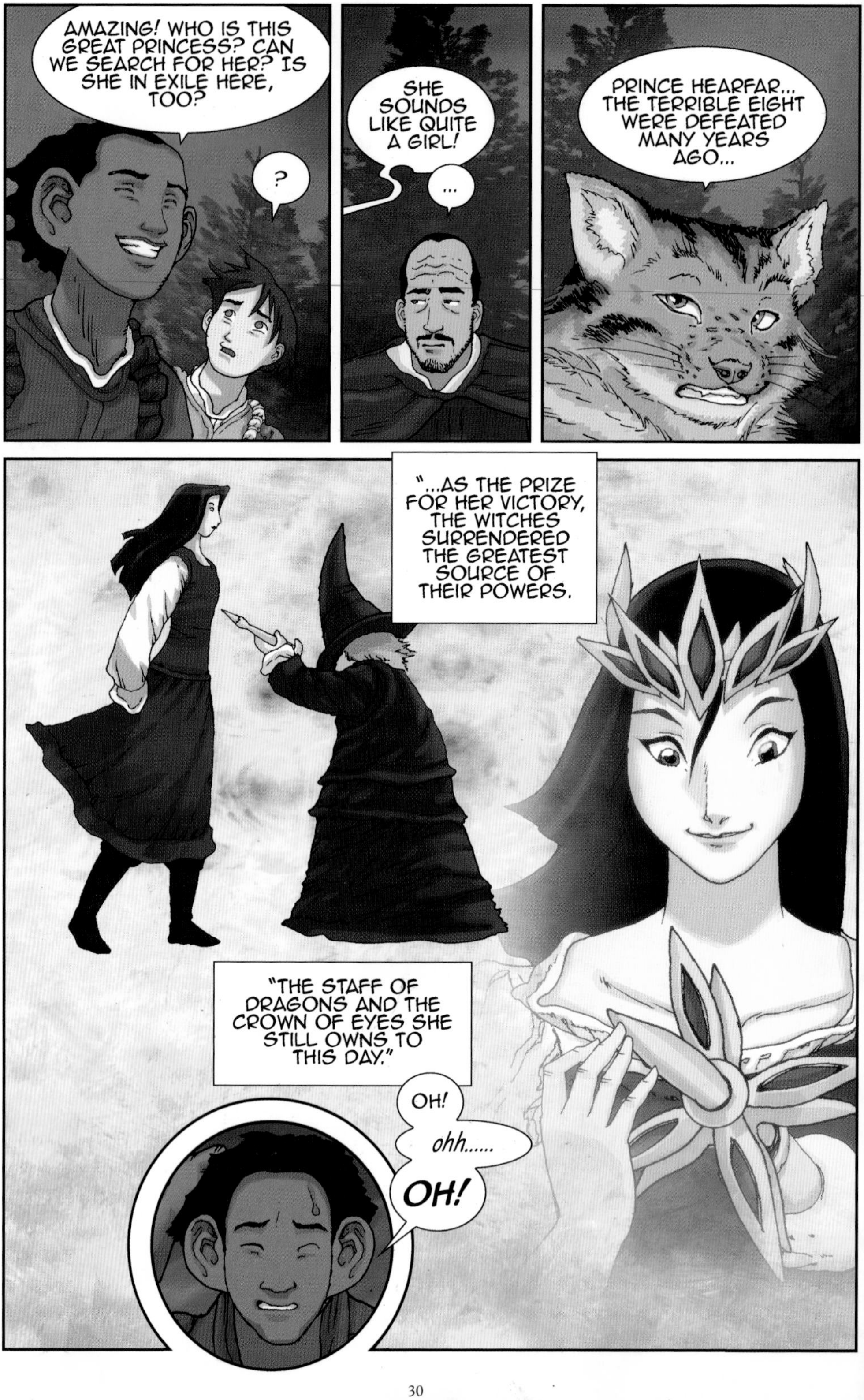
AMAZING! WHO IS THIS GREAT PRINCESS? CAN WE SEARCH FOR HER? IS SHE IN EXILE HERE, TOO?
?
SHE SOUNDS LIKE QUITE A GIRL!
...
PRINCE HEARFAR... THE TERRIBLE EIGHT WERE DEFEATED MANY YEARS AGO...
"...AS THE PRIZE FOR HER VICTORY, THE WITCHES SURRENDERED THE GREATEST SOURCE OF THEIR POWERS.
"THE STAFF OF DRAGONS AND THE CROWN OF EYES SHE STILL OWNS TO THIS DAY."
OH!
ohh......
OH!

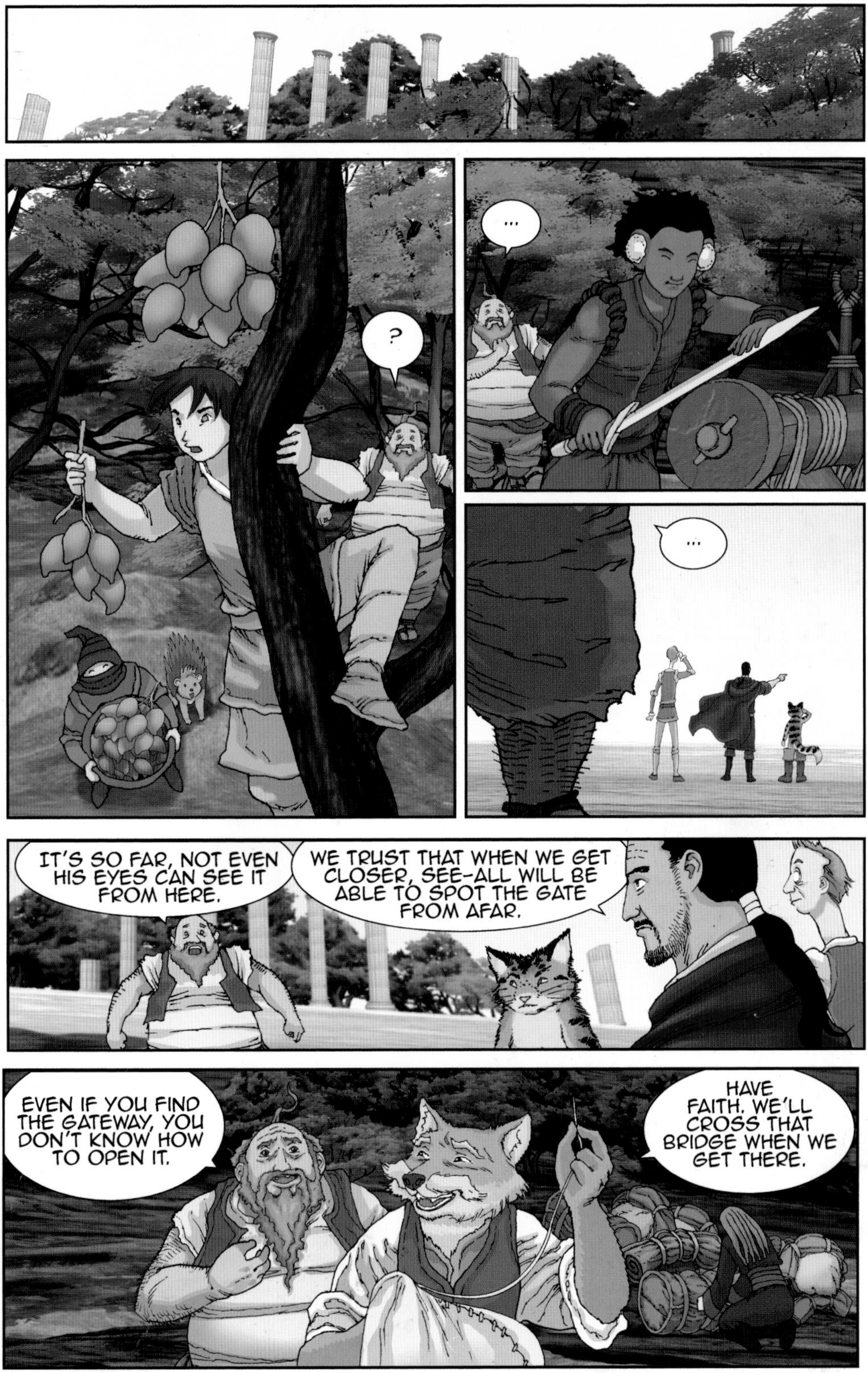
?
...
...
IT'S SO FAR, NOT EVEN HIS EYES CAN SEE IT FROM HERE.
WE TRUST THAT WHEN WE GET CLOSER, SEE-ALL WILL BE ABLE TO SPOT THE GATE FROM AFAR.
EVEN IF YOU FIND THE GATEWAY, YOU DON'T KNOW HOW TO OPEN IT.
HAVE FAITH. WE'LL CROSS THAT BRIDGE WHEN WE GET THERE.

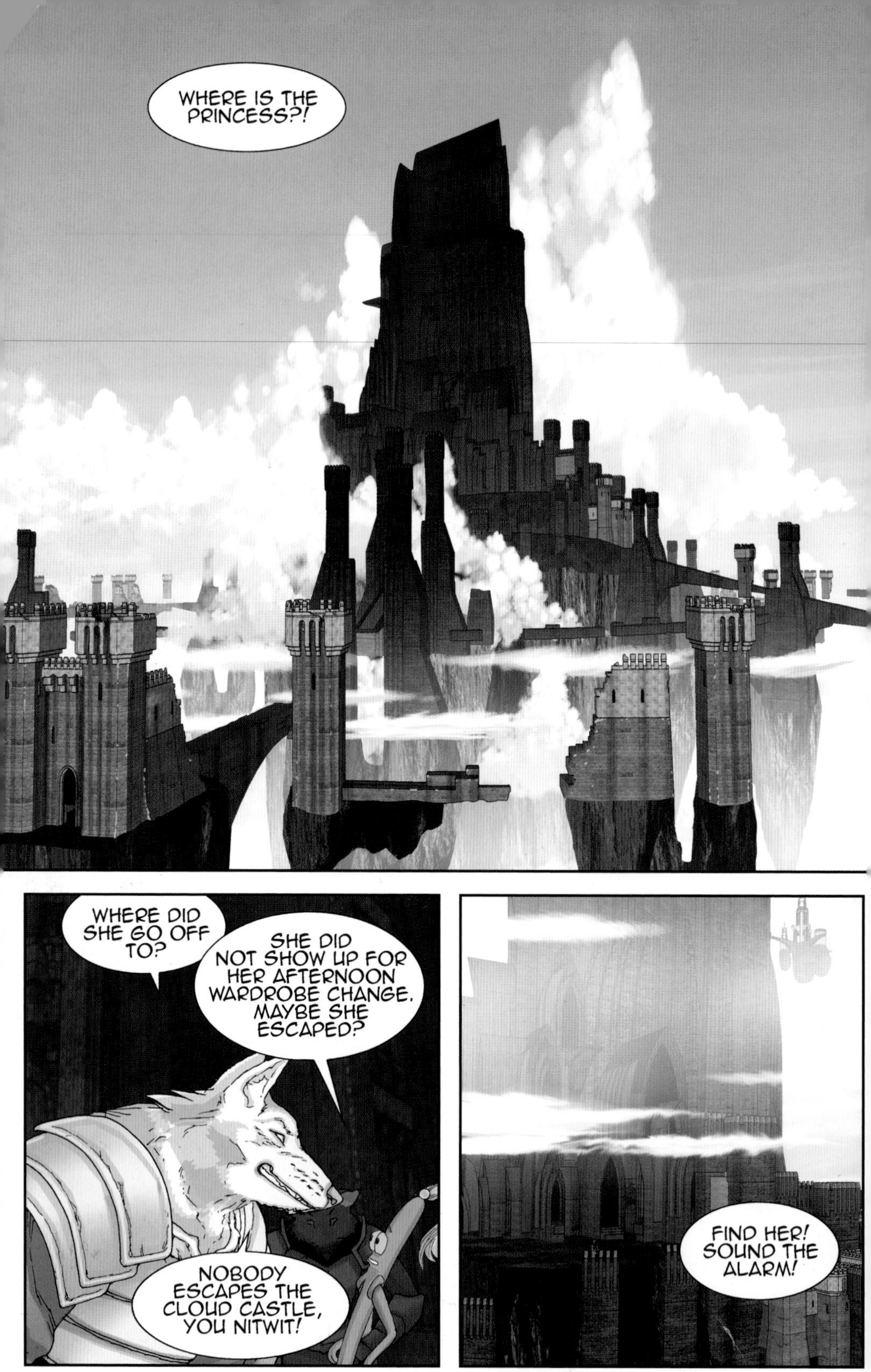
WHERE IS THE PRINCESS?!
WHERE DID SHE GO OFF TO?
SHE DID NOT SHOW UP FOR HER AFTERNOON WARDROBE CHANGE. MAYBE SHE ESCAPED?
NOBODY ESCAPES THE CLOUD CASTLE, YOU NITWIT!
FIND HER! SOUND THE ALARM!

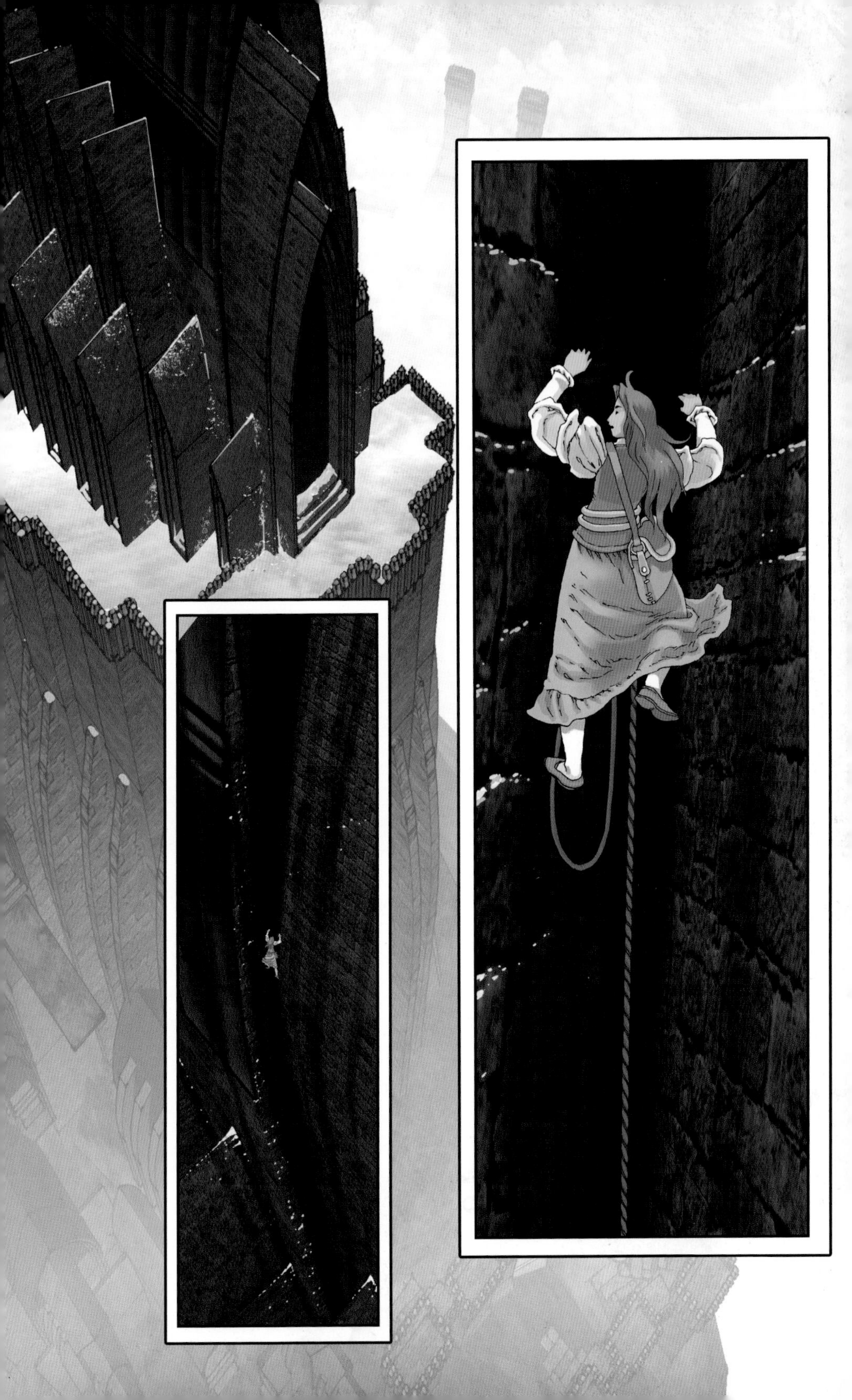

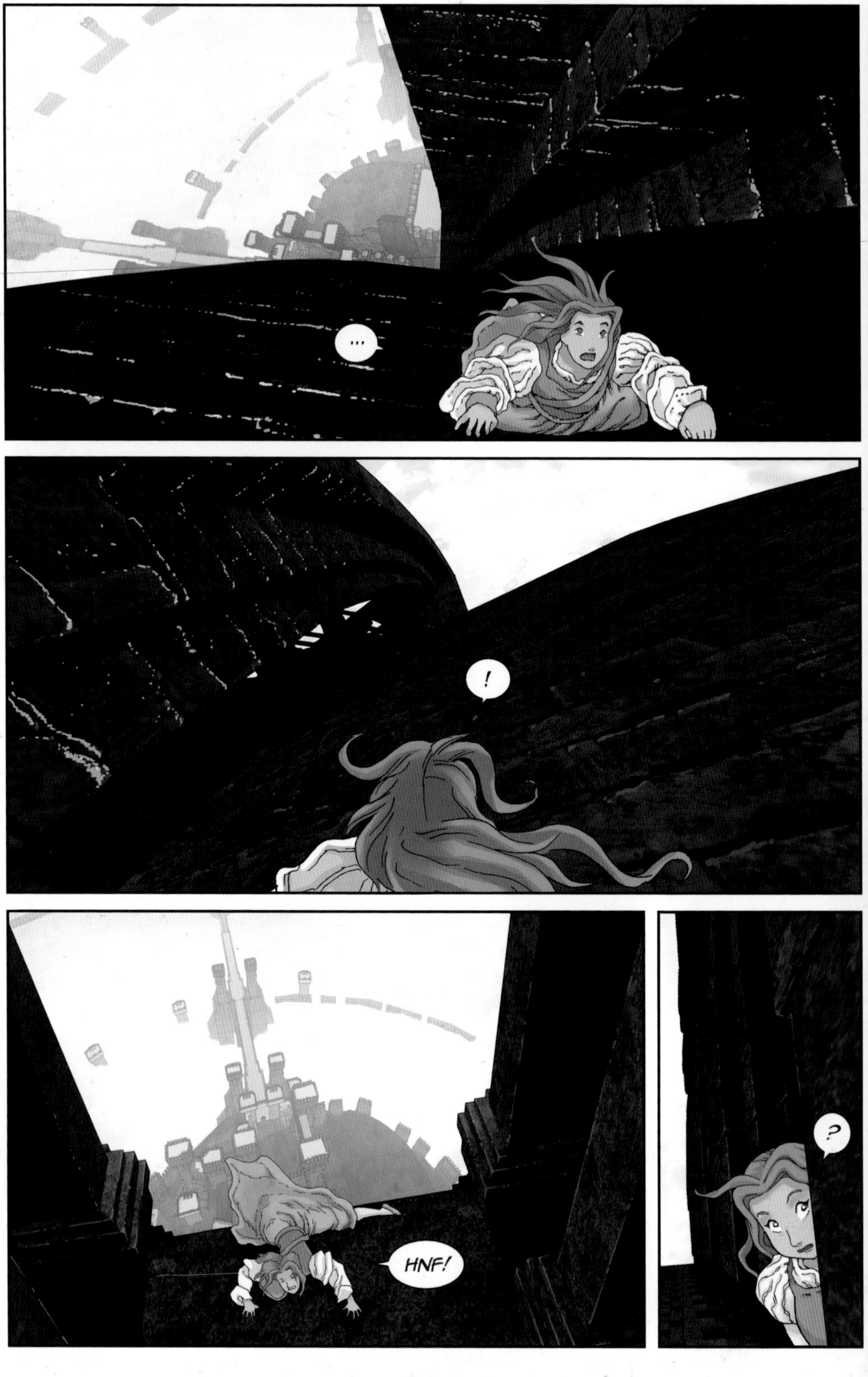
...
!
HNF!
?

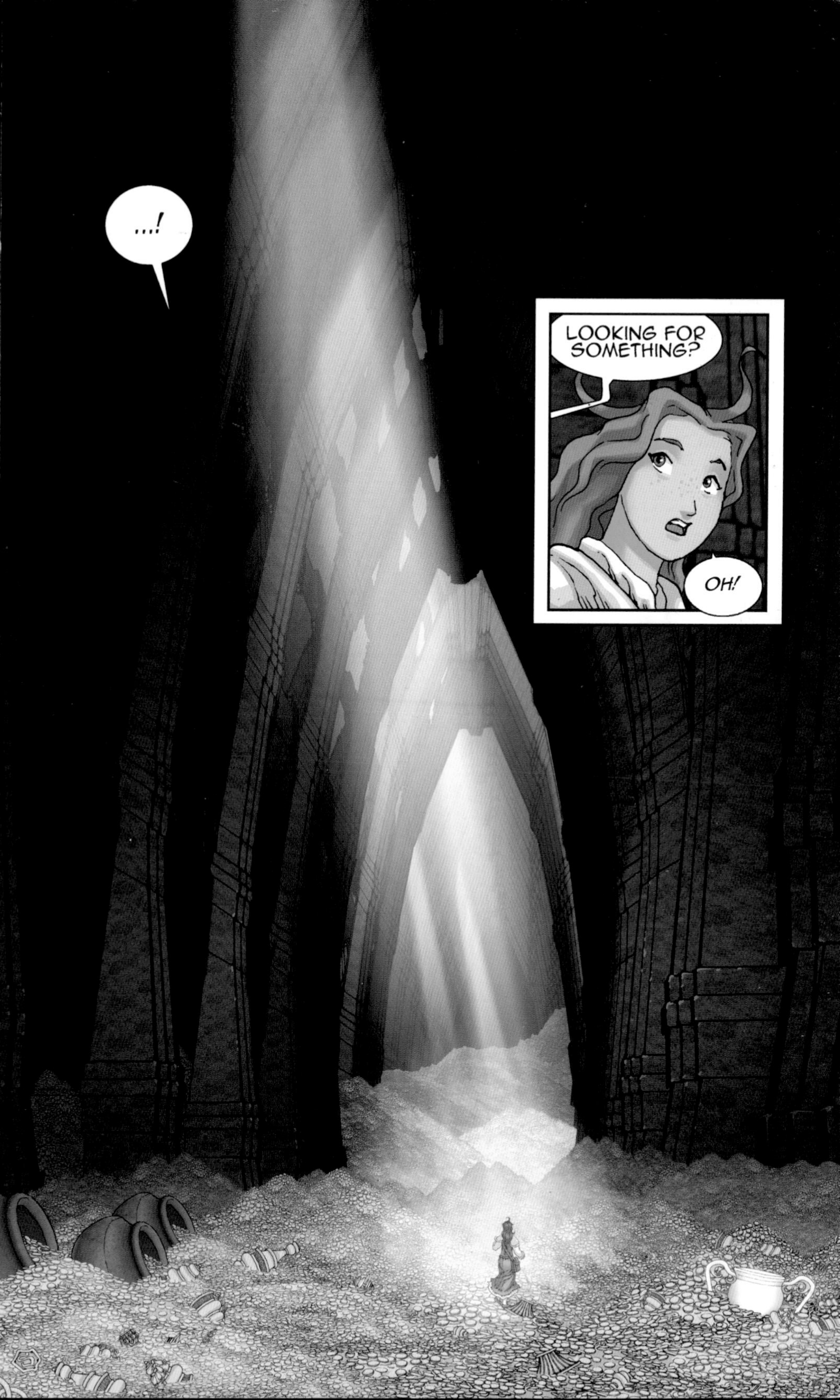
...!
LOOKING FOR SOMETHING?
OH!

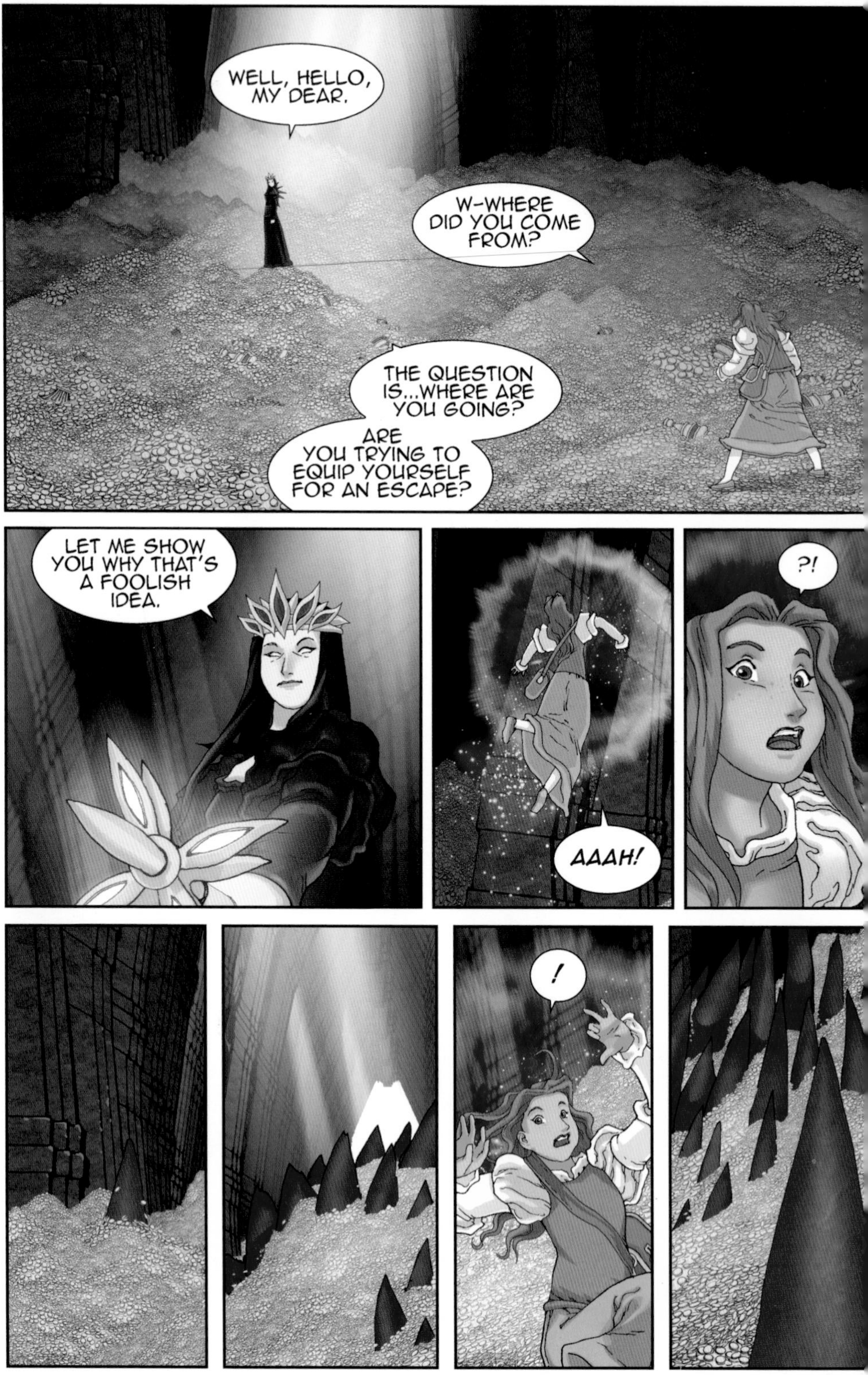

WELL, HELLO, MY DEAR.
W-WHERE DID YOU COME FROM?
THE QUESTION IS...WHERE ARE YOU GOING?
ARE YOU TRYING TO EQUIP YOURSELF FOR AN ESCAPE?
LET ME SHOW YOU WHY THAT'S A FOOLISH IDEA.
AAAH!
?!
!

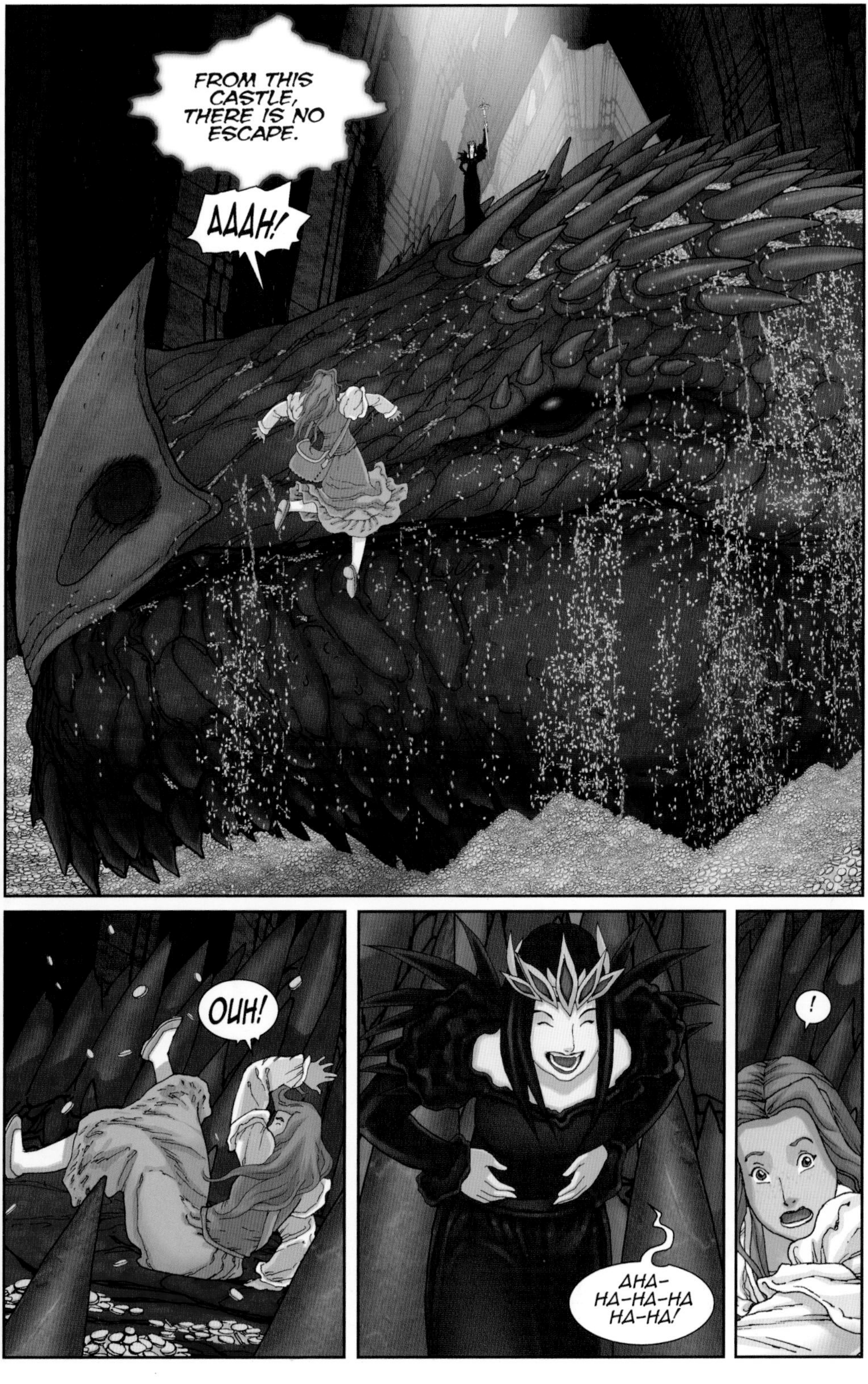
FROM THIS CASTLE, THERE IS NO ESCAPE.
AAAH!
OUH!
AHA-HA-HA-HA HA-HA!
!

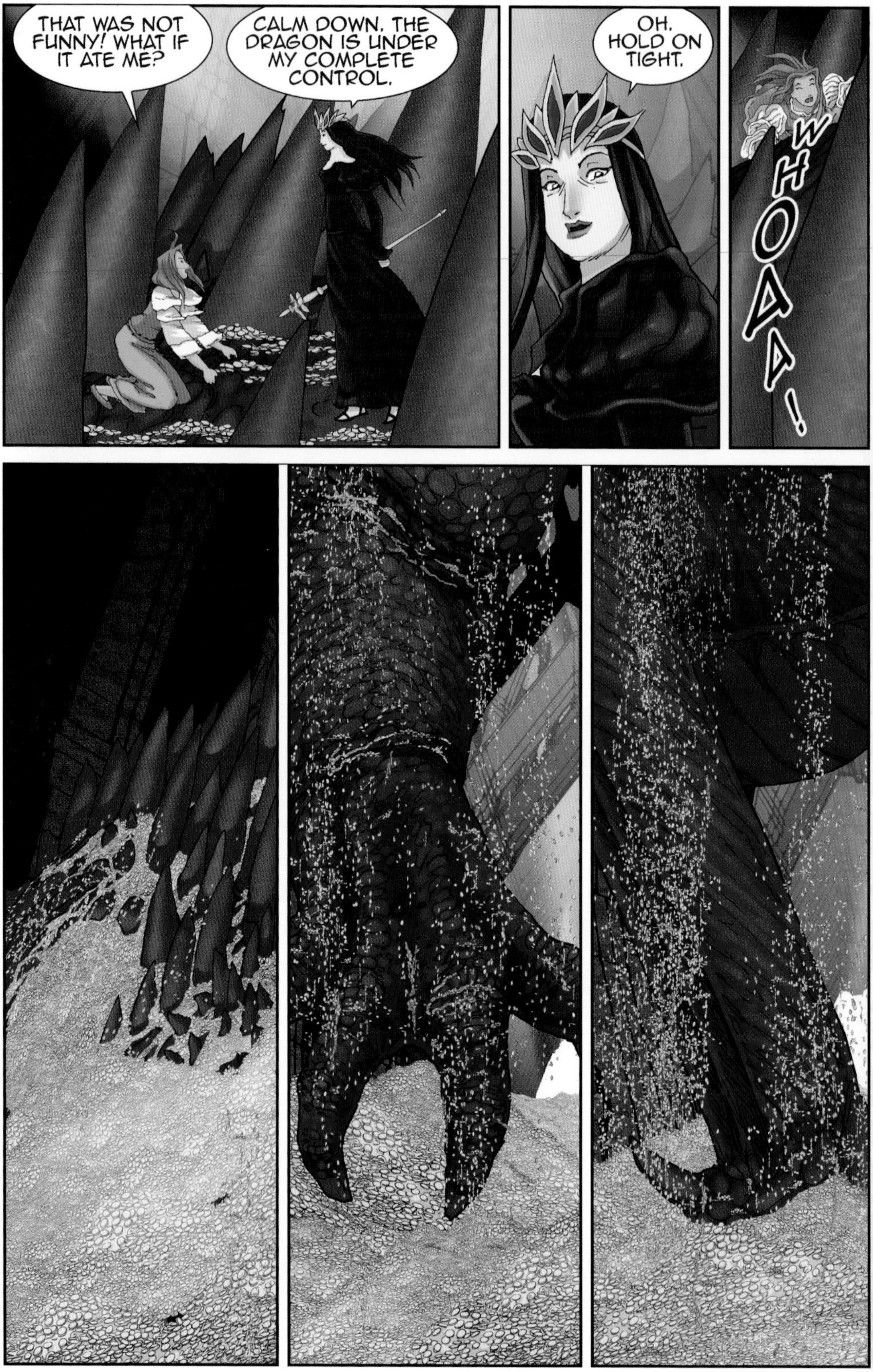
THAT WAS NOT FUNNY! WHAT IF IT ATE ME?
CALM DOWN. THE DRAGON IS UNDER MY COMPLETE CONTROL.
OH. HOLD ON TIGHT.
WHOAA!

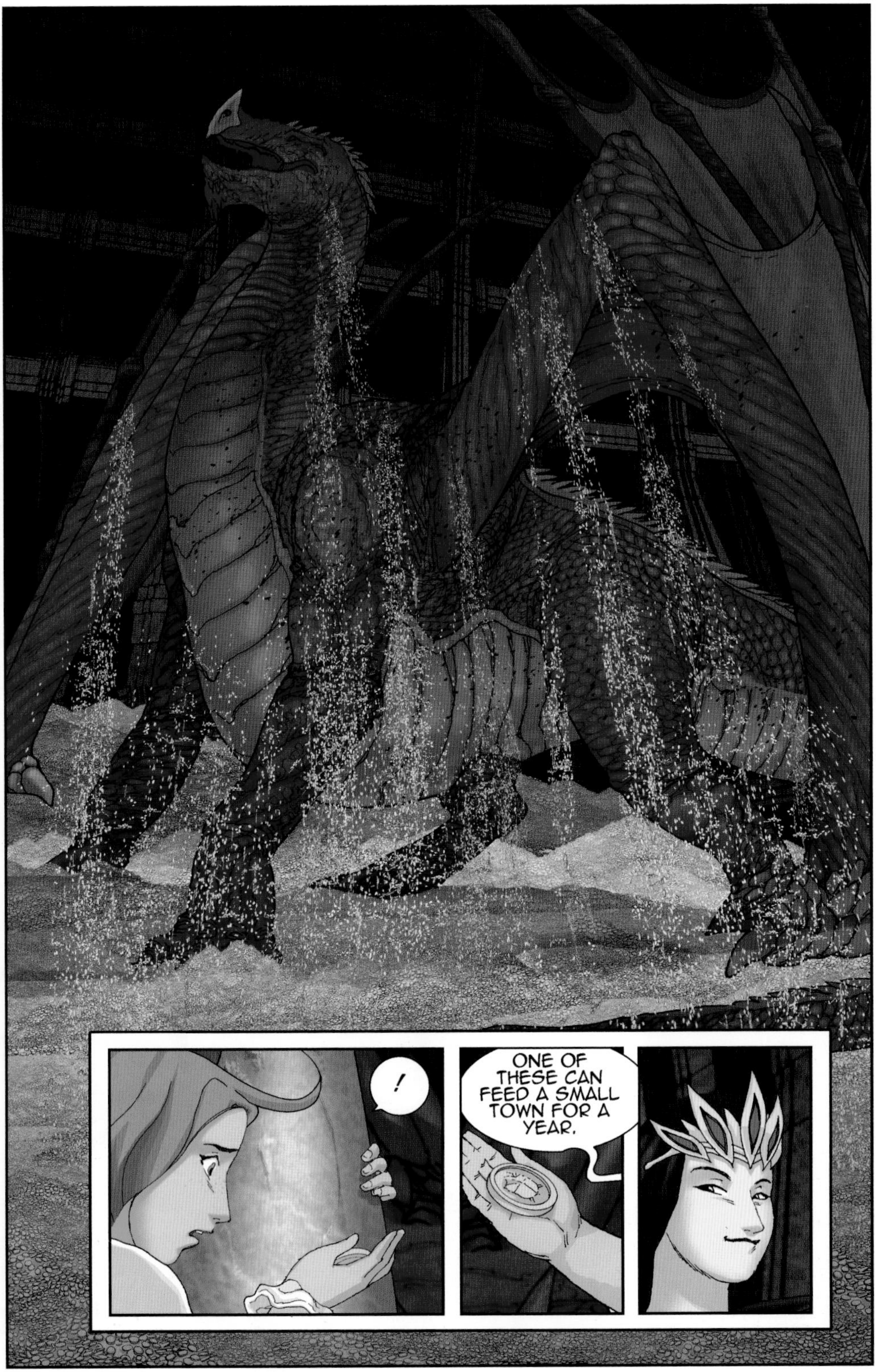
!
ONE OF THESE CAN FEED A SMALL TOWN FOR A YEAR.

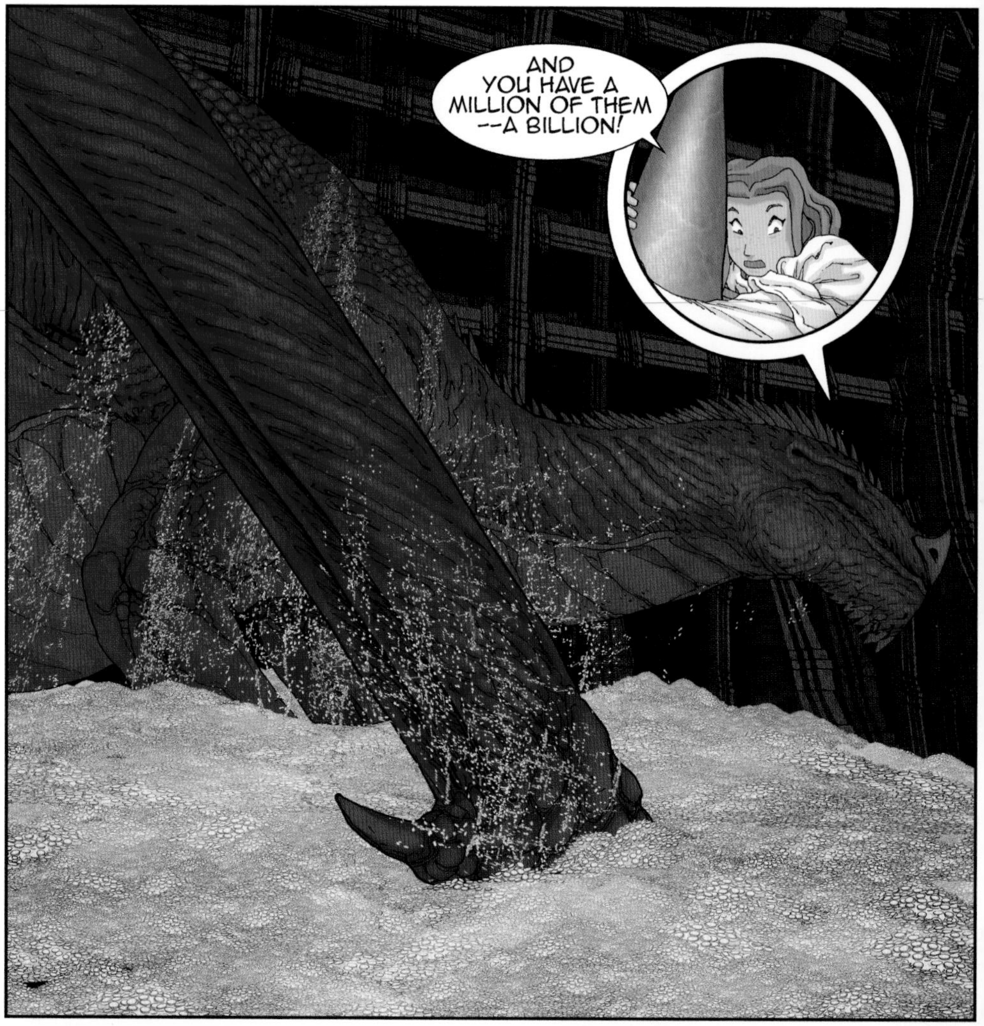
AND YOU HAVE A MILLION OF THEM --A BILLION!

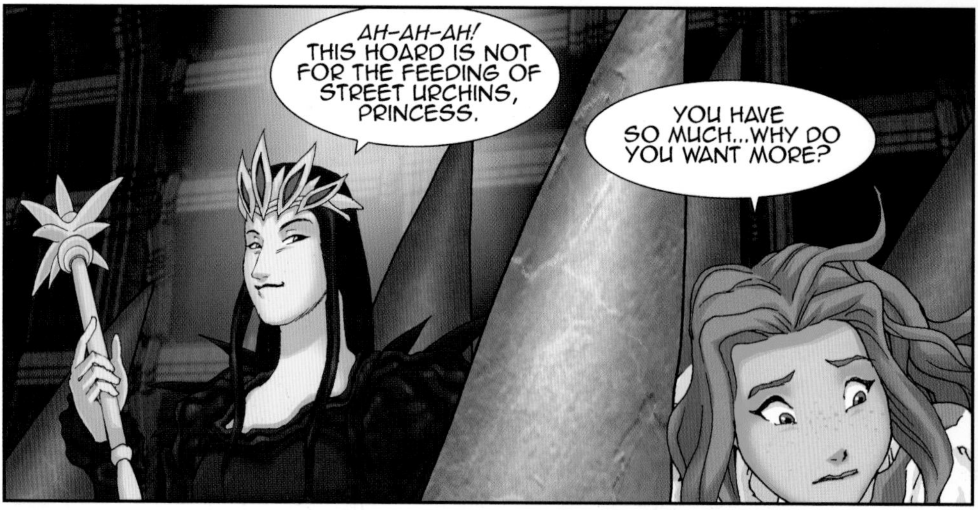
AH-AH-AH! THIS HOARD IS NOT FOR THE FEEDING OF STREET URCHINS, PRINCESS.
YOU HAVE SO MUCH...WHY DO YOU WANT MORE?

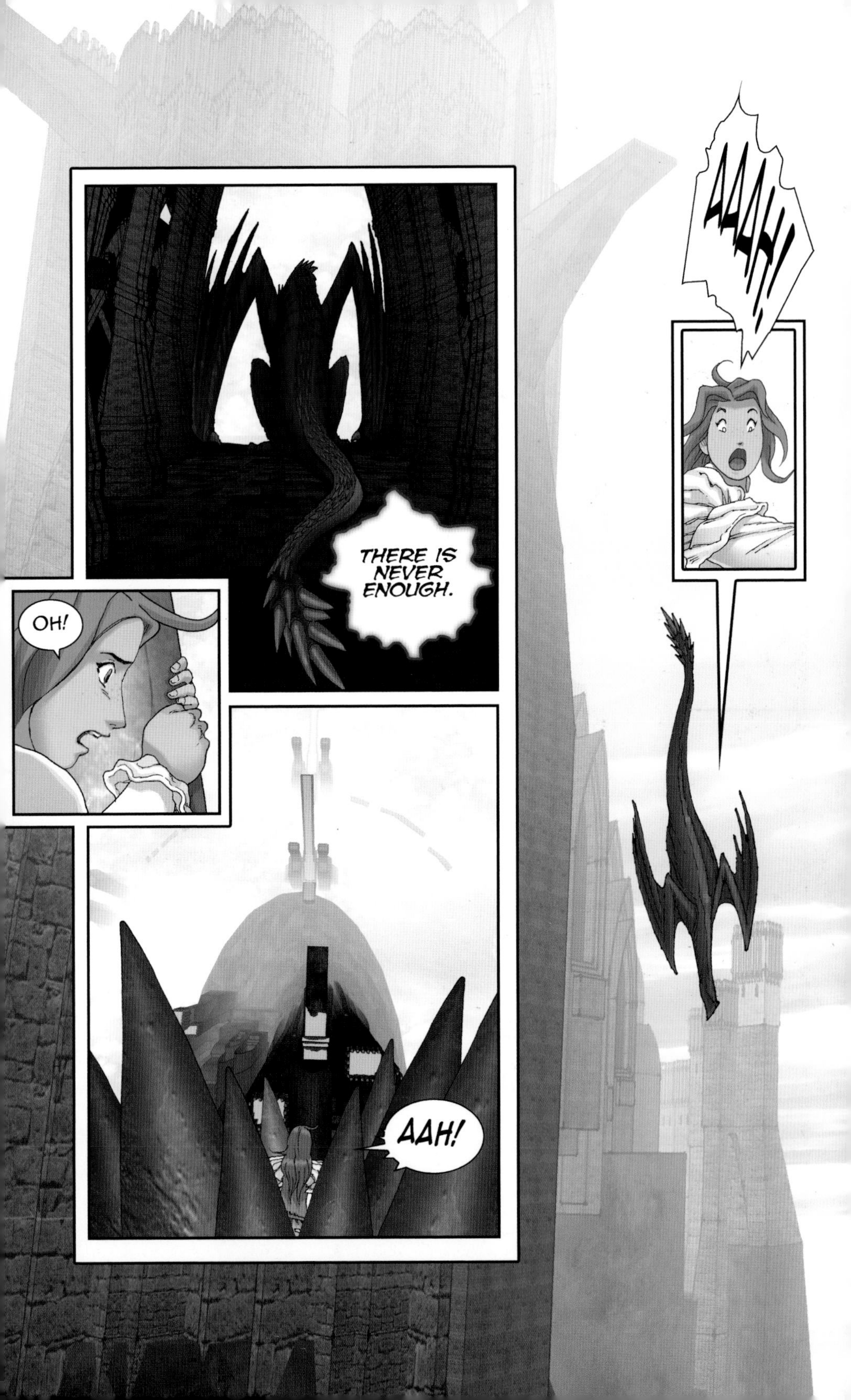
THERE IS NEVER ENOUGH.
OH!
AAH!
AAAH!

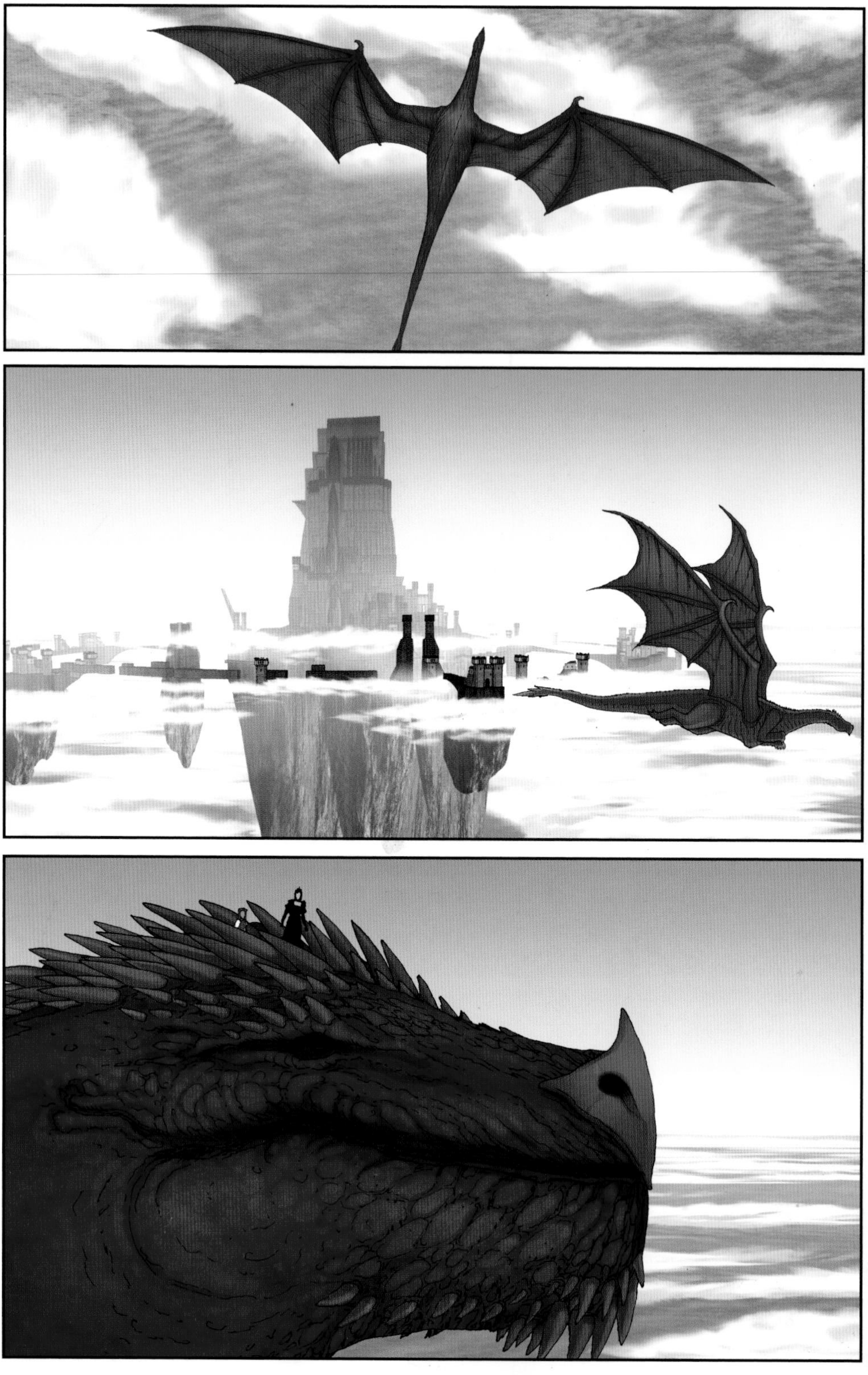

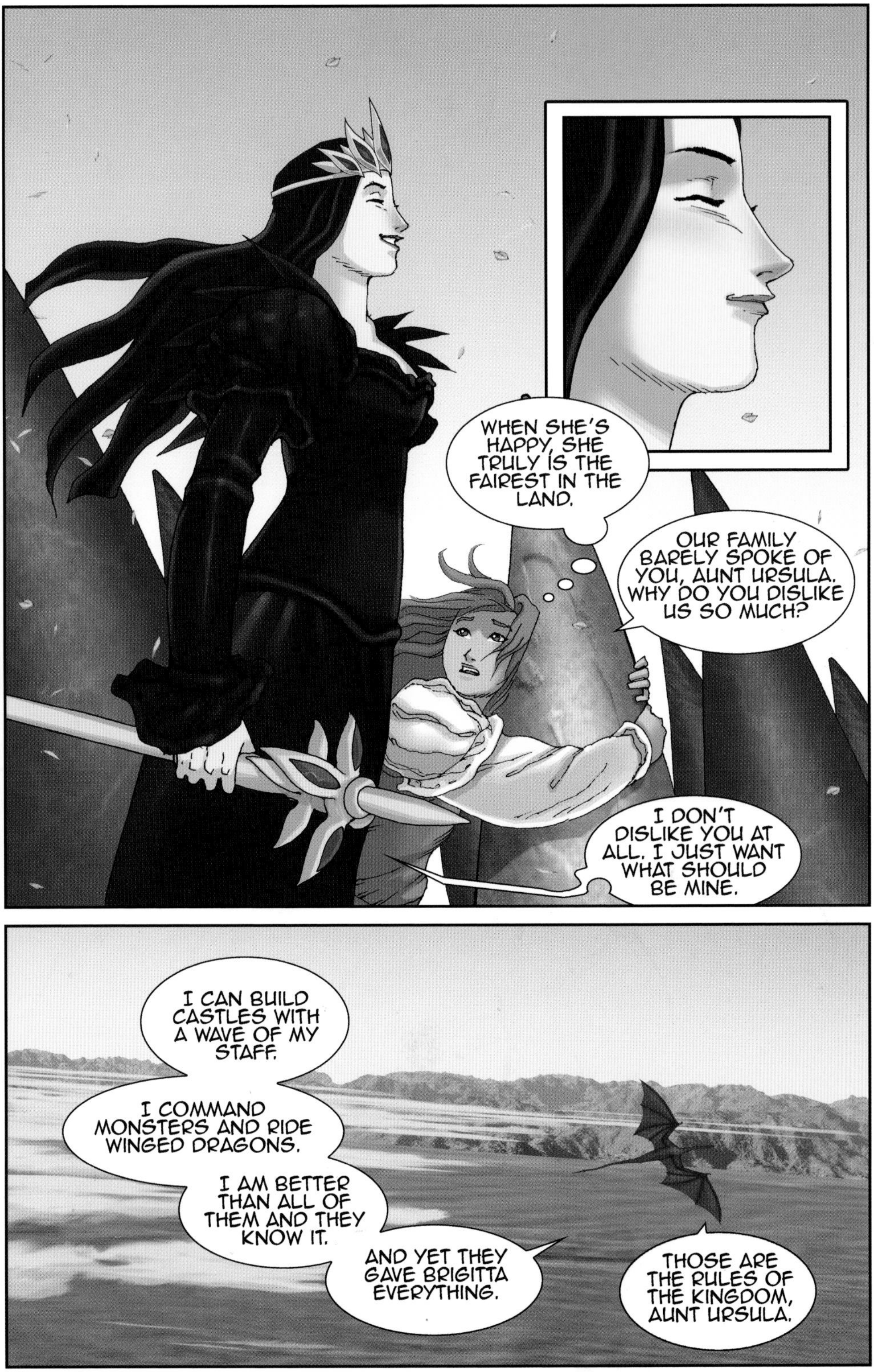
WHEN SHE'S HAPPY, SHE TRULY IS THE FAIREST IN THE LAND.
OUR FAMILY BARELY SPOKE OF YOU, AUNT URSULA. WHY DO YOU DISLIKE US SO MUCH?
I DON'T DISLIKE YOU AT ALL. I JUST WANT WHAT SHOULD BE MINE.
I CAN BUILD CASTLES WITH A WAVE OF MY STAFF.
I COMMAND MONSTERS AND RIDE WINGED DRAGONS.
I AM BETTER THAN ALL OF THEM AND THEY KNOW IT.
AND YET THEY GAVE BRIGITTA EVERYTHING.
THOSE ARE THE RULES OF THE KINGDOM, AUNT URSULA.

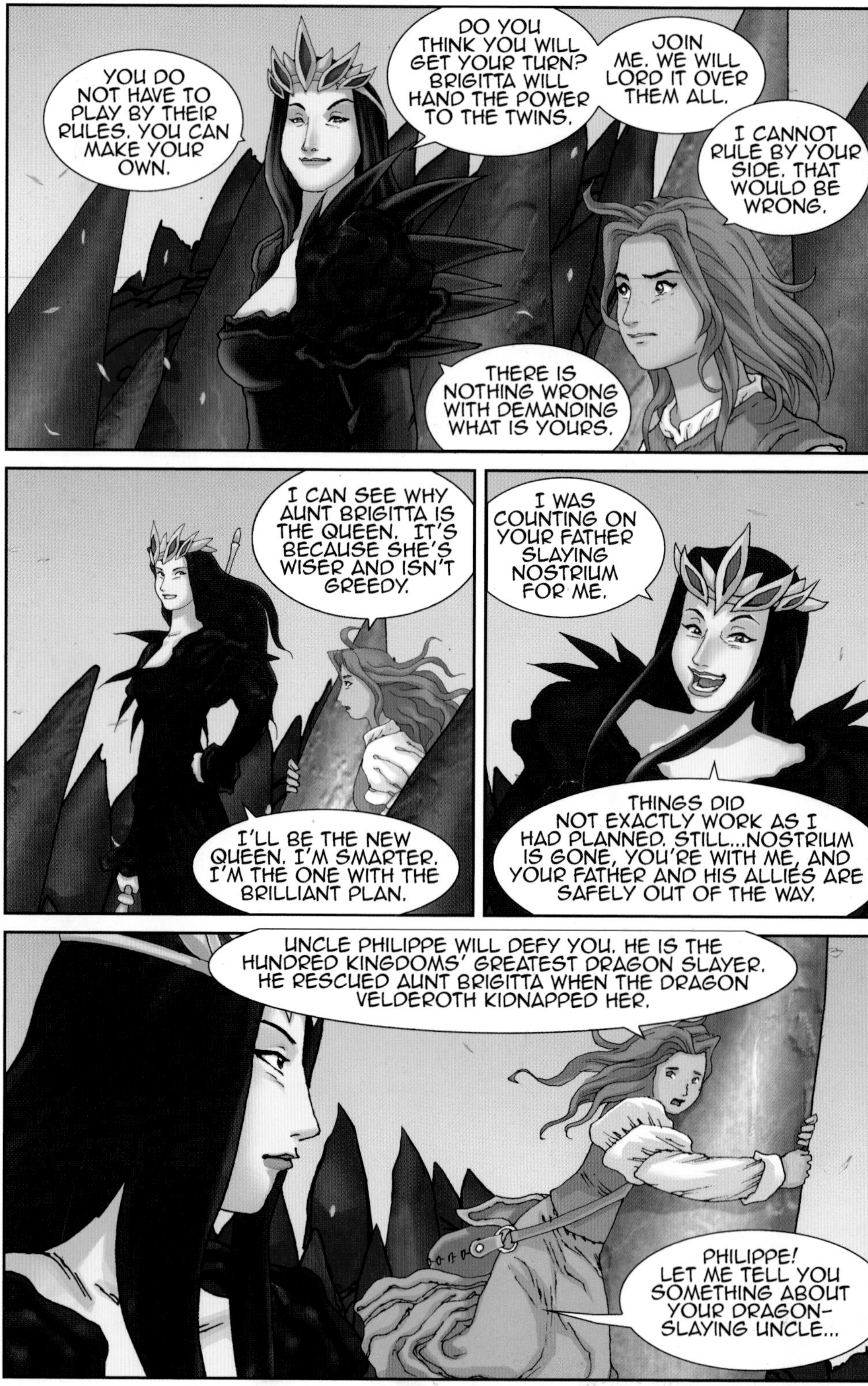
YOU DO NOT HAVE TO PLAY BY THEIR RULES. YOU CAN MAKE YOUR OWN.
DO YOU THINK YOU WILL GET YOUR TURN? BRIGITTA WILL HAND THE POWER TO THE TWINS.
JOIN ME. WE WILL LORD IT OVER THEM ALL.
I CANNOT RULE BY YOUR SIDE. THAT WOULD BE WRONG.
THERE IS NOTHING WRONG WITH DEMANDING WHAT IS YOURS.
I CAN SEE WHY AUNT BRIGITTA IS THE QUEEN. IT'S BECAUSE SHE'S WISER AND ISN'T GREEDY.
I'LL BE THE NEW QUEEN. I'M SMARTER. I'M THE ONE WITH THE BRILLIANT PLAN.
I WAS COUNTING ON YOUR FATHER SLAYING NOSTRIUM FOR ME.
THINGS DID NOT EXACTLY WORK AS I HAD PLANNED. STILL...NOSTRIUM IS GONE, YOU'RE WITH ME, AND YOUR FATHER AND HIS ALLIES ARE SAFELY OUT OF THE WAY.
UNCLE PHILIPPE WILL DEFY YOU. HE IS THE HUNDRED KINGDOMS' GREATEST DRAGON SLAYER. HE RESCUED AUNT BRIGITTA WHEN THE DRAGON VELDEROTH KIDNAPPED HER.
PHILIPPE! LET ME TELL YOU SOMETHING ABOUT YOUR DRAGON-SLAYING UNCLE...

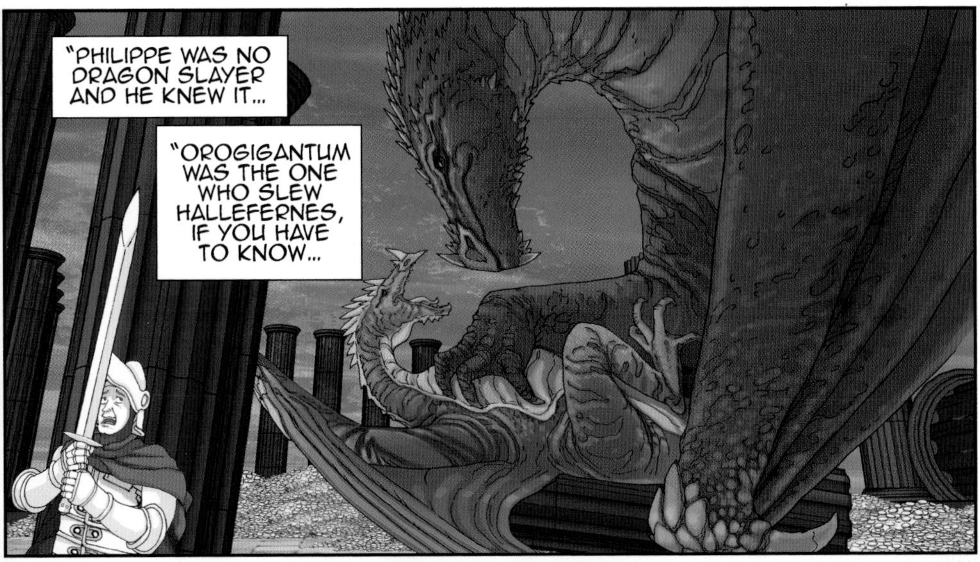
"PHILIPPE WAS NO DRAGON SLAYER AND HE KNEW IT...
"OROGIGANTUM WAS THE ONE WHO SLEW HALLEFERNES, IF YOU HAVE TO KNOW...

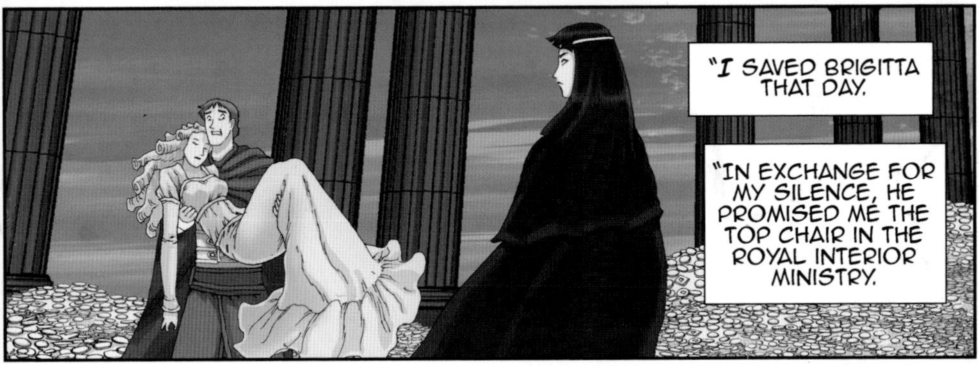
"I SAVED BRIGITTA THAT DAY.
"IN EXCHANGE FOR MY SILENCE, HE PROMISED ME THE TOP CHAIR IN THE ROYAL INTERIOR MINISTRY.

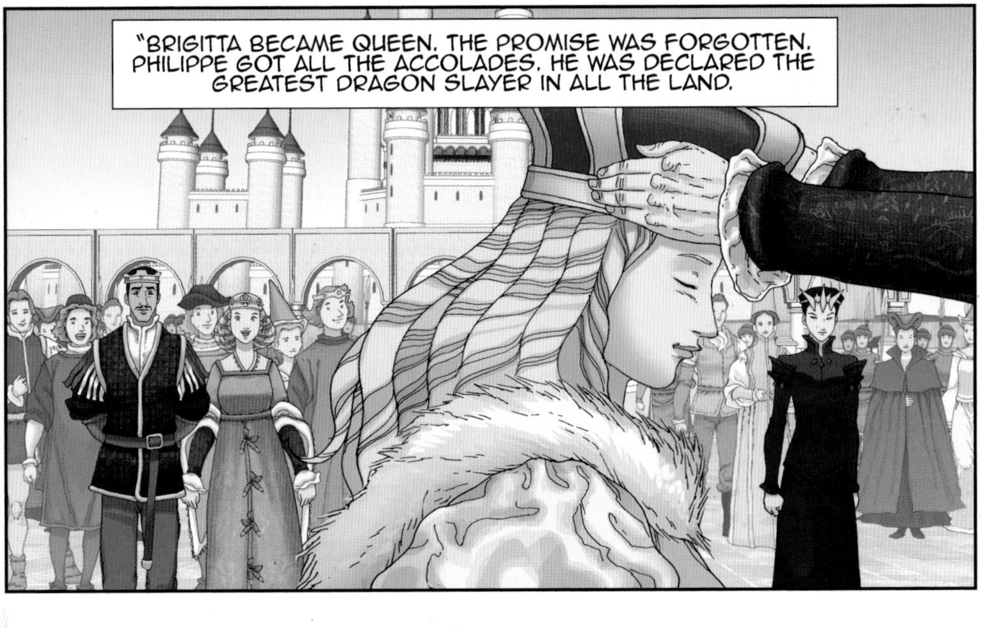
"BRIGITTA BECAME QUEEN. THE PROMISE WAS FORGOTTEN. PHILIPPE GOT ALL THE ACCOLADES. HE WAS DECLARED THE GREATEST DRAGON SLAYER IN ALL THE LAND.

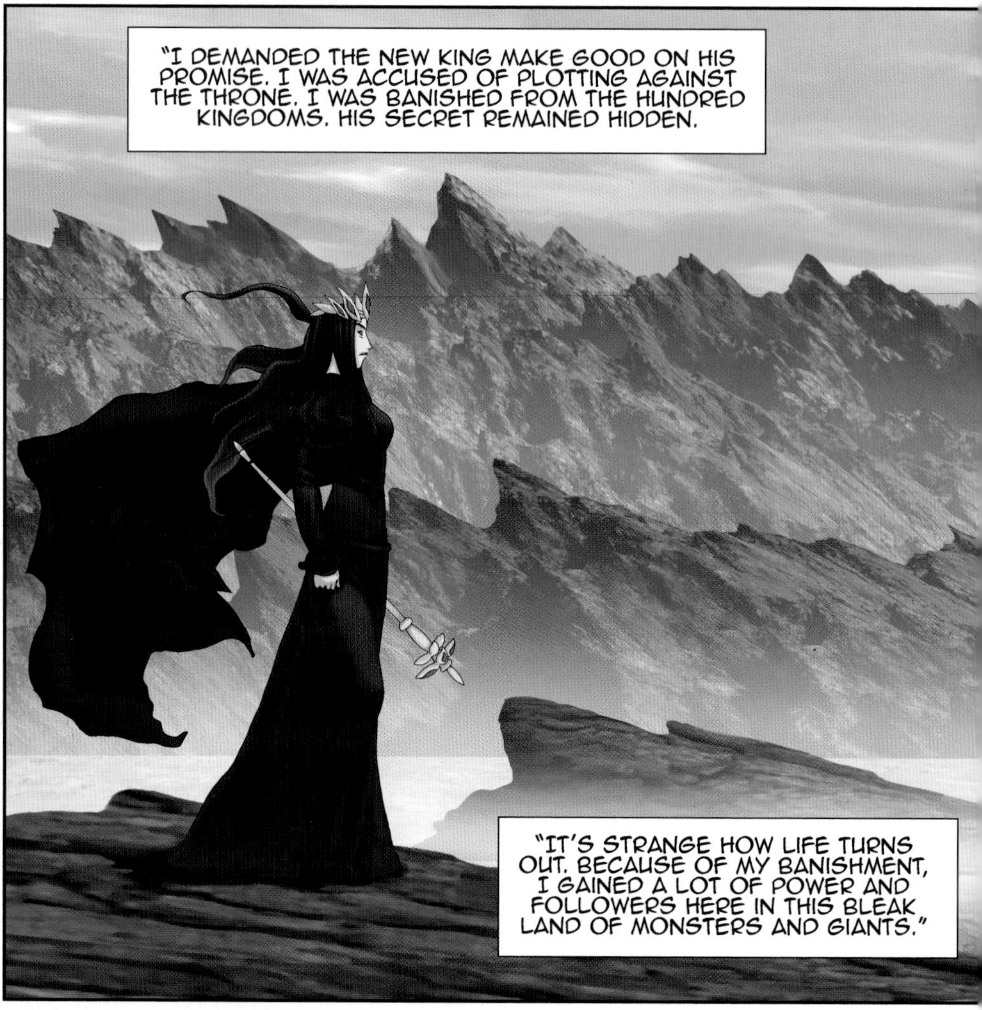
"I DEMANDED THE NEW KING MAKE GOOD ON HIS PROMISE. I WAS ACCUSED OF PLOTTING AGAINST THE THRONE. I WAS BANISHED FROM THE HUNDRED KINGDOMS. HIS SECRET REMAINED HIDDEN.
"IT'S STRANGE HOW LIFE TURNS OUT. BECAUSE OF MY BANISHMENT, I GAINED A LOT OF POWER AND FOLLOWERS HERE IN THIS BLEAK LAND OF MONSTERS AND GIANTS."

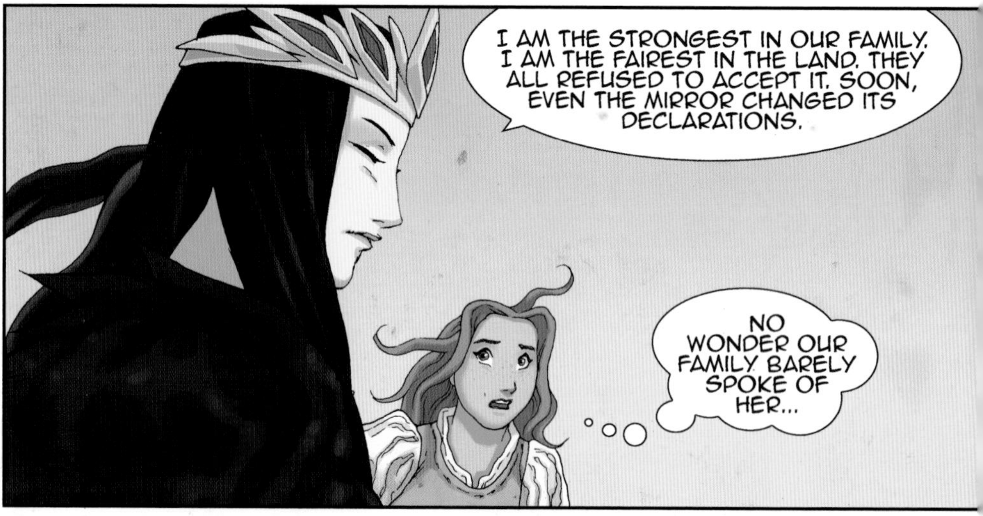
I AM THE STRONGEST IN OUR FAMILY. I AM THE FAIREST IN THE LAND. THEY ALL REFUSED TO ACCEPT IT. SOON, EVEN THE MIRROR CHANGED ITS DECLARATIONS.
NO WONDER OUR FAMILY BARELY SPOKE OF HER...

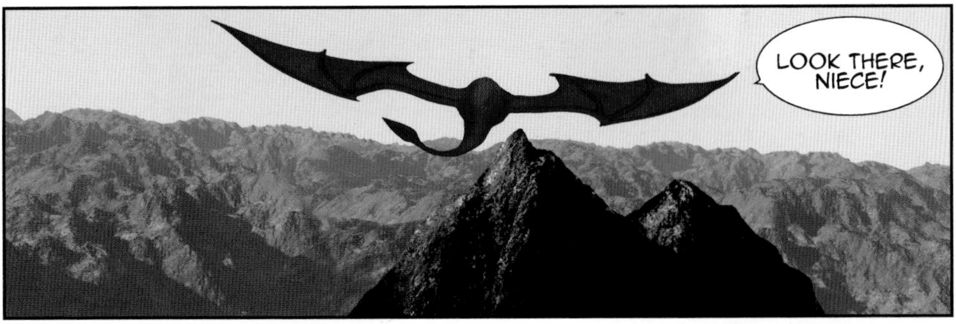
LOOK THERE, NIECE!

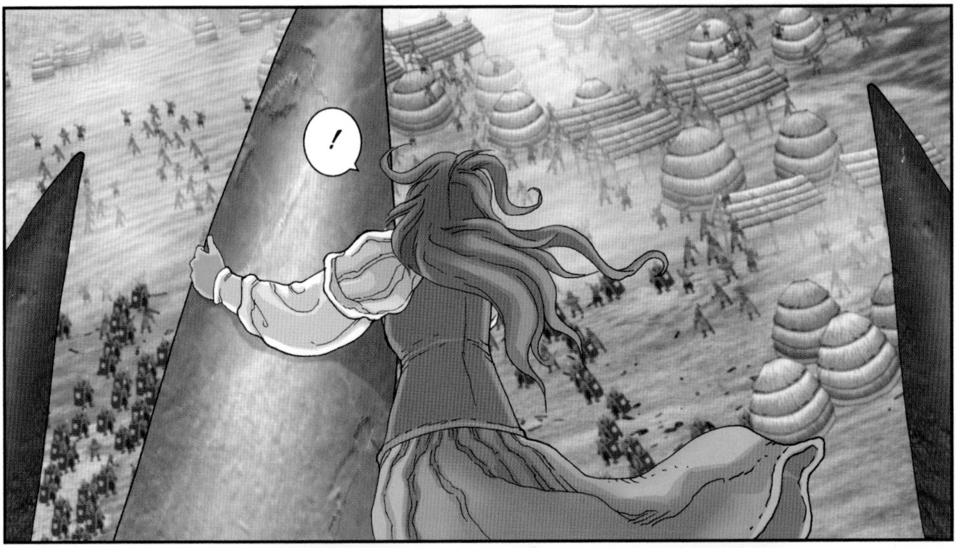
!

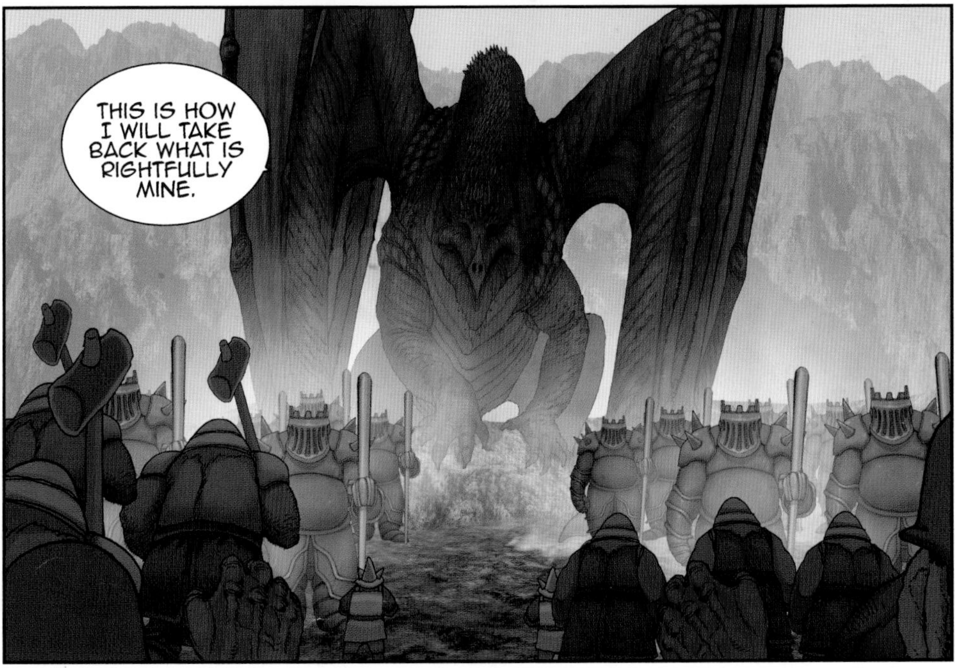
THIS IS HOW I WILL TAKE BACK WHAT IS RIGHTFULLY MINE.

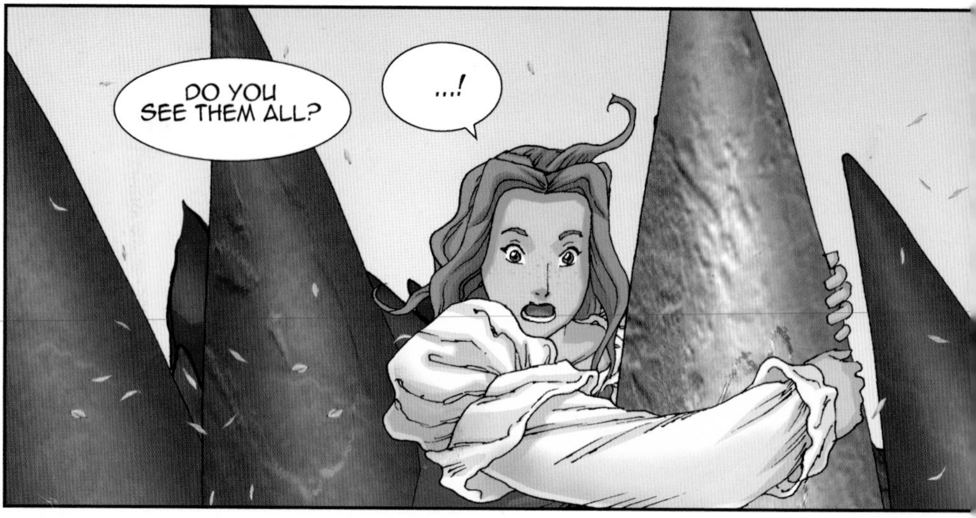
DO YOU SEE THEM ALL?
...!

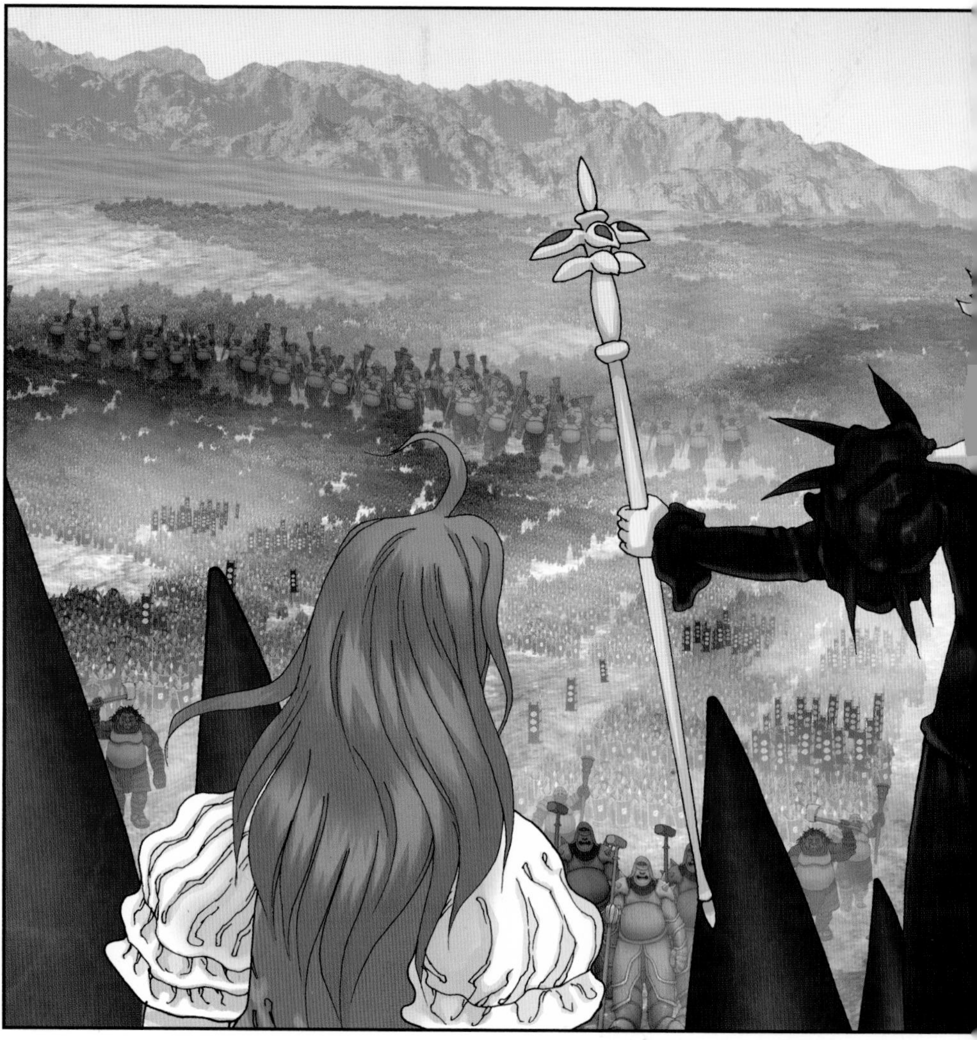

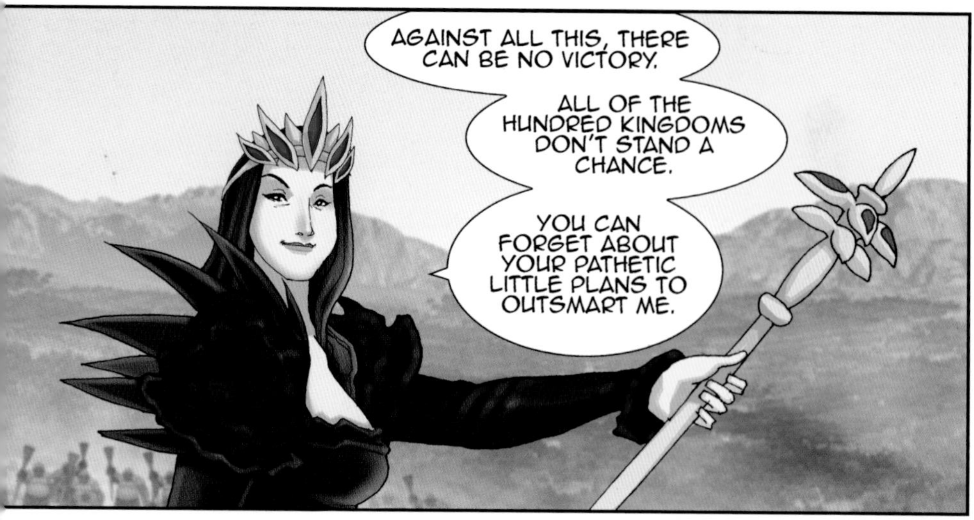
AGAINST ALL THIS, THERE CAN BE NO VICTORY.
ALL OF THE HUNDRED KINGDOMS DON'T STAND A CHANCE.
YOU CAN FORGET ABOUT YOUR PATHETIC LITTLE PLANS TO OUTSMART ME.

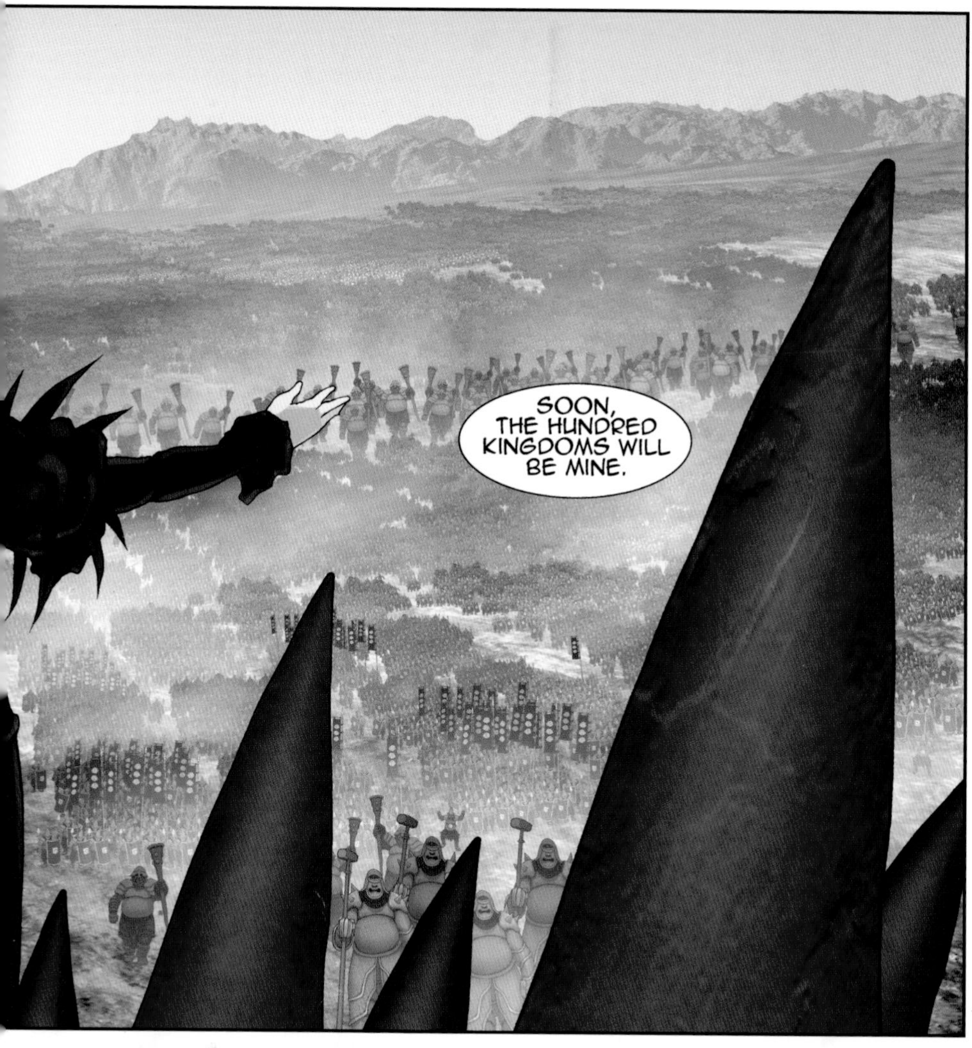
SOON, THE HUNDRED KINGDOMS WILL BE MINE.

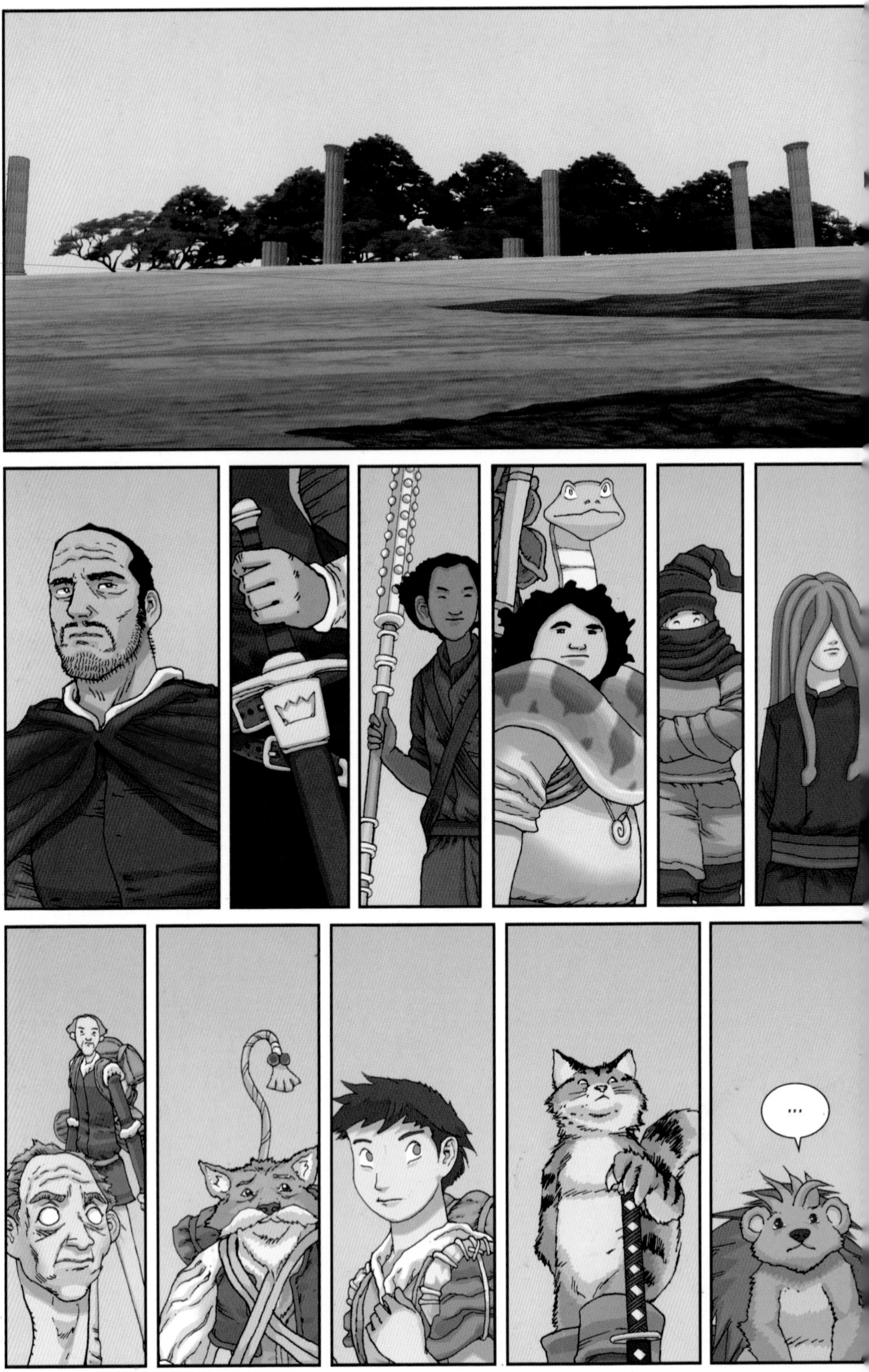
...

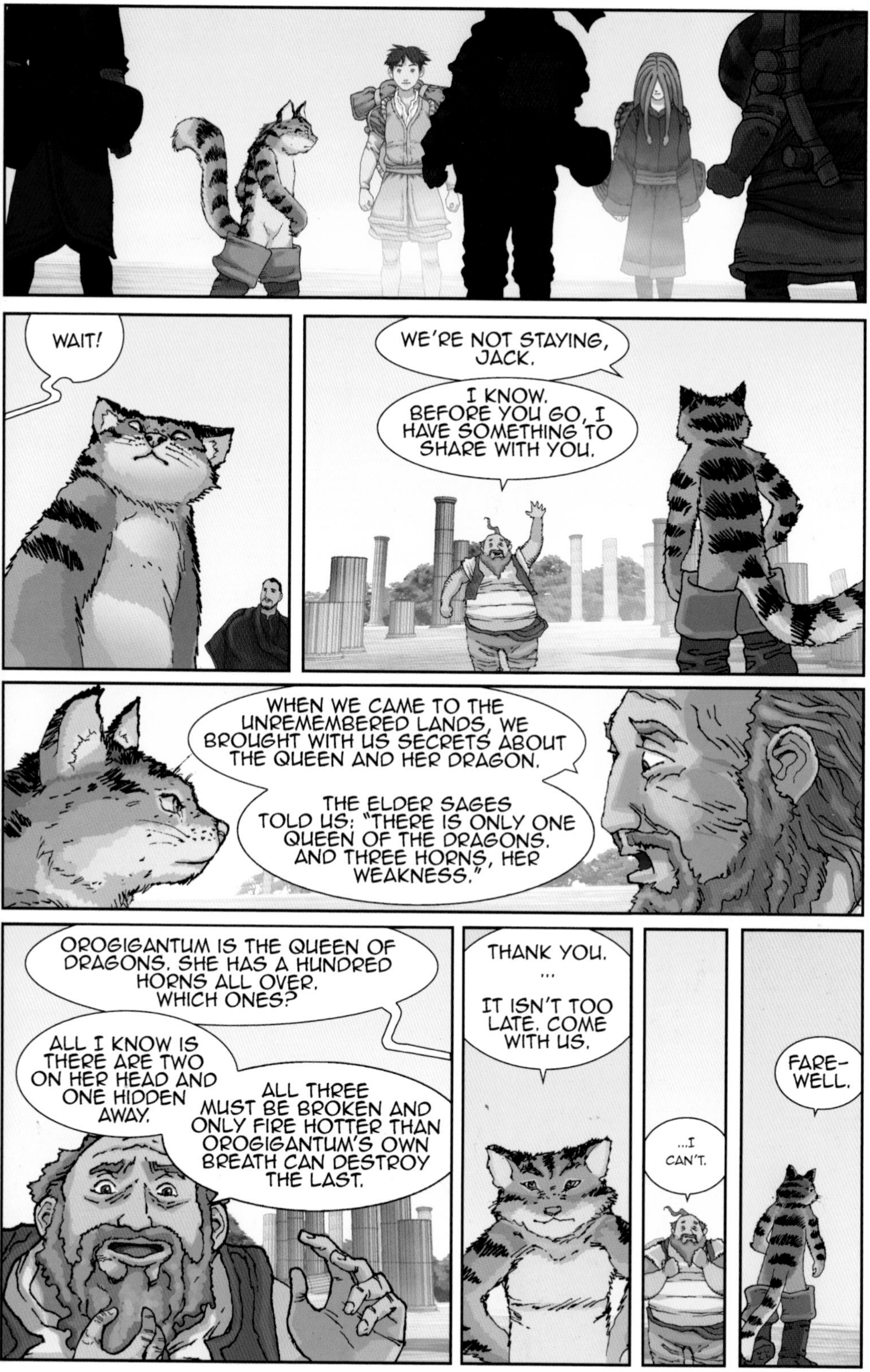
WAIT!
WE'RE NOT STAYING, JACK.
I KNOW. BEFORE YOU GO, I HAVE SOMETHING TO SHARE WITH YOU.
WHEN WE CAME TO THE UNREMEMBERED LANDS, WE BROUGHT WITH US SECRETS ABOUT THE QUEEN AND HER DRAGON.
THE ELDER SAGES TOLD US: "THERE IS ONLY ONE QUEEN OF THE DRAGONS. AND THREE HORNS, HER WEAKNESS."
OROGIGANTUM IS THE QUEEN OF DRAGONS. SHE HAS A HUNDRED HORNS ALL OVER. WHICH ONES?
ALL I KNOW IS THERE ARE TWO ON HER HEAD AND ONE HIDDEN AWAY.
ALL THREE MUST BE BROKEN AND ONLY FIRE HOTTER THAN OROGIGANTUM'S OWN BREATH CAN DESTROY THE LAST.
THANK YOU. ... IT ISN'T TOO LATE. COME WITH US.
...I CAN'T.
FARE-WELL.

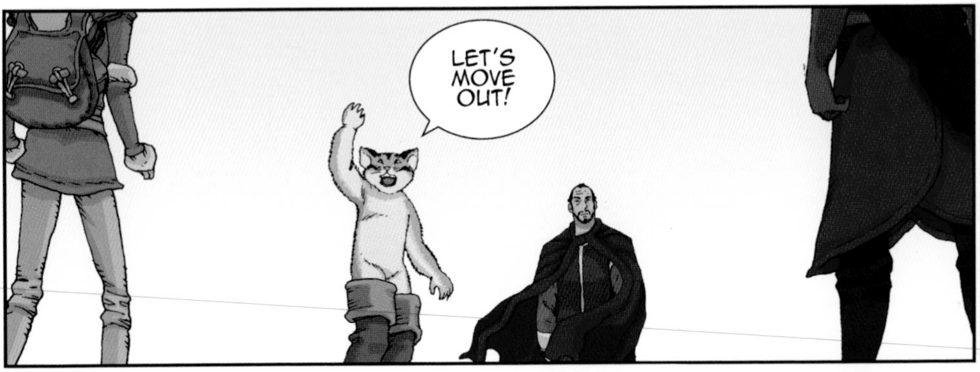
LET'S MOVE OUT!

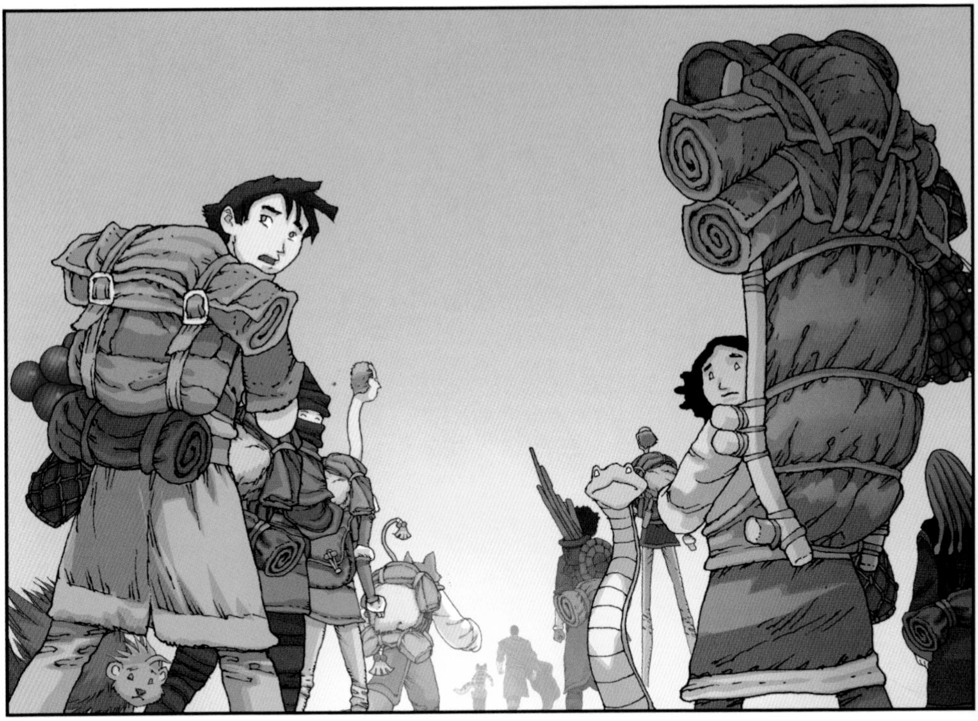

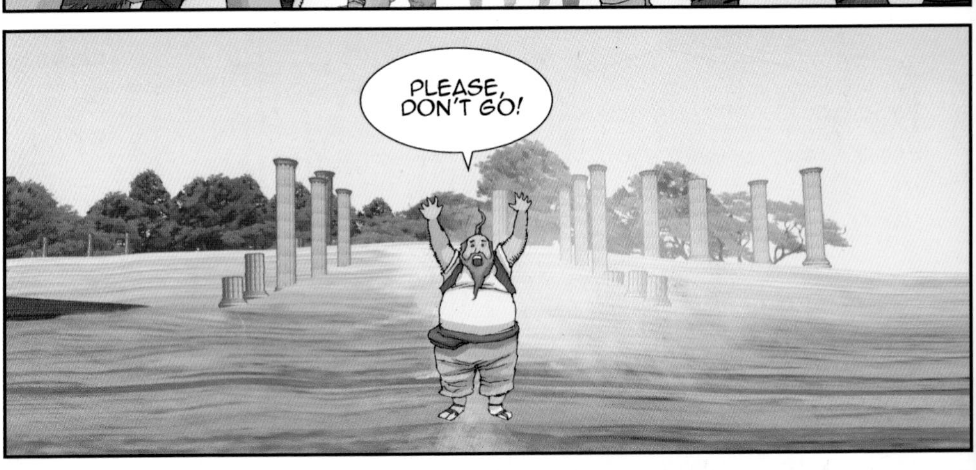
PLEASE, DON'T GO!

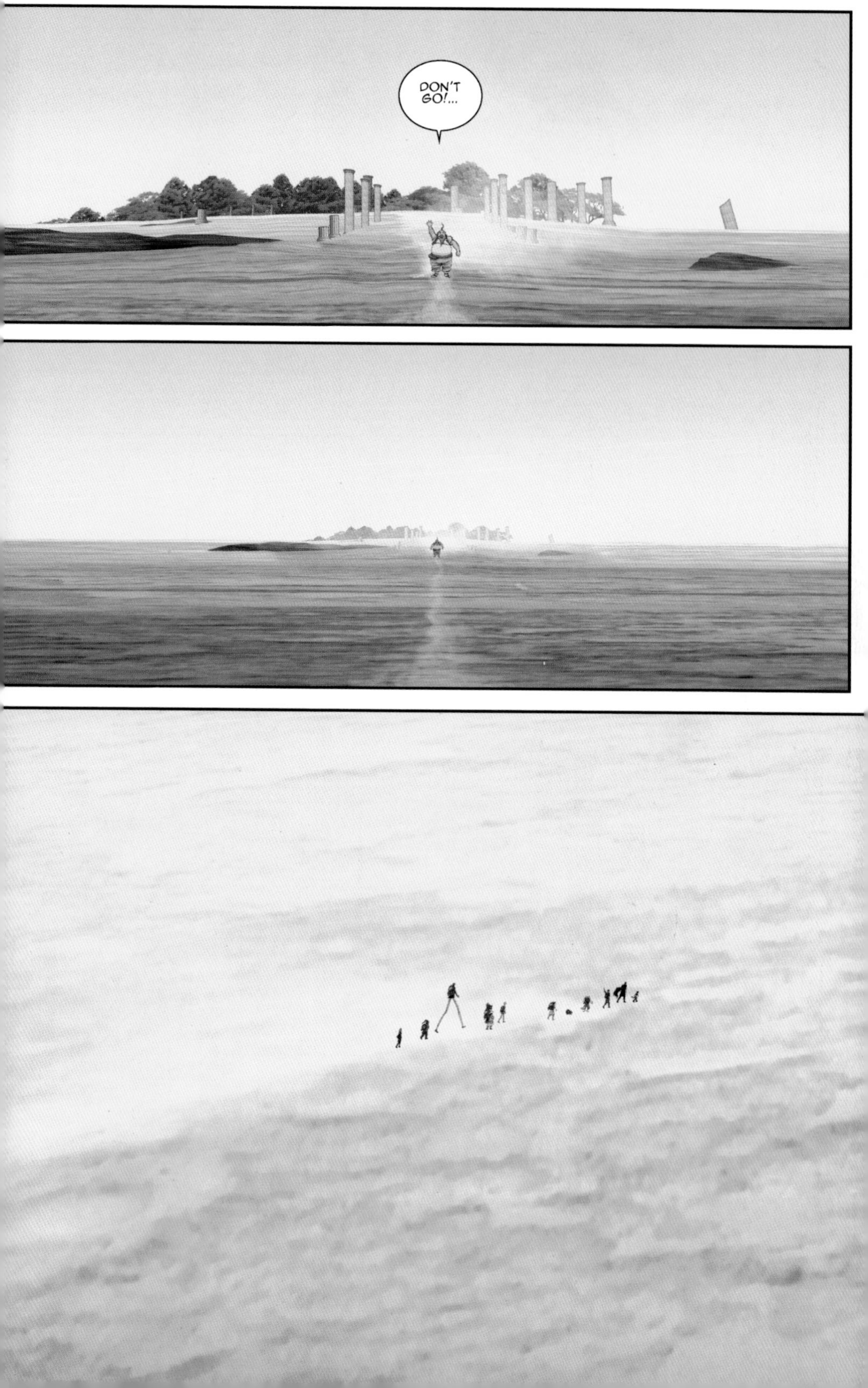
DON'T GO!...

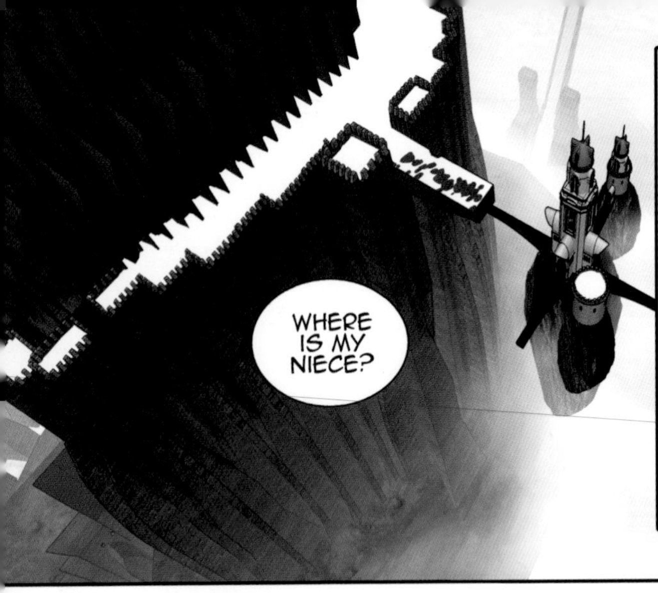
WHERE IS MY NIECE?

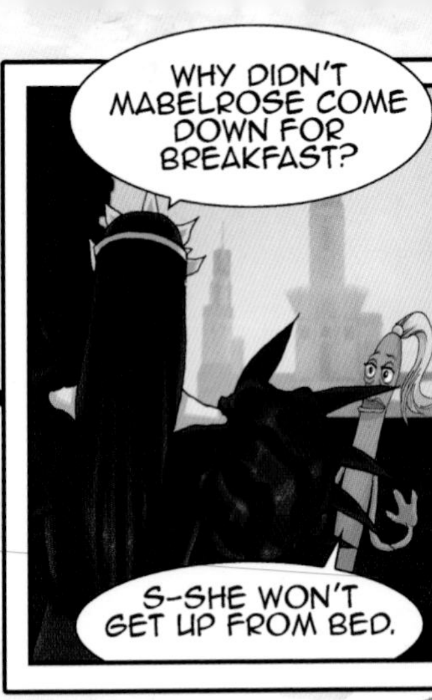
WHY DIDN'T MABELROSE COME DOWN FOR BREAKFAST?
S-SHE WON'T GET UP FROM BED.

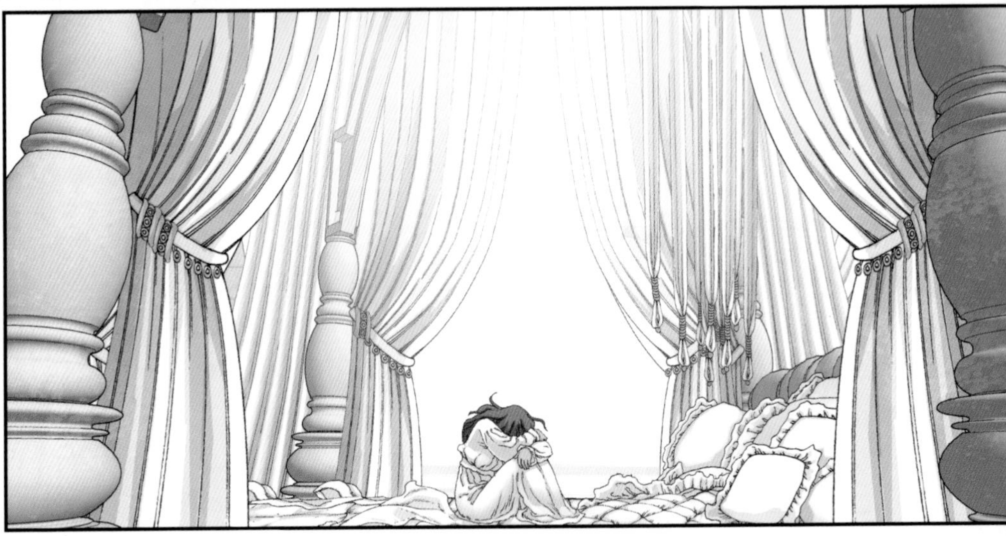

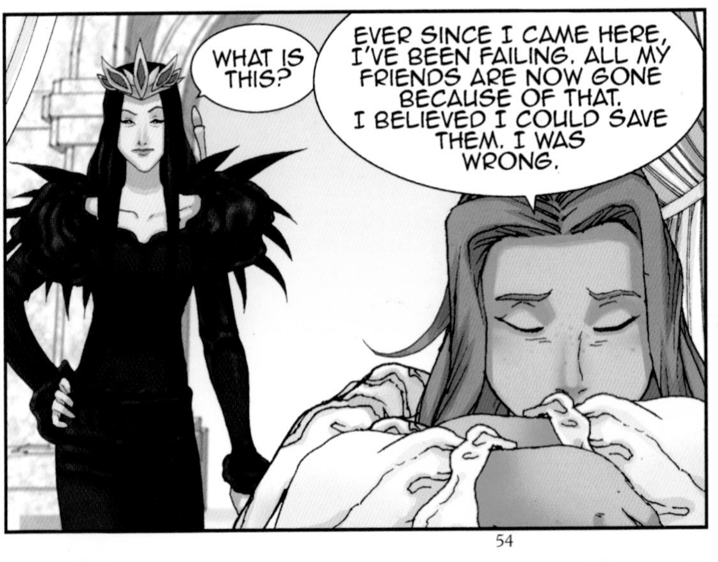
WHAT IS THIS?
EVER SINCE I CAME HERE, I'VE BEEN FAILING. ALL MY FRIENDS ARE NOW GONE BECAUSE OF THAT. I BELIEVED I COULD SAVE THEM. I WAS WRONG.

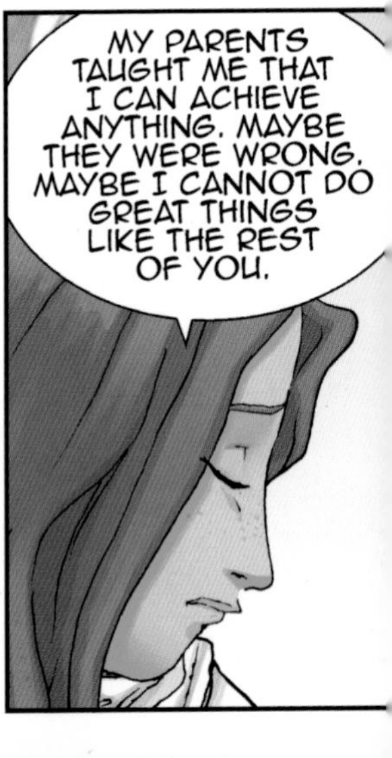
MY PARENTS TAUGHT ME THAT I CAN ACHIEVE ANYTHING. MAYBE THEY WERE WRONG. MAYBE I CANNOT DO GREAT THINGS LIKE THE REST OF YOU.

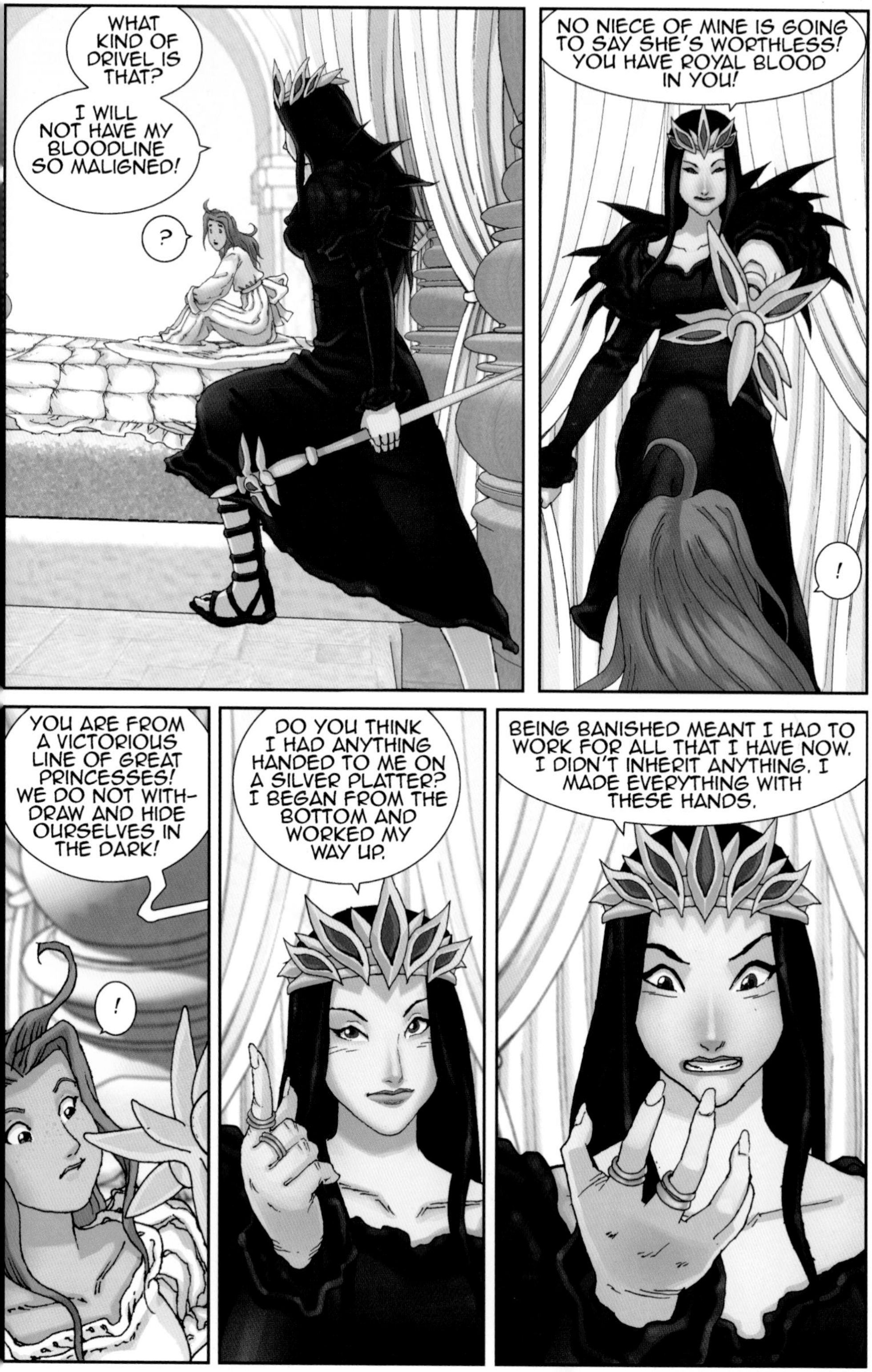
WHAT KIND OF DRIVEL IS THAT?
I WILL NOT HAVE MY BLOODLINE SO MALIGNED!
?
NO NIECE OF MINE IS GOING TO SAY SHE'S WORTHLESS! YOU HAVE ROYAL BLOOD IN YOU!
!
YOU ARE FROM A VICTORIOUS LINE OF GREAT PRINCESSES! WE DO NOT WITH-DRAW AND HIDE OURSELVES IN THE DARK!
!
DO YOU THINK I HAD ANYTHING HANDED TO ME ON A SILVER PLATTER? I BEGAN FROM THE BOTTOM AND WORKED MY WAY UP.
BEING BANISHED MEANT I HAD TO WORK FOR ALL THAT I HAVE NOW. I DIDN'T INHERIT ANYTHING. I MADE EVERYTHING WITH THESE HANDS.

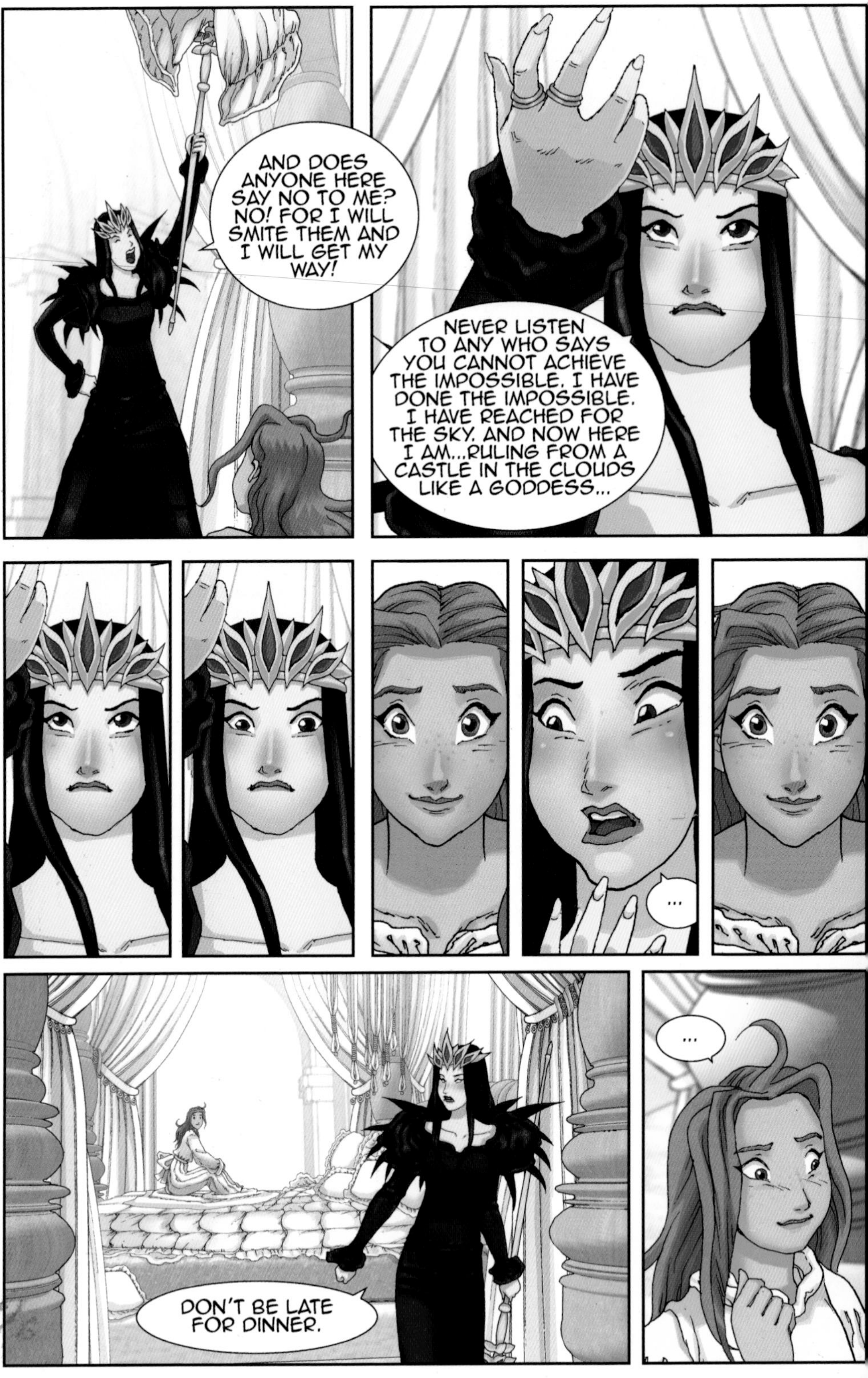
AND DOES ANYONE HERE SAY NO TO ME? NO! FOR I WILL SMITE THEM AND I WILL GET MY WAY!
NEVER LISTEN TO ANY WHO SAYS YOU CANNOT ACHIEVE THE IMPOSSIBLE. I HAVE DONE THE IMPOSSIBLE. I HAVE REACHED FOR THE SKY. AND NOW HERE I AM...RULING FROM A CASTLE IN THE CLOUDS LIKE A GODDESS...
...
...
DON'T BE LATE FOR DINNER.

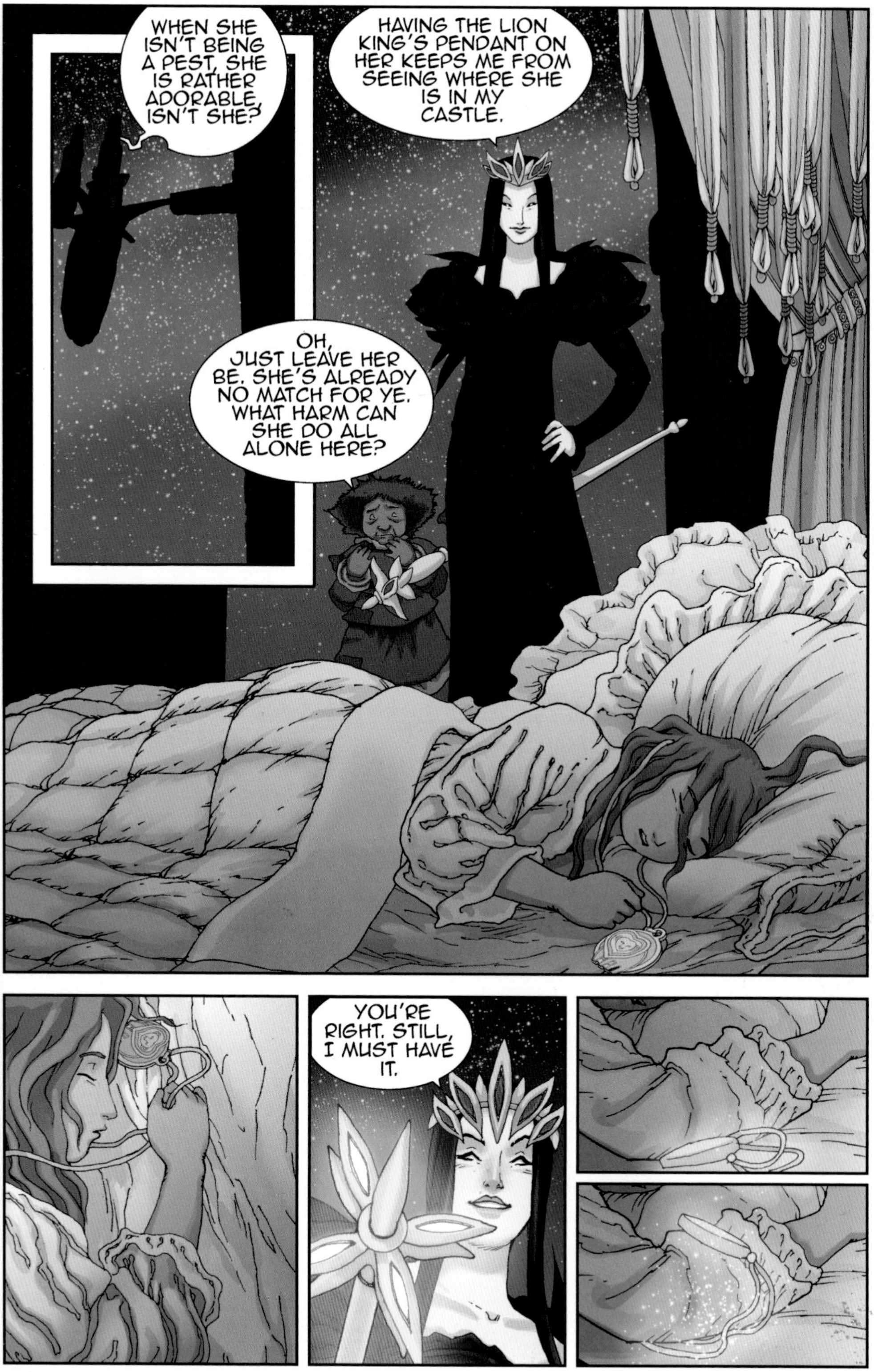
WHEN SHE ISN'T BEING A PEST, SHE IS RATHER ADORABLE, ISN'T SHE?
HAVING THE LION KING'S PENDANT ON HER KEEPS ME FROM SEEING WHERE SHE IS IN MY CASTLE.
OH, JUST LEAVE HER BE. SHE'S ALREADY NO MATCH FOR YE. WHAT HARM CAN SHE DO ALL ALONE HERE?
YOU'RE RIGHT. STILL, I MUST HAVE IT.

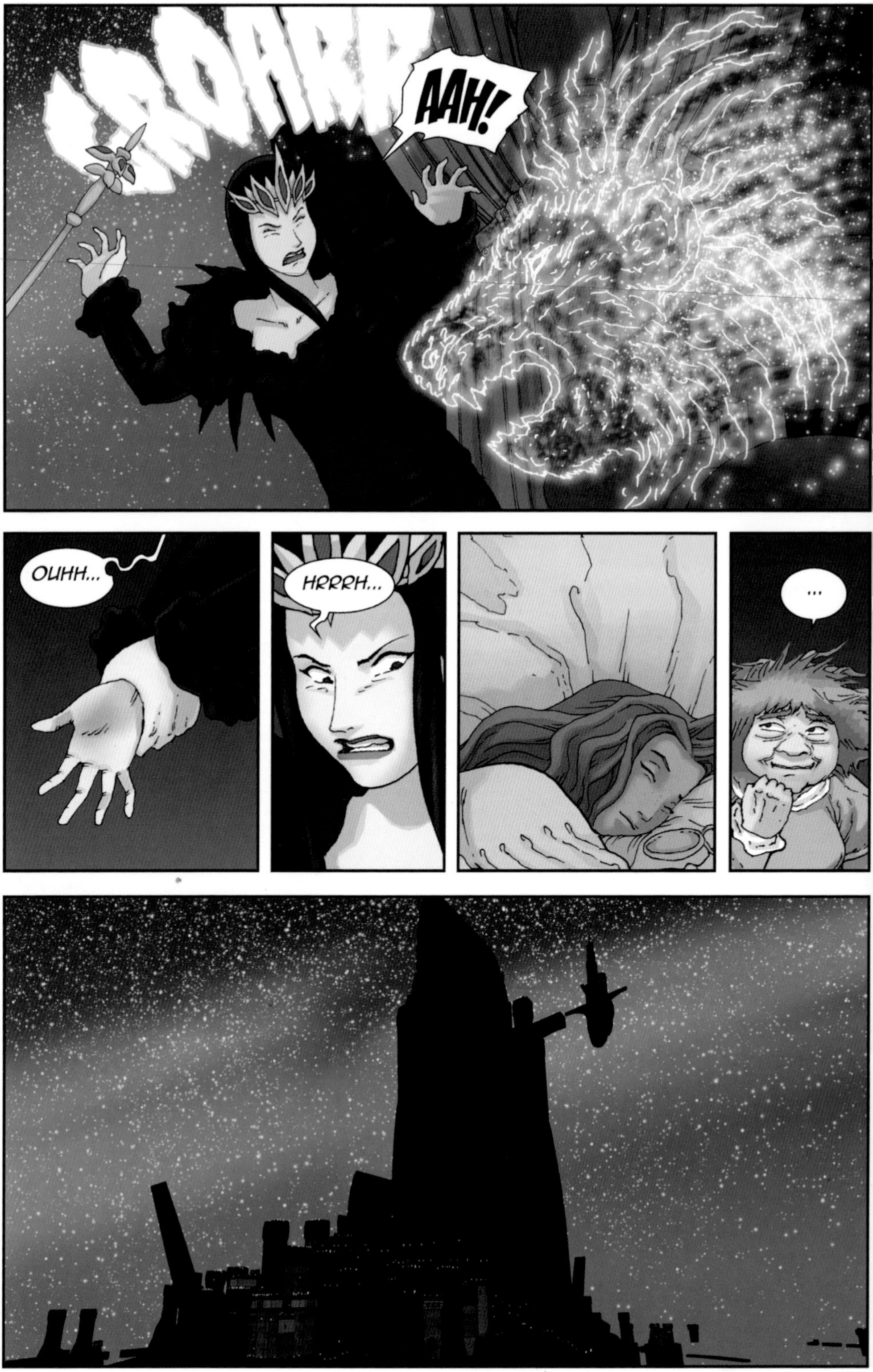
GROARR
AAH!
OUHH...
HRRRH...
...

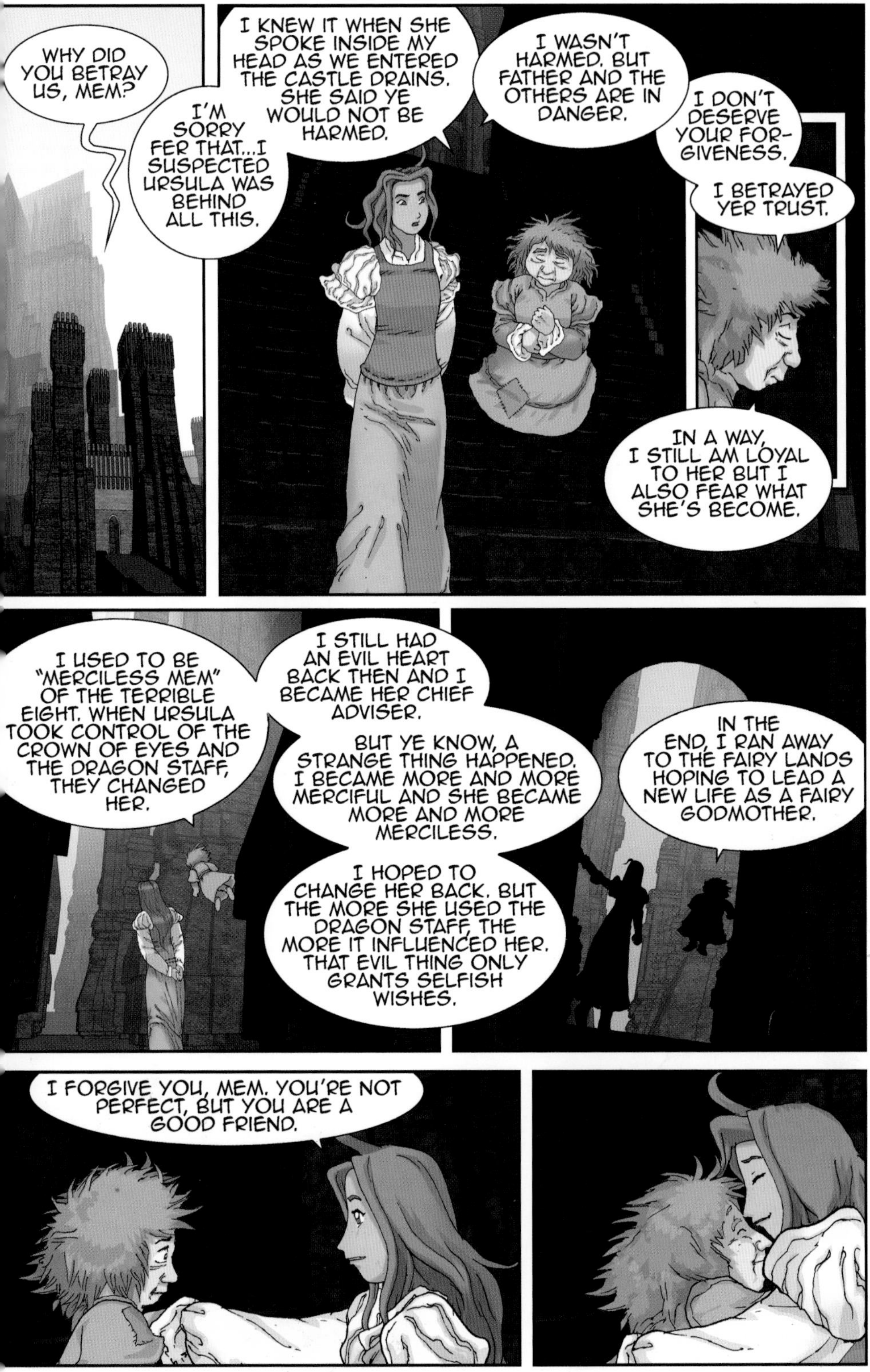
WHY DID YOU BETRAY US, MEM?
I'M SORRY FER THAT...I SUSPECTED URSULA WAS BEHIND ALL THIS.
I KNEW IT WHEN SHE SPOKE INSIDE MY HEAD AS WE ENTERED THE CASTLE DRAINS. SHE SAID YE WOULD NOT BE HARMED.
I WASN'T HARMED. BUT FATHER AND THE OTHERS ARE IN DANGER.
I DON'T DESERVE YOUR FORGIVENESS.
I BETRAYED YER TRUST.
IN A WAY, I STILL AM LOYAL TO HER BUT I ALSO FEAR WHAT SHE'S BECOME.
I USED TO BE "MERCILESS MEM" OF THE TERRIBLE EIGHT. WHEN URSULA TOOK CONTROL OF THE CROWN OF EYES AND THE DRAGON STAFF, THEY CHANGED HER.
I STILL HAD AN EVIL HEART BACK THEN AND I BECAME HER CHIEF ADVISER.
BUT YE KNOW, A STRANGE THING HAPPENED. I BECAME MORE AND MORE MERCIFUL AND SHE BECAME MORE AND MORE MERCILESS.
I HOPED TO CHANGE HER BACK. BUT THE MORE SHE USED THE DRAGON STAFF, THE MORE IT INFLUENCED HER. THAT EVIL THING ONLY GRANTS SELFISH WISHES.
IN THE END, I RAN AWAY TO THE FAIRY LANDS HOPING TO LEAD A NEW LIFE AS A FAIRY GODMOTHER.
I FORGIVE YOU, MEM. YOU'RE NOT PERFECT, BUT YOU ARE A GOOD FRIEND.

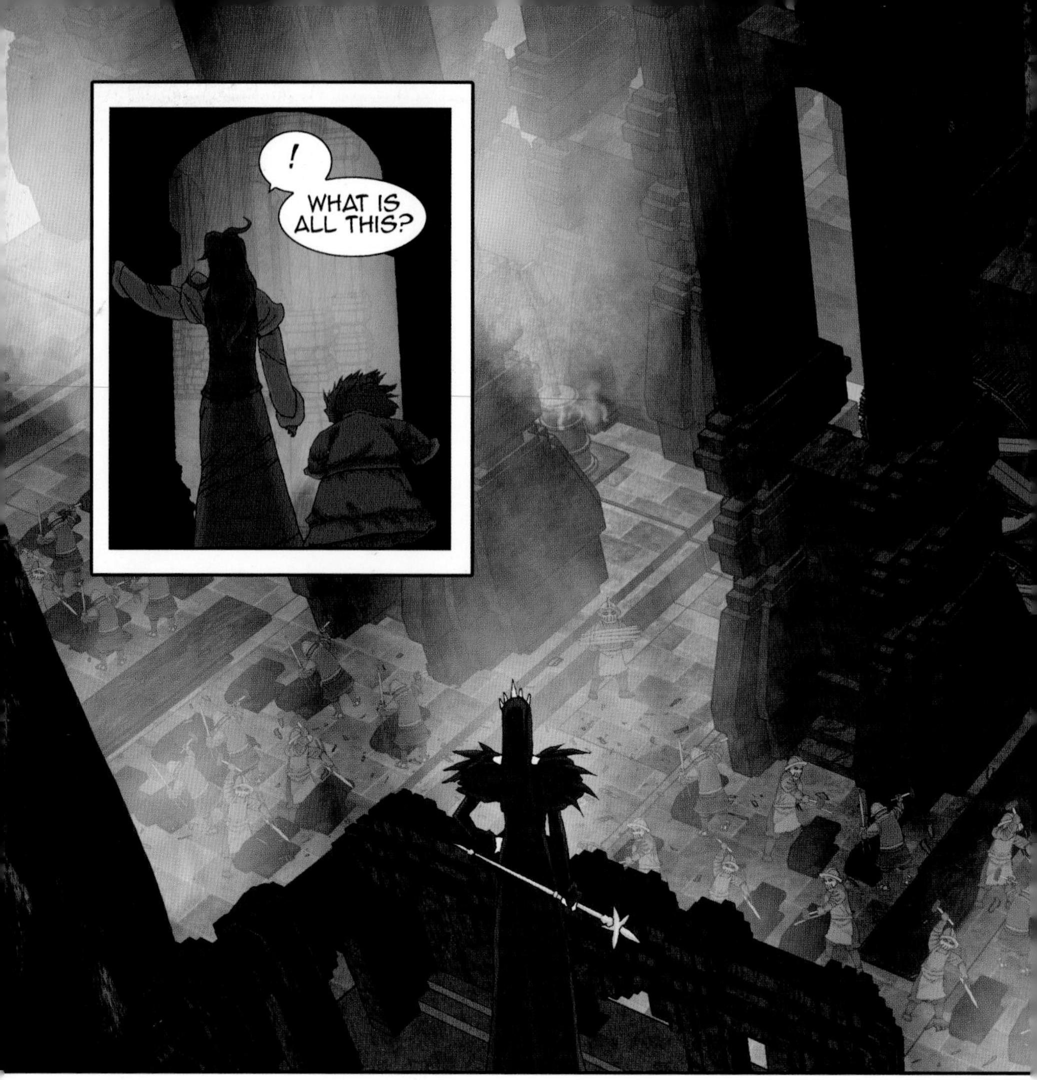
!
WHAT IS ALL THIS?

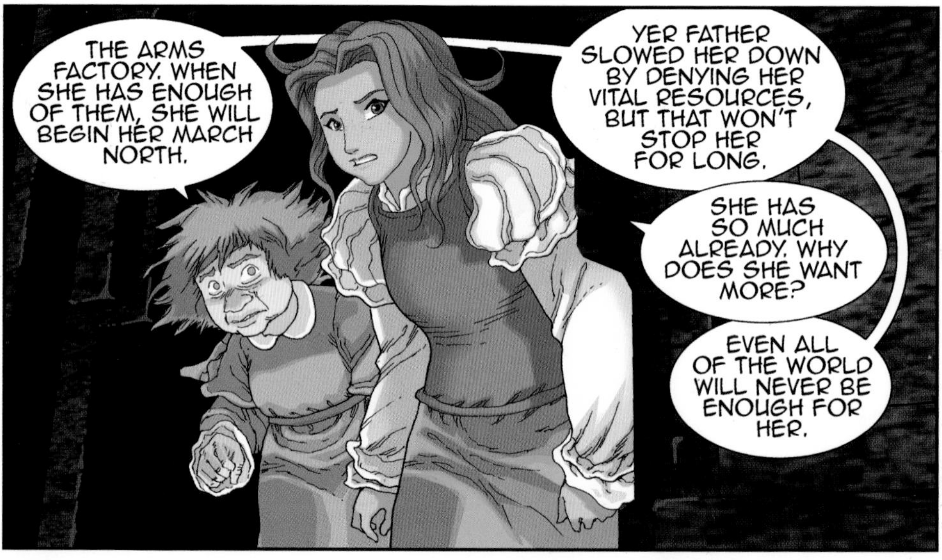
THE ARMS FACTORY. WHEN SHE HAS ENOUGH OF THEM, SHE WILL BEGIN HER MARCH NORTH.
YER FATHER SLOWED HER DOWN BY DENYING HER VITAL RESOURCES, BUT THAT WON'T STOP HER FOR LONG.
SHE HAS SO MUCH ALREADY. WHY DOES SHE WANT MORE?
EVEN ALL OF THE WORLD WILL NEVER BE ENOUGH FOR HER.

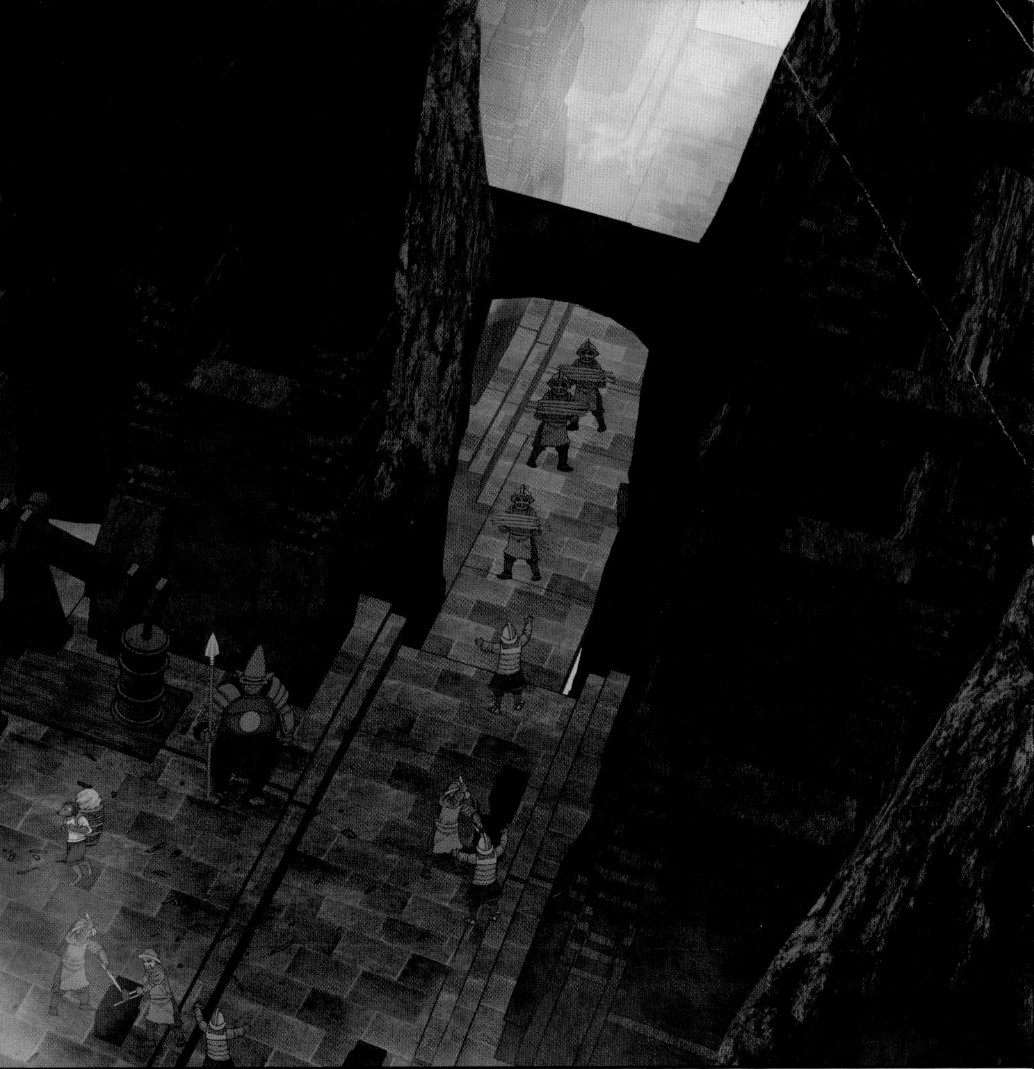

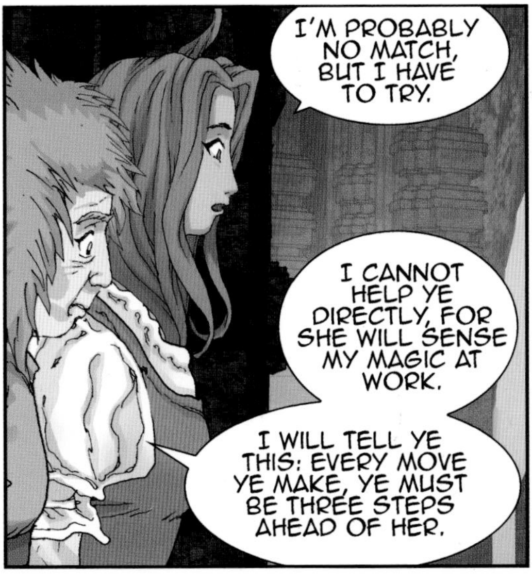
I'M PROBABLY NO MATCH, BUT I HAVE TO TRY.
I CANNOT HELP YE DIRECTLY, FOR SHE WILL SENSE MY MAGIC AT WORK.
I WILL TELL YE THIS: EVERY MOVE YE MAKE, YE MUST BE THREE STEPS AHEAD OF HER.

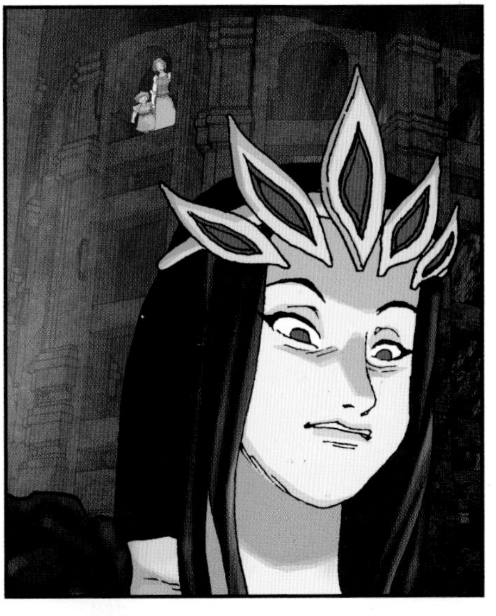

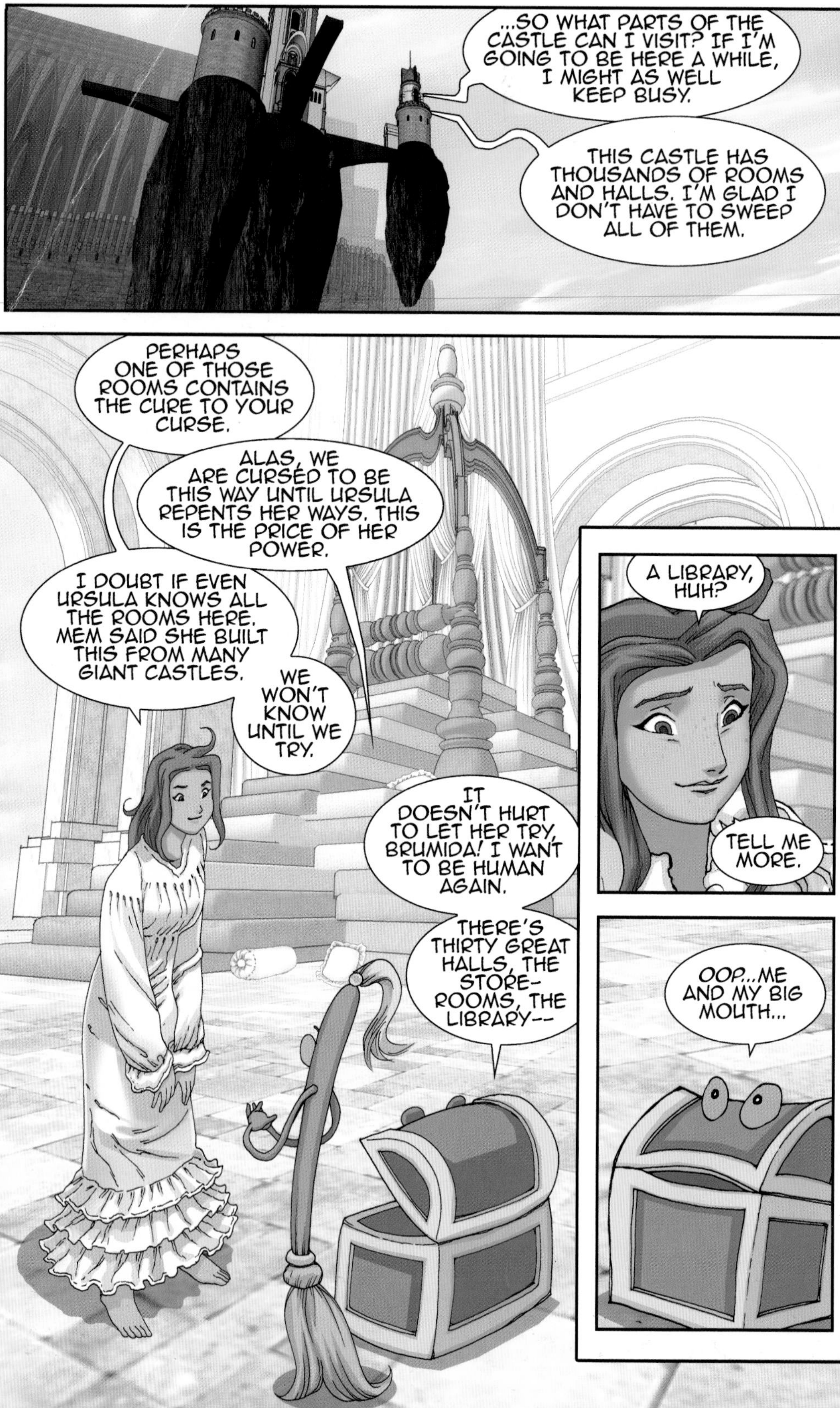
...SO WHAT PARTS OF THE CASTLE CAN I VISIT? IF I'M GOING TO BE HERE A WHILE, I MIGHT AS WELL KEEP BUSY.
THIS CASTLE HAS THOUSANDS OF ROOMS AND HALLS. I'M GLAD I DON'T HAVE TO SWEEP ALL OF THEM.
PERHAPS ONE OF THOSE ROOMS CONTAINS THE CURE TO YOUR CURSE.
ALAS, WE ARE CURSED TO BE THIS WAY UNTIL URSULA REPENTS HER WAYS. THIS IS THE PRICE OF HER POWER.
I DOUBT IF EVEN URSULA KNOWS ALL THE ROOMS HERE. MEM SAID SHE BUILT THIS FROM MANY GIANT CASTLES.
WE WON'T KNOW UNTIL WE TRY.
IT DOESN'T HURT TO LET HER TRY, BRUMIDA! I WANT TO BE HUMAN AGAIN.
THERE'S THIRTY GREAT HALLS, THE STORE-ROOMS, THE LIBRARY--
A LIBRARY, HUH?
TELL ME MORE.
OOP...ME AND MY BIG MOUTH...

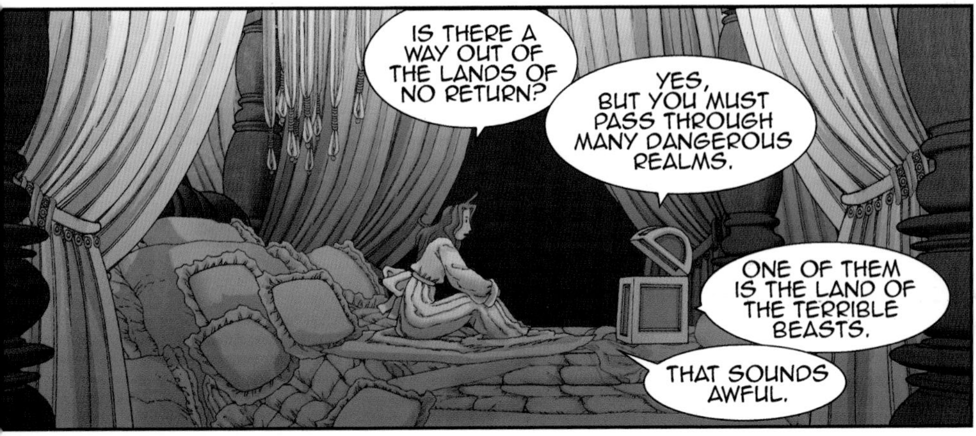
IS THERE A WAY OUT OF THE LANDS OF NO RETURN?
YES, BUT YOU MUST PASS THROUGH MANY DANGEROUS REALMS.
ONE OF THEM IS THE LAND OF THE TERRIBLE BEASTS.
THAT SOUNDS AWFUL.

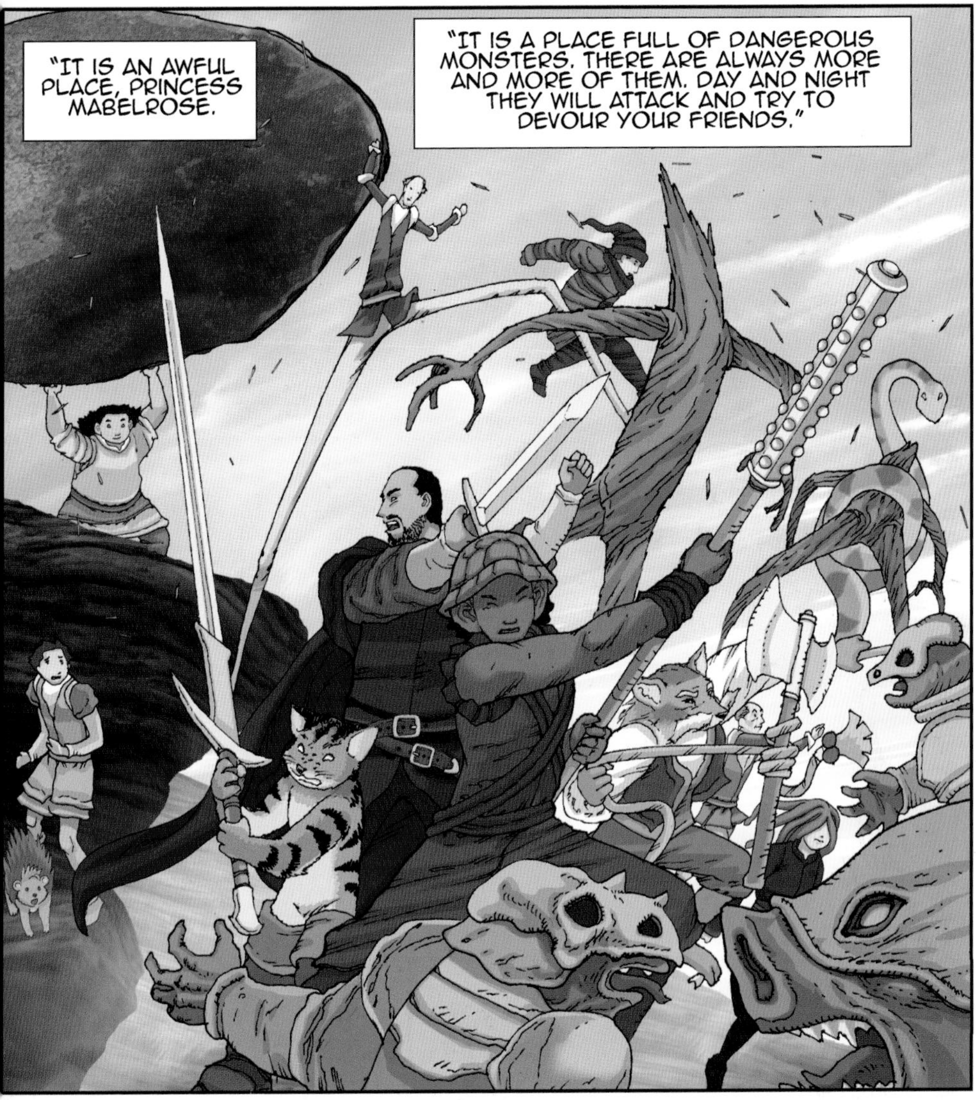
"IT IS AN AWFUL PLACE, PRINCESS MABELROSE.
"IT IS A PLACE FULL OF DANGEROUS MONSTERS. THERE ARE ALWAYS MORE AND MORE OF THEM. DAY AND NIGHT THEY WILL ATTACK AND TRY TO DEVOUR YOUR FRIENDS."

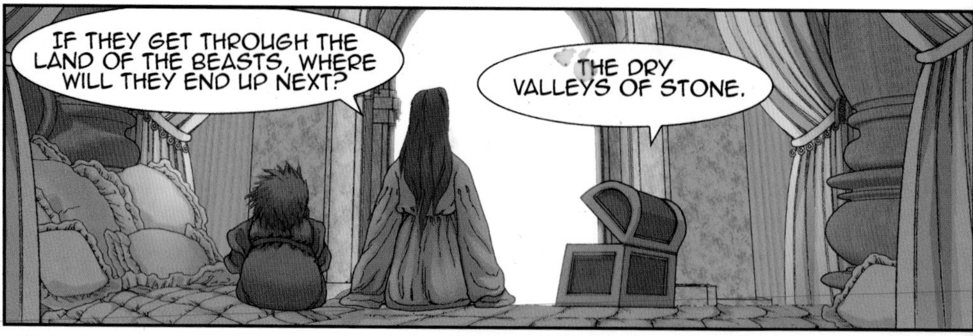
IF THEY GET THROUGH THE LAND OF THE BEASTS, WHERE WILL THEY END UP NEXT?
THE DRY VALLEYS OF STONE.

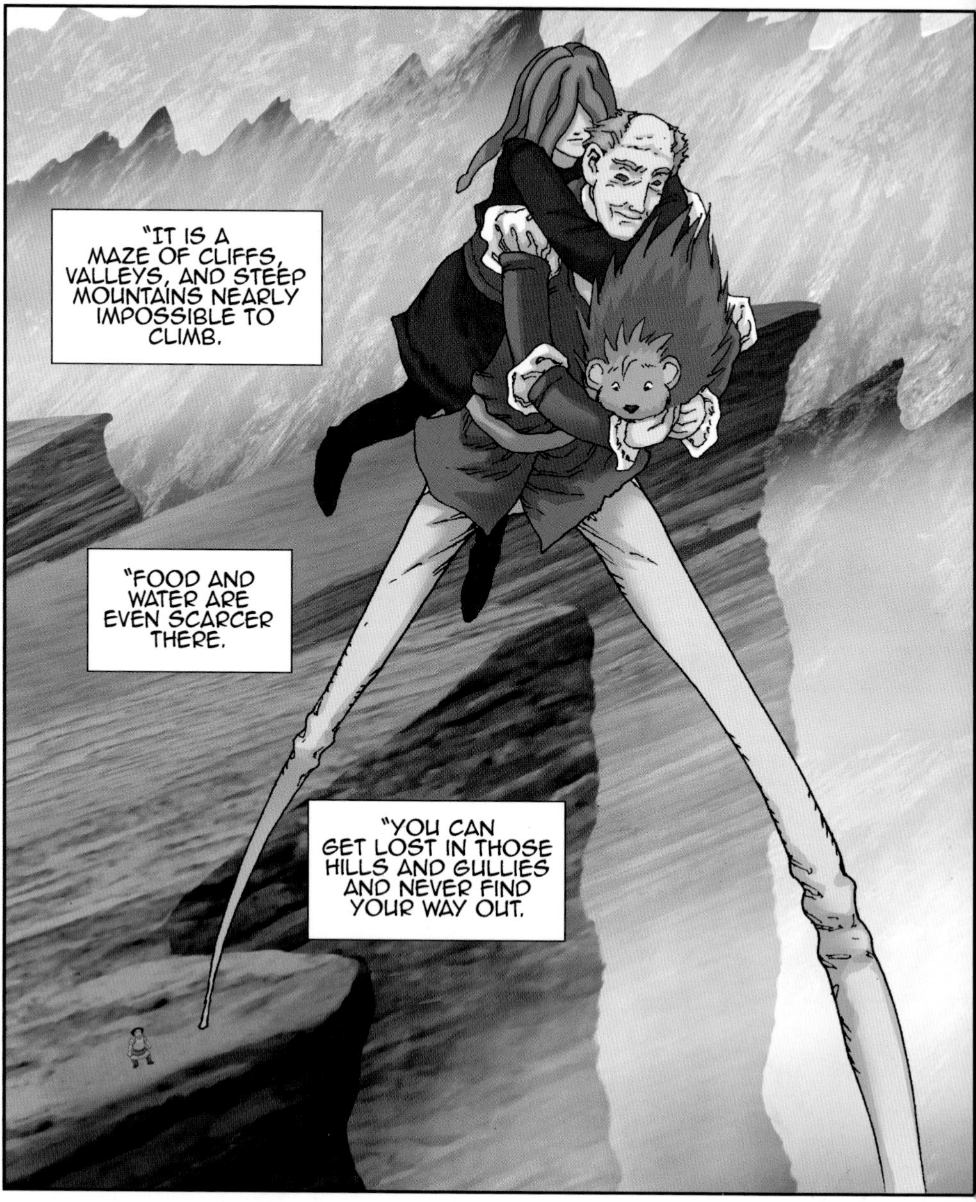
"IT IS A MAZE OF CLIFFS, VALLEYS, AND STEEP MOUNTAINS NEARLY IMPOSSIBLE TO CLIMB.
"FOOD AND WATER ARE EVEN SCARCER THERE.
"YOU CAN GET LOST IN THOSE HILLS AND GULLIES AND NEVER FIND YOUR WAY OUT.

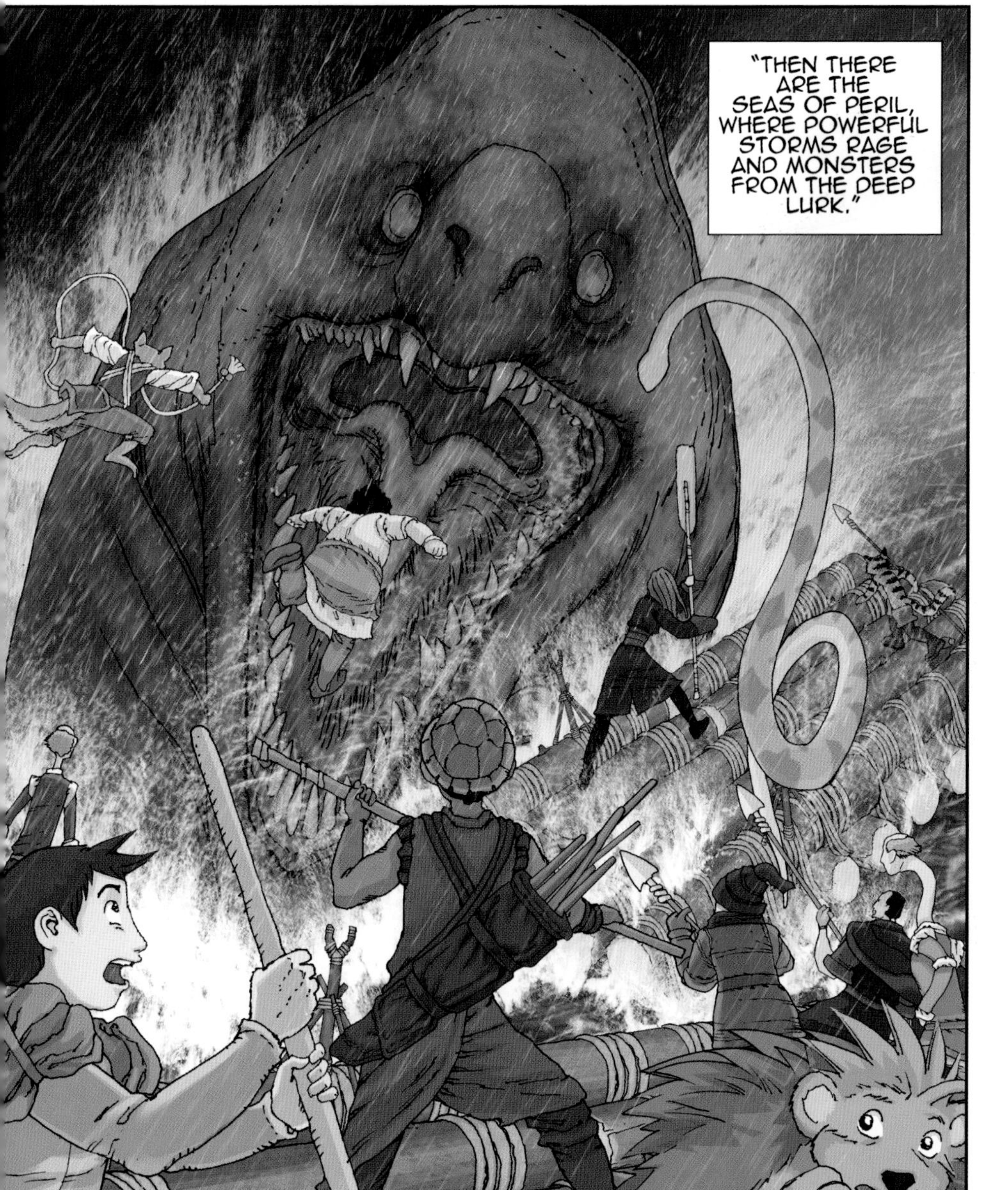
"THEN THERE ARE THE SEAS OF PERIL, WHERE POWERFUL STORMS RAGE AND MONSTERS FROM THE DEEP LURK."

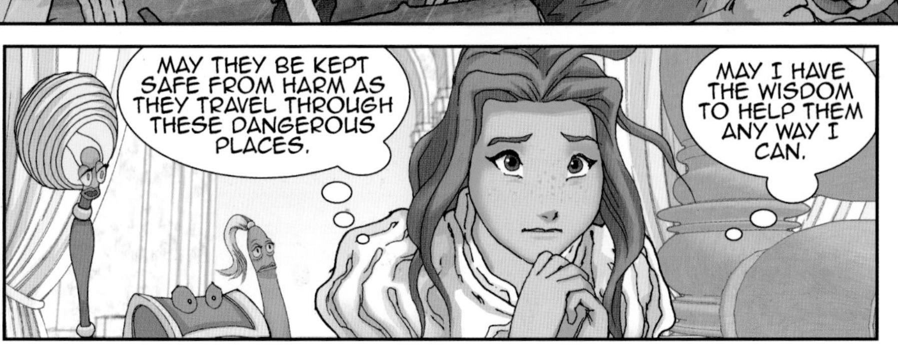
MAY THEY BE KEPT SAFE FROM HARM AS THEY TRAVEL THROUGH THESE DANGEROUS PLACES.
MAY I HAVE THE WISDOM TO HELP THEM ANY WAY I CAN.

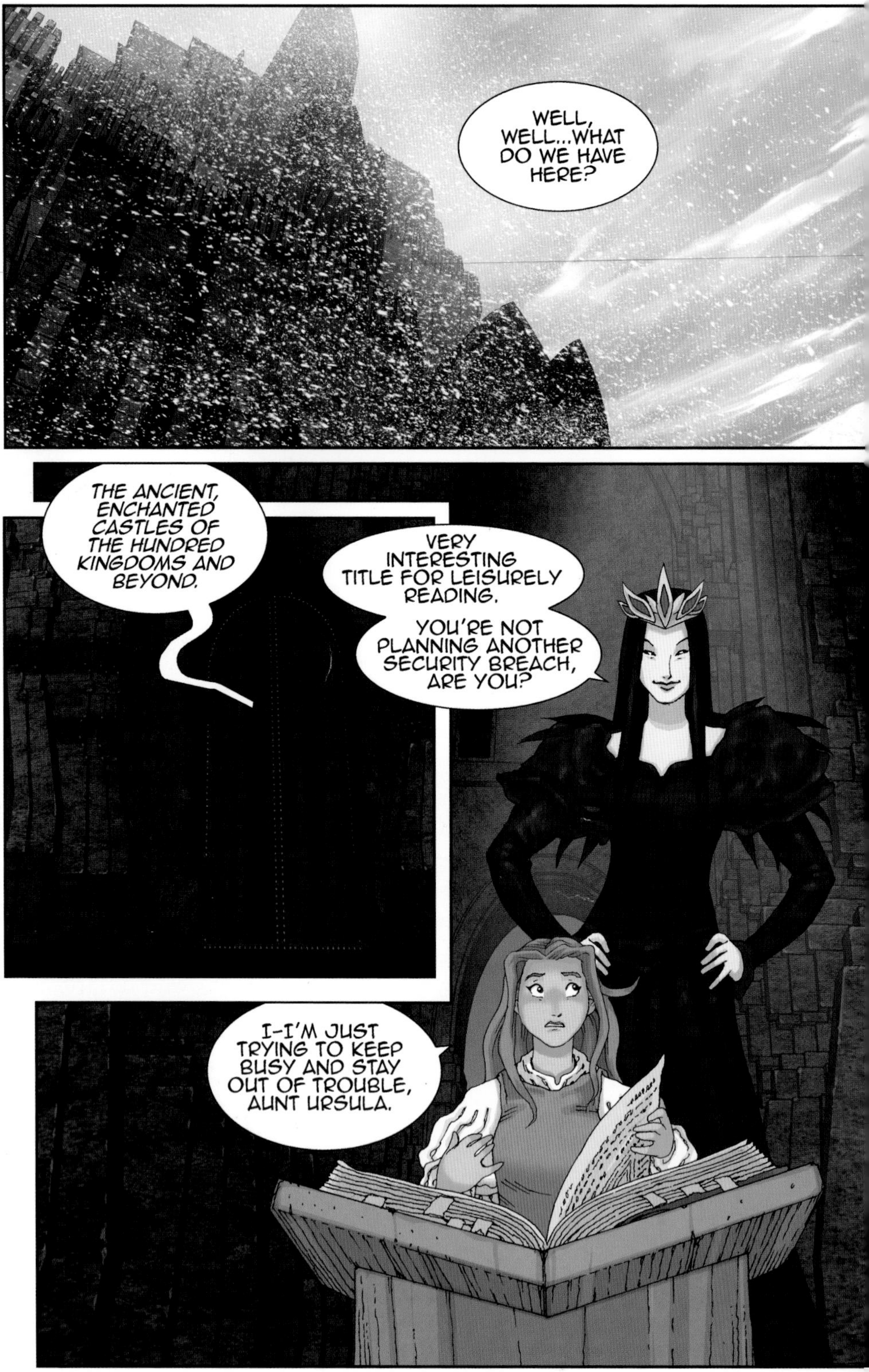
WELL, WELL...WHAT DO WE HAVE HERE?
THE ANCIENT, ENCHANTED CASTLES OF THE HUNDRED KINGDOMS AND BEYOND.
VERY INTERESTING TITLE FOR LEISURELY READING.
YOU'RE NOT PLANNING ANOTHER SECURITY BREACH, ARE YOU?
I-I'M JUST TRYING TO KEEP BUSY AND STAY OUT OF TROUBLE, AUNT URSULA.

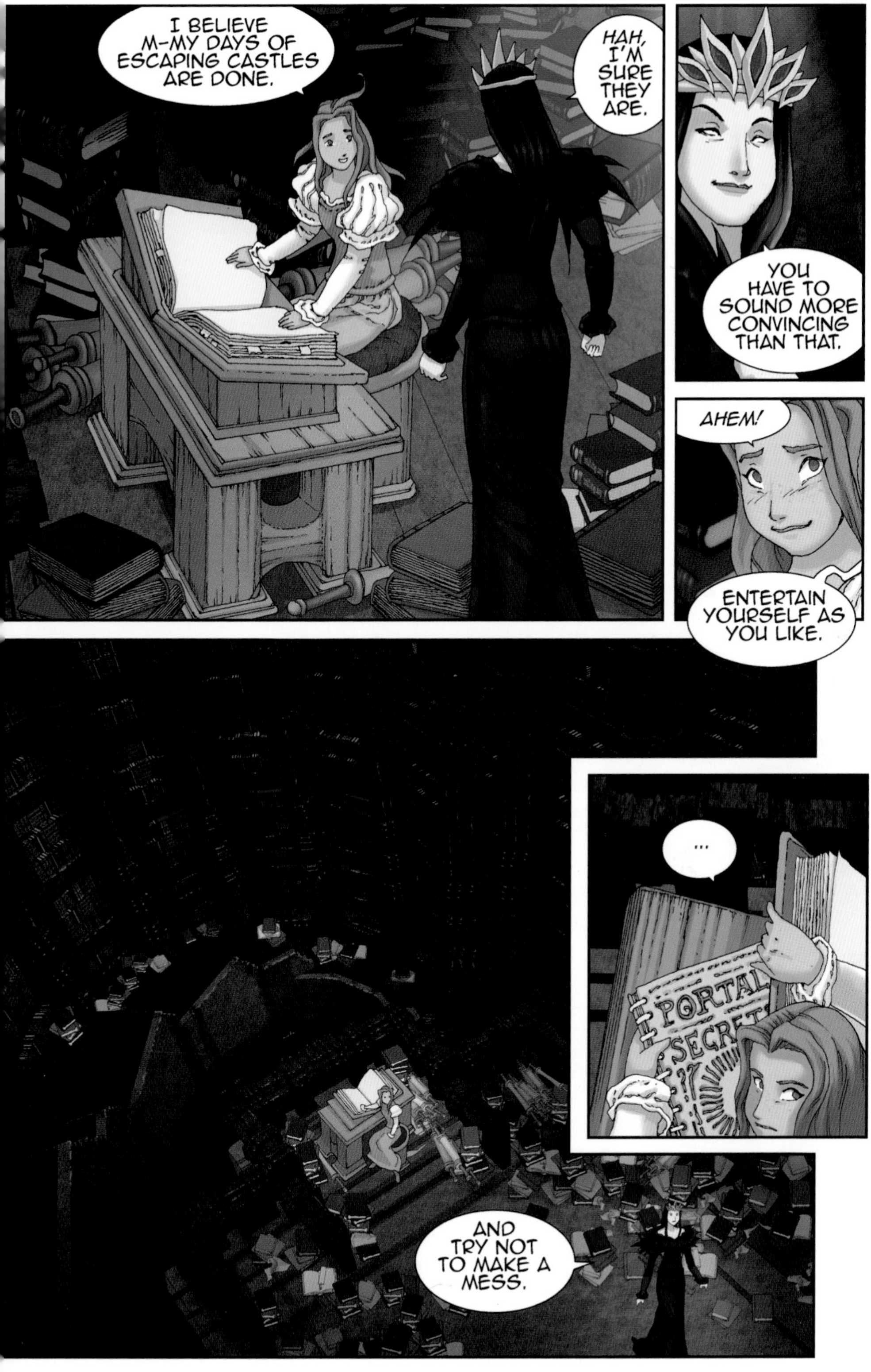
I BELIEVE M-MY DAYS OF ESCAPING CASTLES ARE DONE.
HAH, I'M SURE THEY ARE.
YOU HAVE TO SOUND MORE CONVINCING THAN THAT.
AHEM!
ENTERTAIN YOURSELF AS YOU LIKE.
...
PORTAL SECRET
AND TRY NOT TO MAKE A MESS.

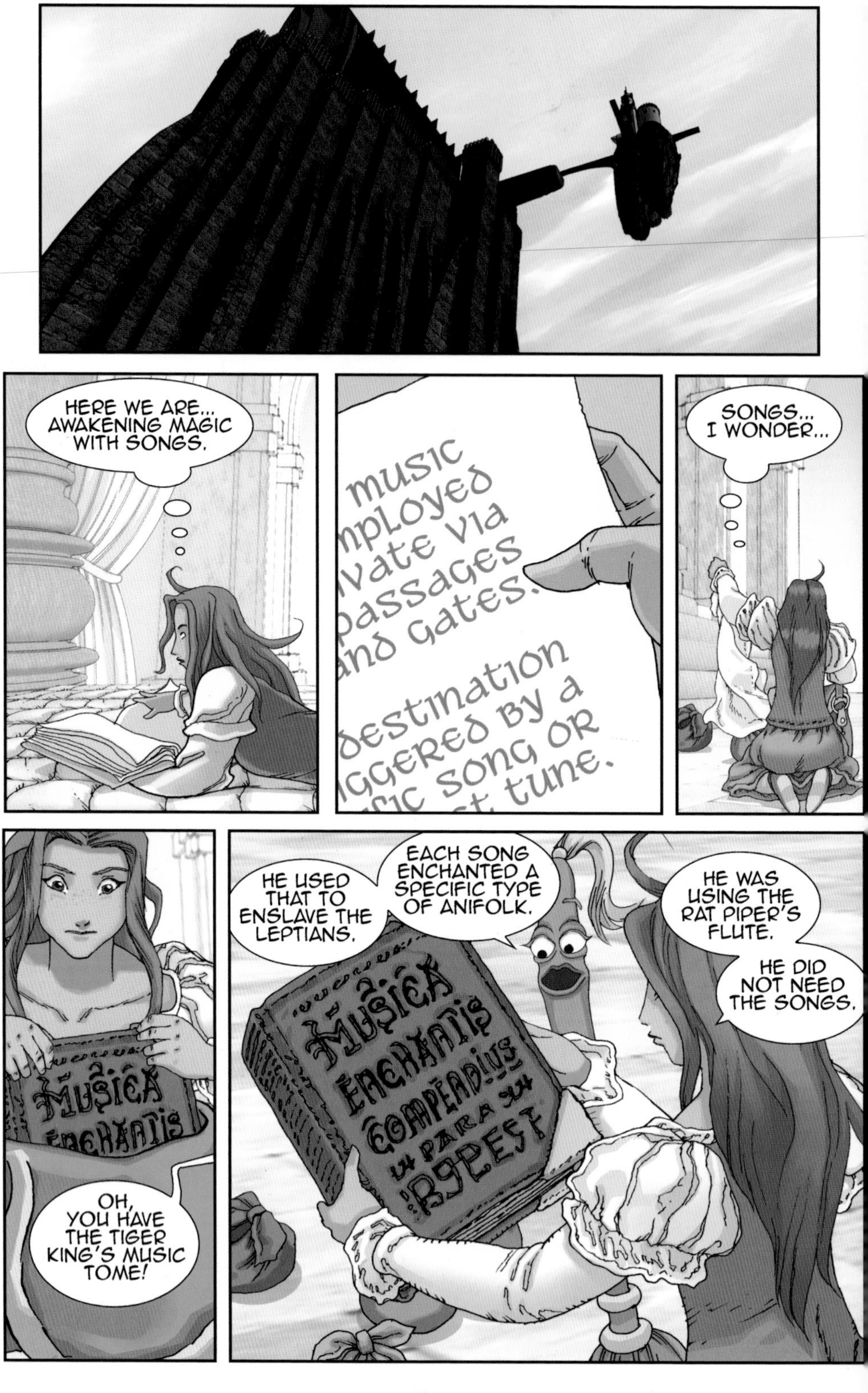
HERE WE ARE... AWAKENING MAGIC WITH SONGS.
music
mployed
ivate via
passages
and gates.
destination
iggered by a
ific song or
SONGS... I WONDER...
MUSICA ENCHANTIS
OH, YOU HAVE THE TIGER KING'S MUSIC TOME!
HE WAS USING THE RAT PIPER'S FLUTE.
HE DID NOT NEED THE SONGS.
EACH SONG ENCHANTED A SPECIFIC TYPE OF ANIFOLK.
HE USED THAT TO ENSLAVE THE LEPTIANS.

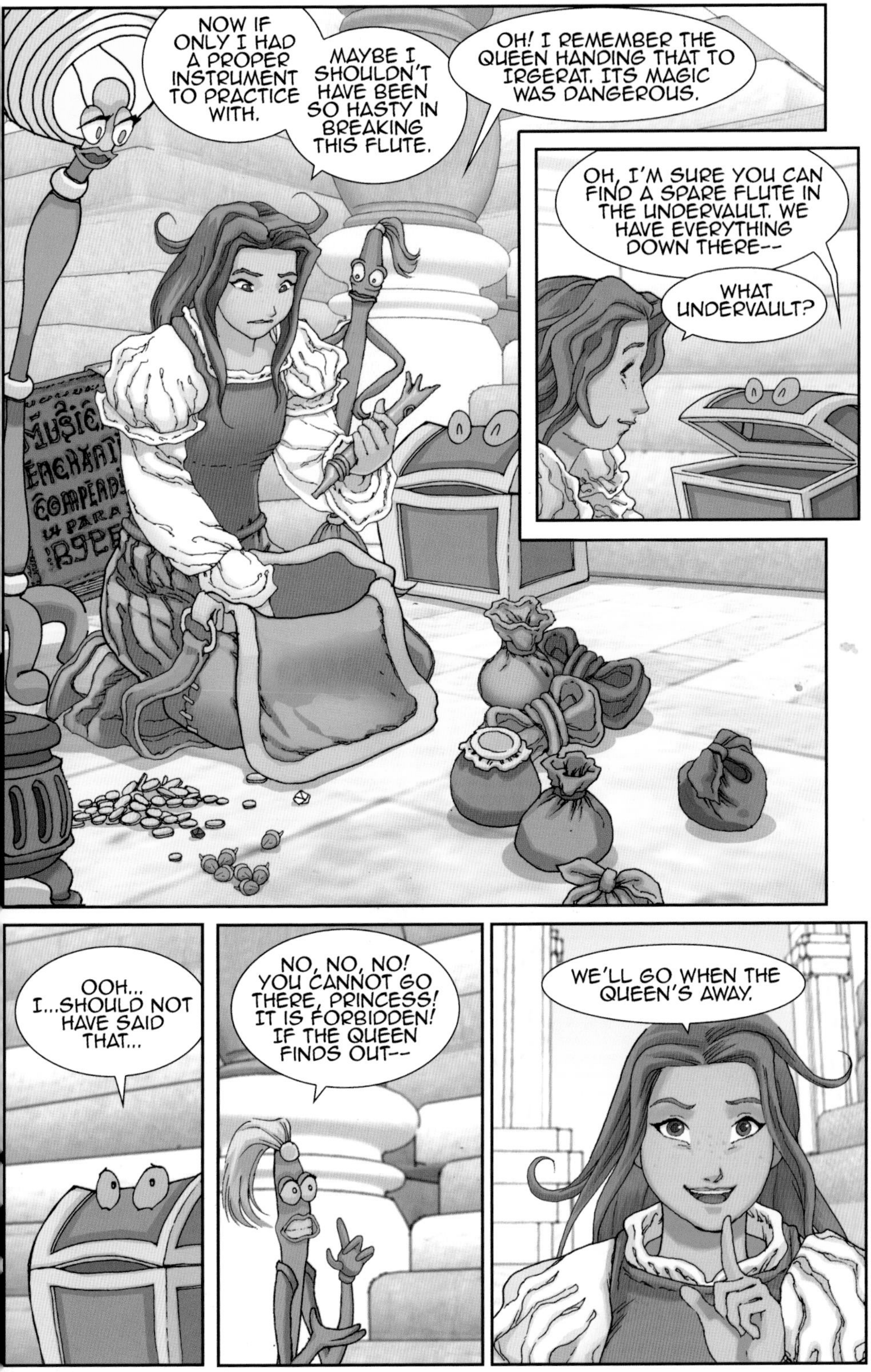
NOW IF ONLY I HAD A PROPER INSTRUMENT TO PRACTICE WITH.
MAYBE I SHOULDN'T HAVE BEEN SO HASTY IN BREAKING THIS FLUTE.
OH! I REMEMBER THE QUEEN HANDING THAT TO IRGERAT. ITS MAGIC WAS DANGEROUS.
OH, I'M SURE YOU CAN FIND A SPARE FLUTE IN THE UNDERVAULT. WE HAVE EVERYTHING DOWN THERE--
WHAT UNDERVAULT?
OOH... I...SHOULD NOT HAVE SAID THAT...
NO, NO, NO! YOU CANNOT GO THERE, PRINCESS! IT IS FORBIDDEN! IF THE QUEEN FINDS OUT--
WE'LL GO WHEN THE QUEEN'S AWAY.

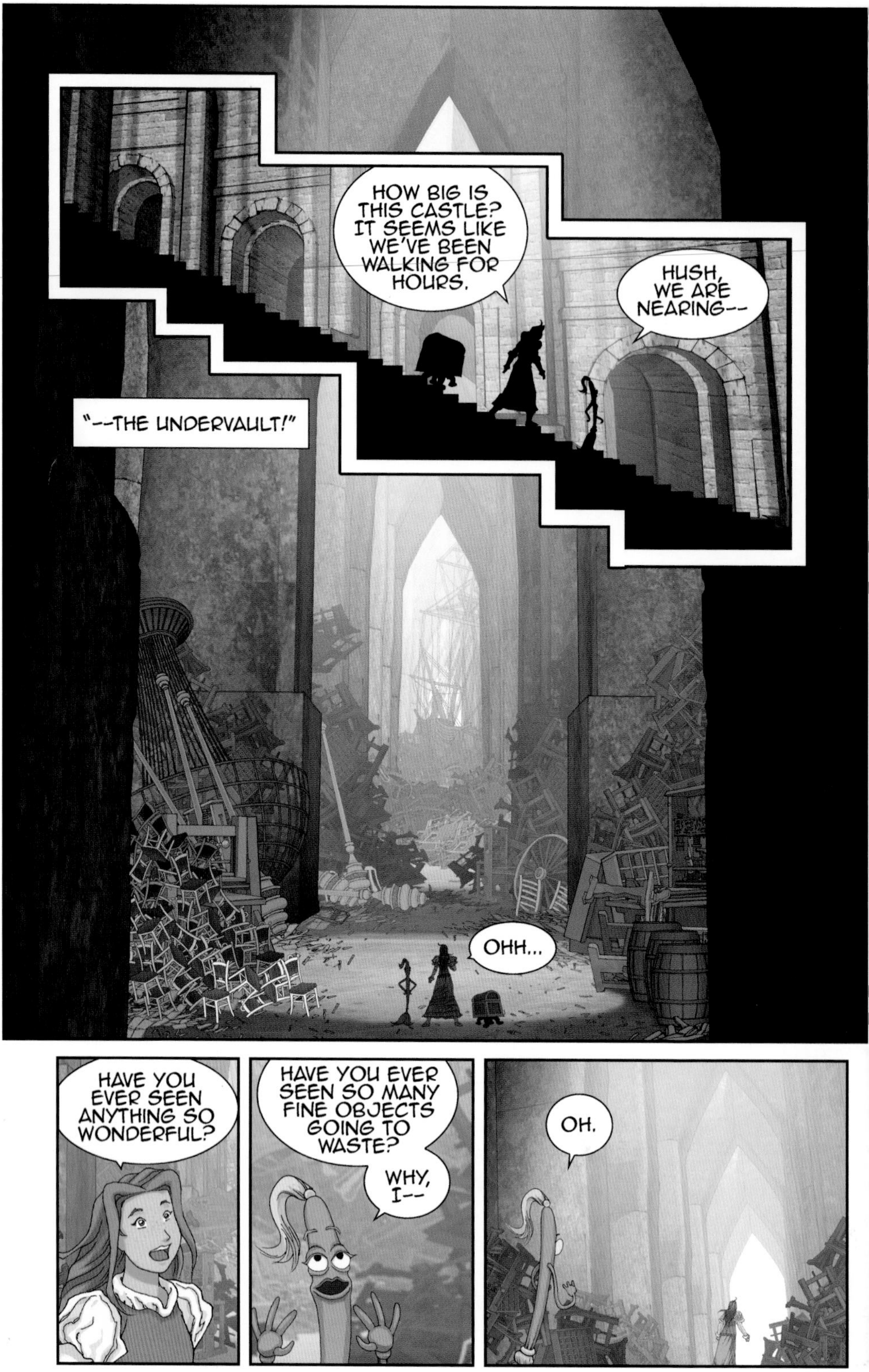
HOW BIG IS THIS CASTLE? IT SEEMS LIKE WE'VE BEEN WALKING FOR HOURS.
HUSH, WE ARE NEARING--
"--THE UNDERVAULT!"
OHH...
HAVE YOU EVER SEEN ANYTHING SO WONDERFUL?
HAVE YOU EVER SEEN SO MANY FINE OBJECTS GOING TO WASTE?
WHY, I--
OH.

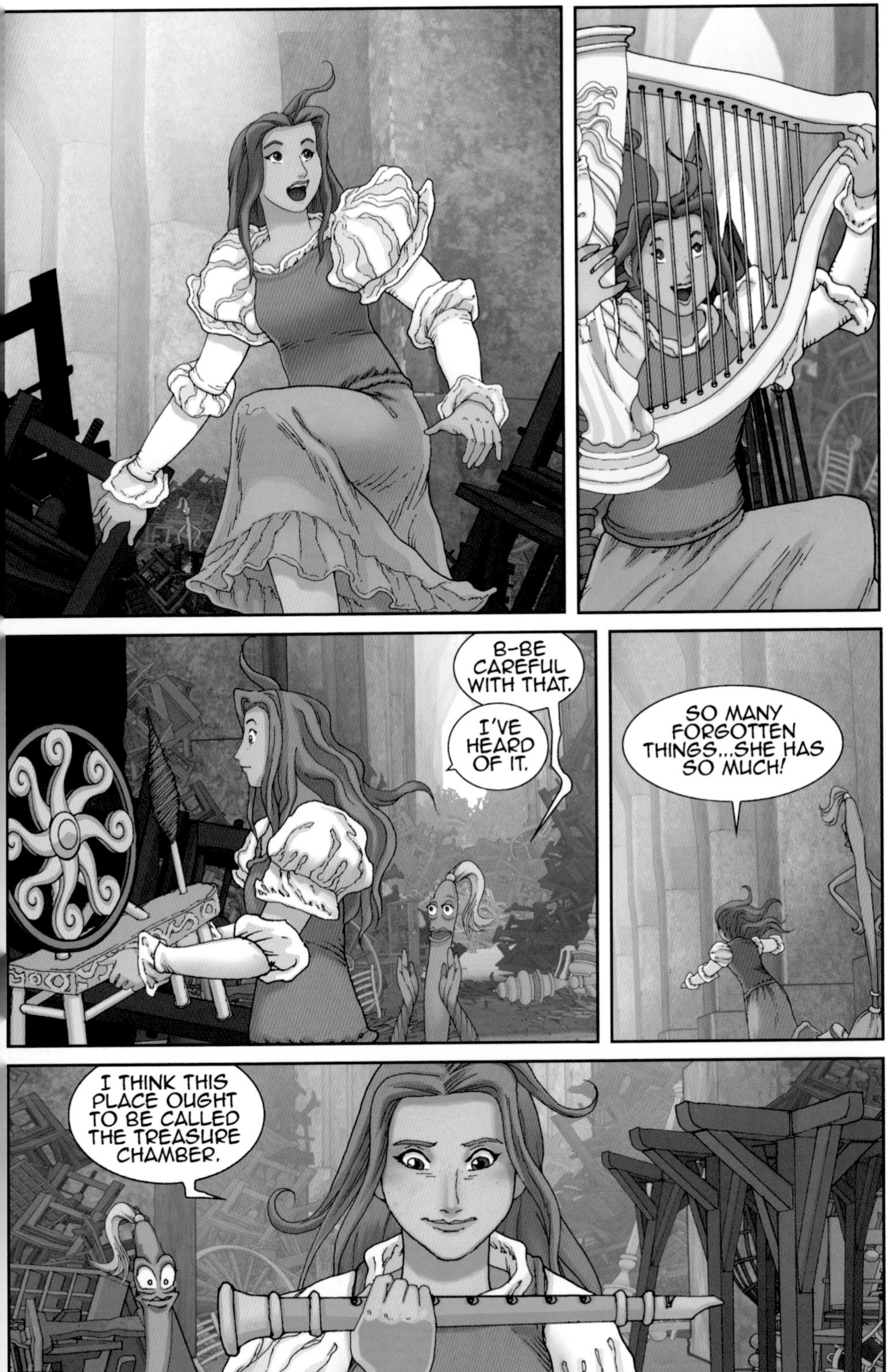
B-BE CAREFUL WITH THAT.
I'VE HEARD OF IT.
SO MANY FORGOTTEN THINGS...SHE HAS SO MUCH!
I THINK THIS PLACE OUGHT TO BE CALLED THE TREASURE CHAMBER.

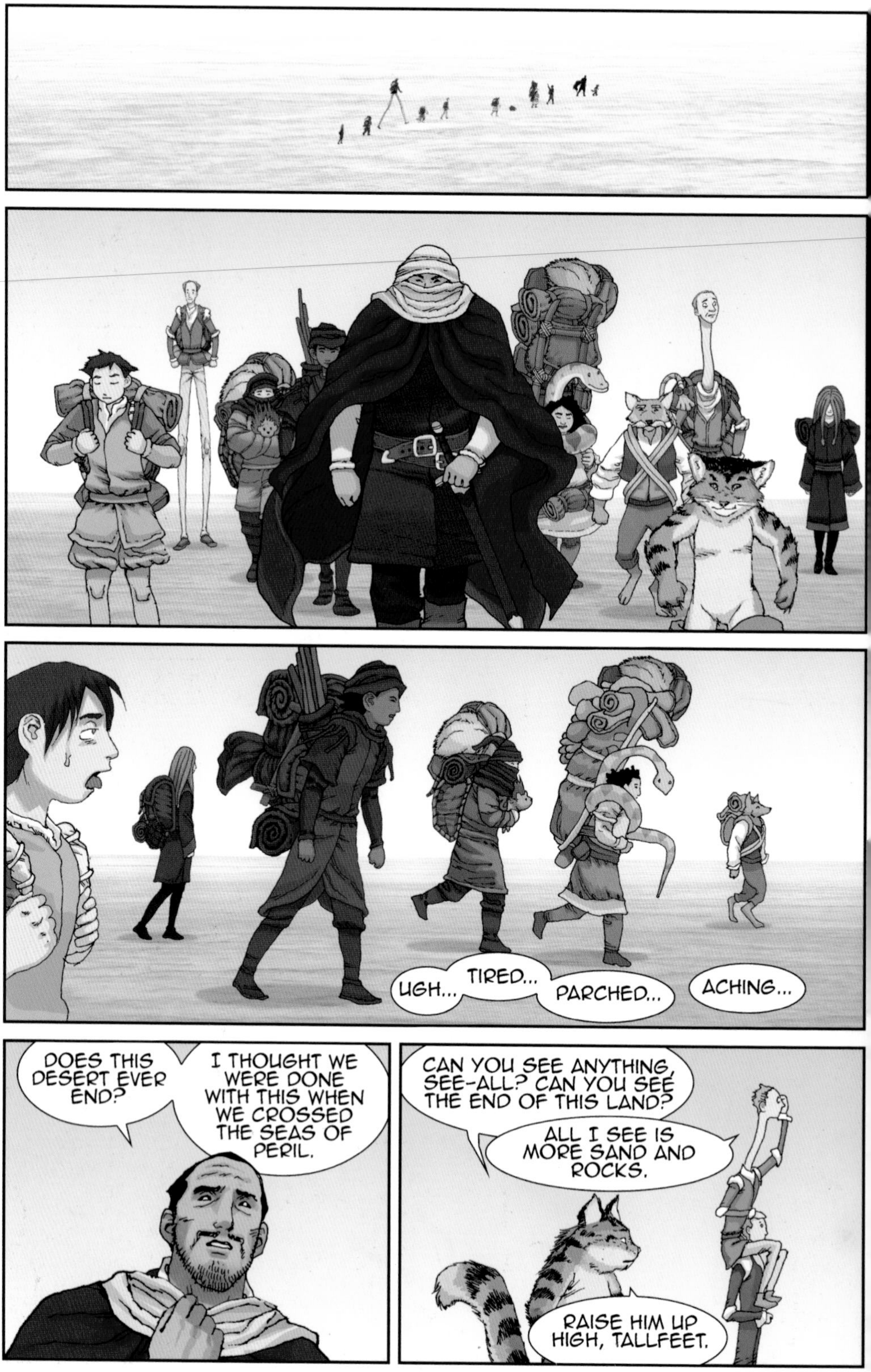
UGH...
TIRED...
PARCHED...
ACHING...
DOES THIS DESERT EVER END?
I THOUGHT WE WERE DONE WITH THIS WHEN WE CROSSED THE SEAS OF PERIL.
CAN YOU SEE ANYTHING, SEE-ALL? CAN YOU SEE THE END OF THIS LAND?
ALL I SEE IS MORE SAND AND ROCKS.
RAISE HIM UP HIGH, TALLFEET.

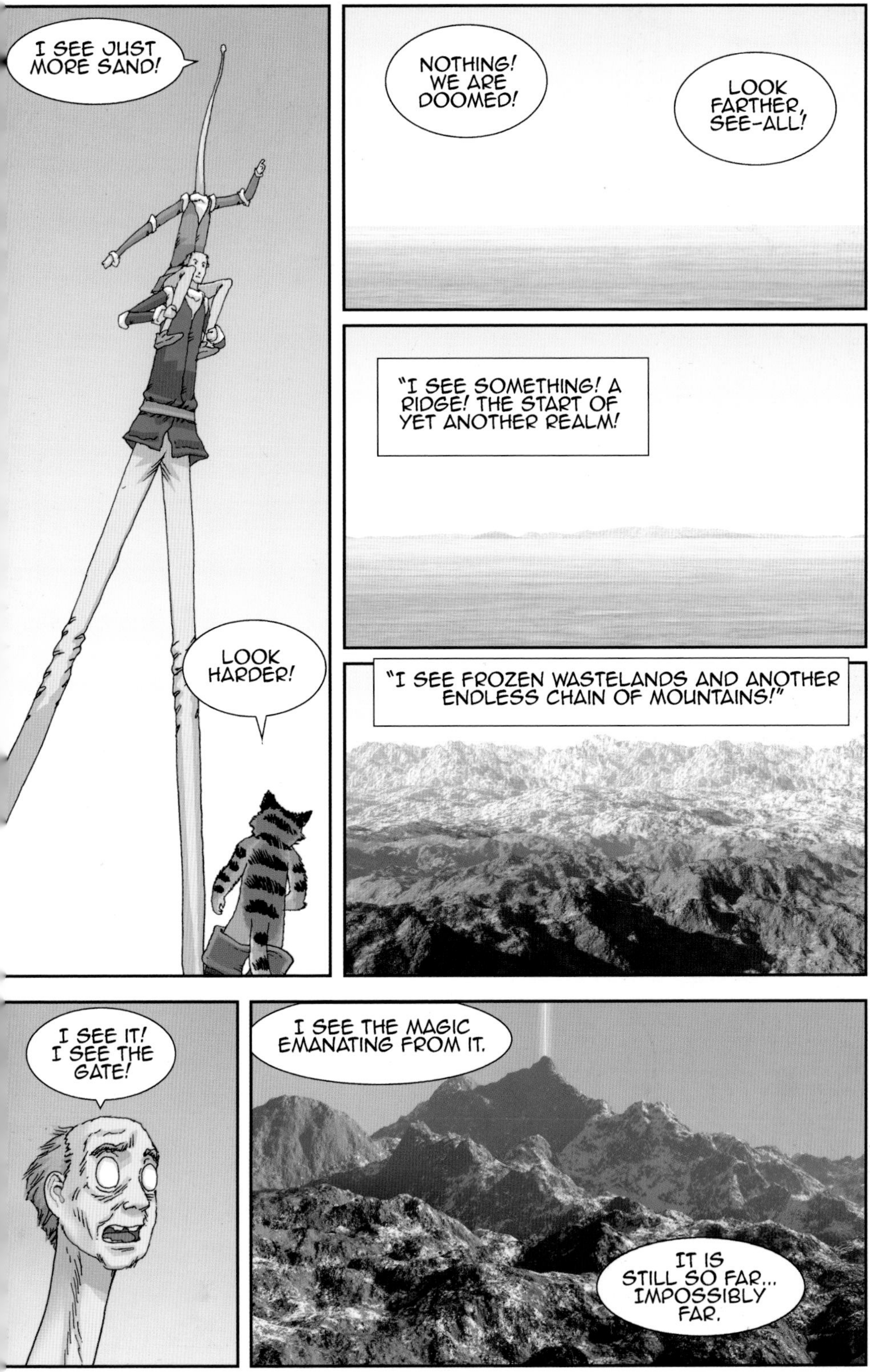
I SEE JUST MORE SAND!
NOTHING! WE ARE DOOMED!
LOOK FARTHER, SEE-ALL!
"I SEE SOMETHING! A RIDGE! THE START OF YET ANOTHER REALM!
LOOK HARDER!
"I SEE FROZEN WASTELANDS AND ANOTHER ENDLESS CHAIN OF MOUNTAINS!"
I SEE IT! I SEE THE GATE!
I SEE THE MAGIC EMANATING FROM IT.
IT IS STILL SO FAR... IMPOSSIBLY FAR.

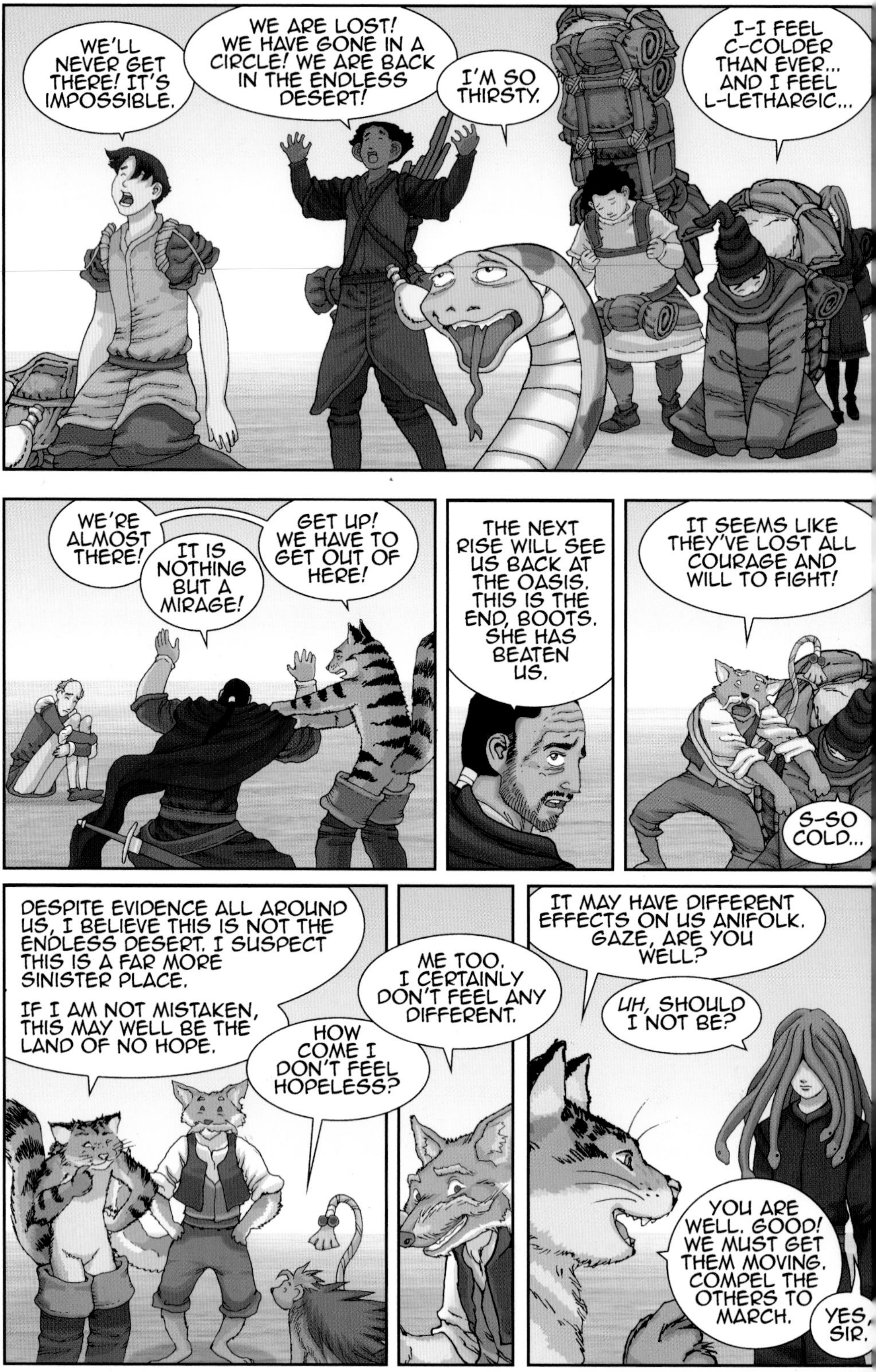
WE'LL NEVER GET THERE! IT'S IMPOSSIBLE.
WE ARE LOST! WE HAVE GONE IN A CIRCLE! WE ARE BACK IN THE ENDLESS DESERT!
I'M SO THIRSTY.
I-I FEEL C-COLDER THAN EVER... AND I FEEL L-LETHARGIC...
WE'RE ALMOST THERE!
IT IS NOTHING BUT A MIRAGE!
GET UP! WE HAVE TO GET OUT OF HERE!
THE NEXT RISE WILL SEE US BACK AT THE OASIS. THIS IS THE END, BOOTS. SHE HAS BEATEN US.
IT SEEMS LIKE THEY'VE LOST ALL COURAGE AND WILL TO FIGHT!
S-SO COLD...
DESPITE EVIDENCE ALL AROUND US, I BELIEVE THIS IS NOT THE ENDLESS DESERT. I SUSPECT THIS IS A FAR MORE SINISTER PLACE.
IF I AM NOT MISTAKEN, THIS MAY WELL BE THE LAND OF NO HOPE.
HOW COME I DON'T FEEL HOPELESS?
ME TOO. I CERTAINLY DON'T FEEL ANY DIFFERENT.
IT MAY HAVE DIFFERENT EFFECTS ON US ANIFOLK. GAZE, ARE YOU WELL?
UH, SHOULD I NOT BE?
YOU ARE WELL. GOOD! WE MUST GET THEM MOVING. COMPEL THE OTHERS TO MARCH.
YES, SIR.

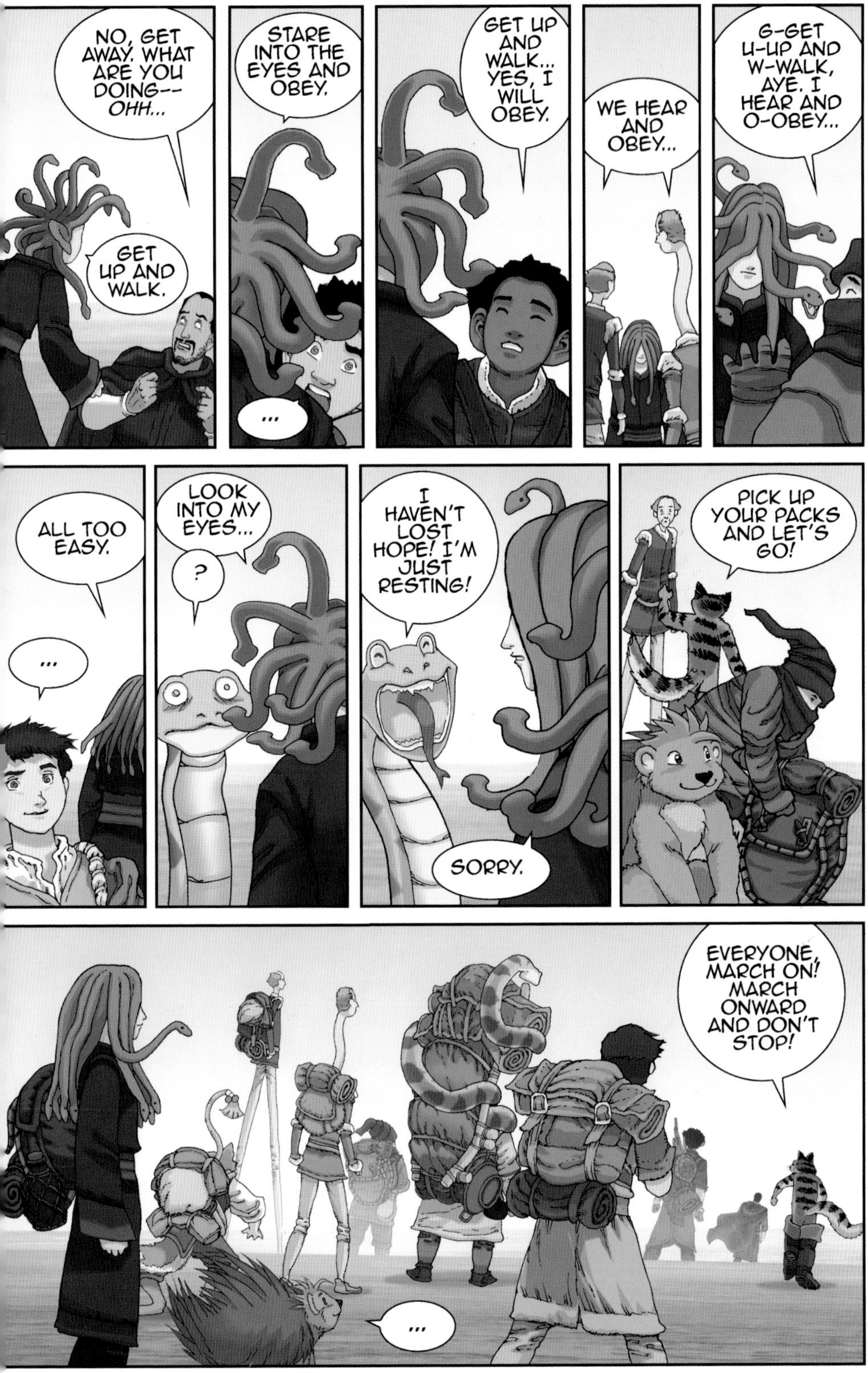
NO, GET AWAY. WHAT ARE YOU DOING-- OHH...
GET UP AND WALK.
STARE INTO THE EYES AND OBEY.
...
GET UP AND WALK... YES, I WILL OBEY.
WE HEAR AND OBEY...
G-GET U-UP AND W-WALK, AYE. I HEAR AND O-OBEY...
ALL TOO EASY.
...
LOOK INTO MY EYES...
?
I HAVEN'T LOST HOPE! I'M JUST RESTING!
SORRY.
PICK UP YOUR PACKS AND LET'S GO!
EVERYONE, MARCH ON! MARCH ONWARD AND DON'T STOP!
...

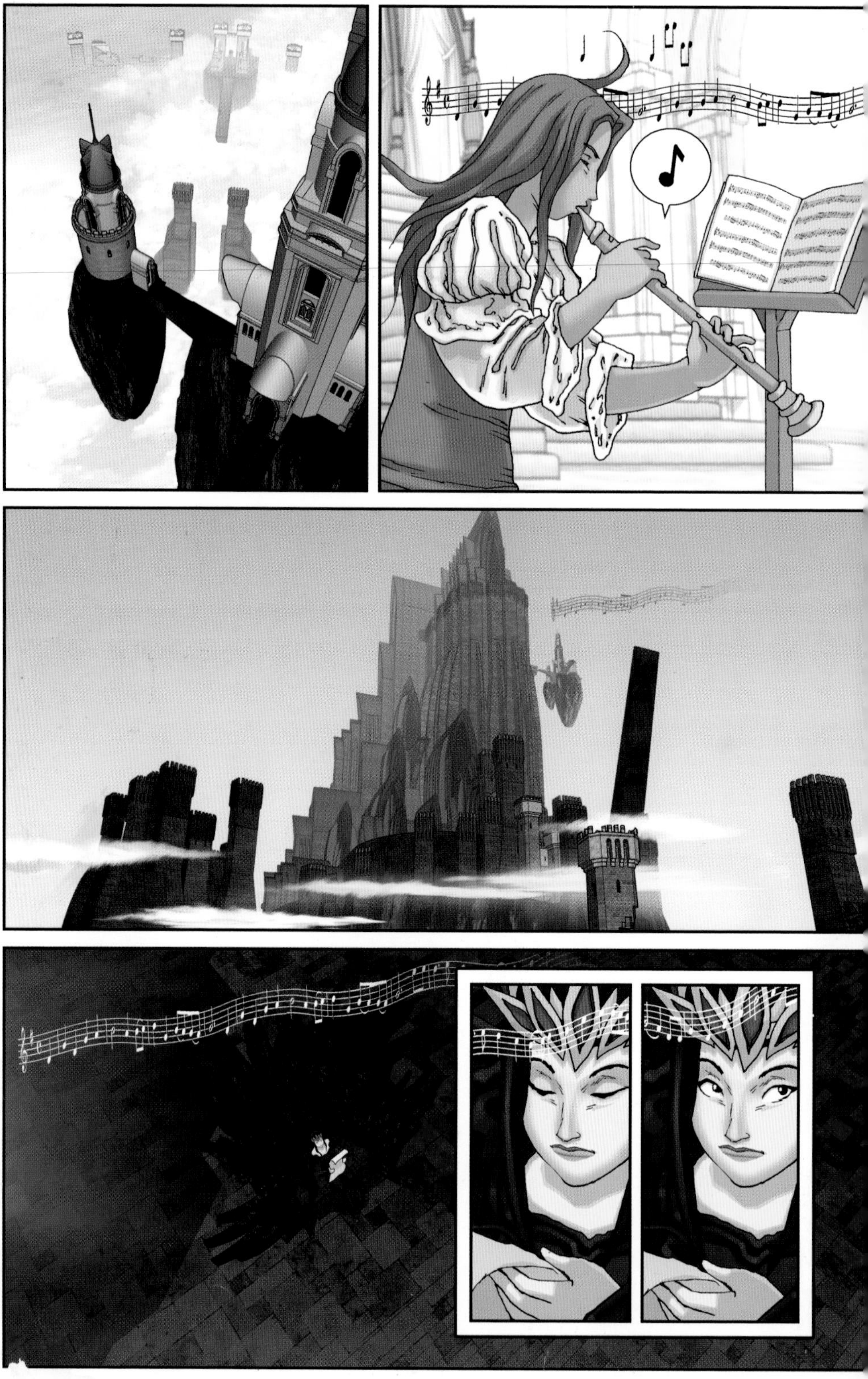

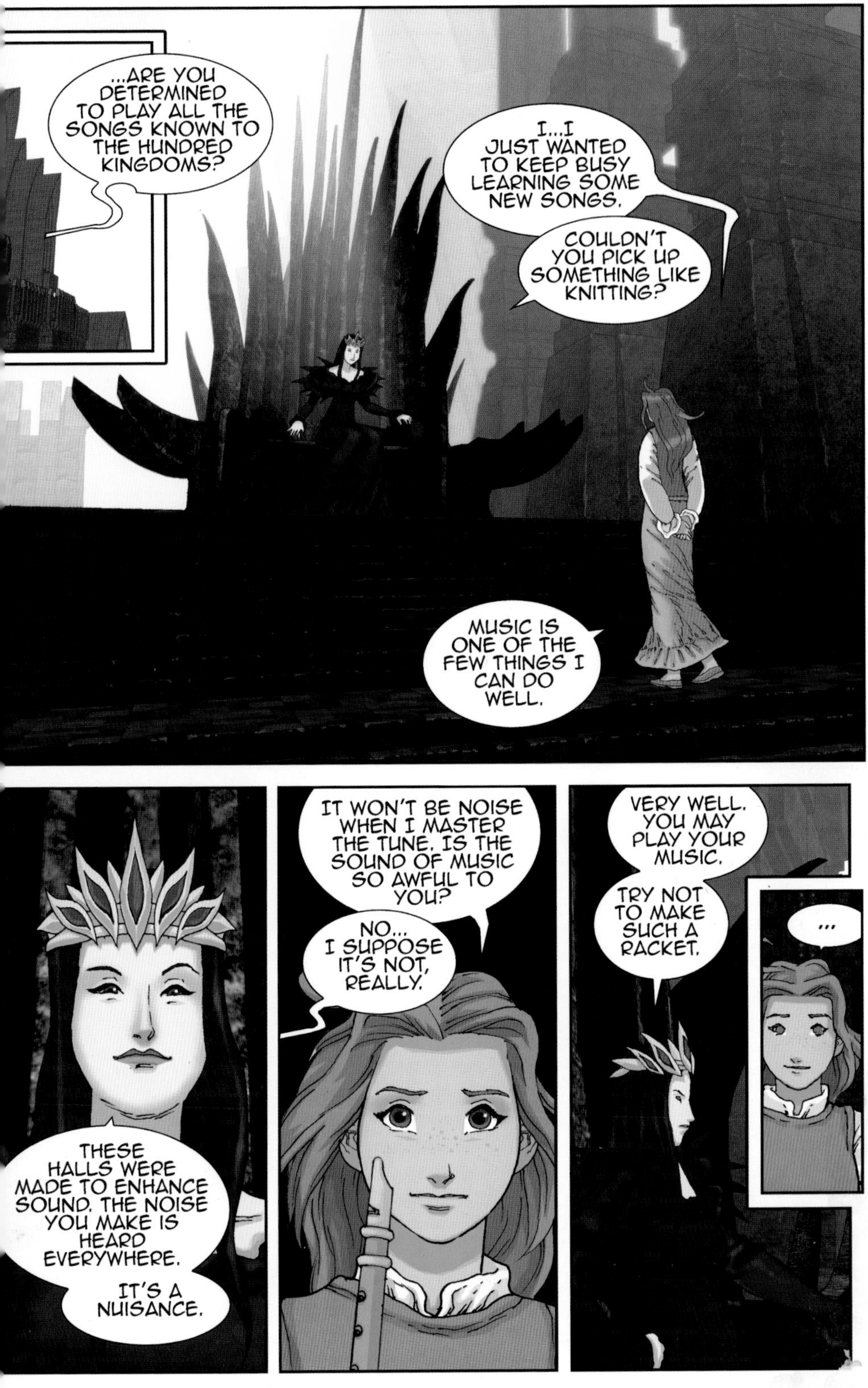
...ARE YOU DETERMINED TO PLAY ALL THE SONGS KNOWN TO THE HUNDRED KINGDOMS?
I...I JUST WANTED TO KEEP BUSY LEARNING SOME NEW SONGS.
COULDN'T YOU PICK UP SOMETHING LIKE KNITTING?
MUSIC IS ONE OF THE FEW THINGS I CAN DO WELL.
THESE HALLS WERE MADE TO ENHANCE SOUND. THE NOISE YOU MAKE IS HEARD EVERYWHERE.
IT'S A NUISANCE.
IT WON'T BE NOISE WHEN I MASTER THE TUNE. IS THE SOUND OF MUSIC SO AWFUL TO YOU?
NO... I SUPPOSE IT'S NOT, REALLY.
VERY WELL. YOU MAY PLAY YOUR MUSIC.
TRY NOT TO MAKE SUCH A RACKET.
...

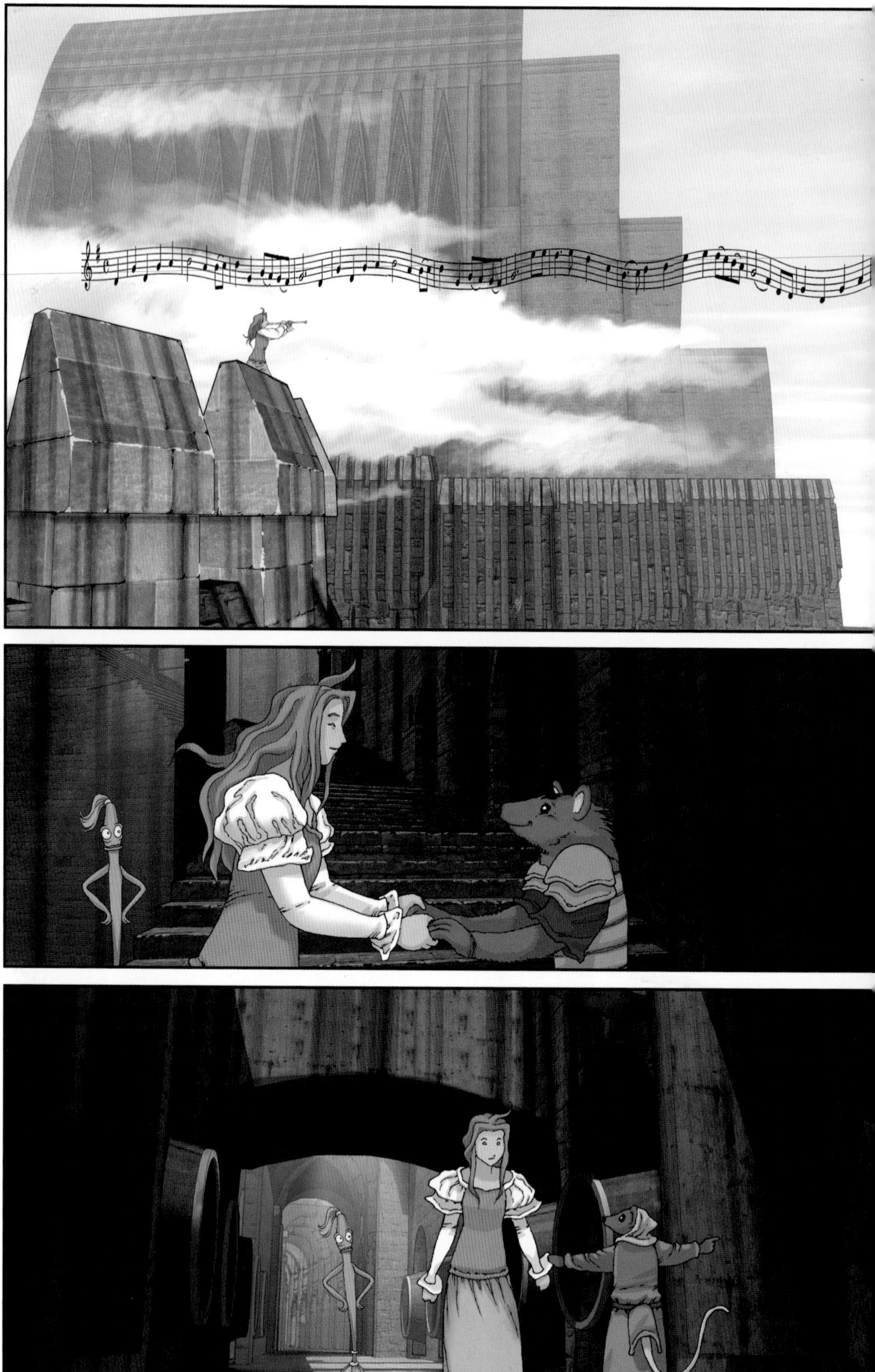

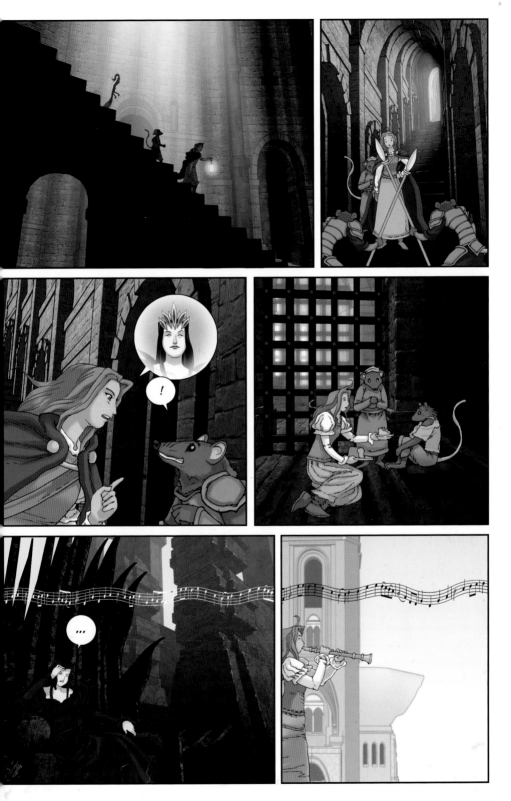

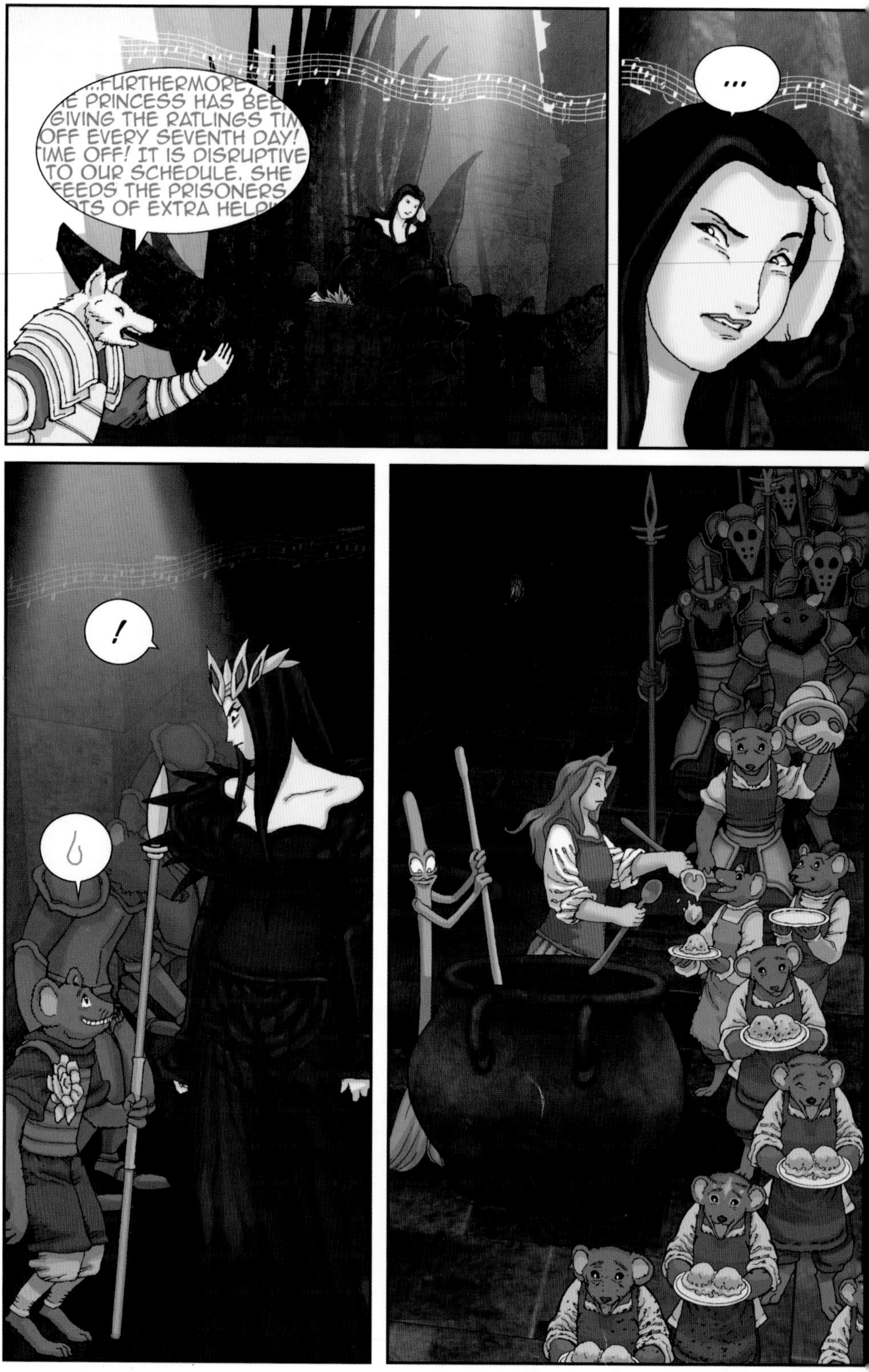
...FURTHERMORE, THE PRINCESS HAS BEEN GIVING THE RATLINGS TIME OFF EVERY SEVENTH DAY! TIME OFF! IT IS DISRUPTIVE TO OUR SCHEDULE. SHE FEEDS THE PRISONERS LOTS OF EXTRA HELP
...
!

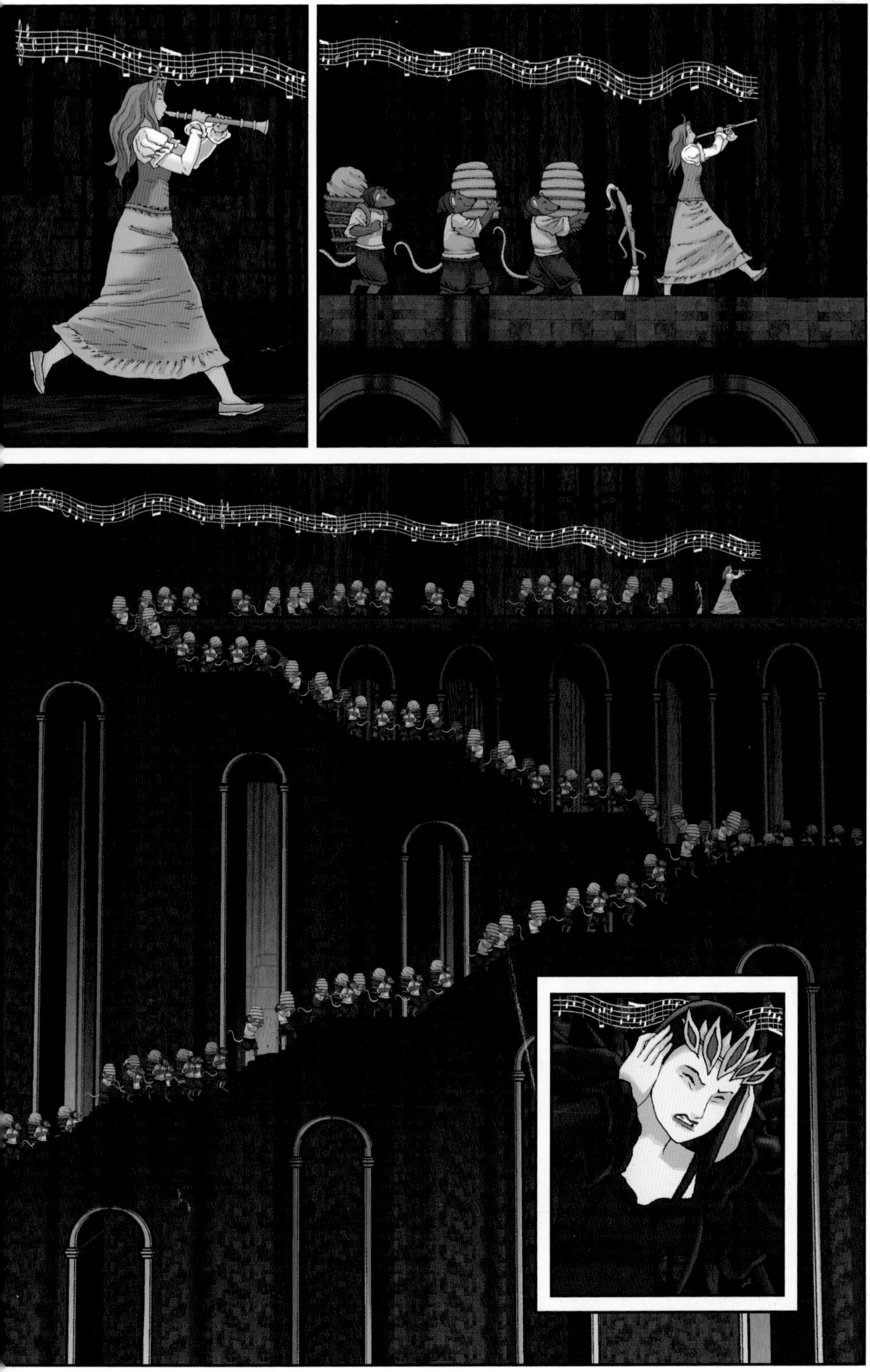

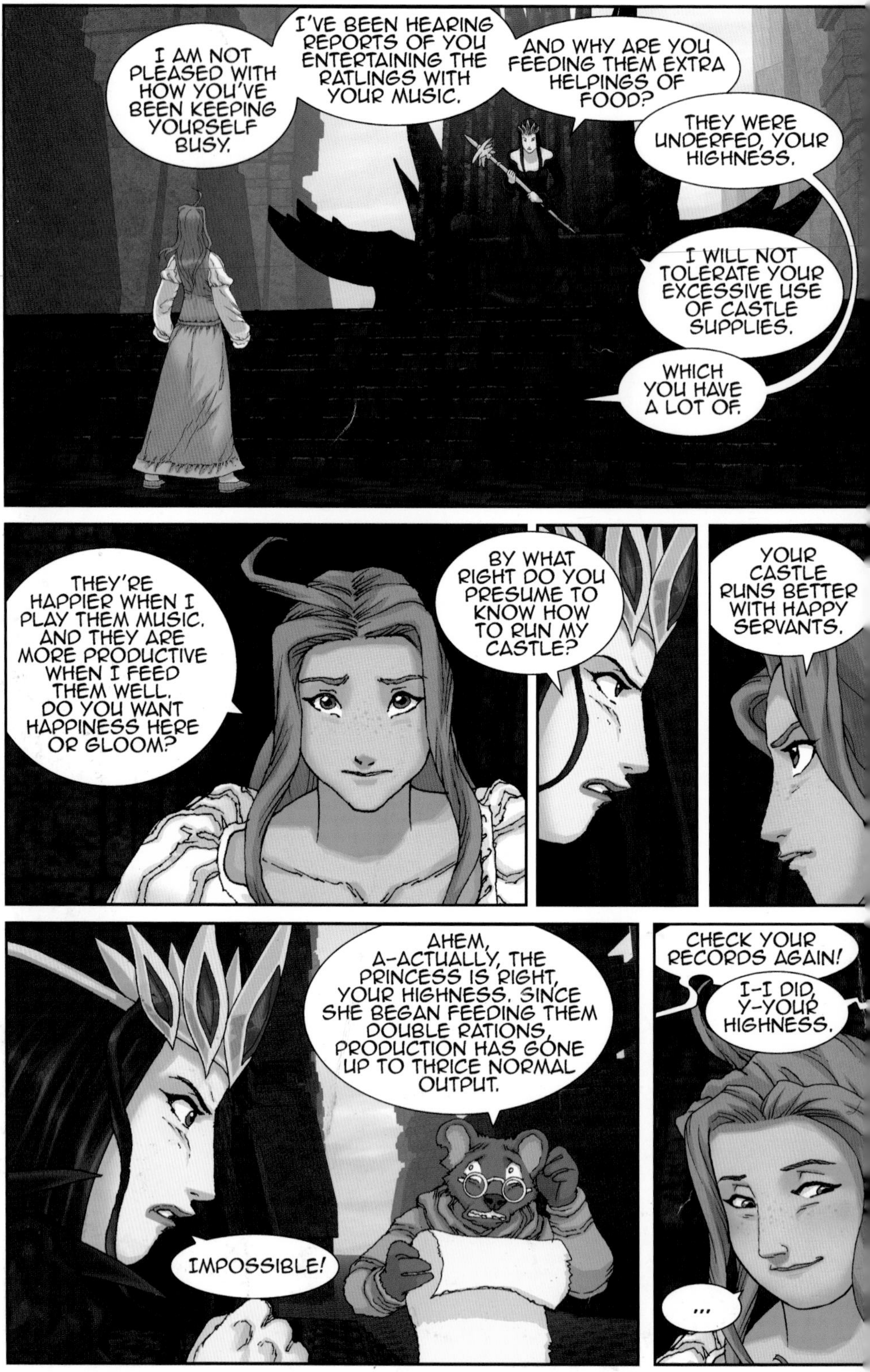

I AM NOT PLEASED WITH HOW YOU'VE BEEN KEEPING YOURSELF BUSY.
I'VE BEEN HEARING REPORTS OF YOU ENTERTAINING THE RATLINGS WITH YOUR MUSIC.
AND WHY ARE YOU FEEDING THEM EXTRA HELPINGS OF FOOD?
THEY WERE UNDERFED, YOUR HIGHNESS.
I WILL NOT TOLERATE YOUR EXCESSIVE USE OF CASTLE SUPPLIES.
WHICH YOU HAVE A LOT OF.
THEY'RE HAPPIER WHEN I PLAY THEM MUSIC. AND THEY ARE MORE PRODUCTIVE WHEN I FEED THEM WELL. DO YOU WANT HAPPINESS HERE OR GLOOM?
BY WHAT RIGHT DO YOU PRESUME TO KNOW HOW TO RUN MY CASTLE?
YOUR CASTLE RUNS BETTER WITH HAPPY SERVANTS.
AHEM, A-ACTUALLY, THE PRINCESS IS RIGHT, YOUR HIGHNESS. SINCE SHE BEGAN FEEDING THEM DOUBLE RATIONS, PRODUCTION HAS GONE UP TO THRICE NORMAL OUTPUT.
IMPOSSIBLE!
CHECK YOUR RECORDS AGAIN!
I-I DID, Y-YOUR HIGHNESS.
...

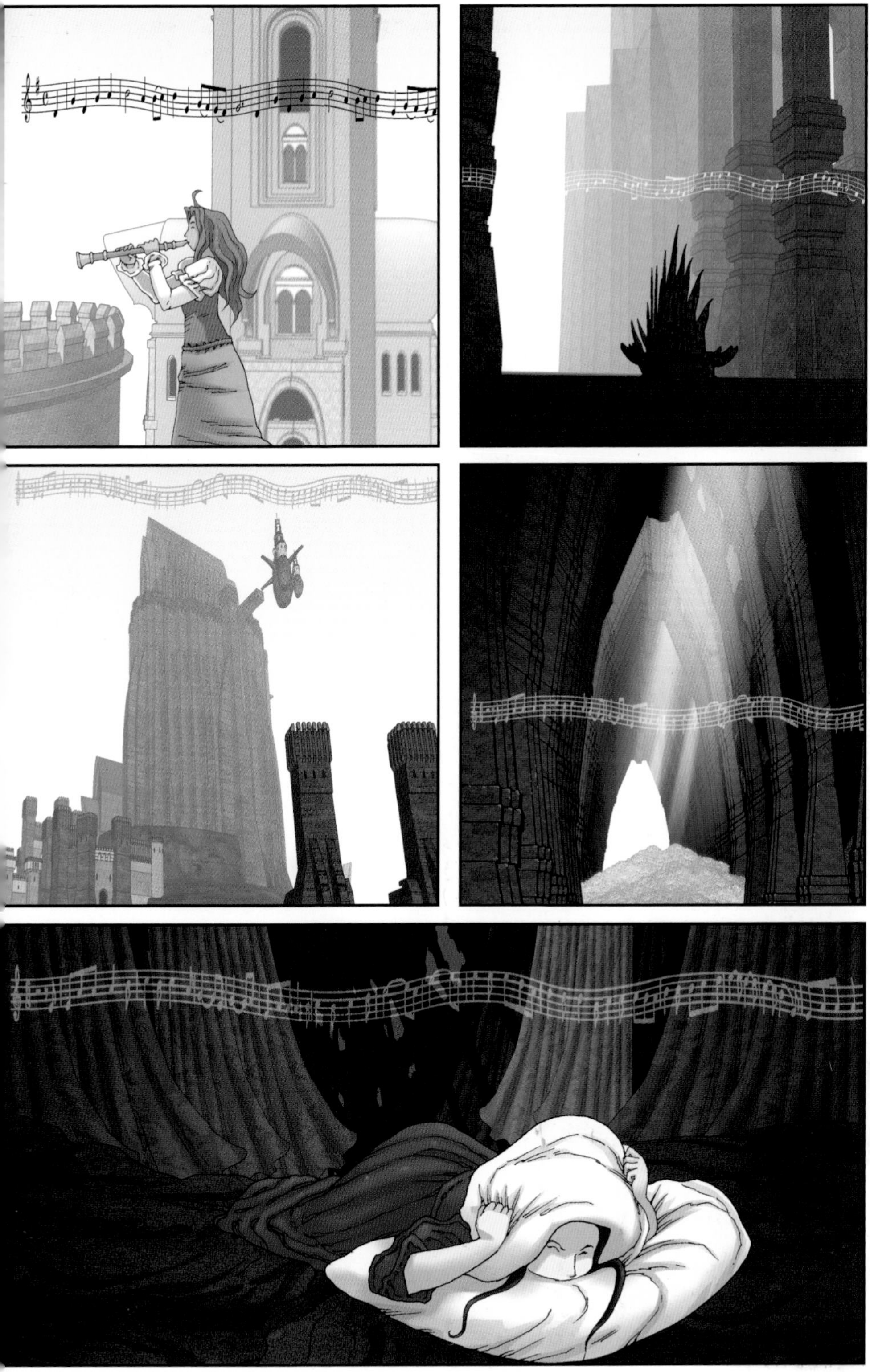

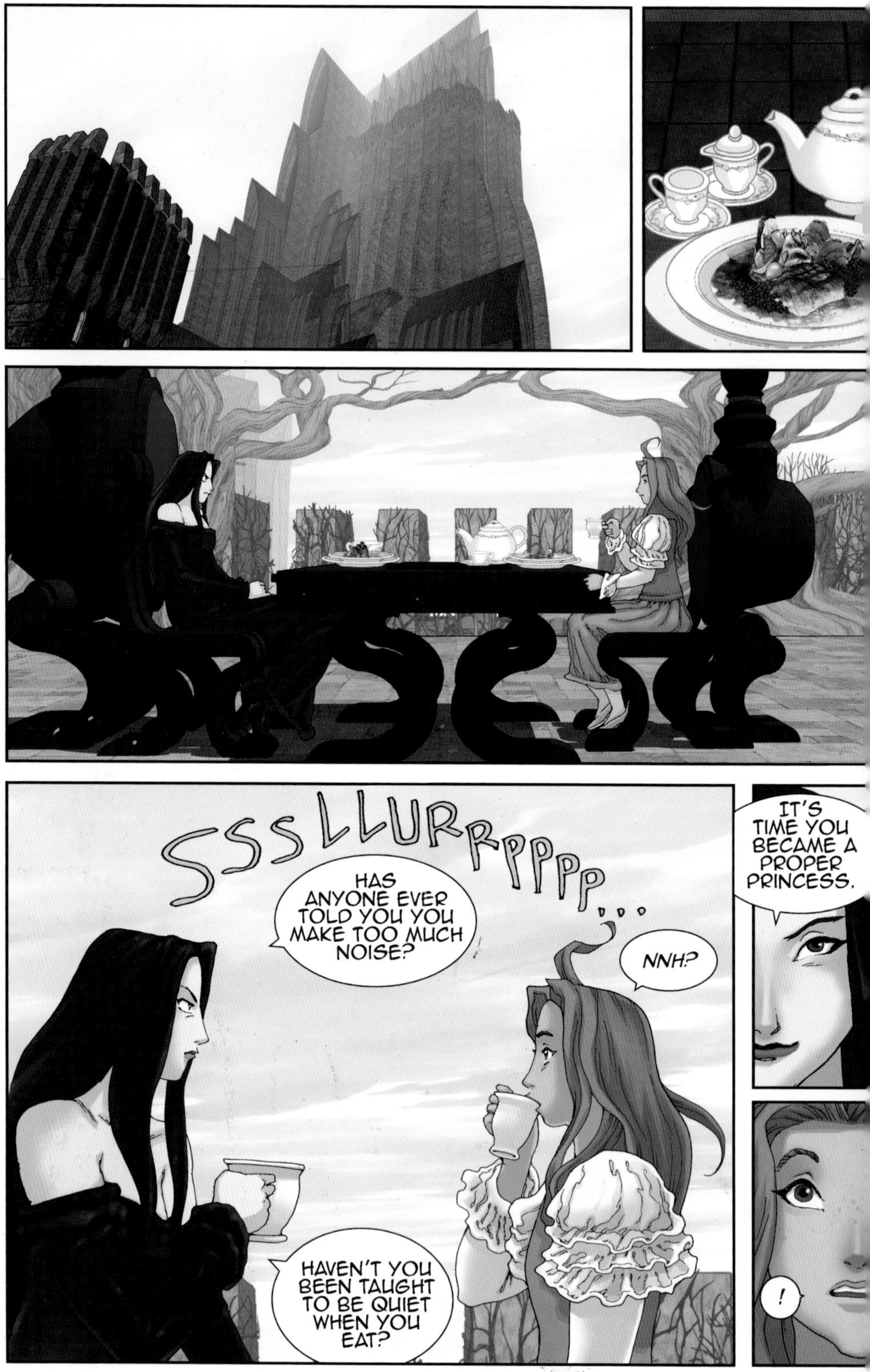
SSSLLURRPPPP...
HAS ANYONE EVER TOLD YOU YOU MAKE TOO MUCH NOISE?
NNH?
HAVEN'T YOU BEEN TAUGHT TO BE QUIET WHEN YOU EAT?
IT'S TIME YOU BECAME A PROPER PRINCESS.
!

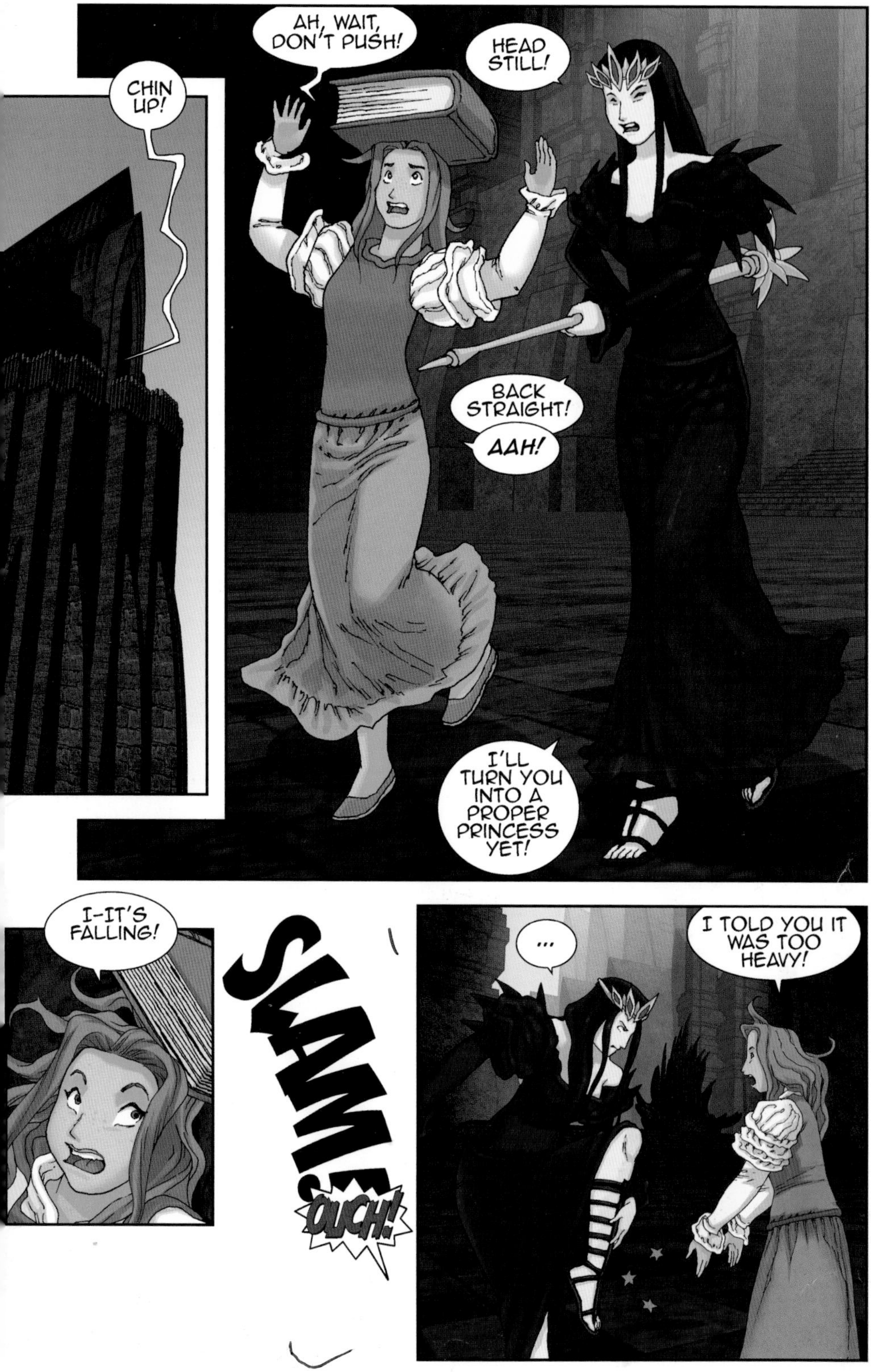
CHIN UP!
AH, WAIT, DON'T PUSH!
HEAD STILL!
BACK STRAIGHT!
AAH!
I'LL TURN YOU INTO A PROPER PRINCESS YET!
I-IT'S FALLING!
SLAM!
OUCH!
...
I TOLD YOU IT WAS TOO HEAVY!

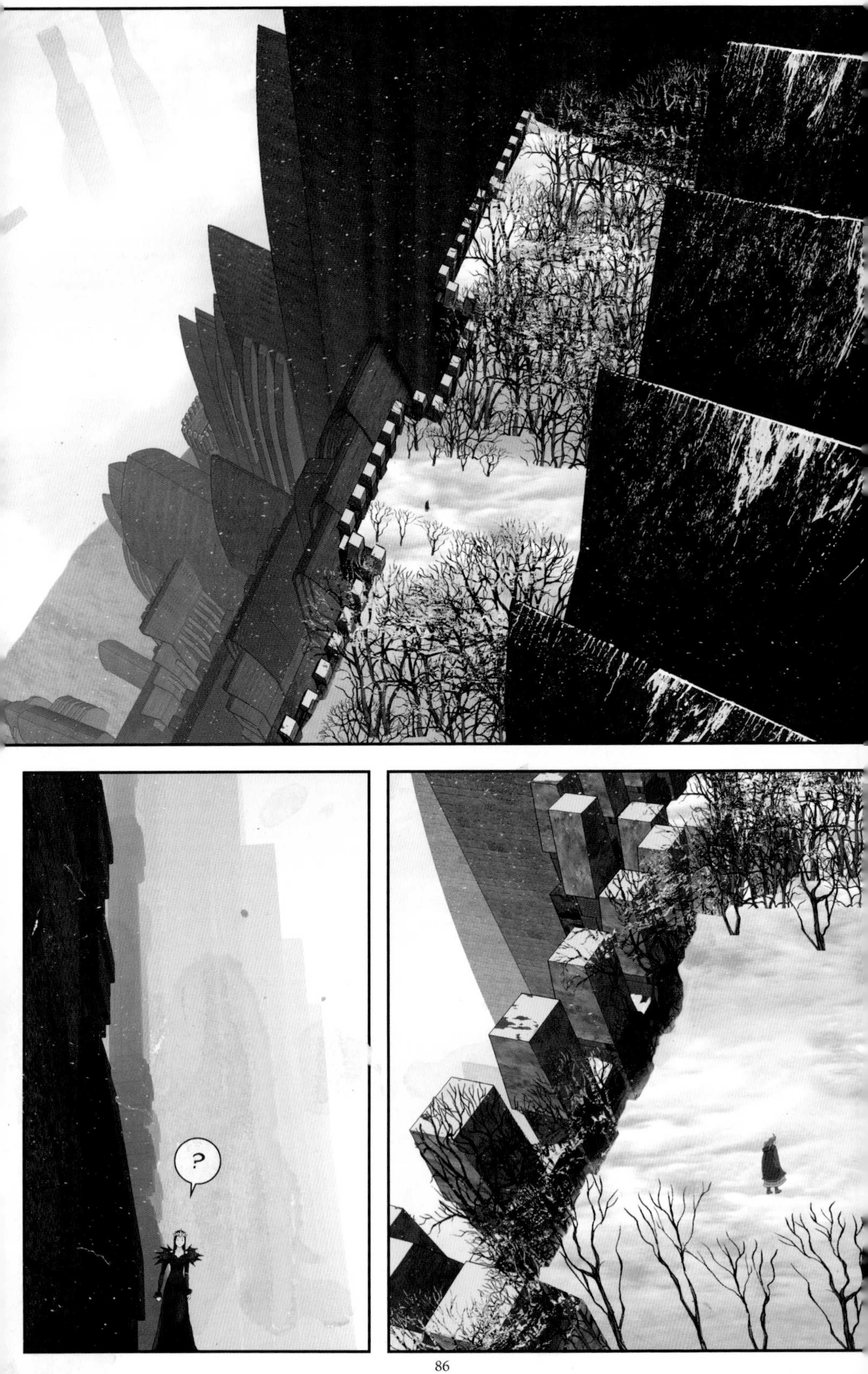
?

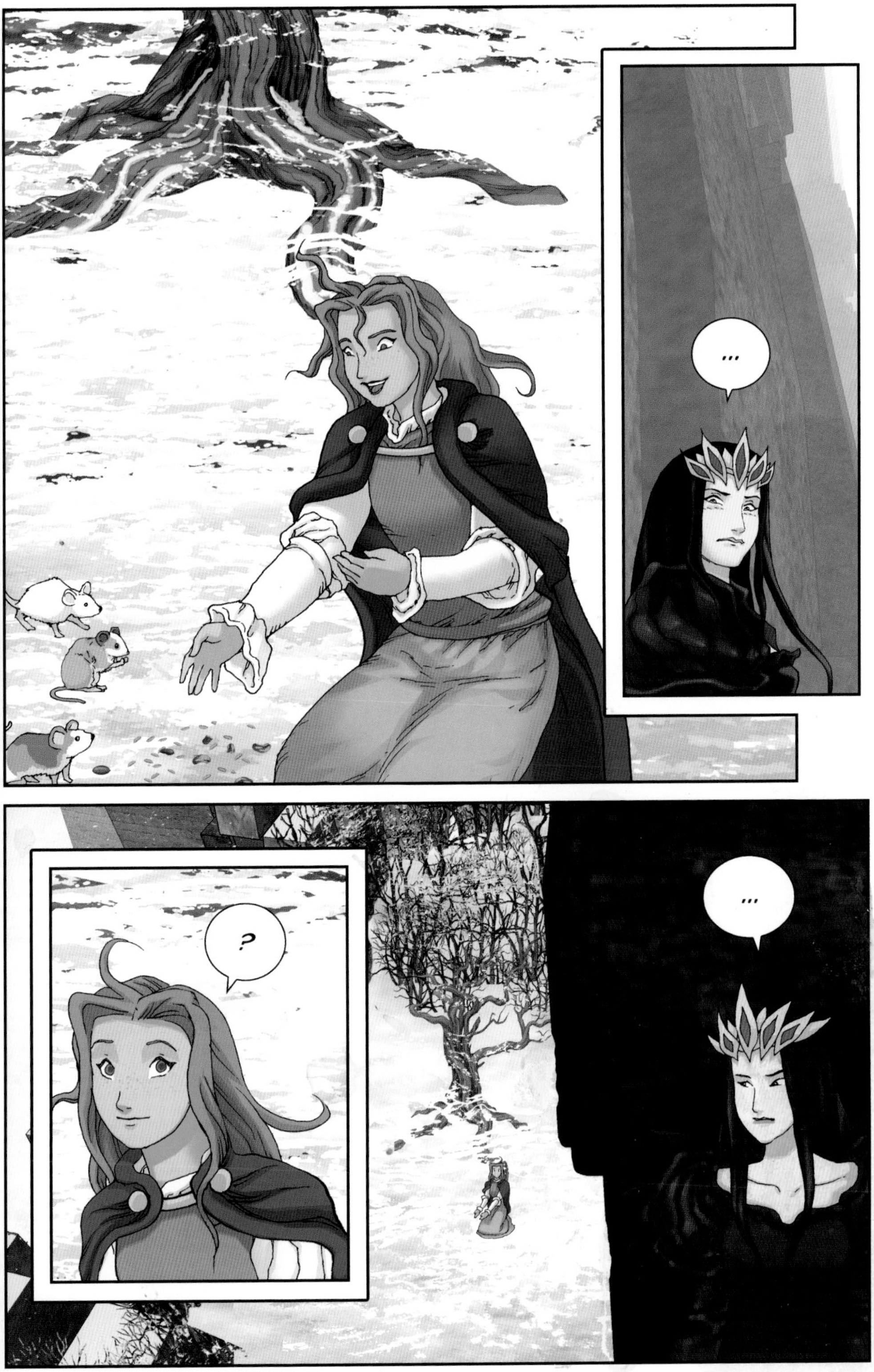
...
?
...

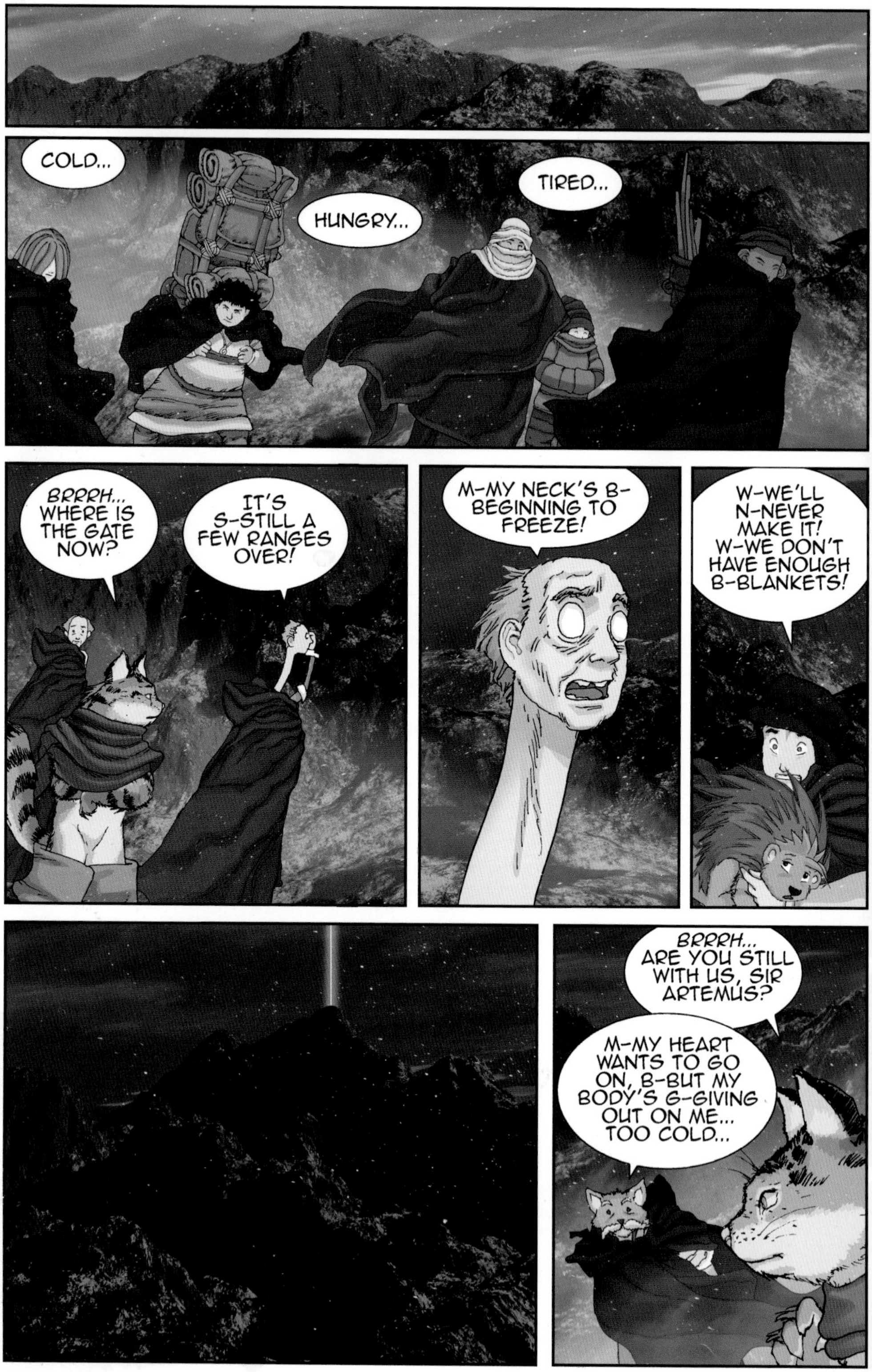
COLD...
HUNGRY...
TIRED...
BRRRH... WHERE IS THE GATE NOW?
IT'S S-STILL A FEW RANGES OVER!
M-MY NECK'S B-BEGINNING TO FREEZE!
W-WE'LL N-NEVER MAKE IT! W-WE DON'T HAVE ENOUGH B-BLANKETS!
BRRRH... ARE YOU STILL WITH US, SIR ARTEMUS?
M-MY HEART WANTS TO GO ON, B-BUT MY BODY'S G-GIVING OUT ON ME... TOO COLD...

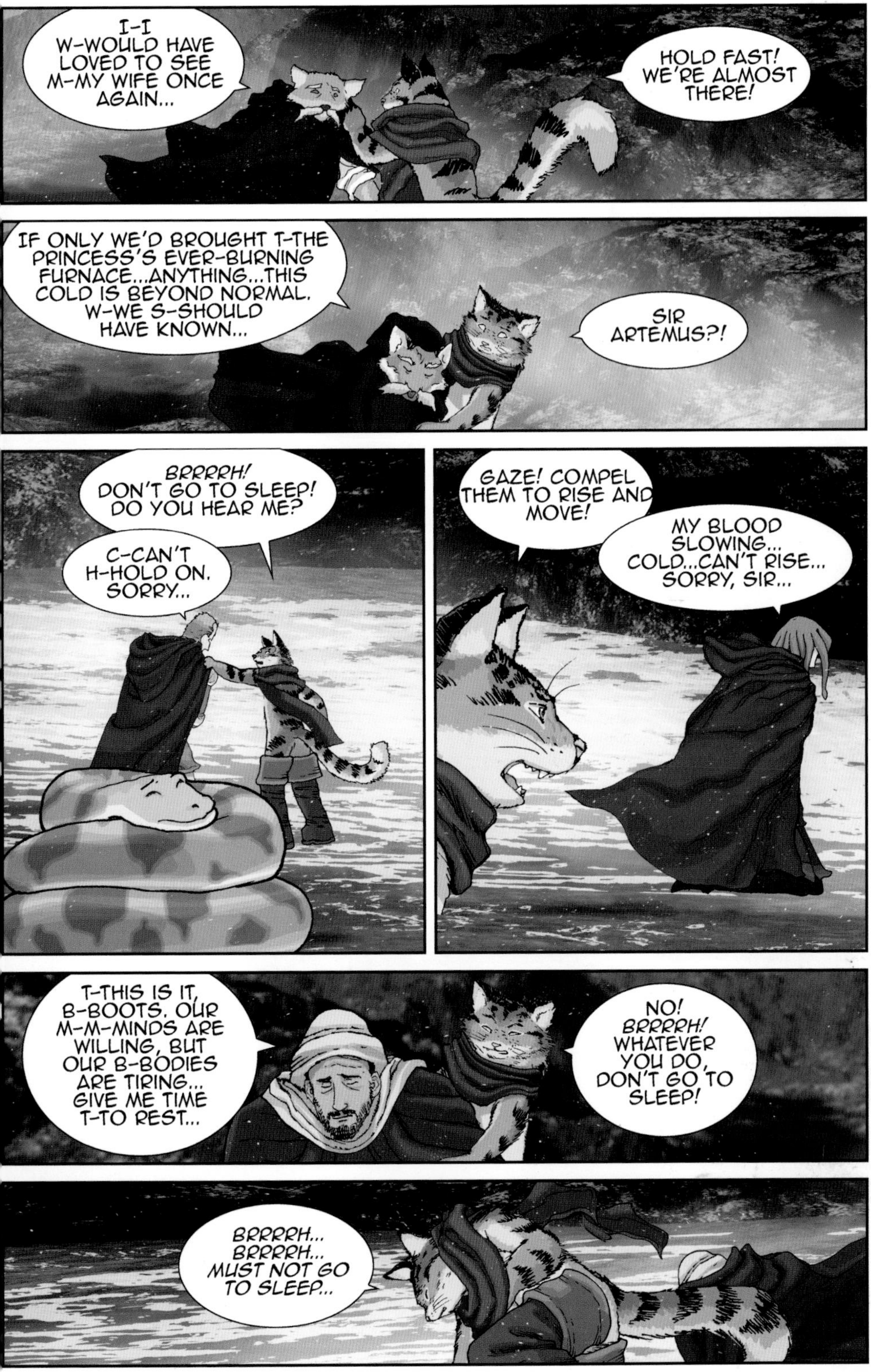
I-I W-WOULD HAVE LOVED TO SEE M-MY WIFE ONCE AGAIN...
HOLD FAST! WE'RE ALMOST THERE!
IF ONLY WE'D BROUGHT T-THE PRINCESS'S EVER-BURNING FURNACE...ANYTHING...THIS COLD IS BEYOND NORMAL. W-WE S-SHOULD HAVE KNOWN...
SIR ARTEMUS?!
BRRRRH! DON'T GO TO SLEEP! DO YOU HEAR ME?
C-CAN'T H-HOLD ON. SORRY...
GAZE! COMPEL THEM TO RISE AND MOVE!
MY BLOOD SLOWING... COLD...CAN'T RISE... SORRY, SIR...
T-THIS IS IT, B-BOOTS. OUR M-M-MINDS ARE WILLING, BUT OUR B-BODIES ARE TIRING... GIVE ME TIME T-TO REST...
NO! BRRRRH! WHATEVER YOU DO, DON'T GO TO SLEEP!
BRRRRH... BRRRRH... MUST NOT GO TO SLEEP...

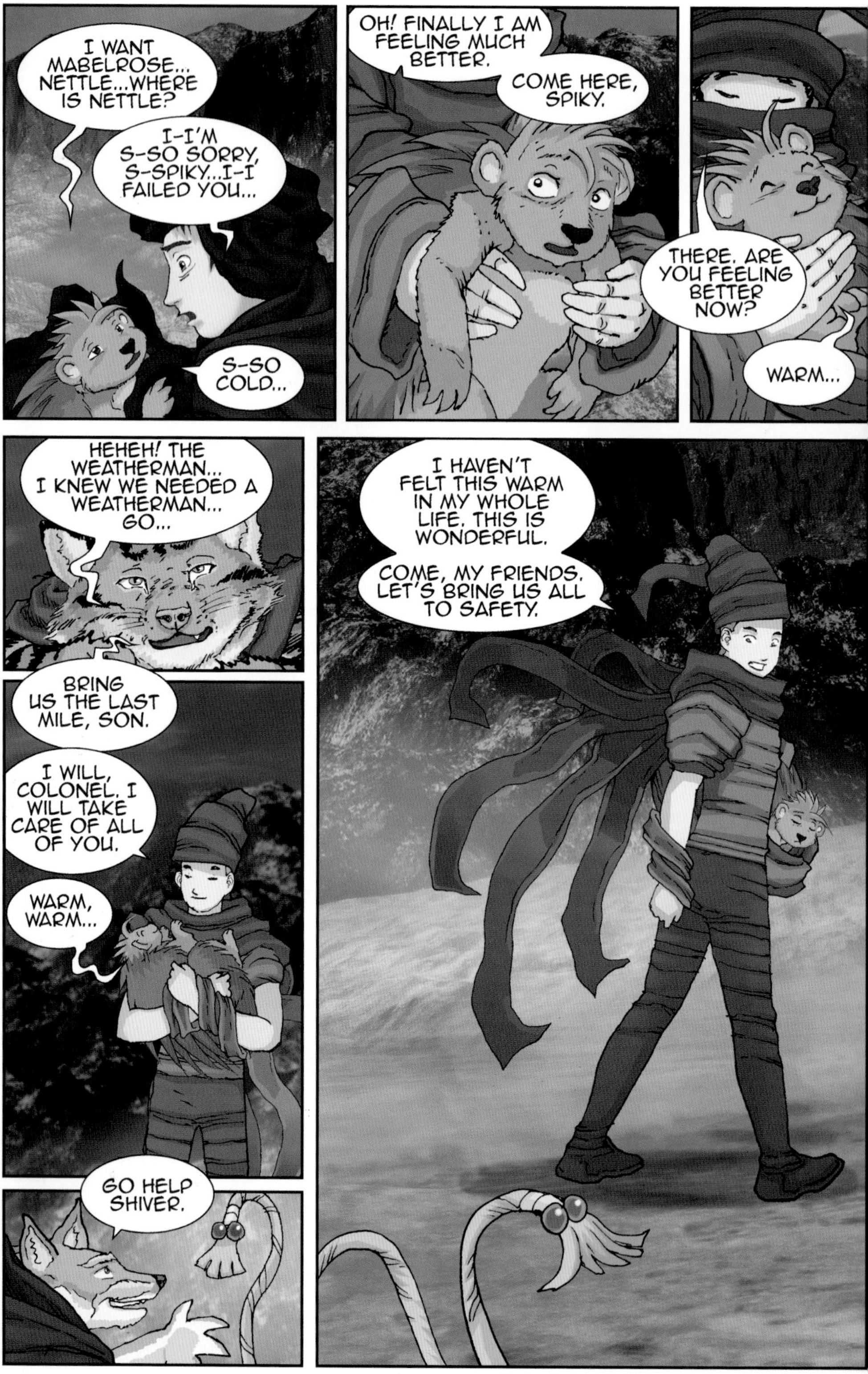
I WANT MABELROSE... NETTLE...WHERE IS NETTLE?
I-I'M S-SO SORRY, S-SPIKY...I-I FAILED YOU...
S-SO COLD...
OH! FINALLY I AM FEELING MUCH BETTER.
COME HERE, SPIKY.
THERE. ARE YOU FEELING BETTER NOW?
WARM...
HEHEH! THE WEATHERMAN... I KNEW WE NEEDED A WEATHERMAN... GO...
BRING US THE LAST MILE, SON.
I WILL, COLONEL. I WILL TAKE CARE OF ALL OF YOU.
WARM, WARM...
GO HELP SHIVER.
I HAVEN'T FELT THIS WARM IN MY WHOLE LIFE. THIS IS WONDERFUL.
COME, MY FRIENDS. LET'S BRING US ALL TO SAFETY.

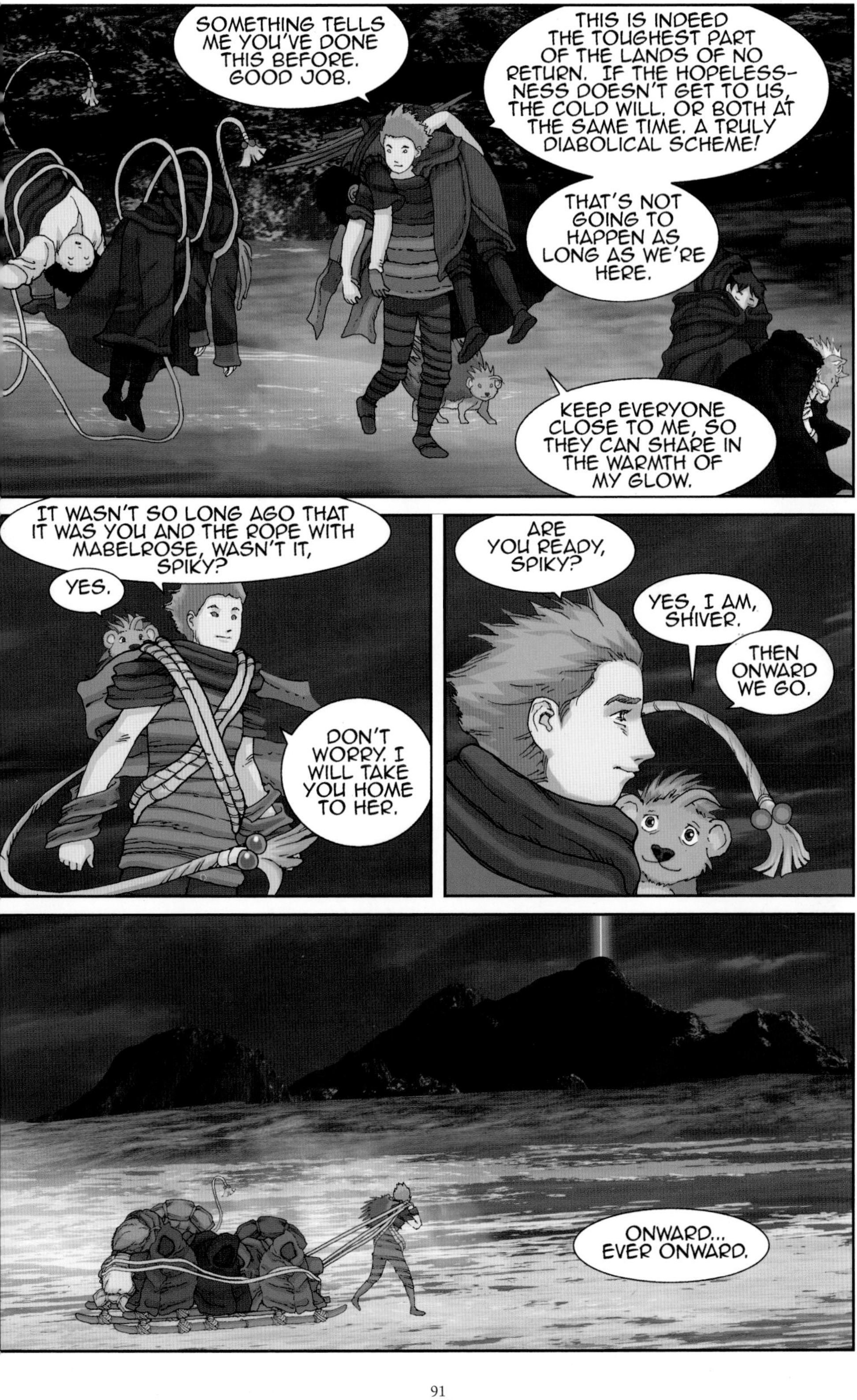
SOMETHING TELLS ME YOU'VE DONE THIS BEFORE. GOOD JOB.
THIS IS INDEED THE TOUGHEST PART OF THE LANDS OF NO RETURN. IF THE HOPELESS-NESS DOESN'T GET TO US, THE COLD WILL, OR BOTH AT THE SAME TIME. A TRULY DIABOLICAL SCHEME!
THAT'S NOT GOING TO HAPPEN AS LONG AS WE'RE HERE.
KEEP EVERYONE CLOSE TO ME, SO THEY CAN SHARE IN THE WARMTH OF MY GLOW.
IT WASN'T SO LONG AGO THAT IT WAS YOU AND THE ROPE WITH MABELROSE, WASN'T IT, SPIKY?
YES.
DON'T WORRY. I WILL TAKE YOU HOME TO HER.
ARE YOU READY, SPIKY?
YES, I AM, SHIVER.
THEN ONWARD WE GO.
ONWARD... EVER ONWARD.

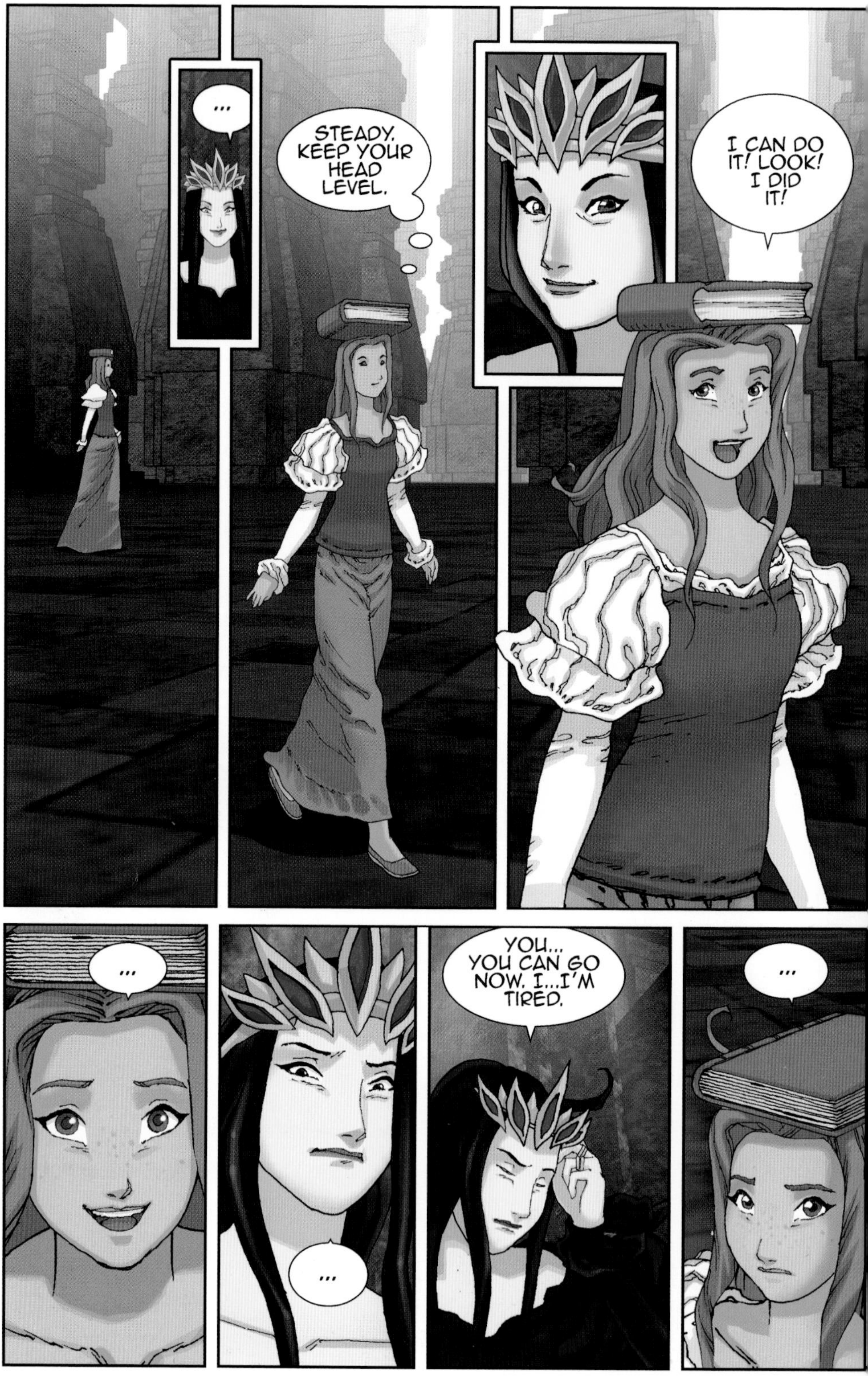
...
STEADY. KEEP YOUR HEAD LEVEL.
I CAN DO IT! LOOK! I DID IT!
...
...
YOU... YOU CAN GO NOW. I...I'M TIRED.
...

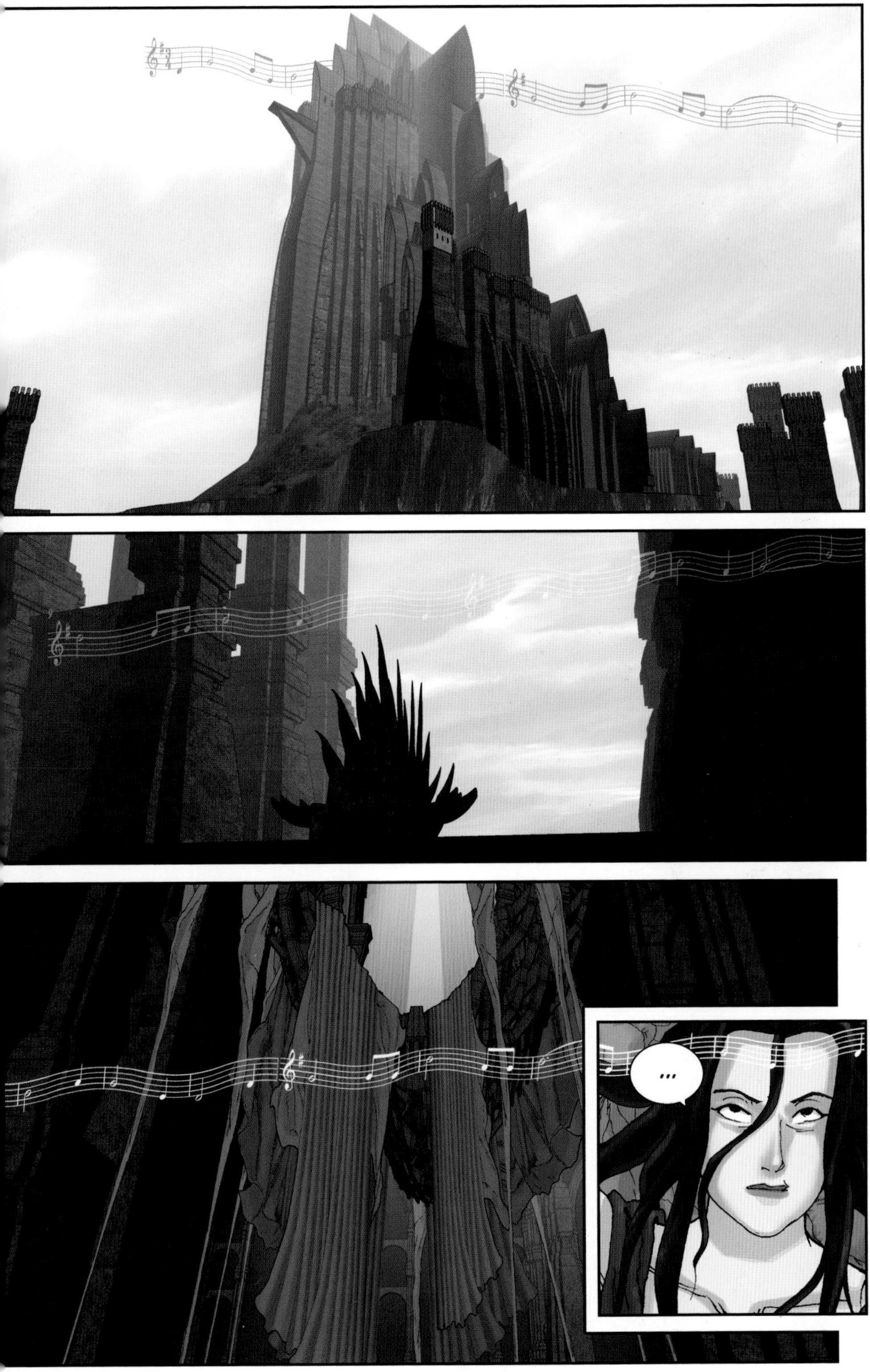
...

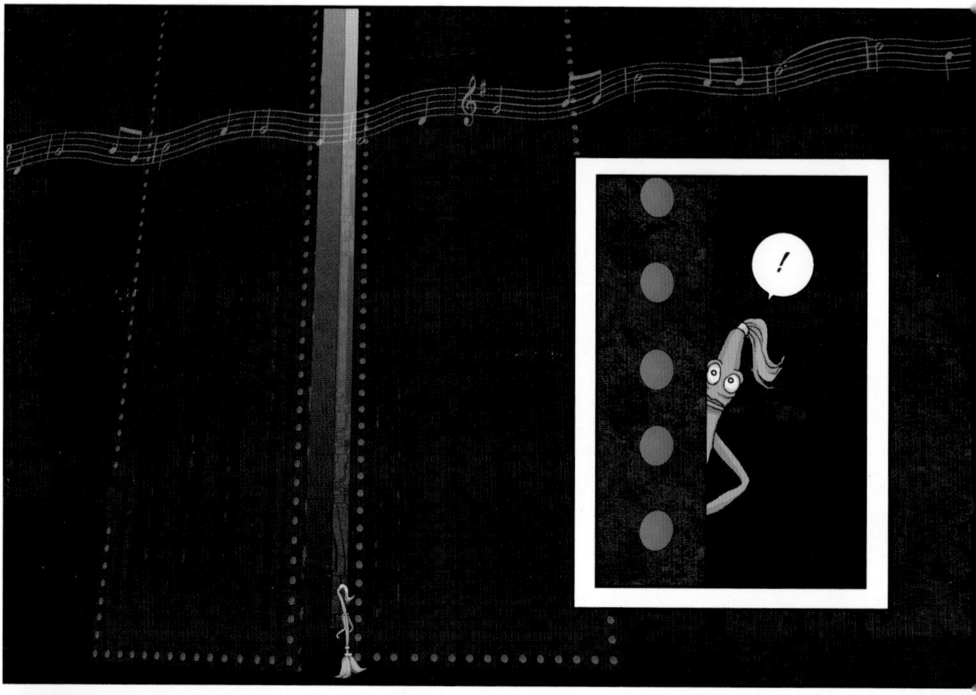
!

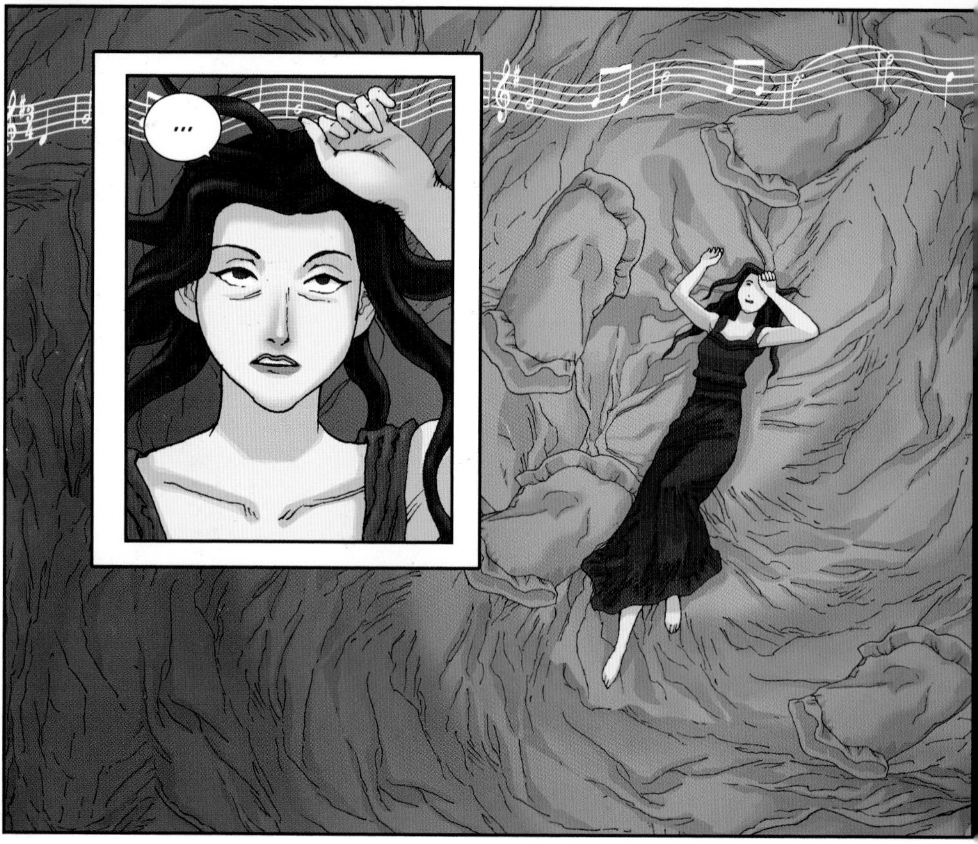
...

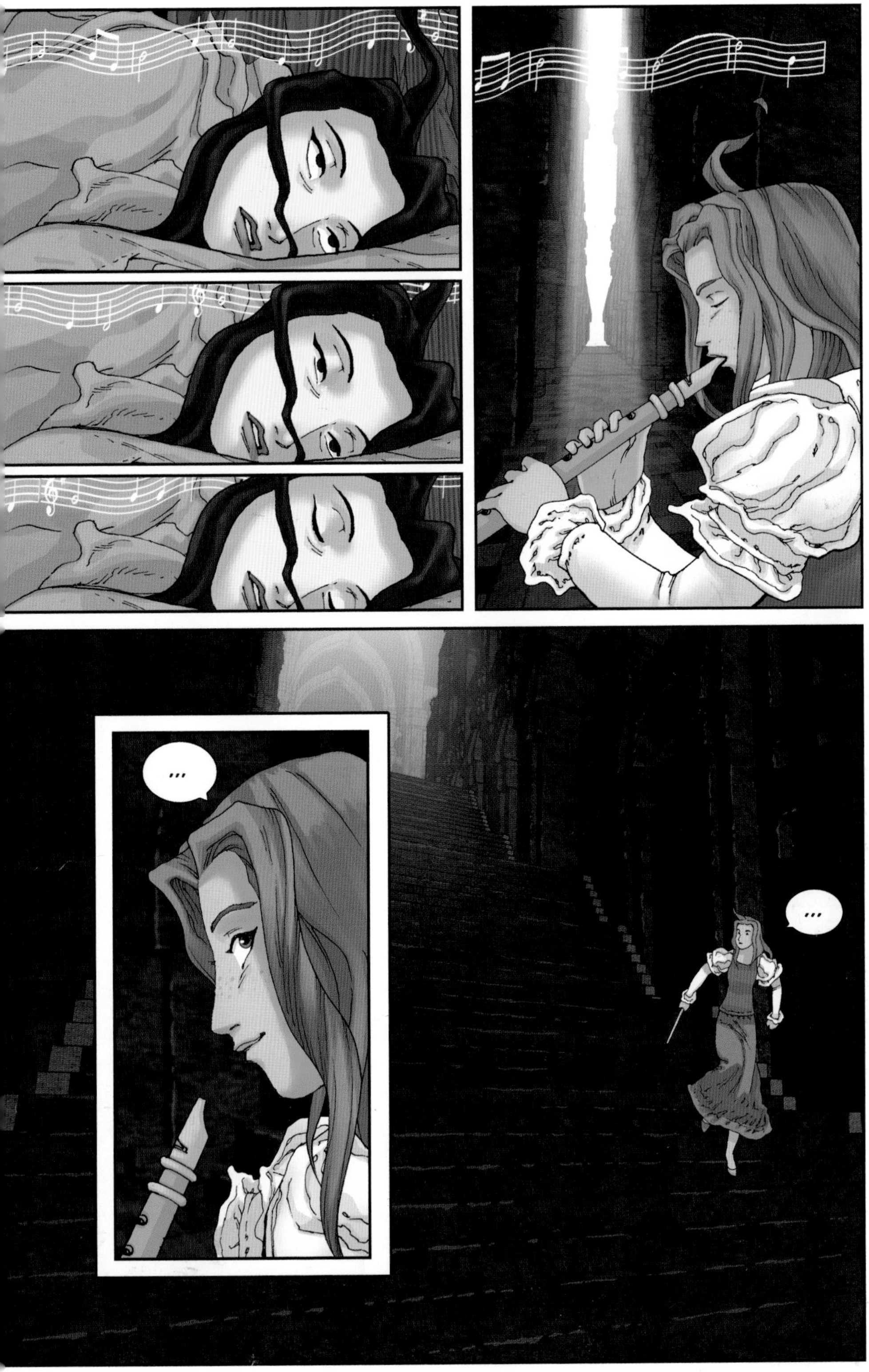
...
...

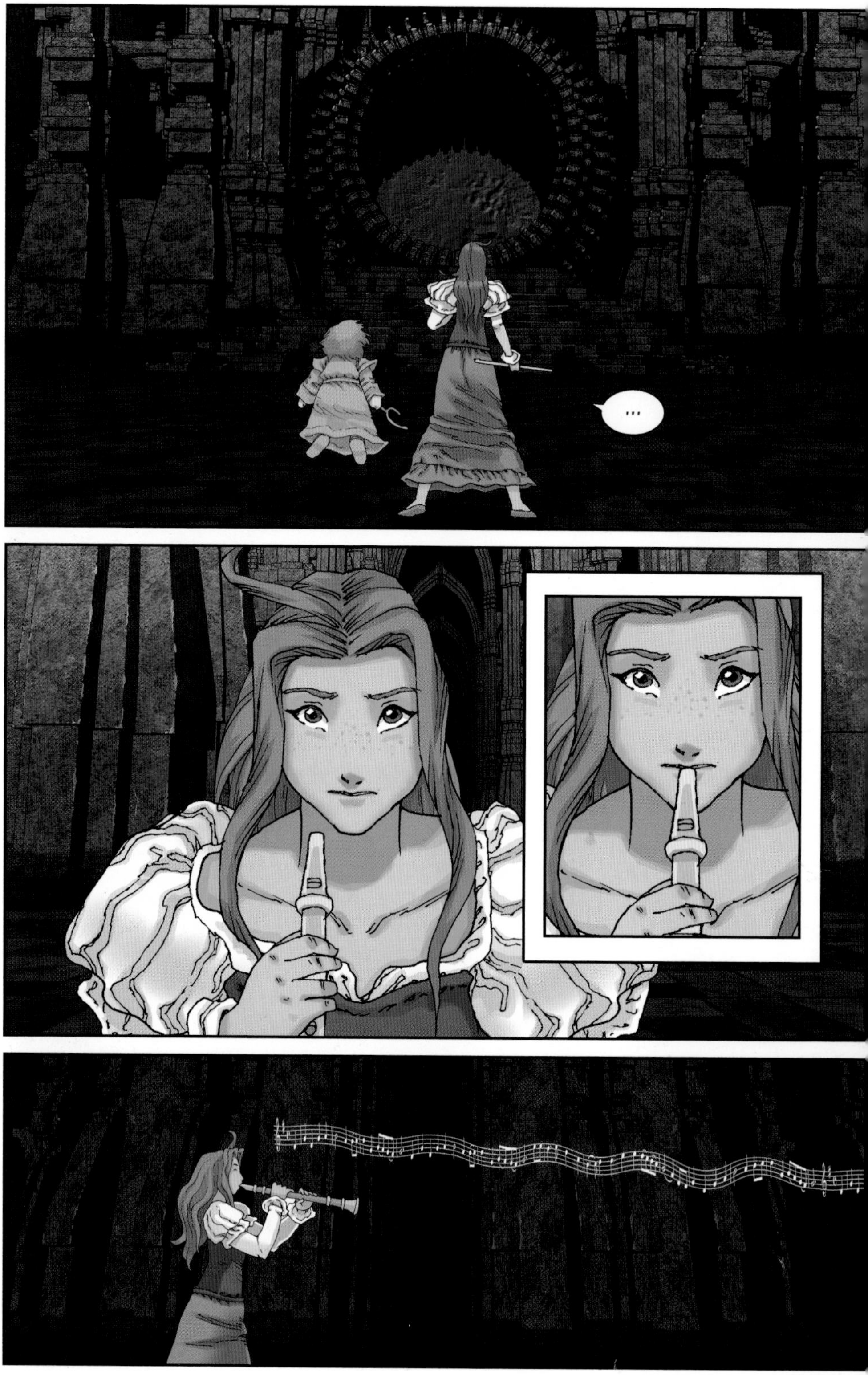
...

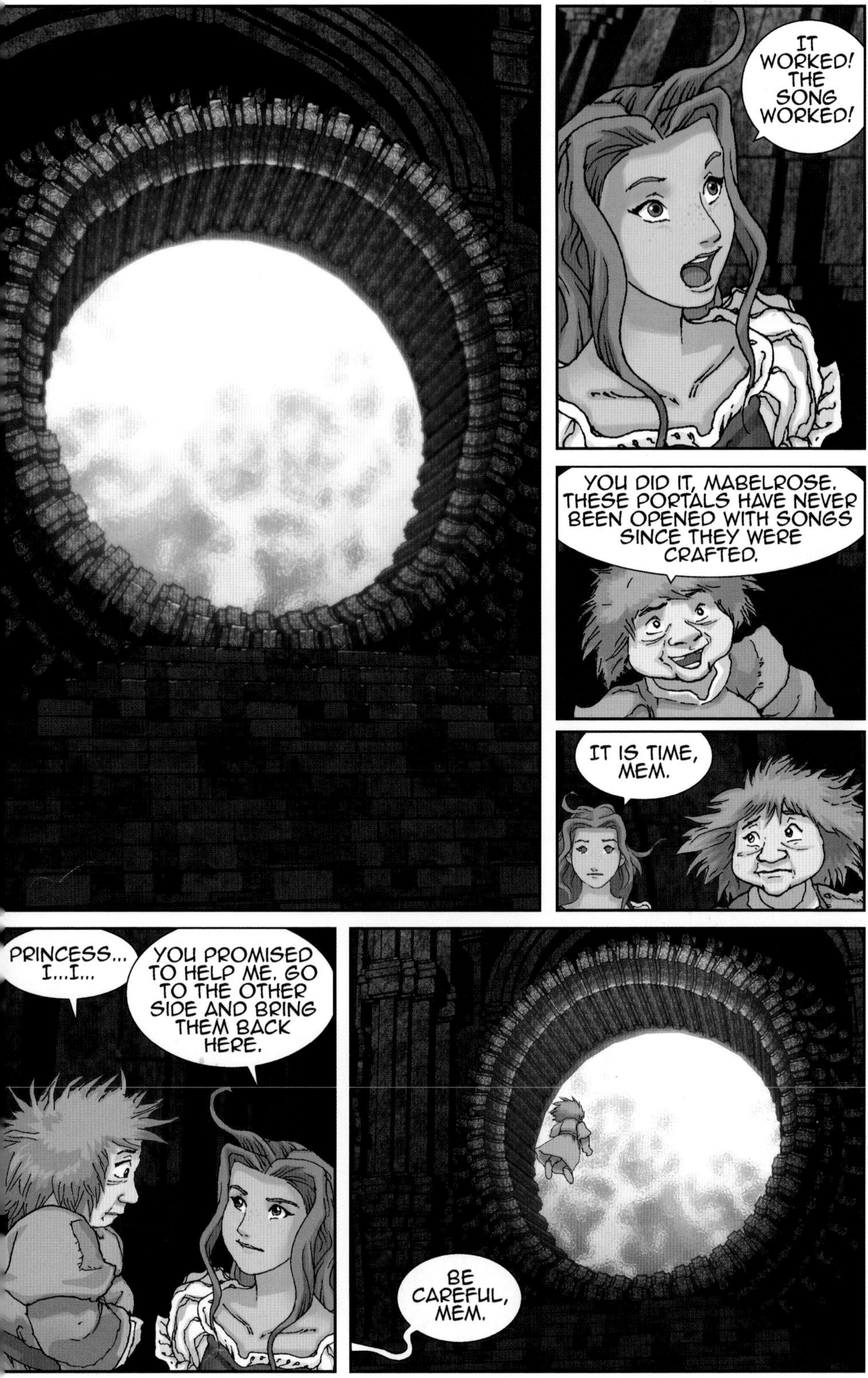
IT WORKED! THE SONG WORKED!
YOU DID IT, MABELROSE. THESE PORTALS HAVE NEVER BEEN OPENED WITH SONGS SINCE THEY WERE CRAFTED.
IT IS TIME, MEM.
PRINCESS... I...I...
YOU PROMISED TO HELP ME. GO TO THE OTHER SIDE AND BRING THEM BACK HERE.
BE CAREFUL, MEM.

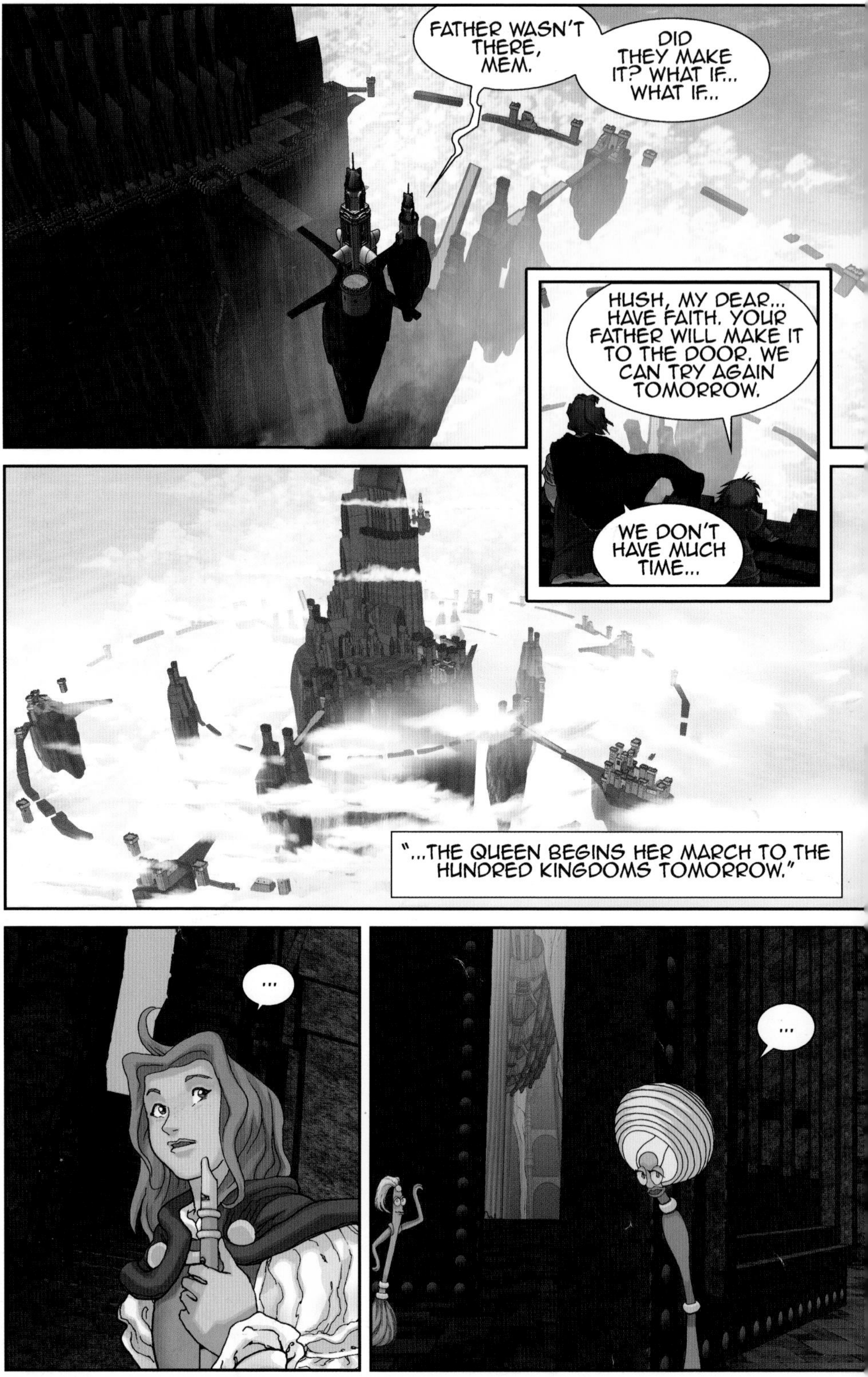
FATHER WASN'T THERE, MEM.
DID THEY MAKE IT? WHAT IF... WHAT IF...
HUSH, MY DEAR... HAVE FAITH. YOUR FATHER WILL MAKE IT TO THE DOOR. WE CAN TRY AGAIN TOMORROW.
WE DON'T HAVE MUCH TIME...
"...THE QUEEN BEGINS HER MARCH TO THE HUNDRED KINGDOMS TOMORROW."
...
...

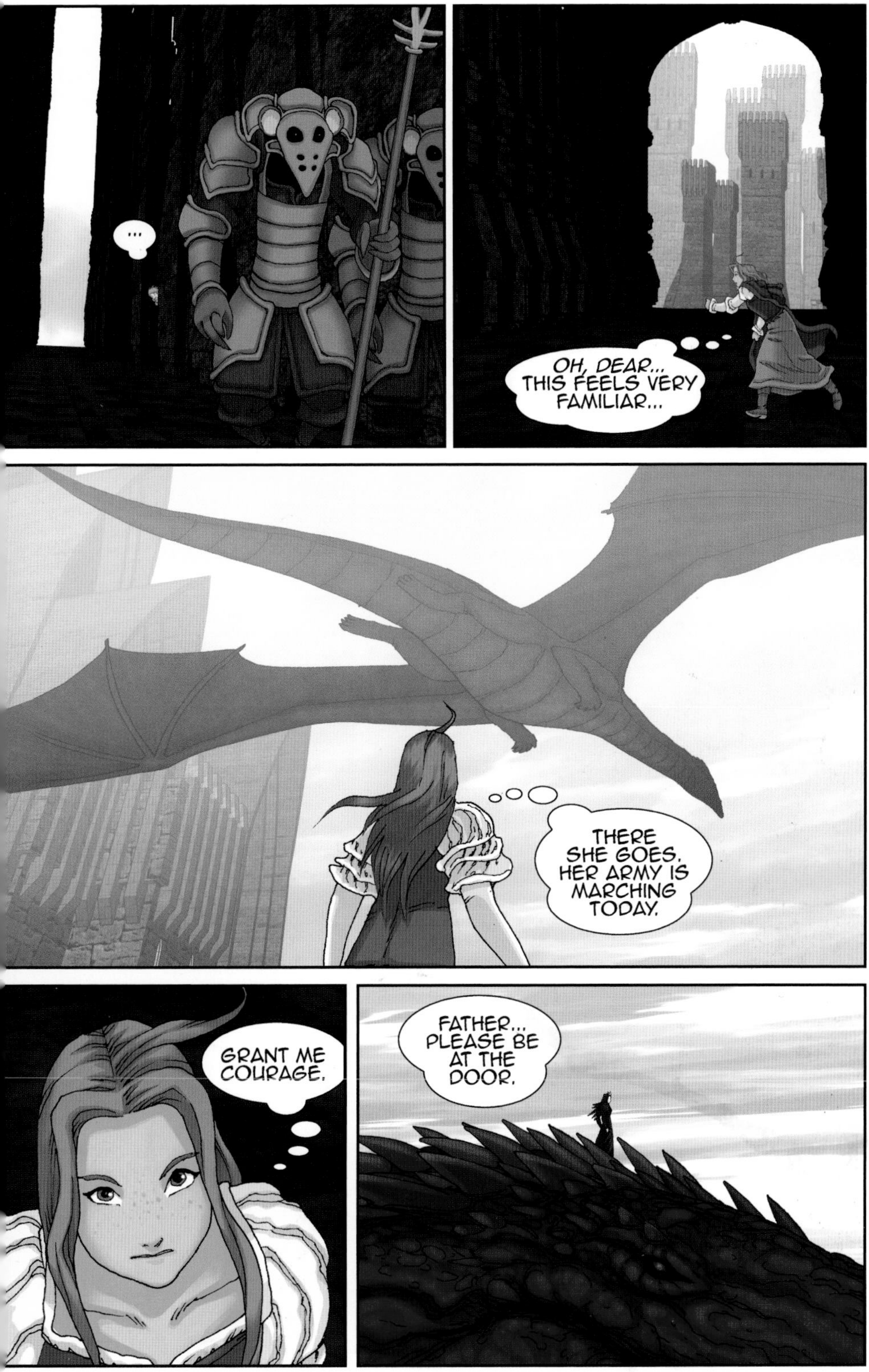
...
OH, DEAR... THIS FEELS VERY FAMILIAR...
THERE SHE GOES. HER ARMY IS MARCHING TODAY.
GRANT ME COURAGE.
FATHER... PLEASE BE AT THE DOOR.

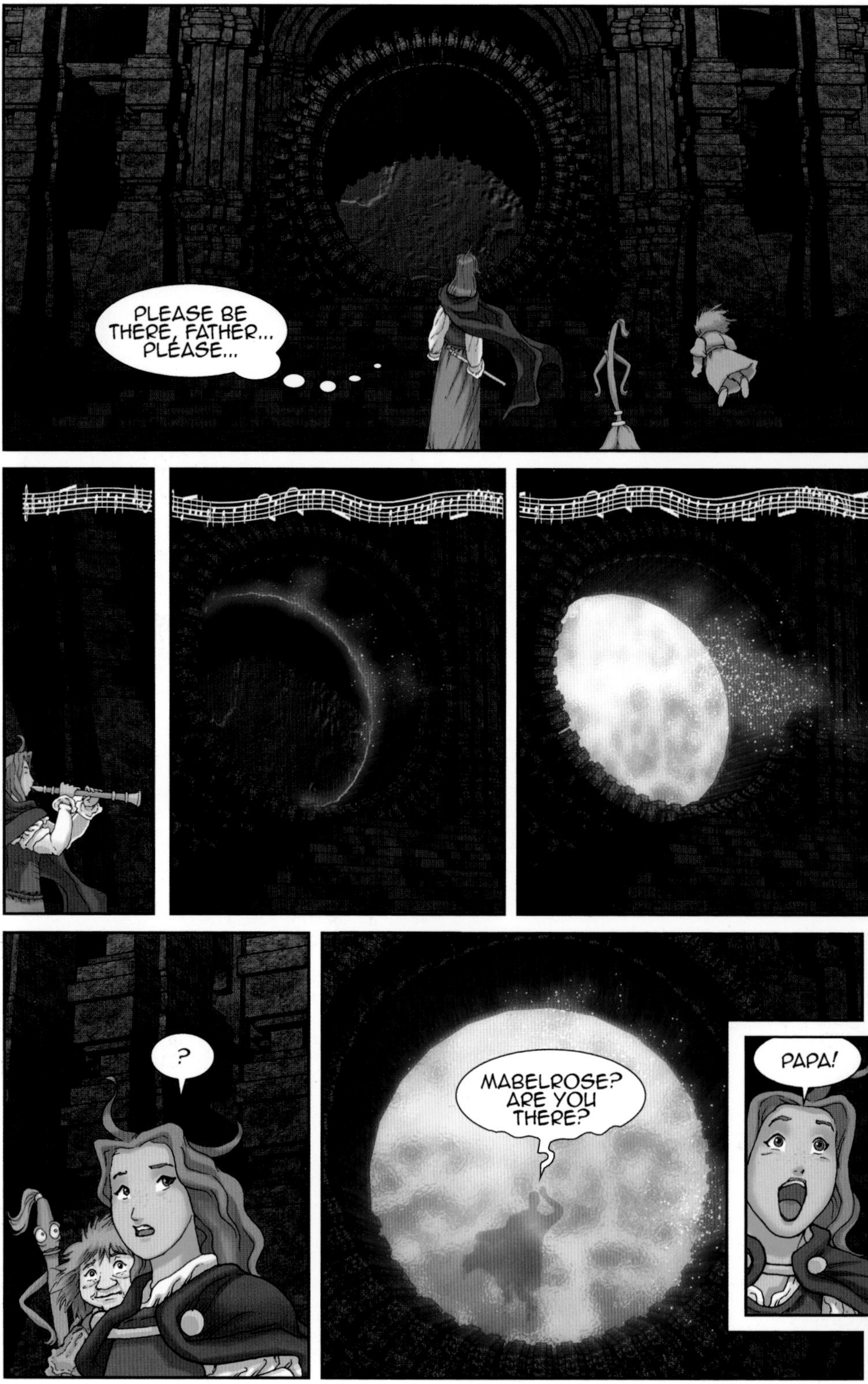
PLEASE BE THERE, FATHER... PLEASE...
?
MABELROSE? ARE YOU THERE?
PAPA!

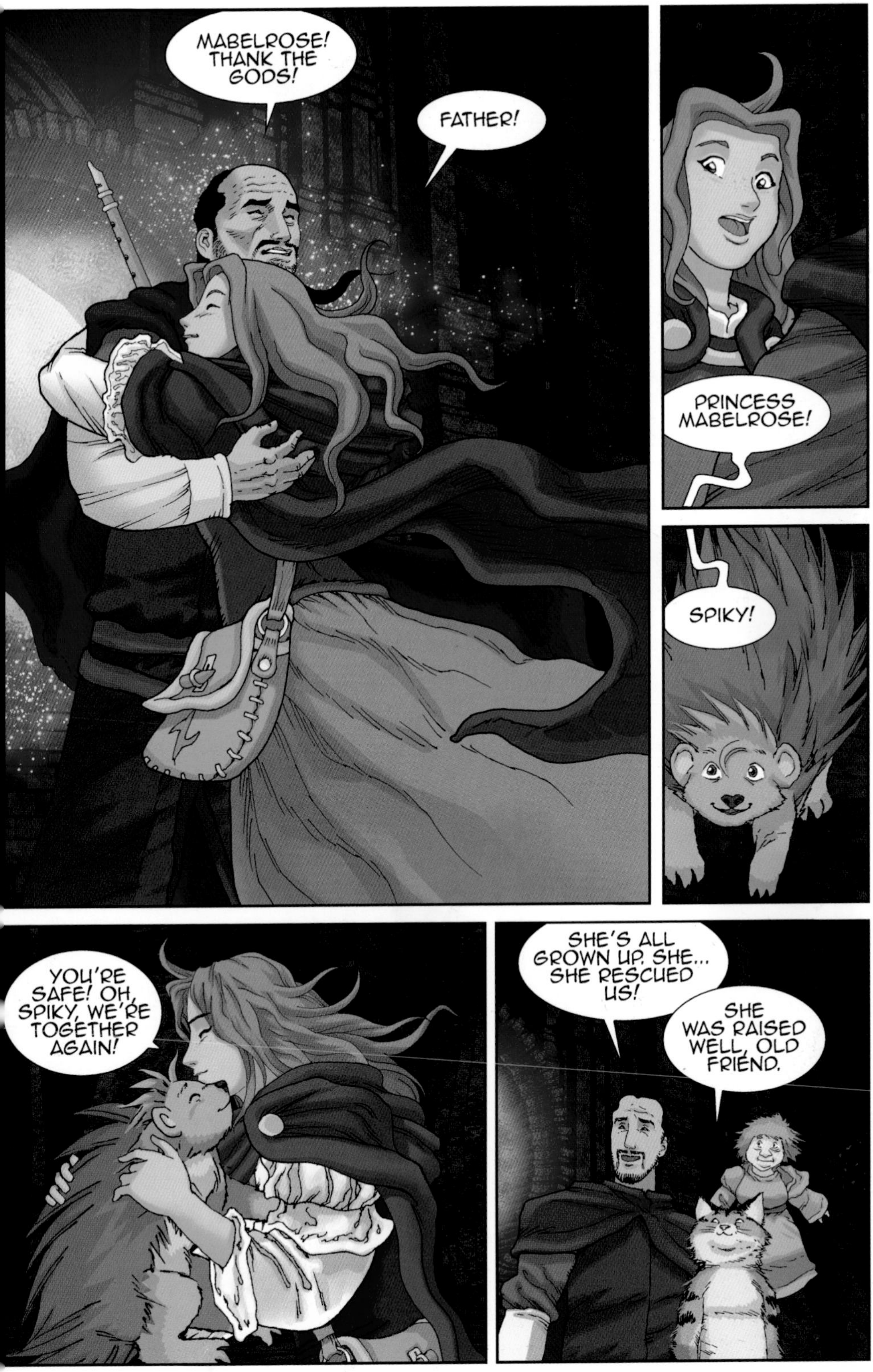
MABELROSE! THANK THE GODS!
FATHER!
PRINCESS MABELROSE!
SPIKY!
YOU'RE SAFE! OH, SPIKY, WE'RE TOGETHER AGAIN!
SHE'S ALL GROWN UP. SHE... SHE RESCUED US!
SHE WAS RAISED WELL, OLD FRIEND.

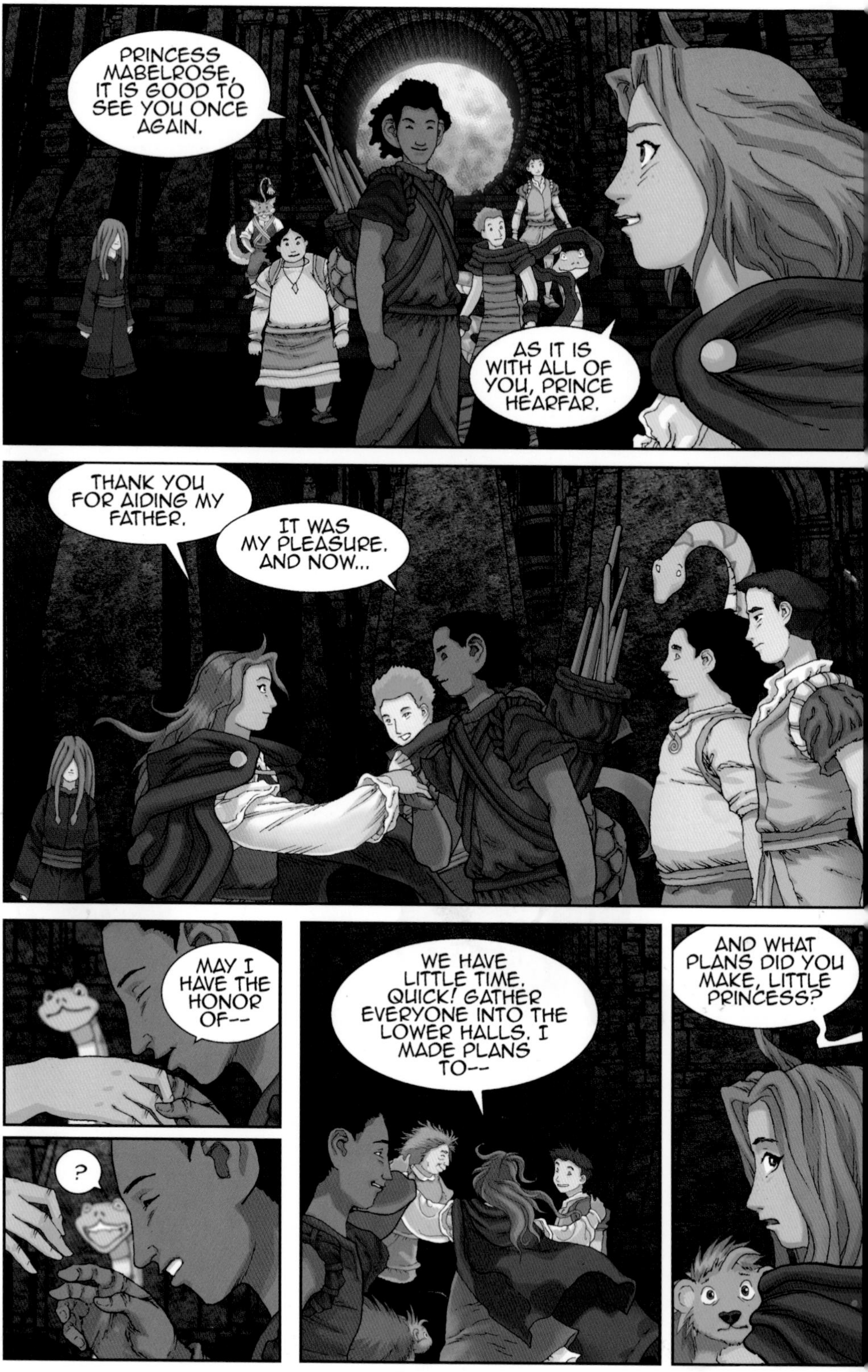
PRINCESS MABELROSE, IT IS GOOD TO SEE YOU ONCE AGAIN.
AS IT IS WITH ALL OF YOU, PRINCE HEARFAR.
THANK YOU FOR AIDING MY FATHER.
IT WAS MY PLEASURE. AND NOW...
MAY I HAVE THE HONOR OF--
?
WE HAVE LITTLE TIME. QUICK! GATHER EVERYONE INTO THE LOWER HALLS. I MADE PLANS TO--
AND WHAT PLANS DID YOU MAKE, LITTLE PRINCESS?

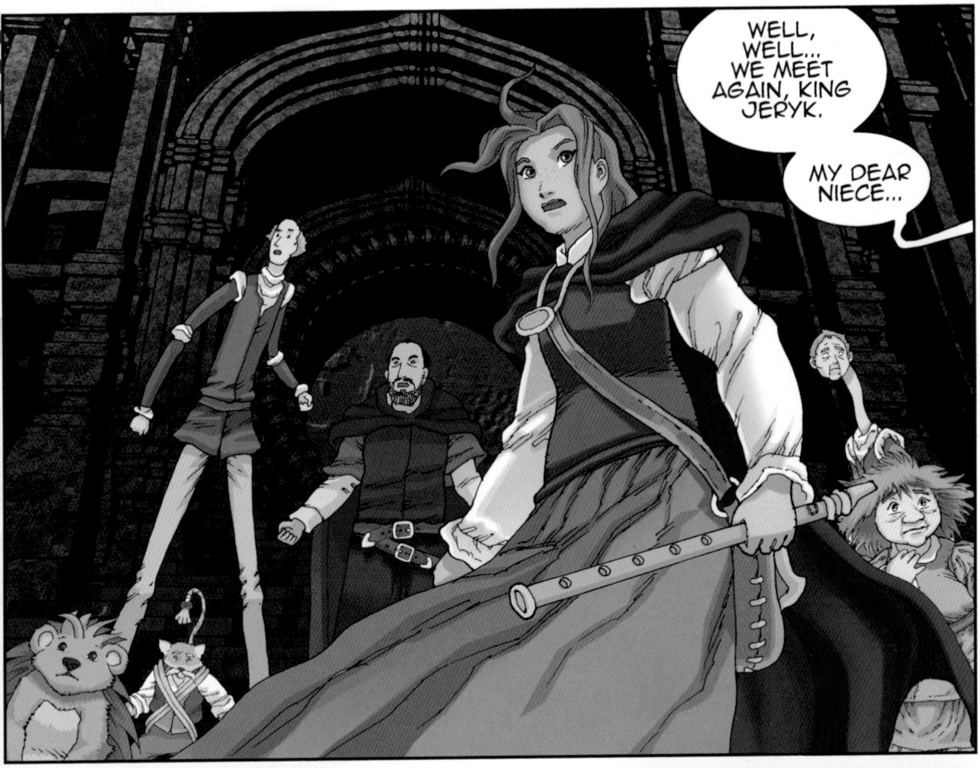
WELL, WELL... WE MEET AGAIN, KING JERYK.
MY DEAR NIECE...

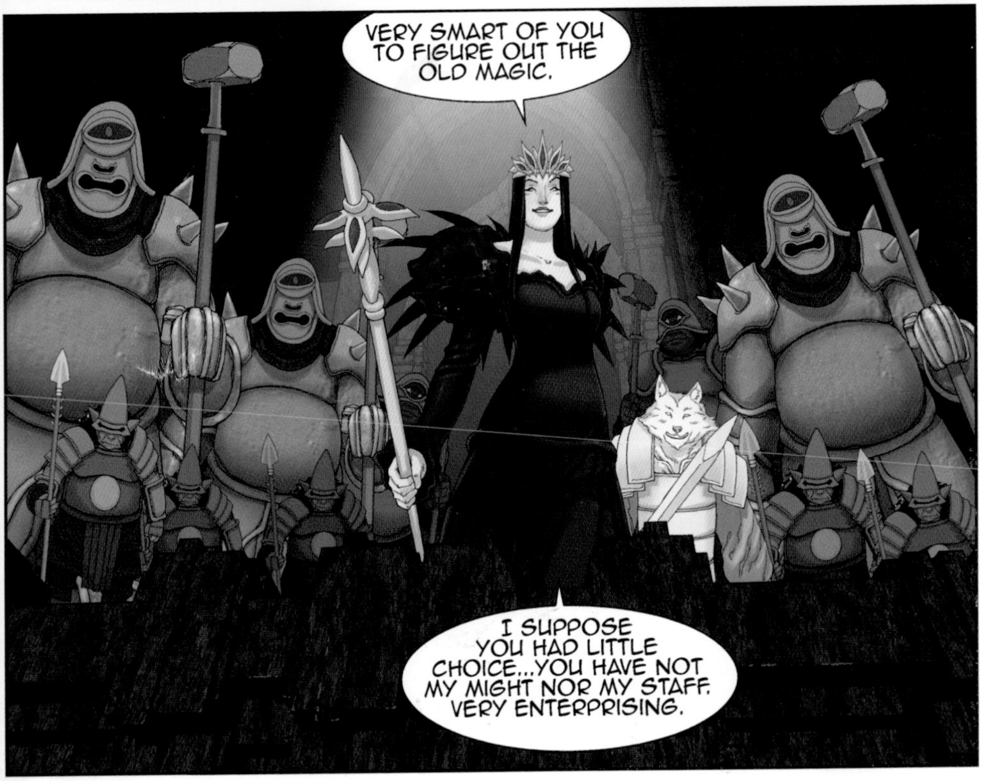
VERY SMART OF YOU TO FIGURE OUT THE OLD MAGIC.
I SUPPOSE YOU HAD LITTLE CHOICE...YOU HAVE NOT MY MIGHT NOR MY STAFF. VERY ENTERPRISING.

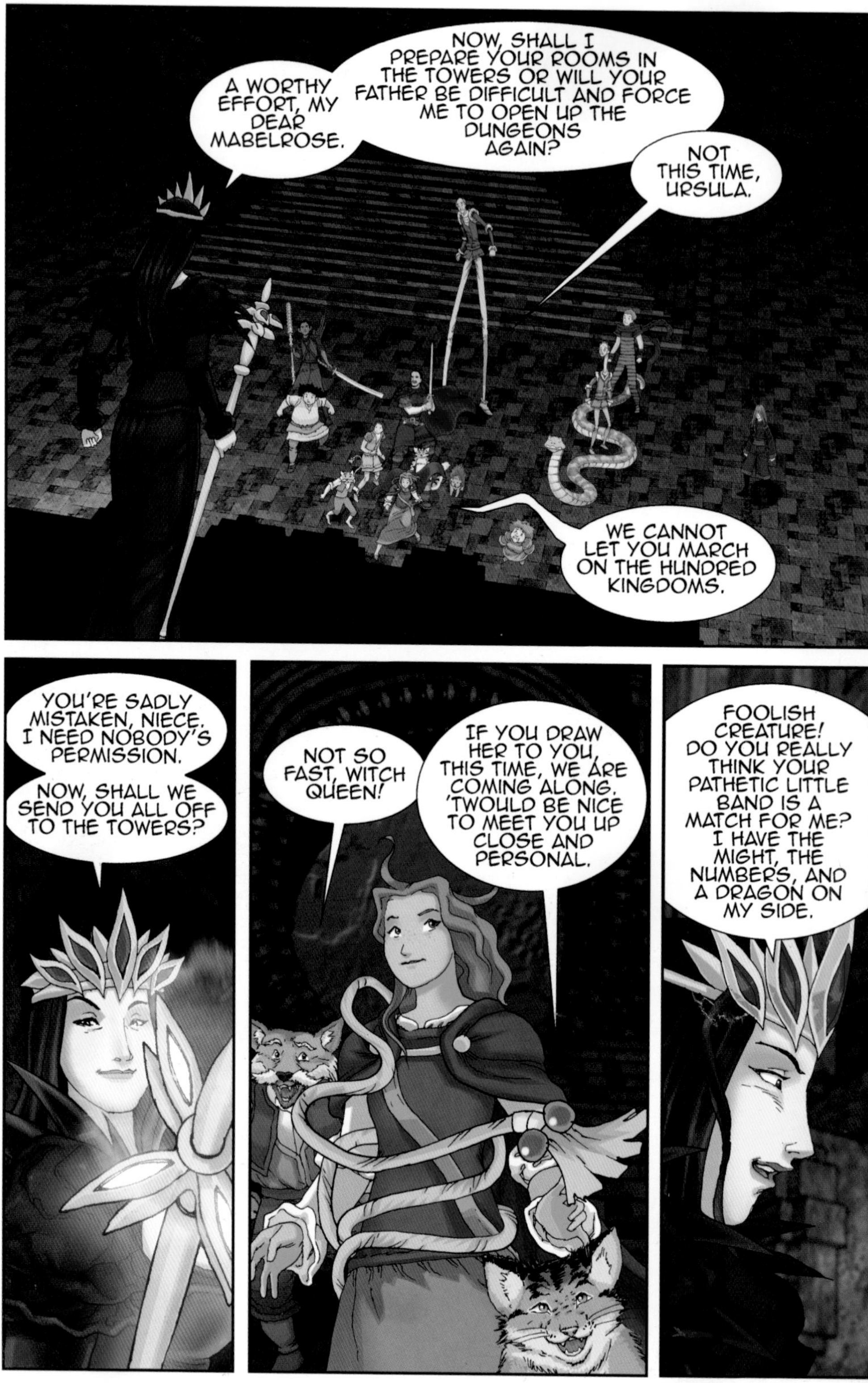
A WORTHY EFFORT, MY DEAR MABELROSE.
NOW, SHALL I PREPARE YOUR ROOMS IN THE TOWERS OR WILL YOUR FATHER BE DIFFICULT AND FORCE ME TO OPEN UP THE DUNGEONS AGAIN?
NOT THIS TIME, URSULA.
WE CANNOT LET YOU MARCH ON THE HUNDRED KINGDOMS.
YOU'RE SADLY MISTAKEN, NIECE. I NEED NOBODY'S PERMISSION.
NOW, SHALL WE SEND YOU ALL OFF TO THE TOWERS?
NOT SO FAST, WITCH QUEEN!
IF YOU DRAW HER TO YOU, THIS TIME, WE ARE COMING ALONG. 'TWOULD BE NICE TO MEET YOU UP CLOSE AND PERSONAL.
FOOLISH CREATURE! DO YOU REALLY THINK YOUR PATHETIC LITTLE BAND IS A MATCH FOR ME? I HAVE THE MIGHT, THE NUMBERS, AND A DRAGON ON MY SIDE.

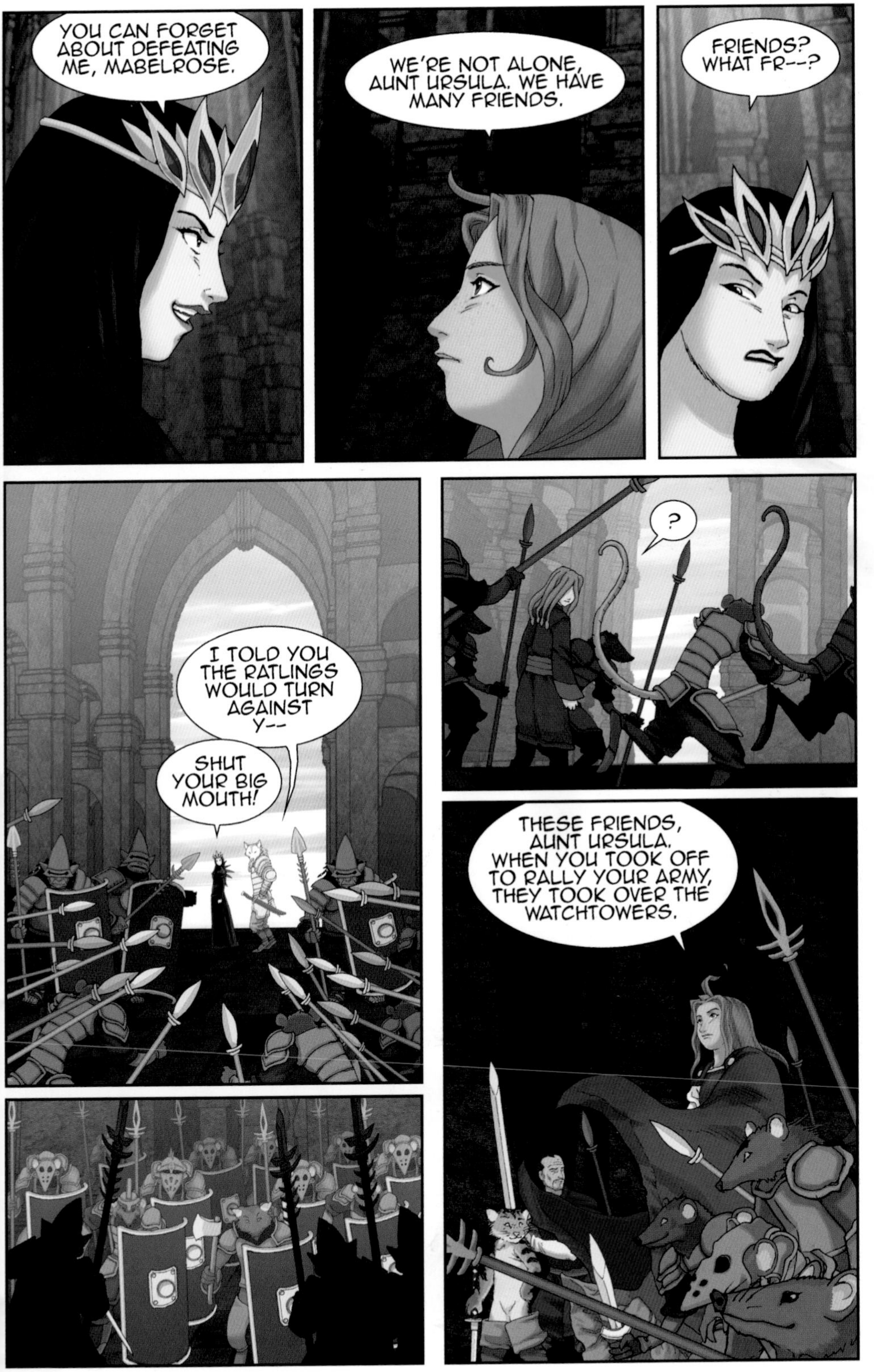
YOU CAN FORGET ABOUT DEFEATING ME, MABELROSE.
WE'RE NOT ALONE, AUNT URSULA. WE HAVE MANY FRIENDS.
FRIENDS? WHAT FR--?
I TOLD YOU THE RATLINGS WOULD TURN AGAINST Y--
SHUT YOUR BIG MOUTH!
?
THESE FRIENDS, AUNT URSULA. WHEN YOU TOOK OFF TO RALLY YOUR ARMY, THEY TOOK OVER THE WATCHTOWERS.

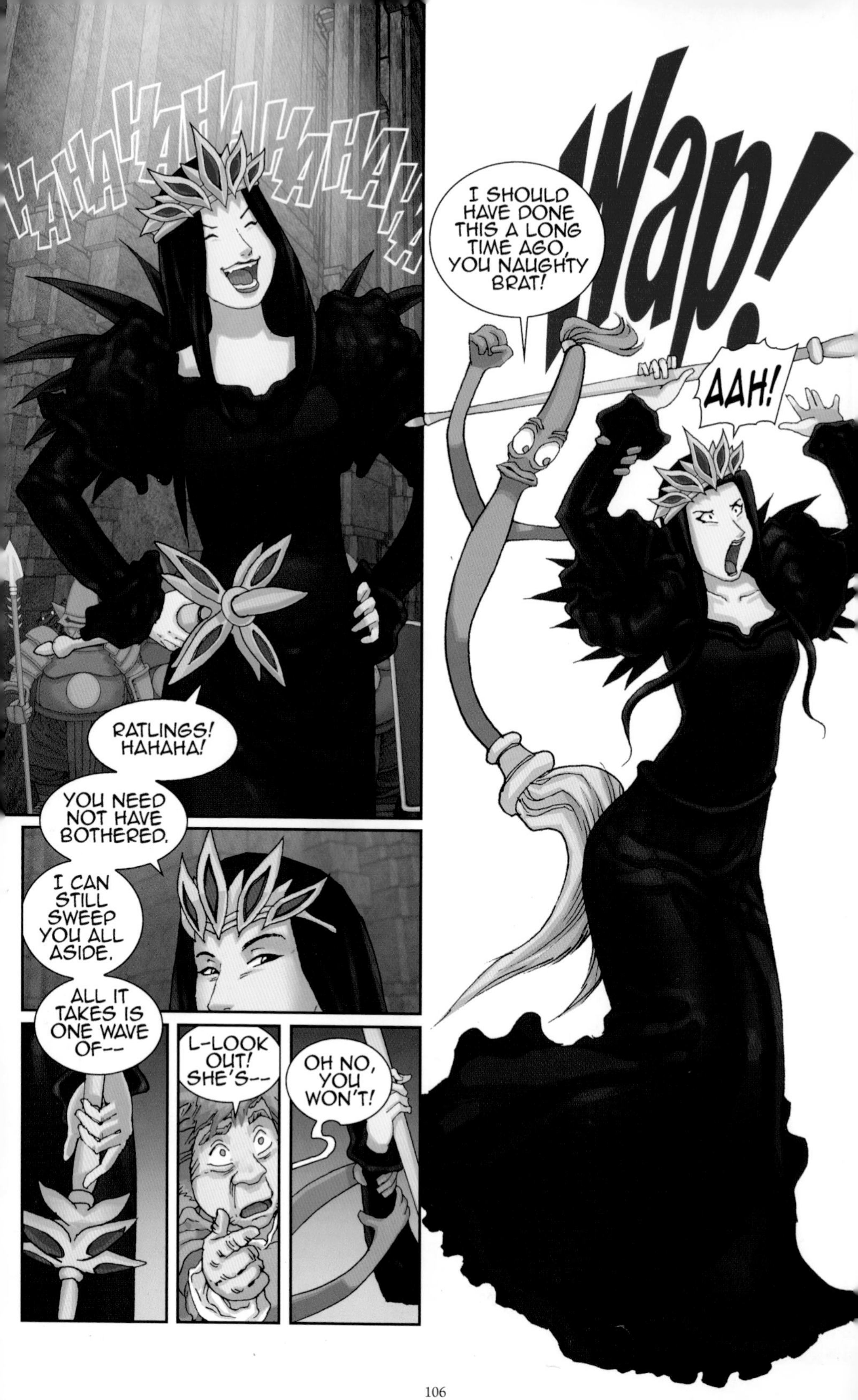
HAHAHAHAHAHAHAHAHA!
RATLINGS! HAHAHA!
YOU NEED NOT HAVE BOTHERED.
I CAN STILL SWEEP YOU ALL ASIDE.
ALL IT TAKES IS ONE WAVE OF--
L-LOOK OUT! SHE'S--
OH NO, YOU WON'T!
WAP!
I SHOULD HAVE DONE THIS A LONG TIME AGO, YOU NAUGHTY BRAT!
AAH!

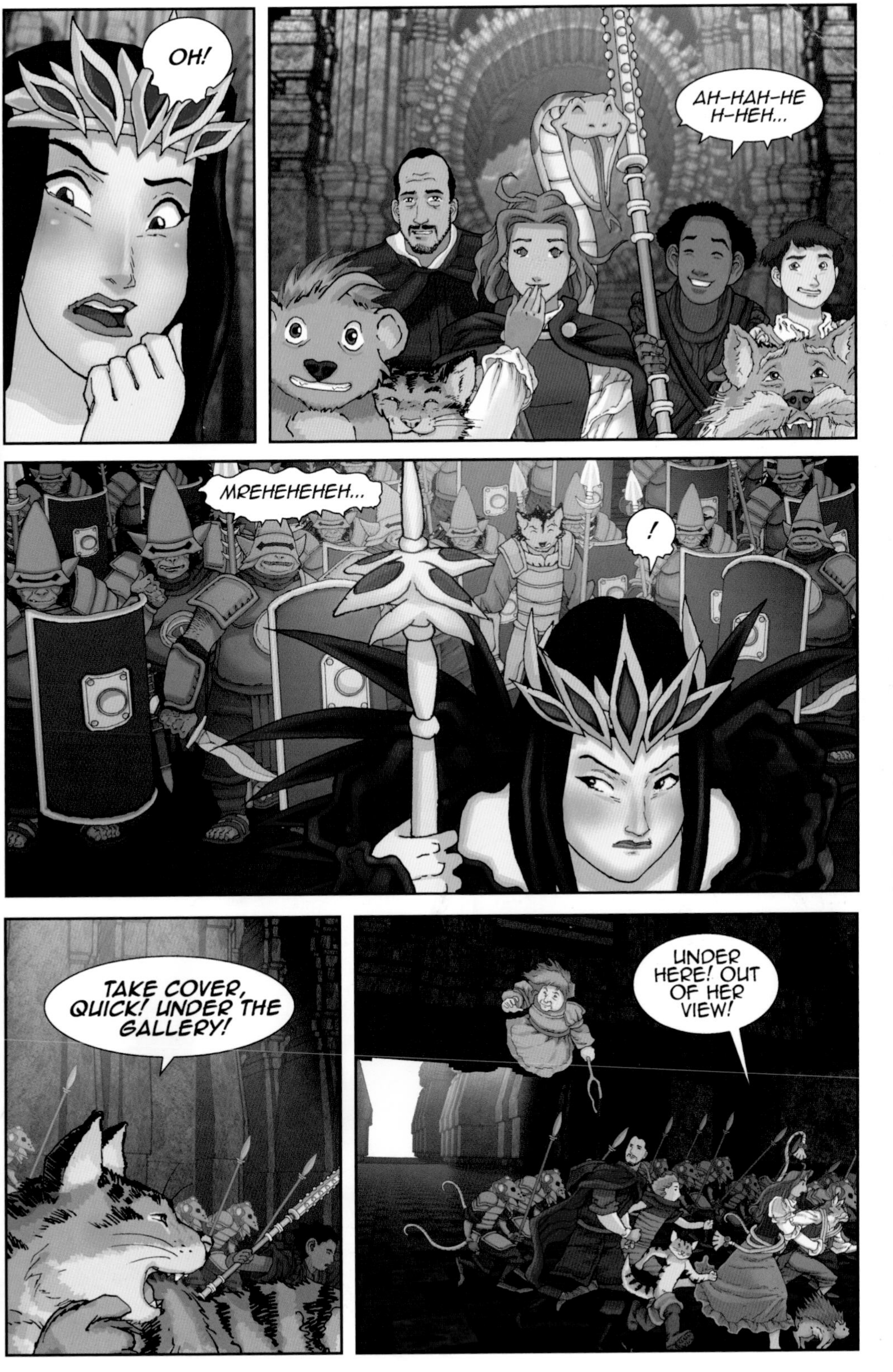
OH!
AH-HAH-HE H-HEH...
MREHEHEHEH...
!
TAKE COVER, QUICK! UNDER THE GALLERY!
UNDER HERE! OUT OF HER VIEW!

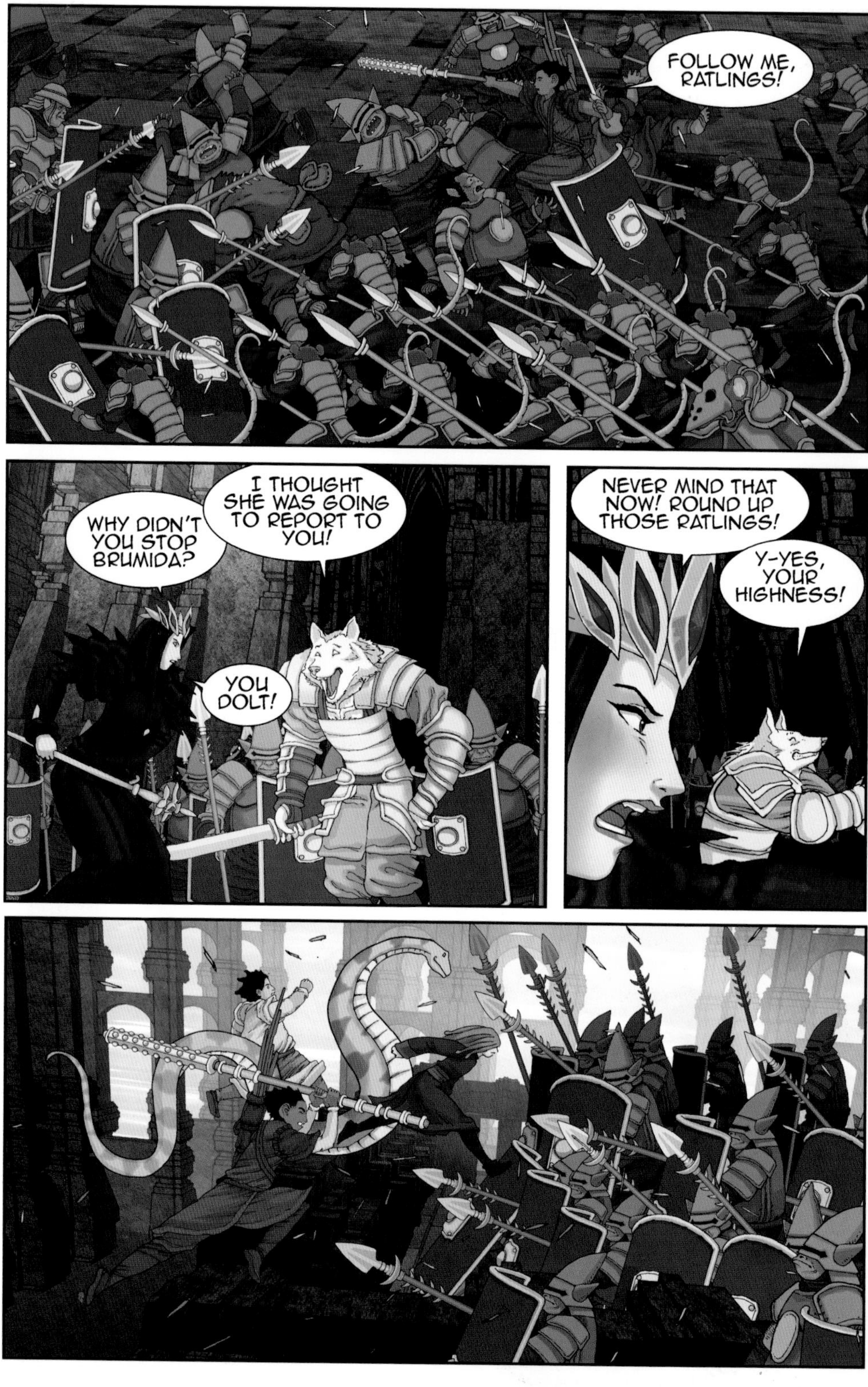
FOLLOW ME, RATLINGS!
WHY DIDN'T YOU STOP BRUMIDA?
I THOUGHT SHE WAS GOING TO REPORT TO YOU!
YOU DOLT!
NEVER MIND THAT NOW! ROUND UP THOSE RATLINGS!
Y-YES, YOUR HIGHNESS!

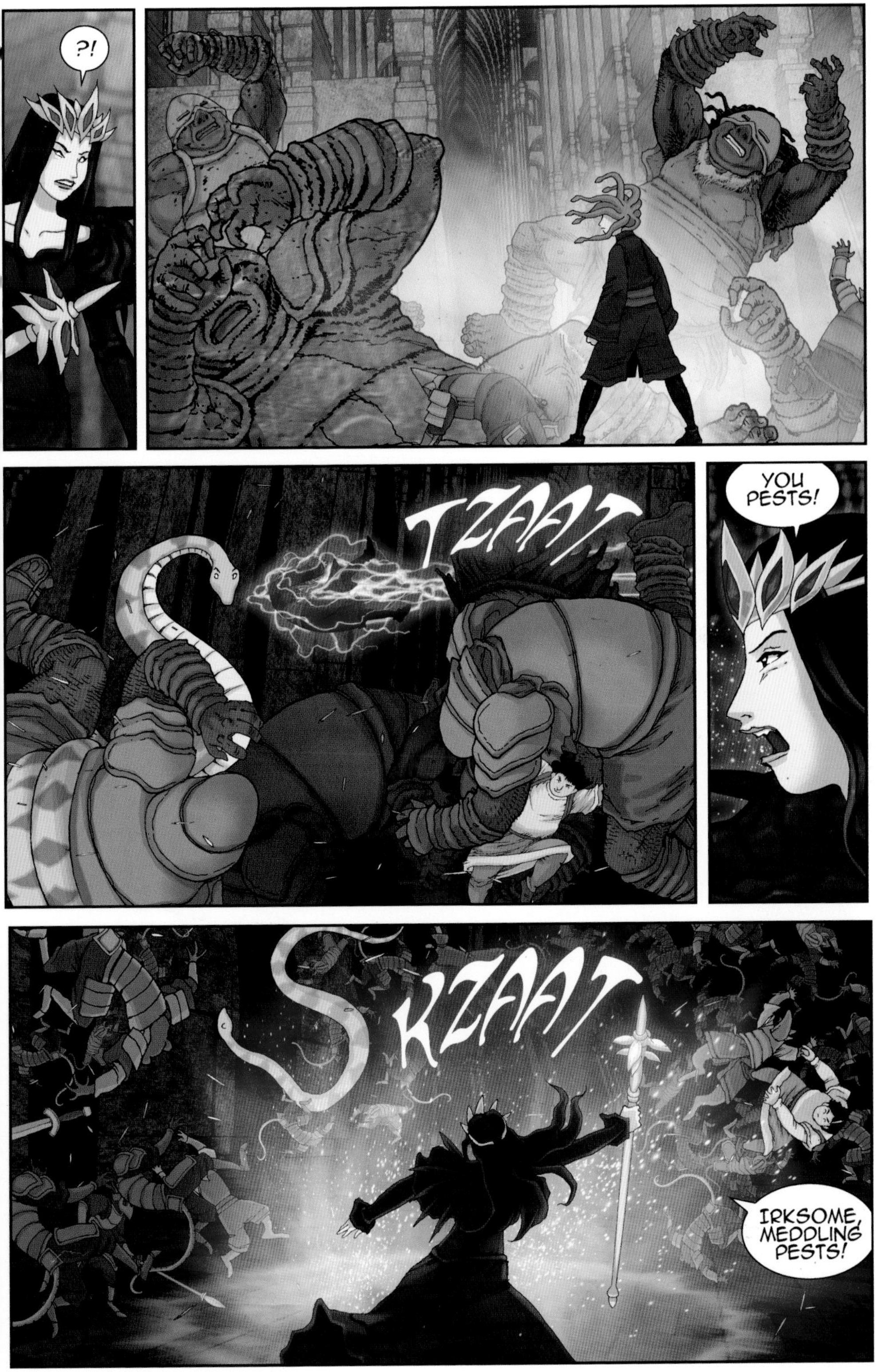
?!
TZAAT
YOU PESTS!
SKZAAT
IRKSOME, MEDDLING PESTS!

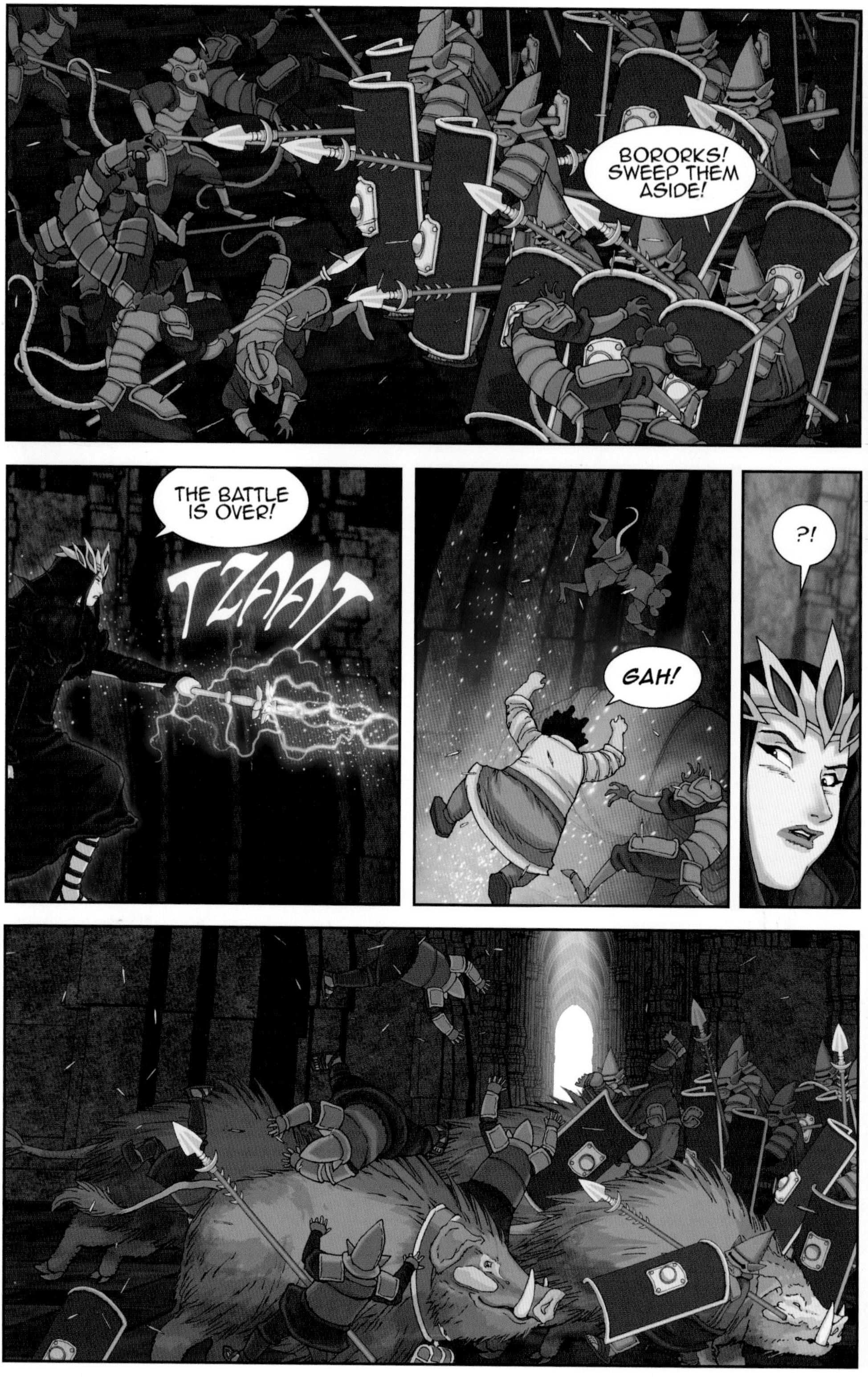
BORORKS! SWEEP THEM ASIDE!
THE BATTLE IS OVER!
TZAAT
GAH!
?!

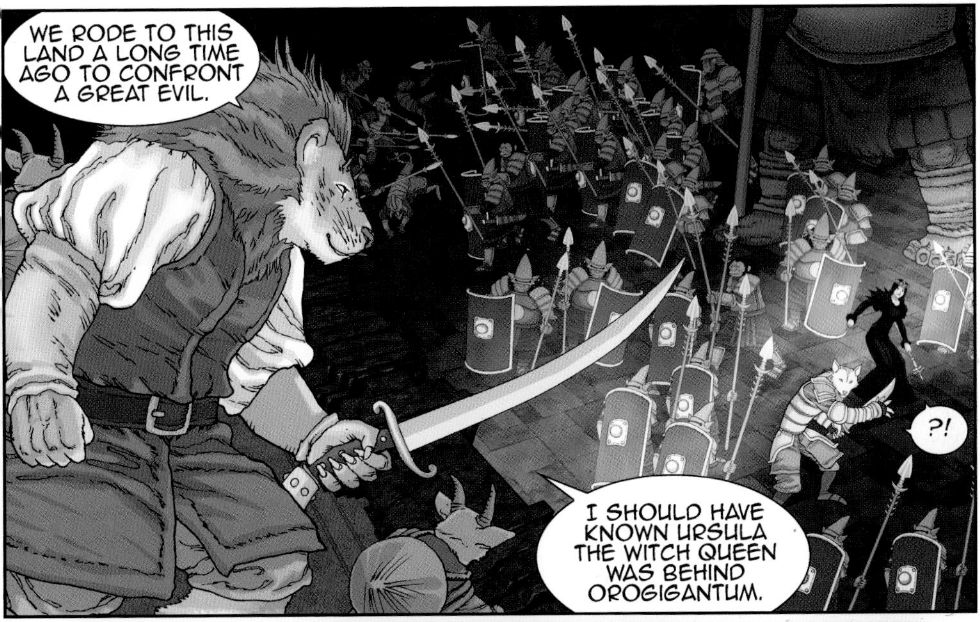
WE RODE TO THIS LAND A LONG TIME AGO TO CONFRONT A GREAT EVIL.
?!
I SHOULD HAVE KNOWN URSULA THE WITCH QUEEN WAS BEHIND OROGIGANTUM.

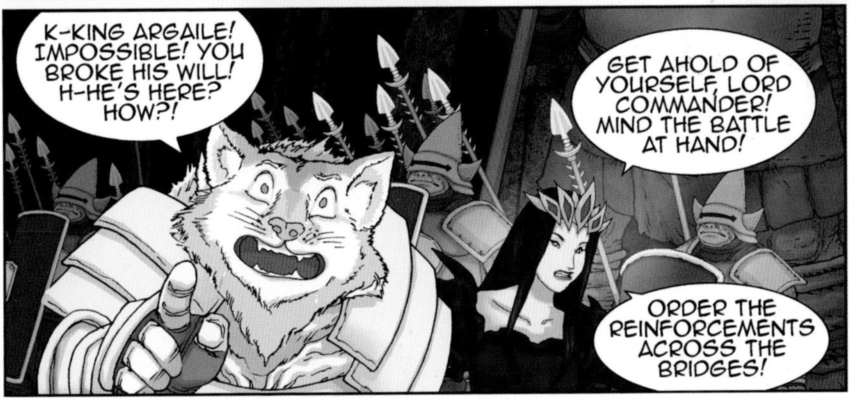
K-KING ARGAILE! IMPOSSIBLE! YOU BROKE HIS WILL! H-HE'S HERE? HOW?!
GET AHOLD OF YOURSELF, LORD COMMANDER! MIND THE BATTLE AT HAND!
ORDER THE REINFORCEMENTS ACROSS THE BRIDGES!

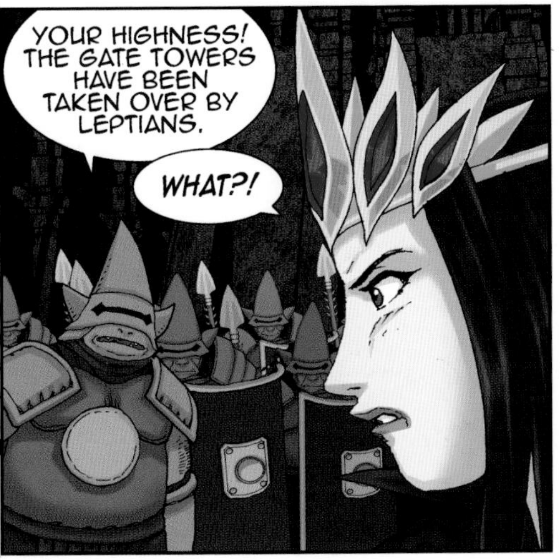
YOUR HIGHNESS! THE GATE TOWERS HAVE BEEN TAKEN OVER BY LEPTIANS.
WHAT?!

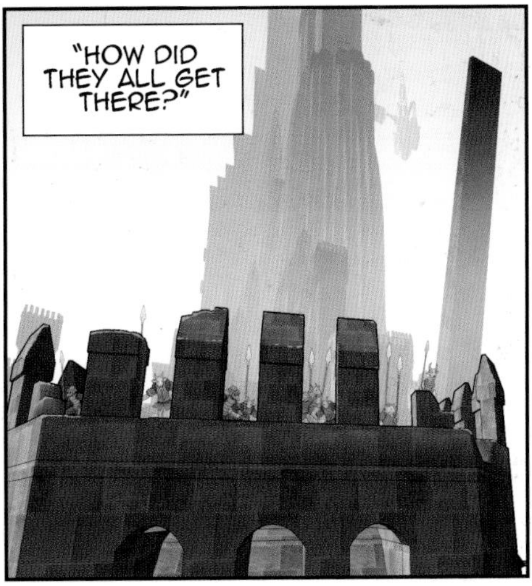
"HOW DID THEY ALL GET THERE?"

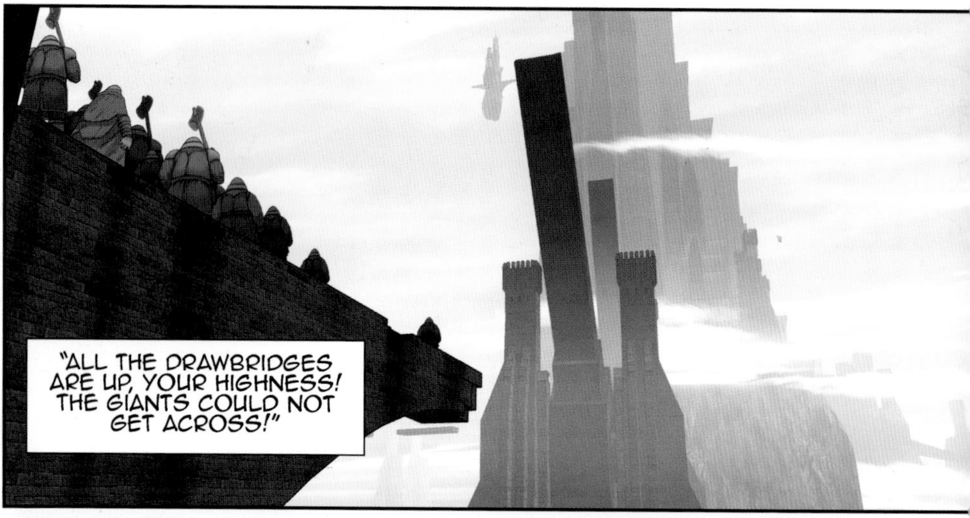
"ALL THE DRAWBRIDGES ARE UP, YOUR HIGHNESS! THE GIANTS COULD NOT GET ACROSS!"

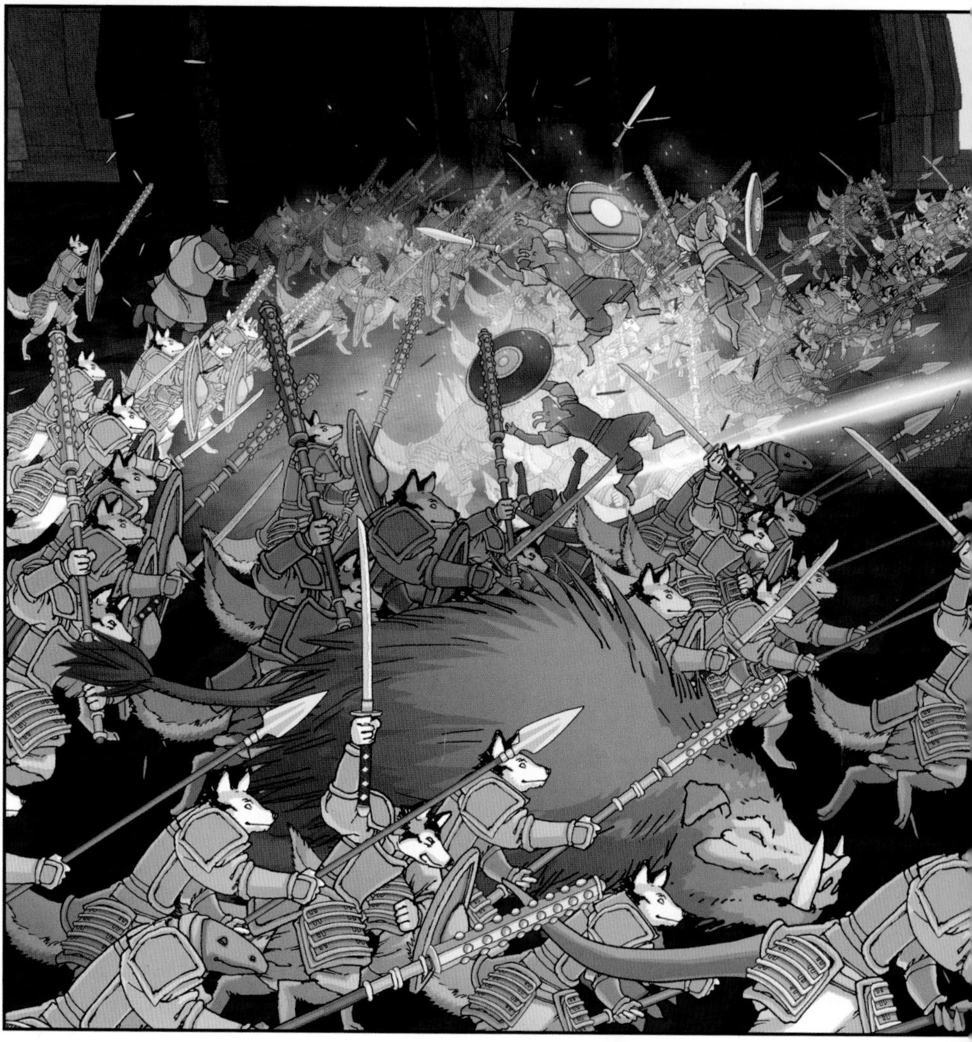

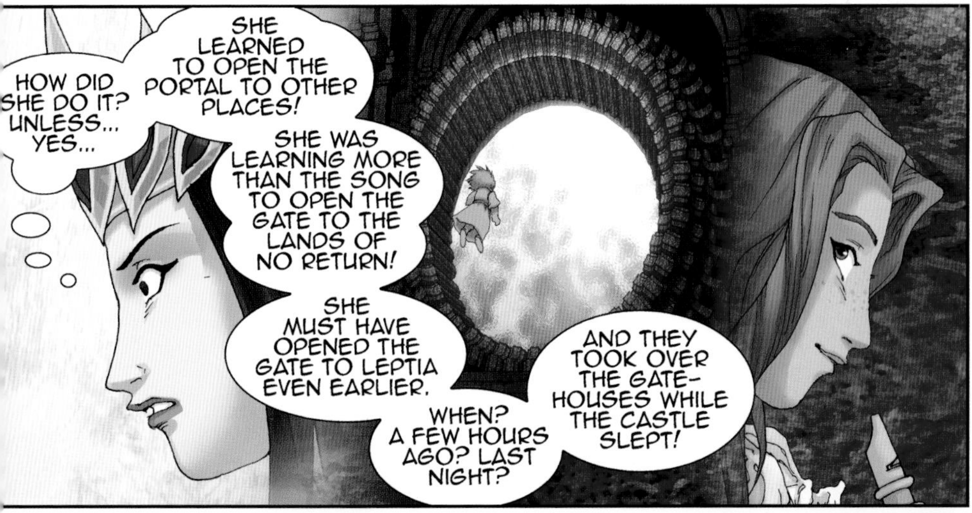
HOW DID SHE DO IT? UNLESS... YES...
SHE LEARNED TO OPEN THE PORTAL TO OTHER PLACES!
SHE WAS LEARNING MORE THAN THE SONG TO OPEN THE GATE TO THE LANDS OF NO RETURN!
SHE MUST HAVE OPENED THE GATE TO LEPTIA EVEN EARLIER.
WHEN? A FEW HOURS AGO? LAST NIGHT?
AND THEY TOOK OVER THE GATE-HOUSES WHILE THE CASTLE SLEPT!

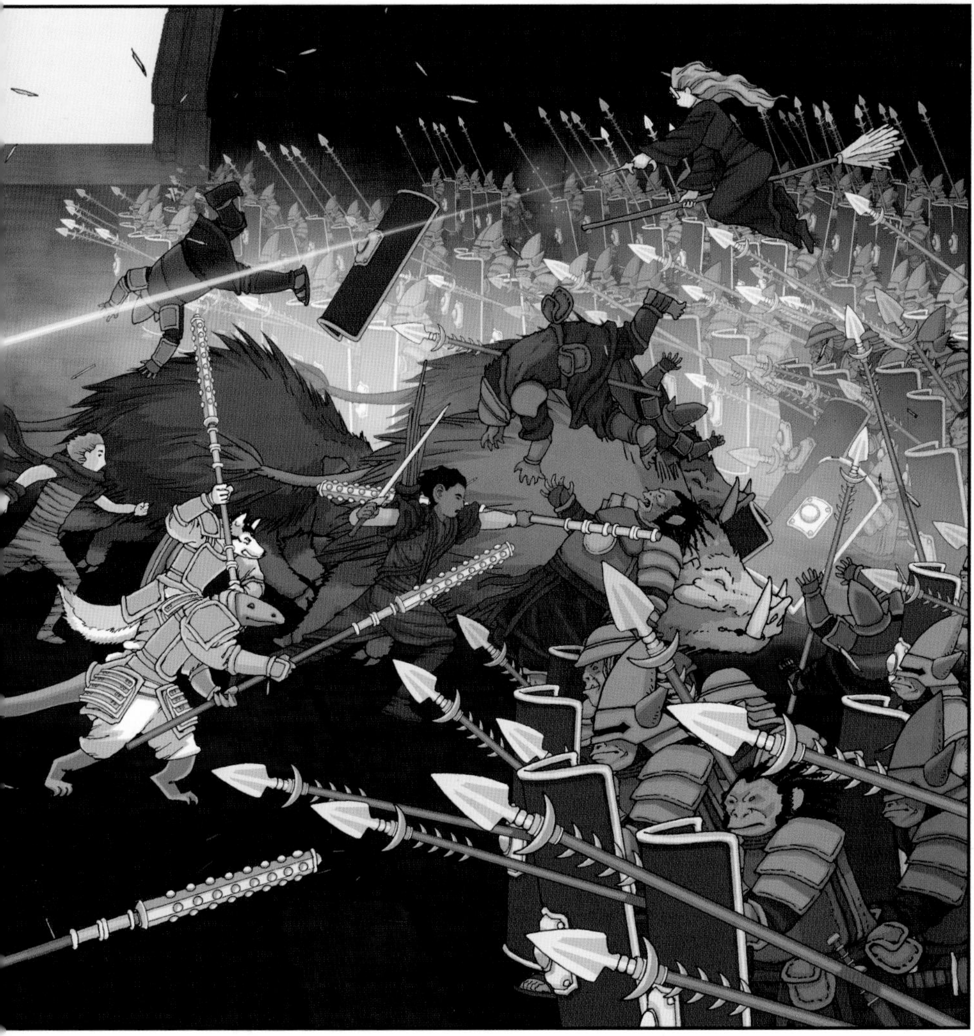

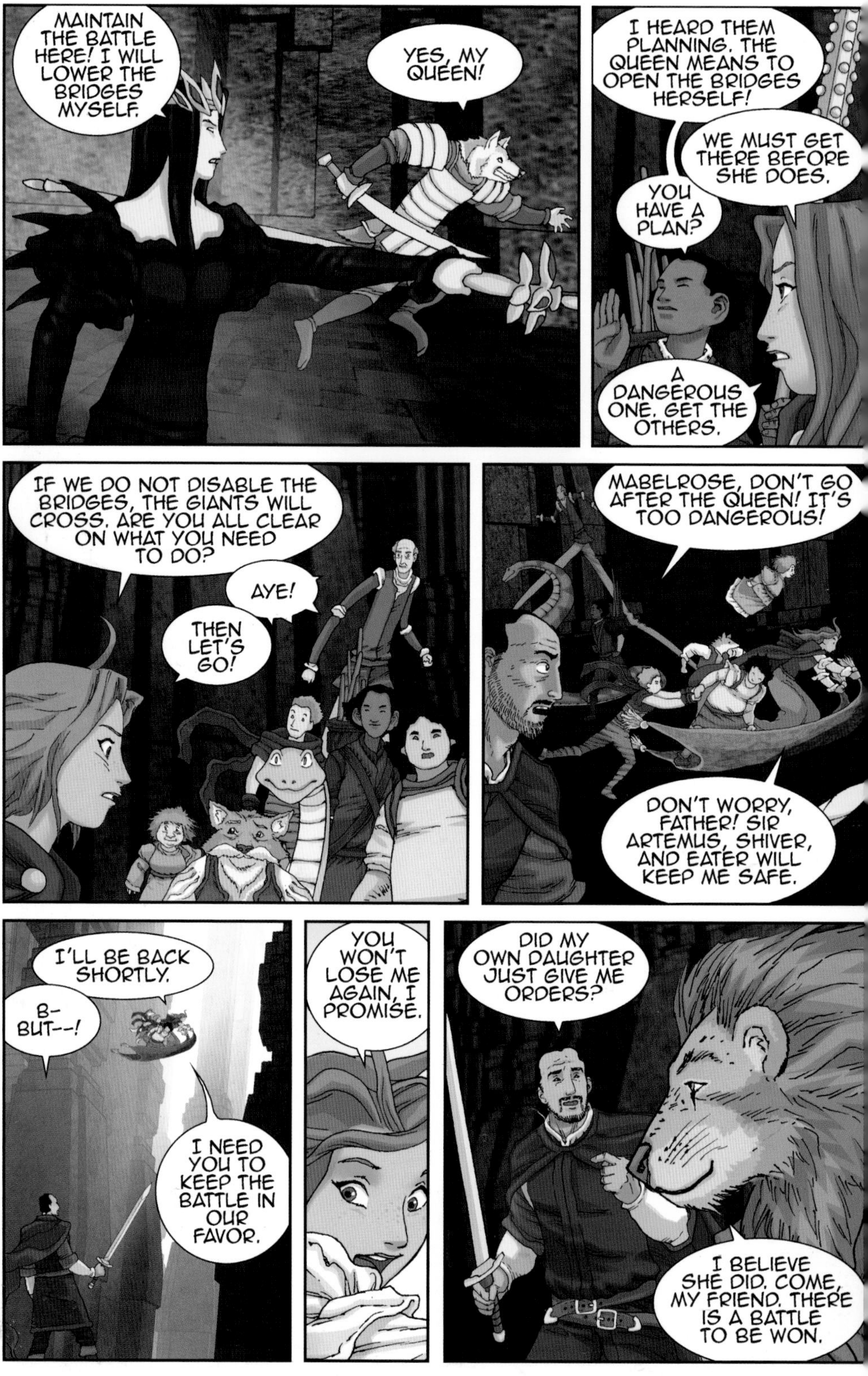
MAINTAIN THE BATTLE HERE! I WILL LOWER THE BRIDGES MYSELF.
YES, MY QUEEN!
I HEARD THEM PLANNING. THE QUEEN MEANS TO OPEN THE BRIDGES HERSELF!
WE MUST GET THERE BEFORE SHE DOES.
YOU HAVE A PLAN?
A DANGEROUS ONE. GET THE OTHERS.
IF WE DO NOT DISABLE THE BRIDGES, THE GIANTS WILL CROSS. ARE YOU ALL CLEAR ON WHAT YOU NEED TO DO?
AYE!
THEN LET'S GO!
MABELROSE, DON'T GO AFTER THE QUEEN! IT'S TOO DANGEROUS!
DON'T WORRY, FATHER! SIR ARTEMUS, SHIVER, AND EATER WILL KEEP ME SAFE.
I'LL BE BACK SHORTLY.
B-BUT--!
I NEED YOU TO KEEP THE BATTLE IN OUR FAVOR.
YOU WON'T LOSE ME AGAIN, I PROMISE.
DID MY OWN DAUGHTER JUST GIVE ME ORDERS?
I BELIEVE SHE DID. COME, MY FRIEND. THERE IS A BATTLE TO BE WON.

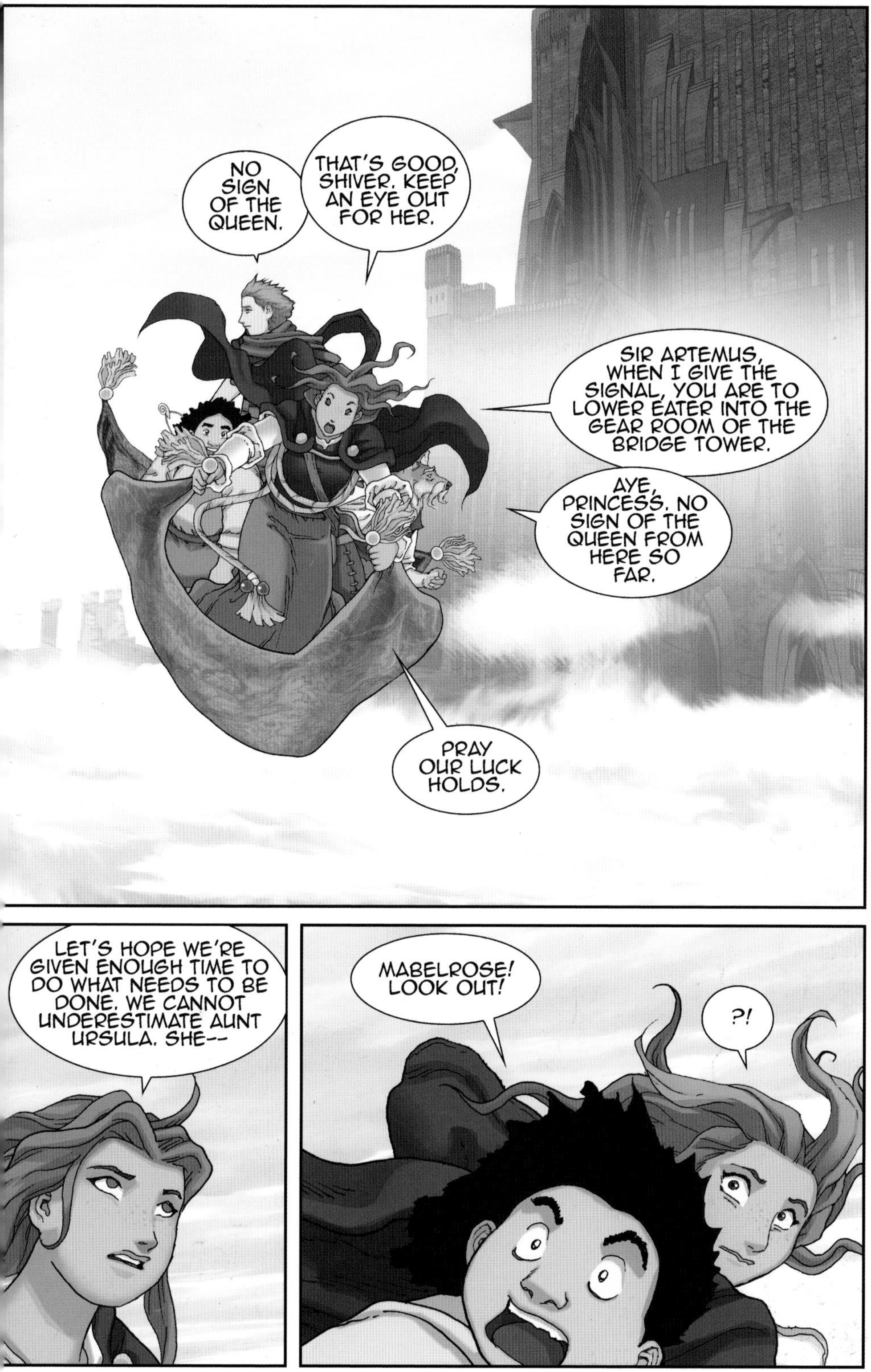
NO SIGN OF THE QUEEN.
THAT'S GOOD, SHIVER. KEEP AN EYE OUT FOR HER.
SIR ARTEMUS, WHEN I GIVE THE SIGNAL, YOU ARE TO LOWER EATER INTO THE GEAR ROOM OF THE BRIDGE TOWER.
AYE, PRINCESS. NO SIGN OF THE QUEEN FROM HERE SO FAR.
PRAY OUR LUCK HOLDS.
LET'S HOPE WE'RE GIVEN ENOUGH TIME TO DO WHAT NEEDS TO BE DONE. WE CANNOT UNDERESTIMATE AUNT URSULA. SHE--
MABELROSE! LOOK OUT!
?!

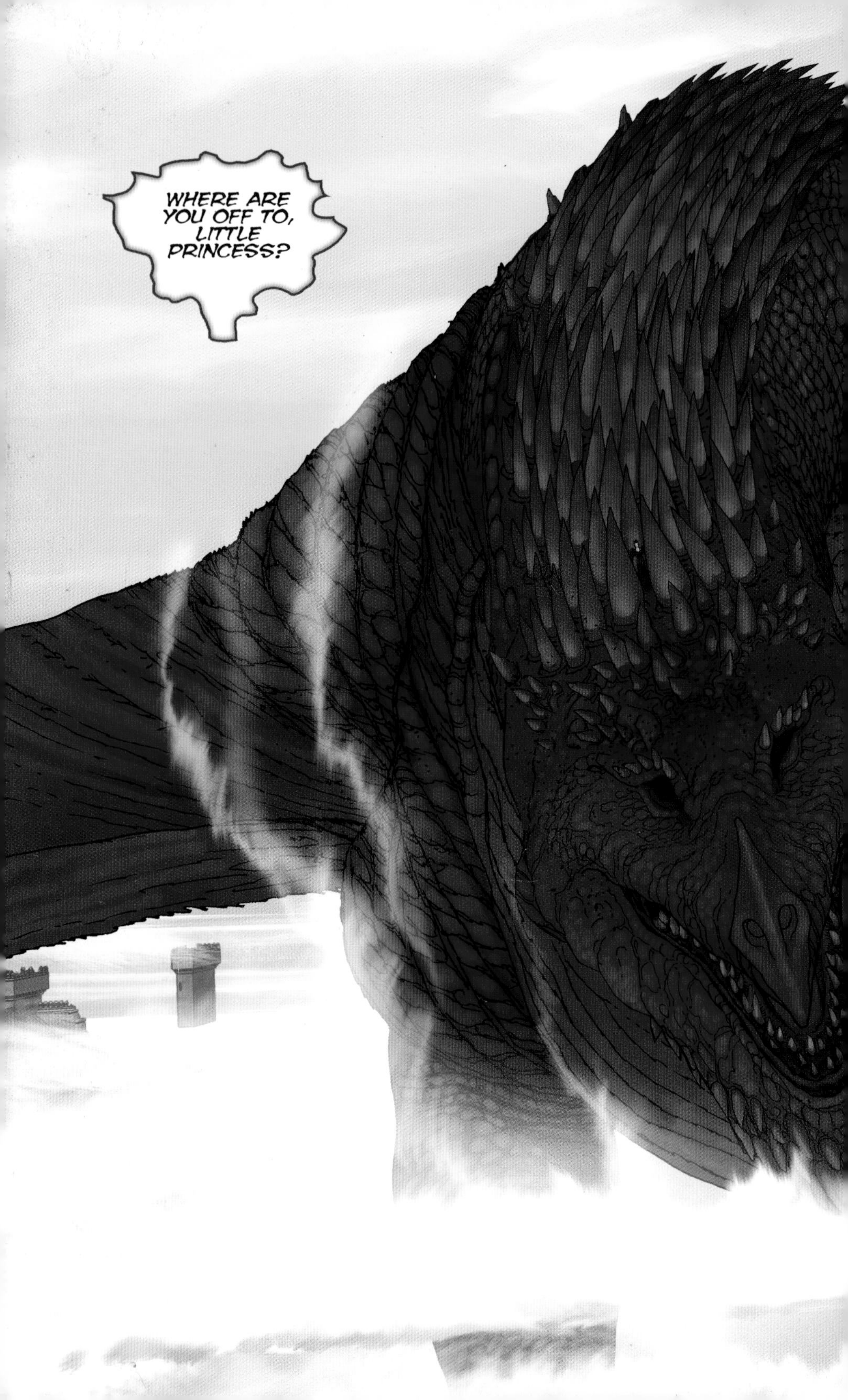
WHERE ARE YOU OFF TO, LITTLE PRINCESS?

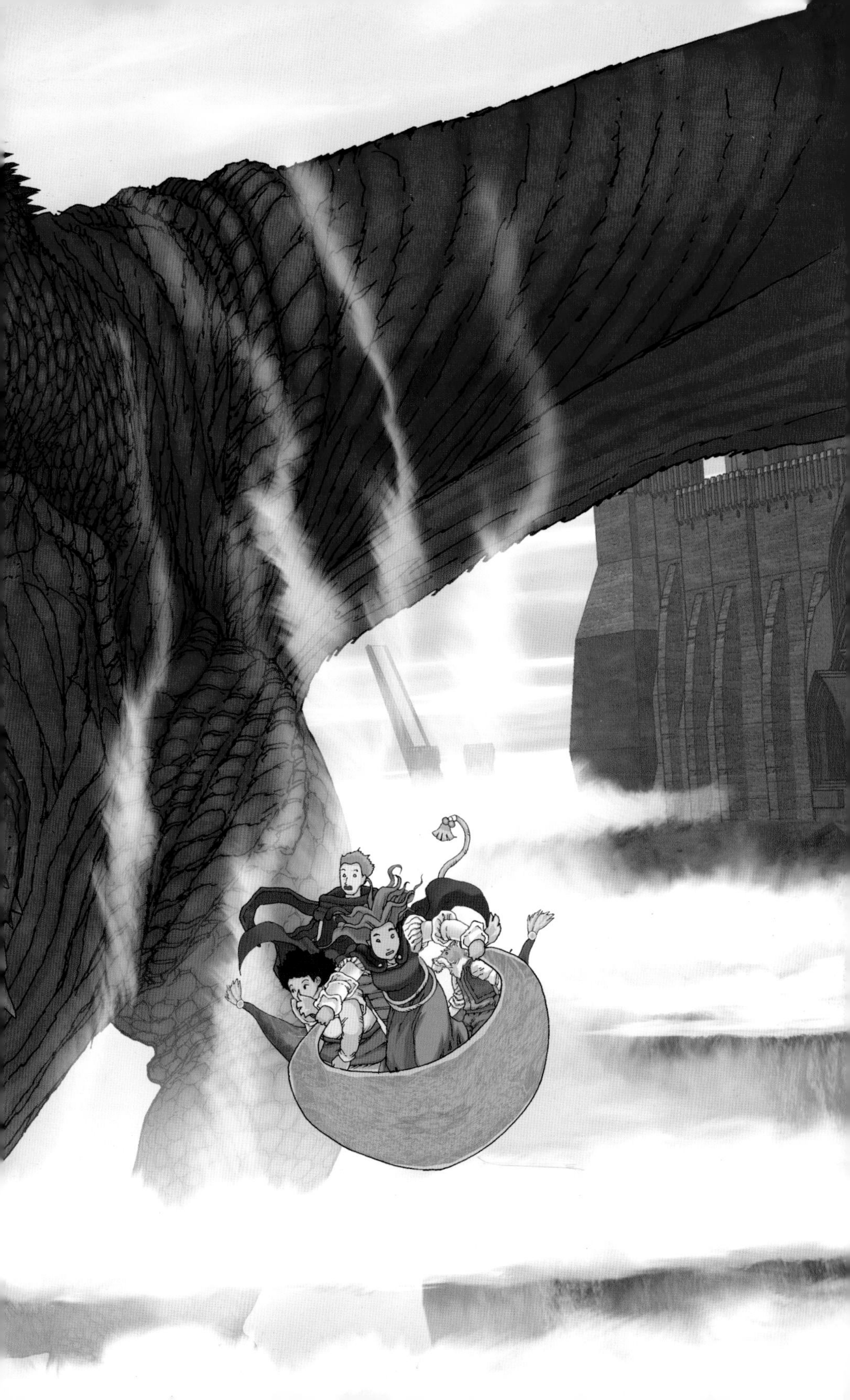

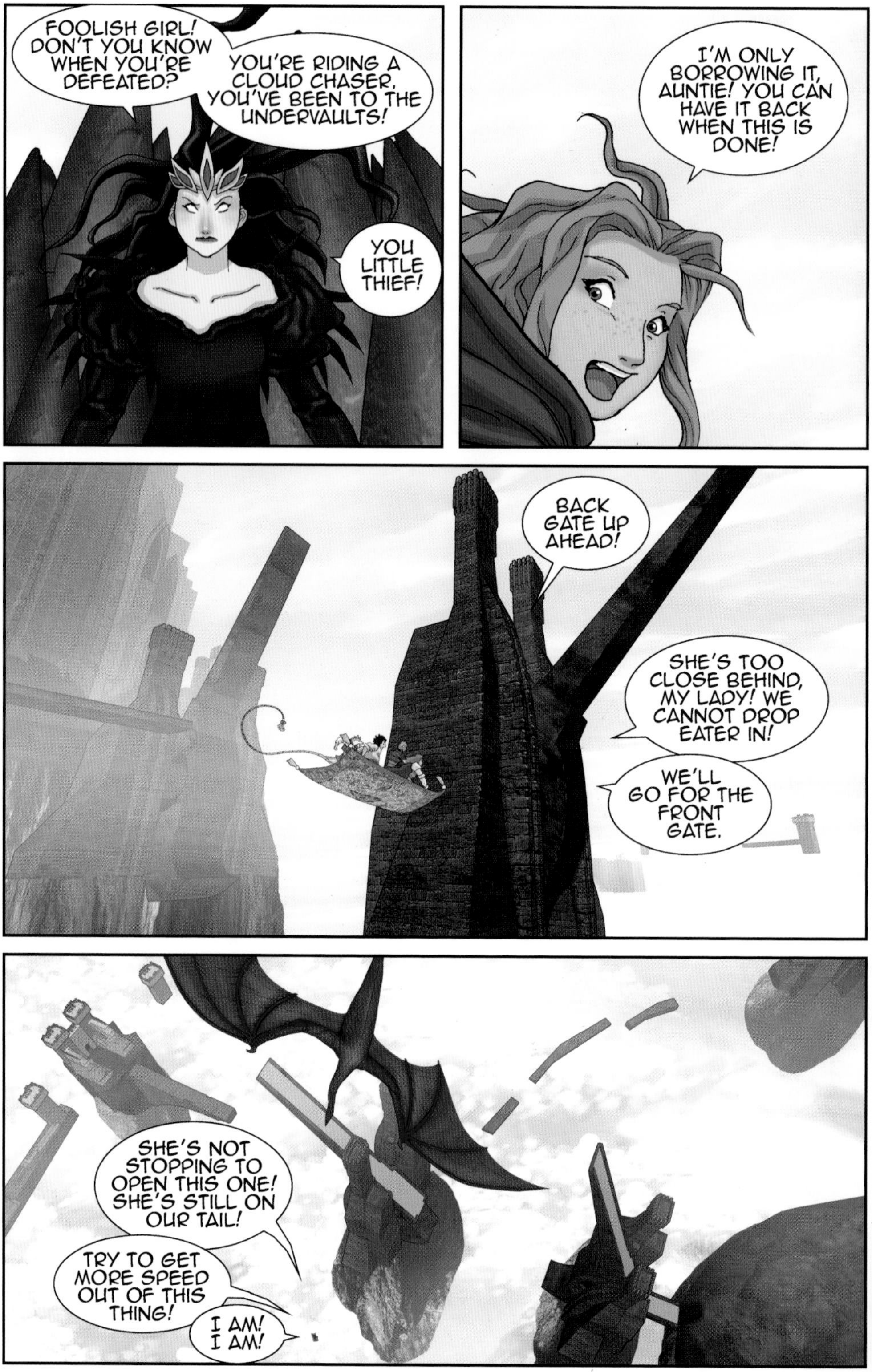
FOOLISH GIRL! DON'T YOU KNOW WHEN YOU'RE DEFEATED?
YOU'RE RIDING A CLOUD CHASER. YOU'VE BEEN TO THE UNDERVAULTS!
YOU LITTLE THIEF!
I'M ONLY BORROWING IT, AUNTIE! YOU CAN HAVE IT BACK WHEN THIS IS DONE!
BACK GATE UP AHEAD!
SHE'S TOO CLOSE BEHIND, MY LADY! WE CANNOT DROP EATER IN!
WE'LL GO FOR THE FRONT GATE.
SHE'S NOT STOPPING TO OPEN THIS ONE! SHE'S STILL ON OUR TAIL!
TRY TO GET MORE SPEED OUT OF THIS THING!
I AM! I AM!

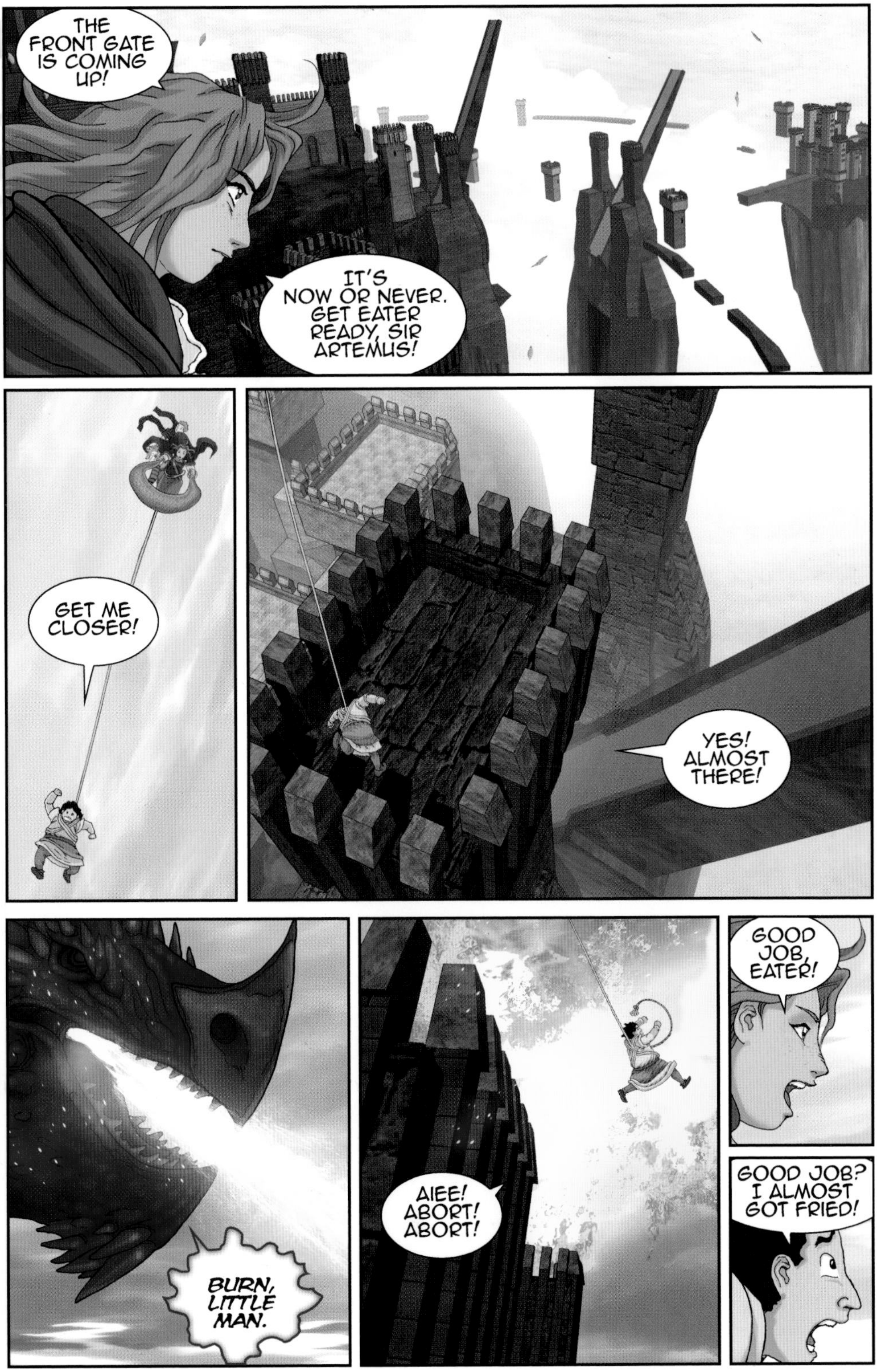
THE FRONT GATE IS COMING UP!
IT'S NOW OR NEVER. GET EATER READY, SIR ARTEMUS!
GET ME CLOSER!
YES! ALMOST THERE!
BURN, LITTLE MAN.
AIEE! ABORT! ABORT!
GOOD JOB, EATER!
GOOD JOB? I ALMOST GOT FRIED!

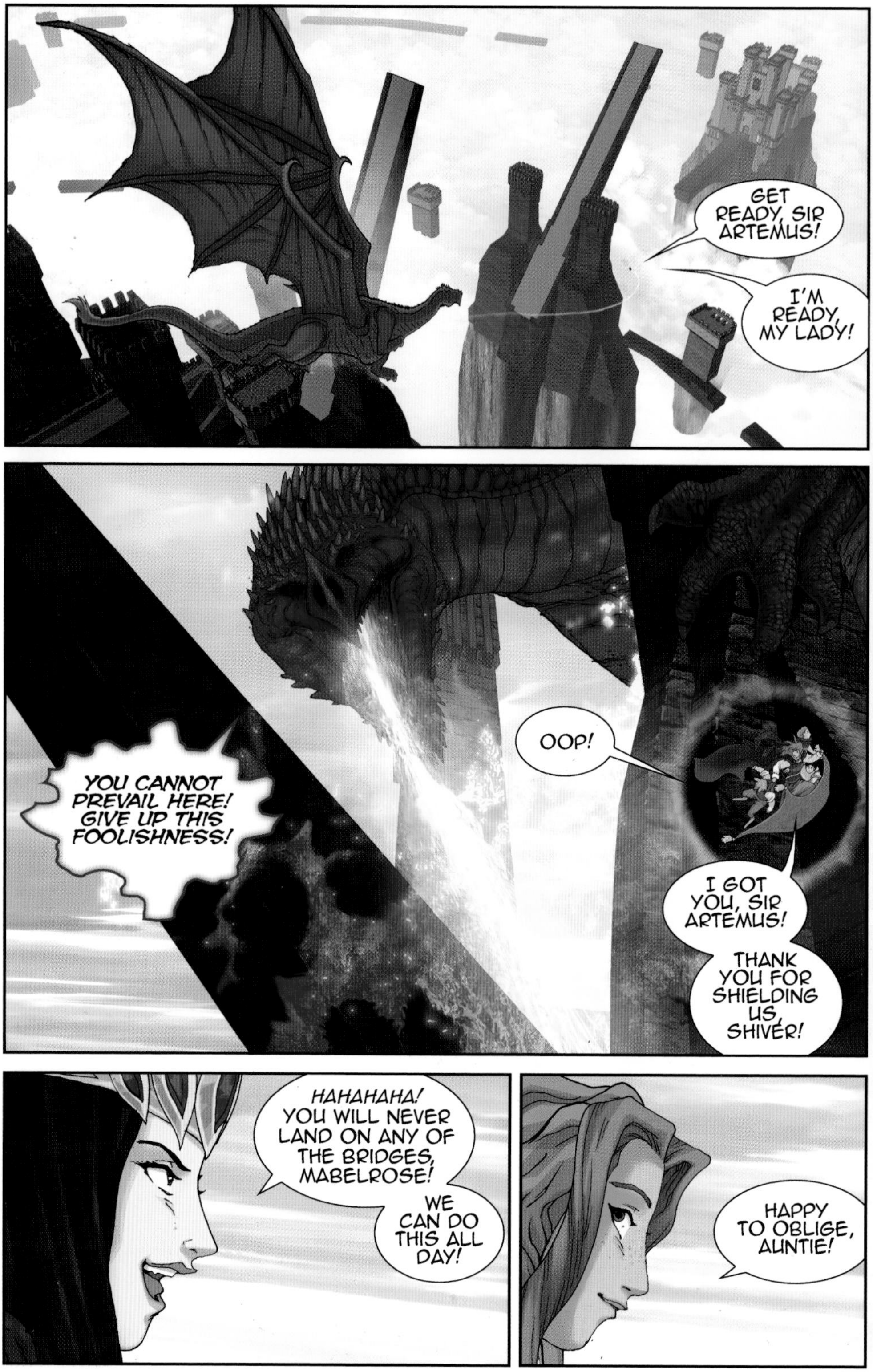
GET READY, SIR ARTEMUS!
I'M READY, MY LADY!
YOU CANNOT PREVAIL HERE! GIVE UP THIS FOOLISHNESS!
OOP!
I GOT YOU, SIR ARTEMUS!
THANK YOU FOR SHIELDING US, SHIVER!
HAHAHAHA! YOU WILL NEVER LAND ON ANY OF THE BRIDGES, MABELROSE!
WE CAN DO THIS ALL DAY!
HAPPY TO OBLIGE, AUNTIE!

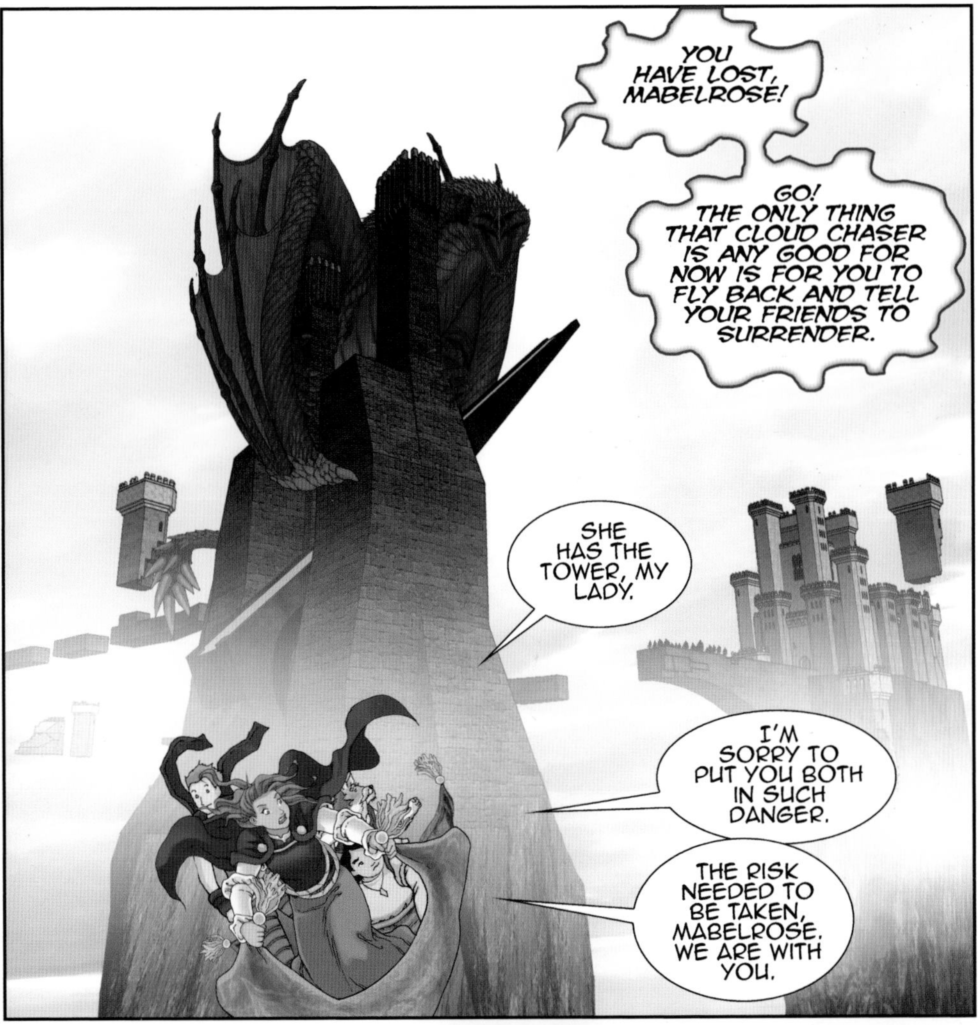
YOU HAVE LOST, MABELROSE!
GO! THE ONLY THING THAT CLOUD CHASER IS ANY GOOD FOR NOW IS FOR YOU TO FLY BACK AND TELL YOUR FRIENDS TO SURRENDER.
SHE HAS THE TOWER, MY LADY.
I'M SORRY TO PUT YOU BOTH IN SUCH DANGER.
THE RISK NEEDED TO BE TAKEN, MABELROSE. WE ARE WITH YOU.

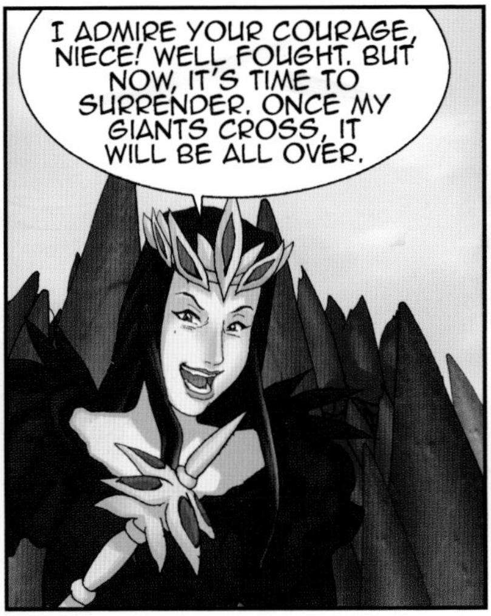
I ADMIRE YOUR COURAGE, NIECE! WELL FOUGHT. BUT NOW, IT'S TIME TO SURRENDER. ONCE MY GIANTS CROSS, IT WILL BE ALL OVER.

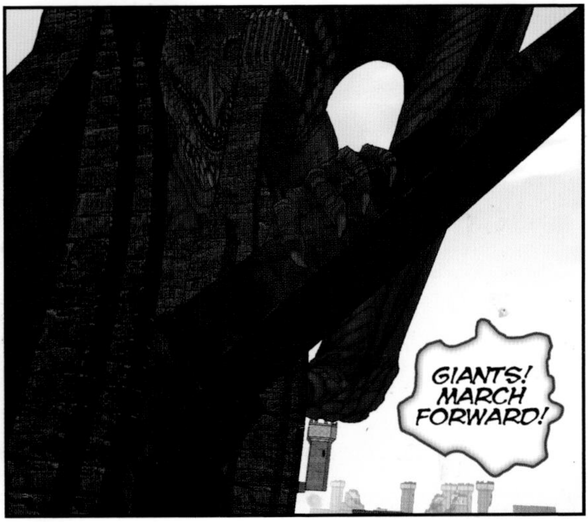
GIANTS! MARCH FORWARD!

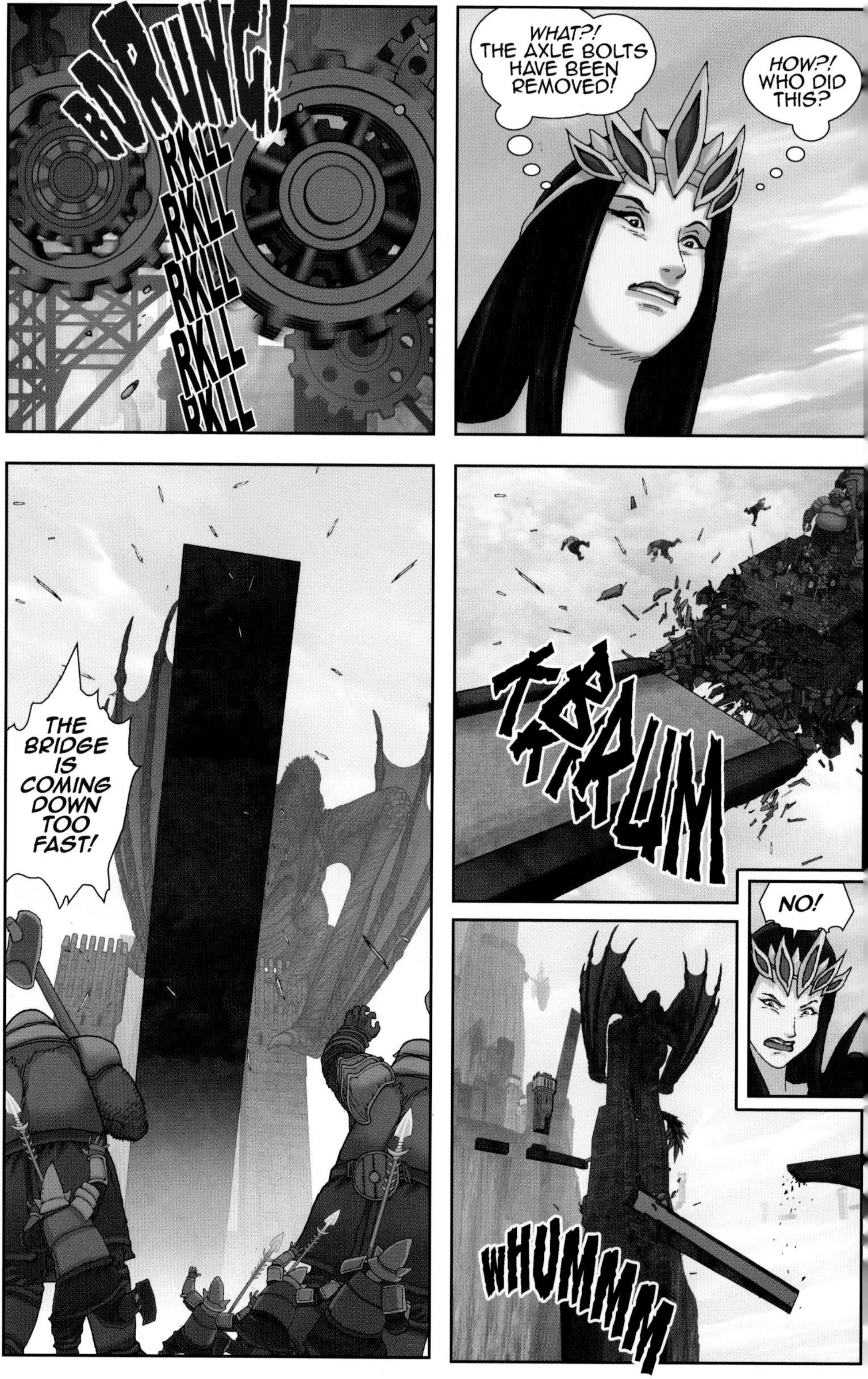
BDRUNG!
RKLL RKLL RKLL RKLL RKLL RKLL
WHAT?! THE AXLE BOLTS HAVE BEEN REMOVED!
HOW?! WHO DID THIS?
THE BRIDGE IS COMING DOWN TOO FAST!
TKRRUM
NO!
WHUMMMM

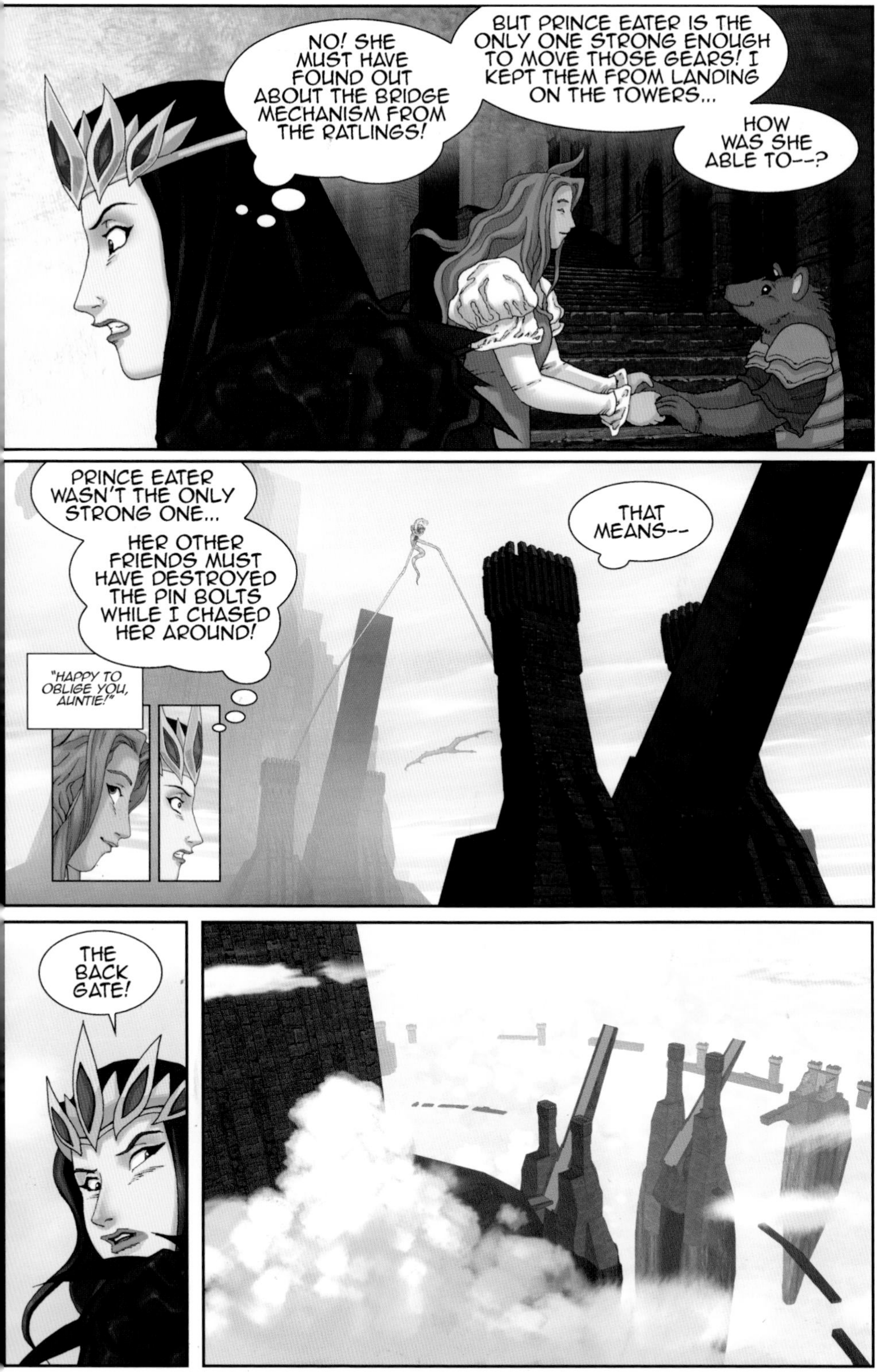
NO! SHE MUST HAVE FOUND OUT ABOUT THE BRIDGE MECHANISM FROM THE RATLINGS!
BUT PRINCE EATER IS THE ONLY ONE STRONG ENOUGH TO MOVE THOSE GEARS! I KEPT THEM FROM LANDING ON THE TOWERS...
HOW WAS SHE ABLE TO--?
PRINCE EATER WASN'T THE ONLY STRONG ONE...
HER OTHER FRIENDS MUST HAVE DESTROYED THE PIN BOLTS WHILE I CHASED HER AROUND!
"HAPPY TO OBLIGE YOU, AUNTIE!"
THAT MEANS--
THE BACK GATE!

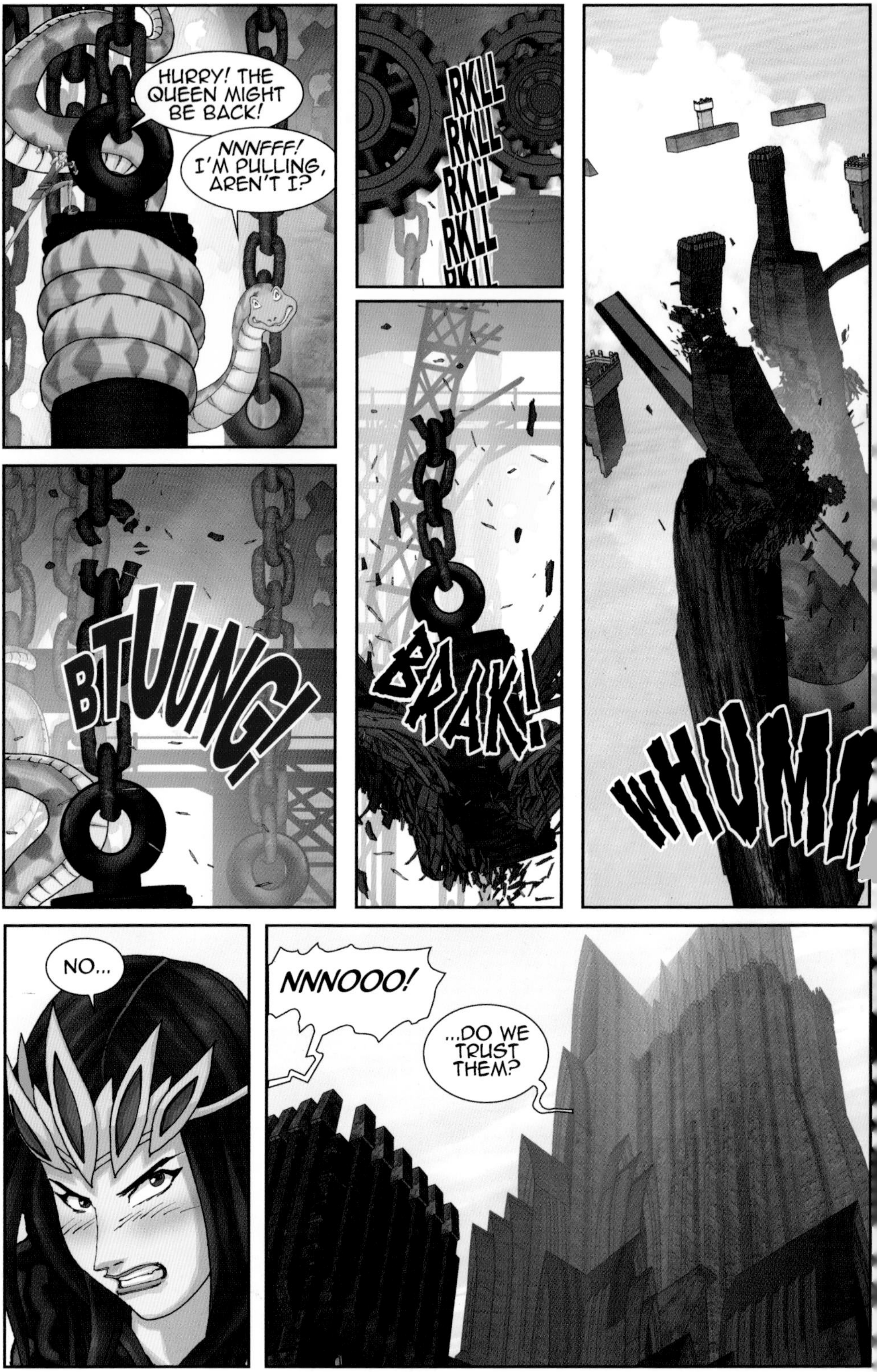
HURRY! THE QUEEN MIGHT BE BACK!
NNNFFF! I'M PULLING, AREN'T I?
RKLL RKLL RKLL RKLL
BTUUNG!
BRAK!
WHUMM
NO...
NNNOOO!
...DO WE TRUST THEM?

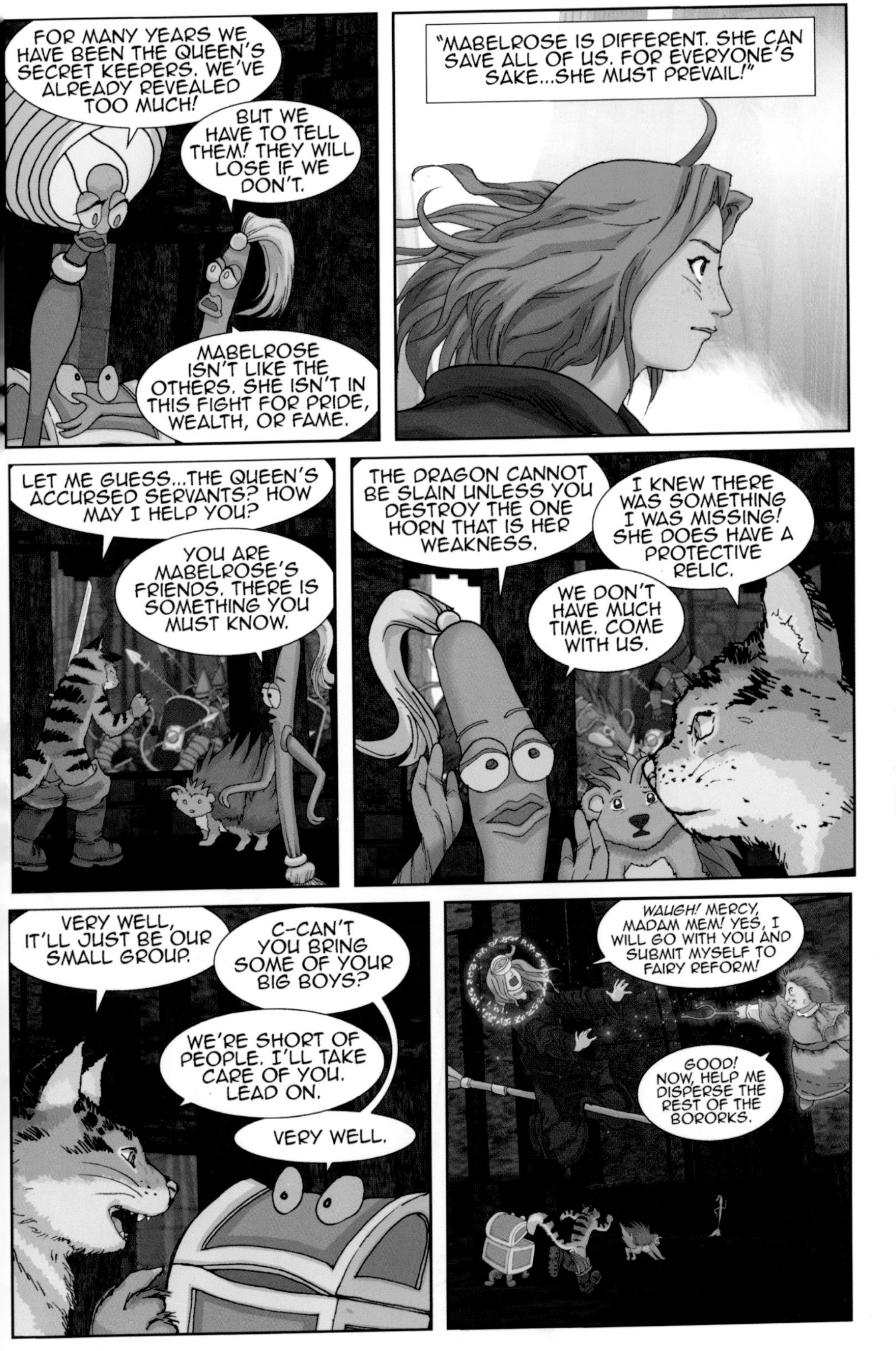
FOR MANY YEARS WE HAVE BEEN THE QUEEN'S SECRET KEEPERS. WE'VE ALREADY REVEALED TOO MUCH!
BUT WE HAVE TO TELL THEM! THEY WILL LOSE IF WE DON'T.
MABELROSE ISN'T LIKE THE OTHERS. SHE ISN'T IN THIS FIGHT FOR PRIDE, WEALTH, OR FAME.
"MABELROSE IS DIFFERENT. SHE CAN SAVE ALL OF US. FOR EVERYONE'S SAKE...SHE MUST PREVAIL!"
LET ME GUESS...THE QUEEN'S ACCURSED SERVANTS? HOW MAY I HELP YOU?
YOU ARE MABELROSE'S FRIENDS. THERE IS SOMETHING YOU MUST KNOW.
THE DRAGON CANNOT BE SLAIN UNLESS YOU DESTROY THE ONE HORN THAT IS HER WEAKNESS.
I KNEW THERE WAS SOMETHING I WAS MISSING! SHE DOES HAVE A PROTECTIVE RELIC.
WE DON'T HAVE MUCH TIME. COME WITH US.
VERY WELL, IT'LL JUST BE OUR SMALL GROUP.
C-CAN'T YOU BRING SOME OF YOUR BIG BOYS?
WE'RE SHORT OF PEOPLE. I'LL TAKE CARE OF YOU. LEAD ON.
VERY WELL.
WAUGH! MERCY, MADAM MEM! YES, I WILL GO WITH YOU AND SUBMIT MYSELF TO FAIRY REFORM!
GOOD! NOW, HELP ME DISPERSE THE REST OF THE BORORKS.

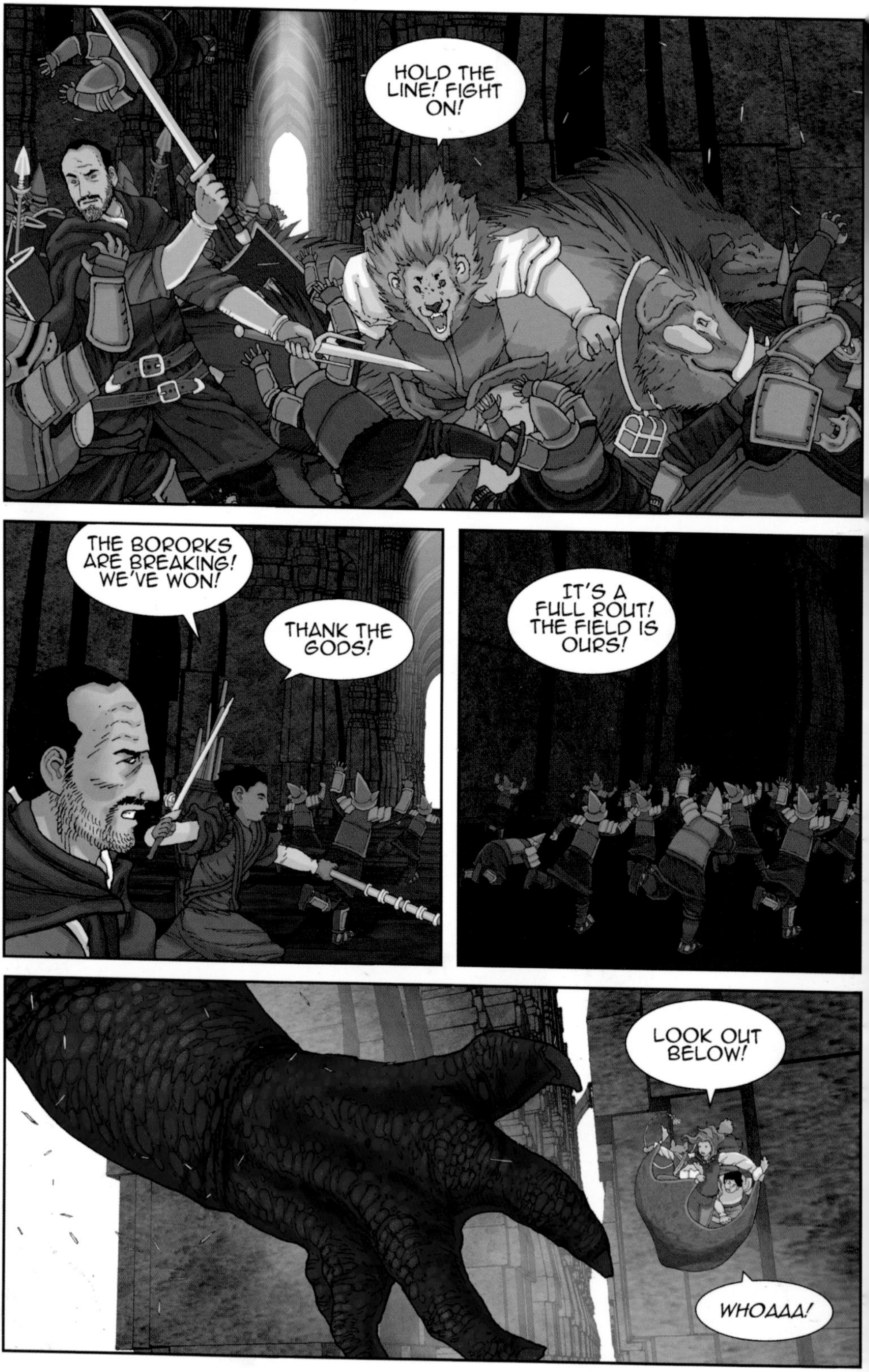
HOLD THE LINE! FIGHT ON!
THE BORORKS ARE BREAKING! WE'VE WON!
THANK THE GODS!
IT'S A FULL ROUT! THE FIELD IS OURS!
LOOK OUT BELOW!
WHOAAA!

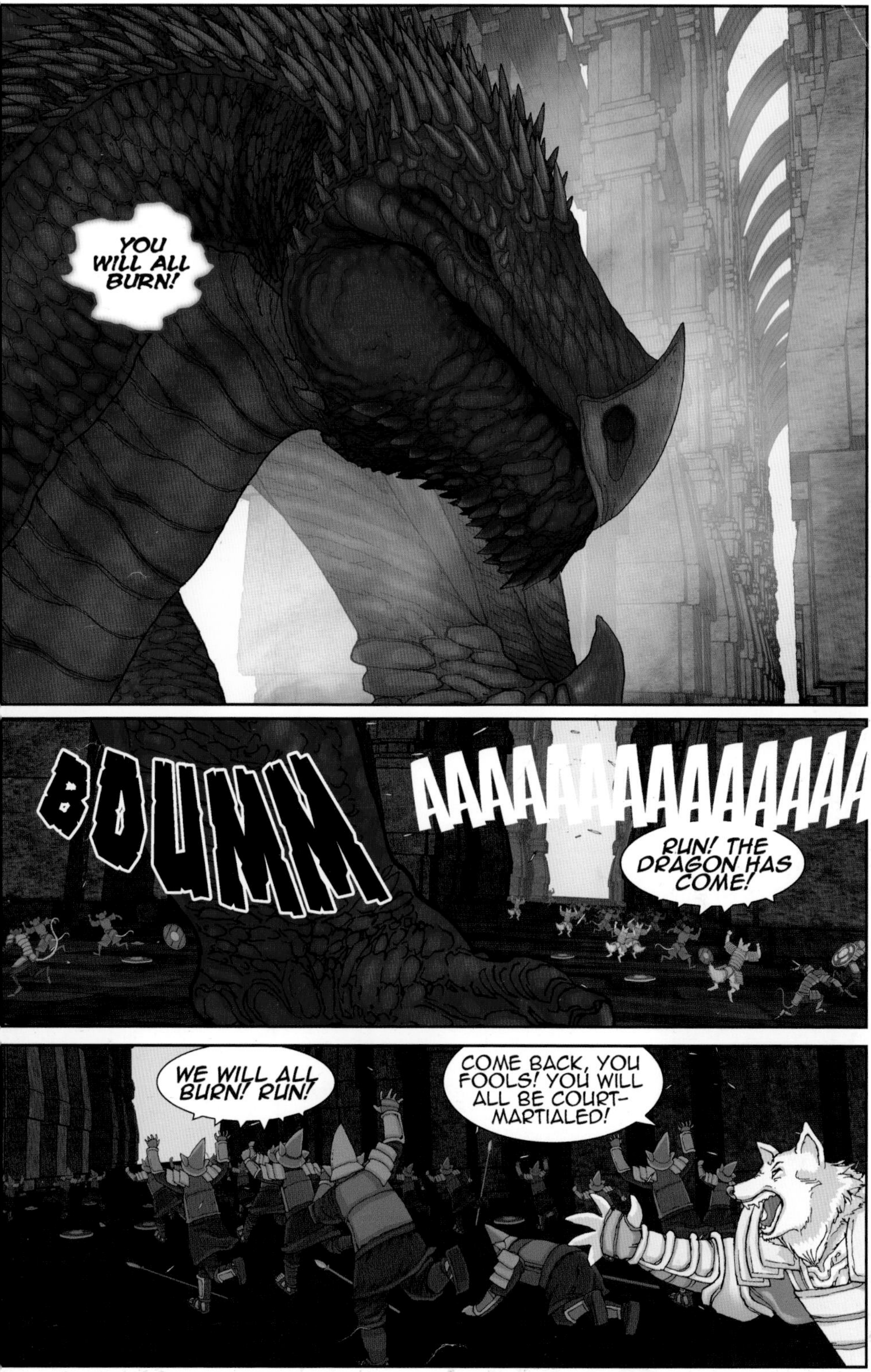
YOU WILL ALL BURN!
BOUMM
AAAAAAAAAAAAA
RUN! THE DRAGON HAS COME!
WE WILL ALL BURN! RUN!
COME BACK, YOU FOOLS! YOU WILL ALL BE COURT-MARTIALED!

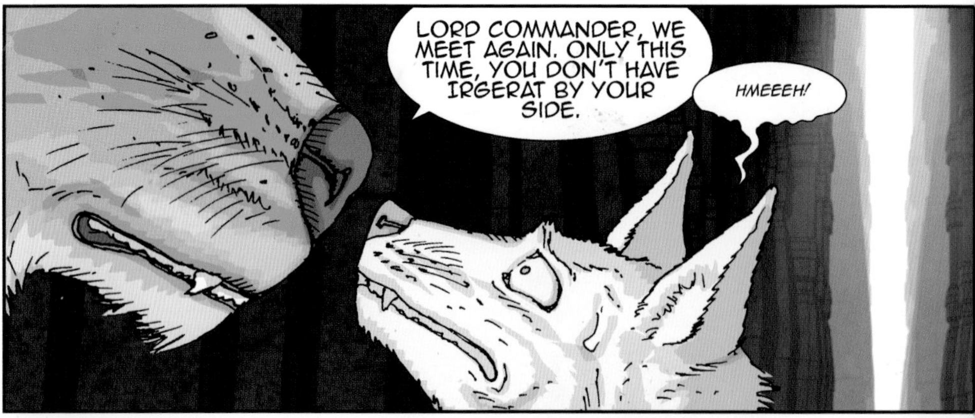
LORD COMMANDER, WE MEET AGAIN. ONLY THIS TIME, YOU DON'T HAVE IRGERAT BY YOUR SIDE.
HMEEEH!

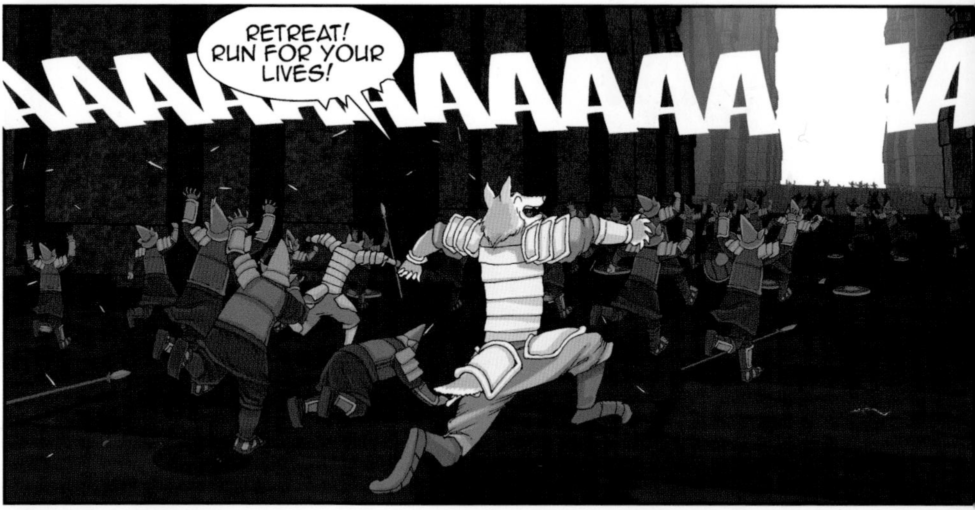
RETREAT! RUN FOR YOUR LIVES!
AAAAAAAAAAAAAA

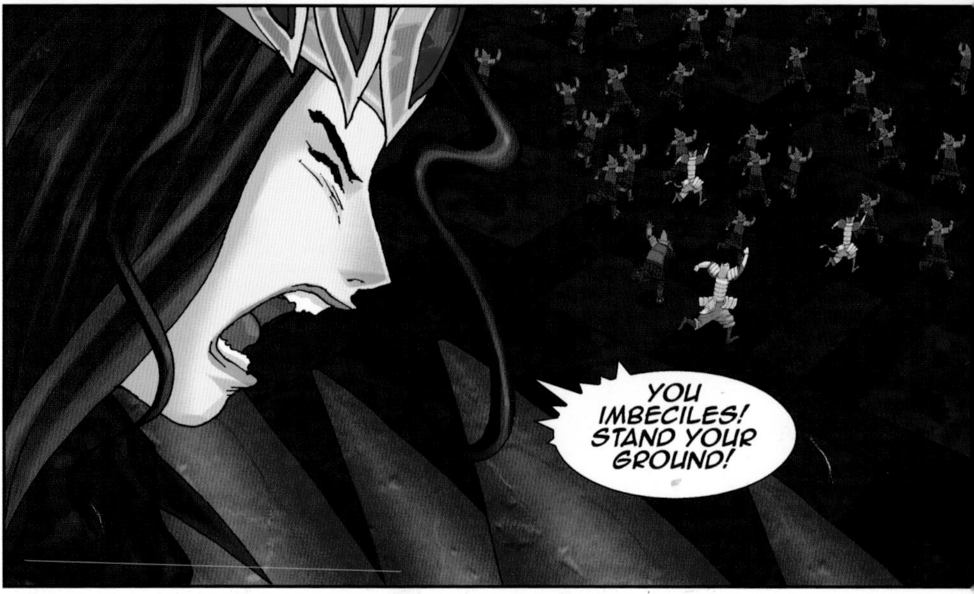
YOU IMBECILES! STAND YOUR GROUND!

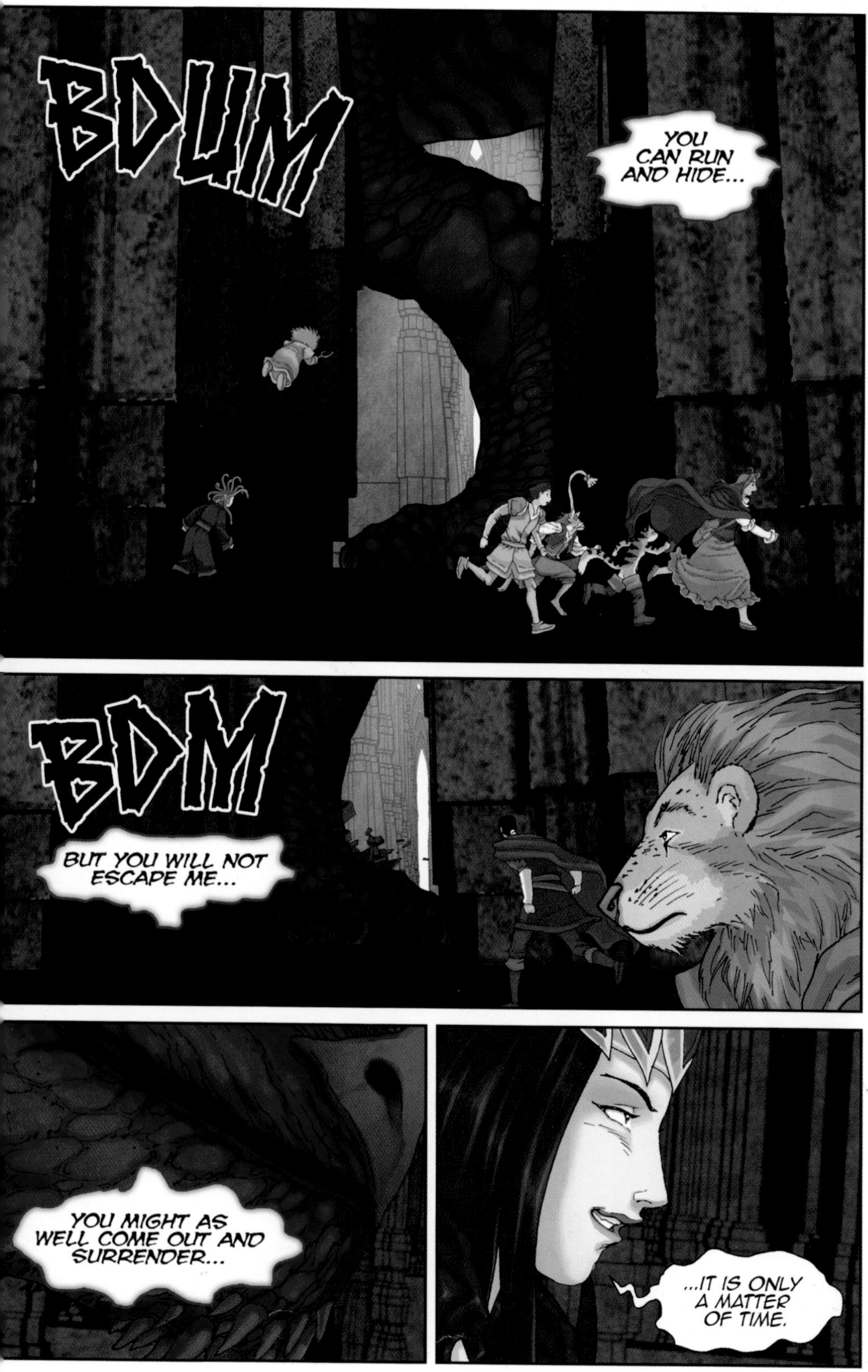
BDUM
YOU CAN RUN AND HIDE...
BDM
BUT YOU WILL NOT ESCAPE ME...
YOU MIGHT AS WELL COME OUT AND SURRENDER...
...IT IS ONLY A MATTER OF TIME.

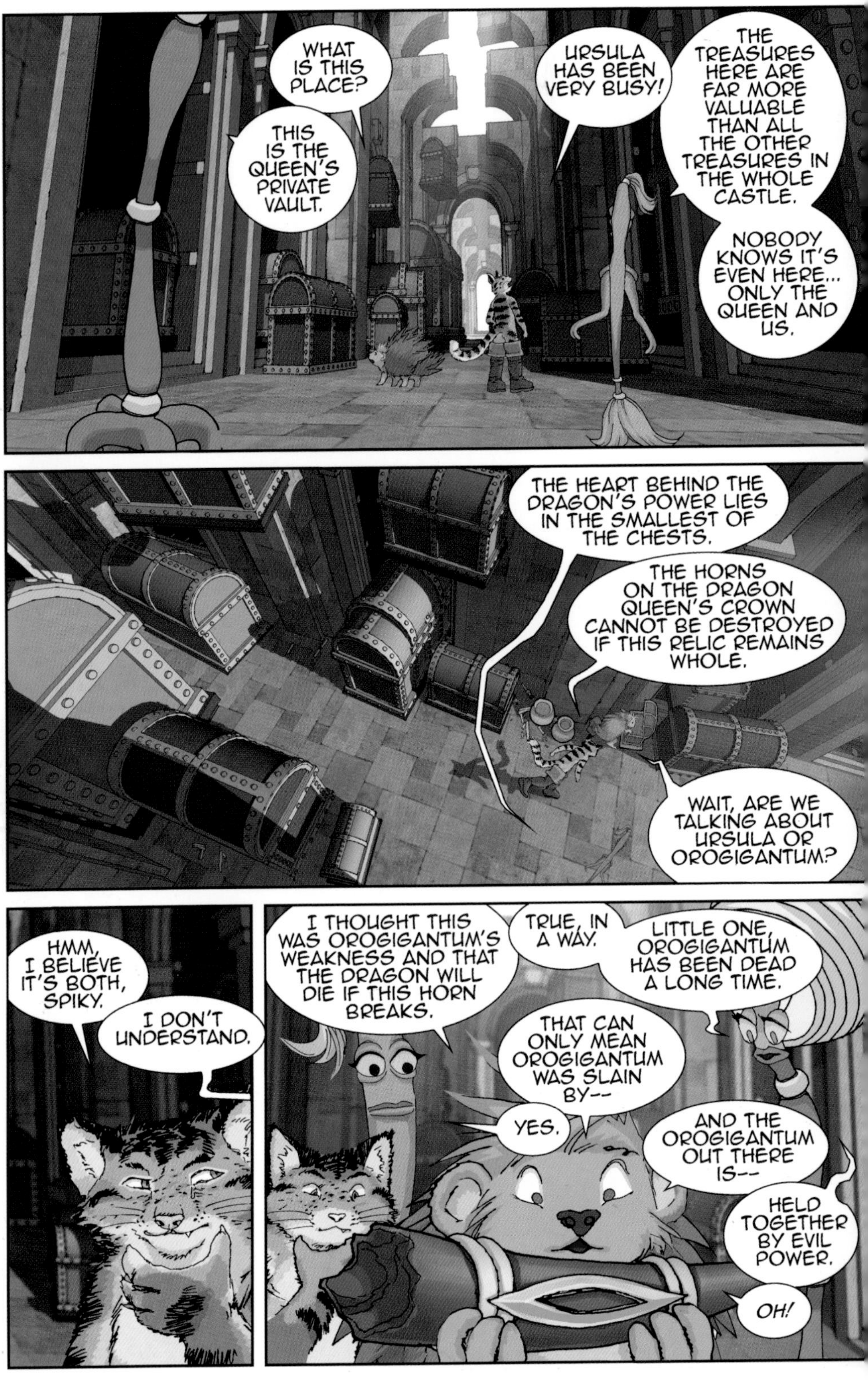
WHAT IS THIS PLACE?
THIS IS THE QUEEN'S PRIVATE VAULT.
URSULA HAS BEEN VERY BUSY!
THE TREASURES HERE ARE FAR MORE VALUABLE THAN ALL THE OTHER TREASURES IN THE WHOLE CASTLE.
NOBODY KNOWS IT'S EVEN HERE... ONLY THE QUEEN AND US.
THE HEART BEHIND THE DRAGON'S POWER LIES IN THE SMALLEST OF THE CHESTS.
THE HORNS ON THE DRAGON QUEEN'S CROWN CANNOT BE DESTROYED IF THIS RELIC REMAINS WHOLE.
WAIT, ARE WE TALKING ABOUT URSULA OR OROGIGANTUM?
HMM, I BELIEVE IT'S BOTH, SPIKY.
I DON'T UNDERSTAND.
I THOUGHT THIS WAS OROGIGANTUM'S WEAKNESS AND THAT THE DRAGON WILL DIE IF THIS HORN BREAKS.
TRUE, IN A WAY.
LITTLE ONE, OROGIGANTUM HAS BEEN DEAD A LONG TIME.
THAT CAN ONLY MEAN OROGIGANTUM WAS SLAIN BY--
YES.
AND THE OROGIGANTUM OUT THERE IS--
HELD TOGETHER BY EVIL POWER.
OH!

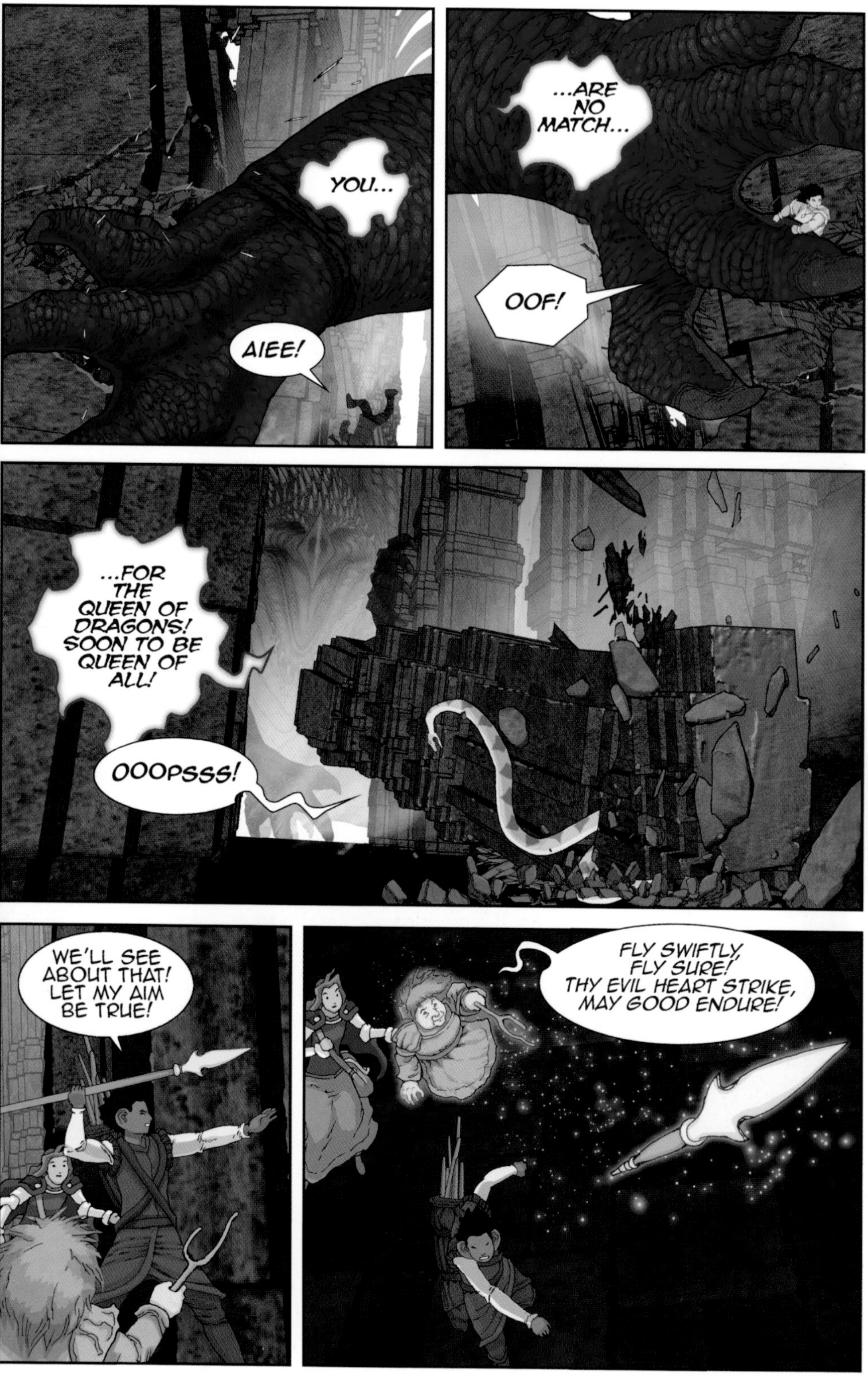
YOU...
AIEE!
...ARE NO MATCH...
OOF!
...FOR THE QUEEN OF DRAGONS! SOON TO BE QUEEN OF ALL!
OOOPSSS!
WE'LL SEE ABOUT THAT! LET MY AIM BE TRUE!
FLY SWIFTLY, FLY SURE! THY EVIL HEART STRIKE, MAY GOOD ENDURE!

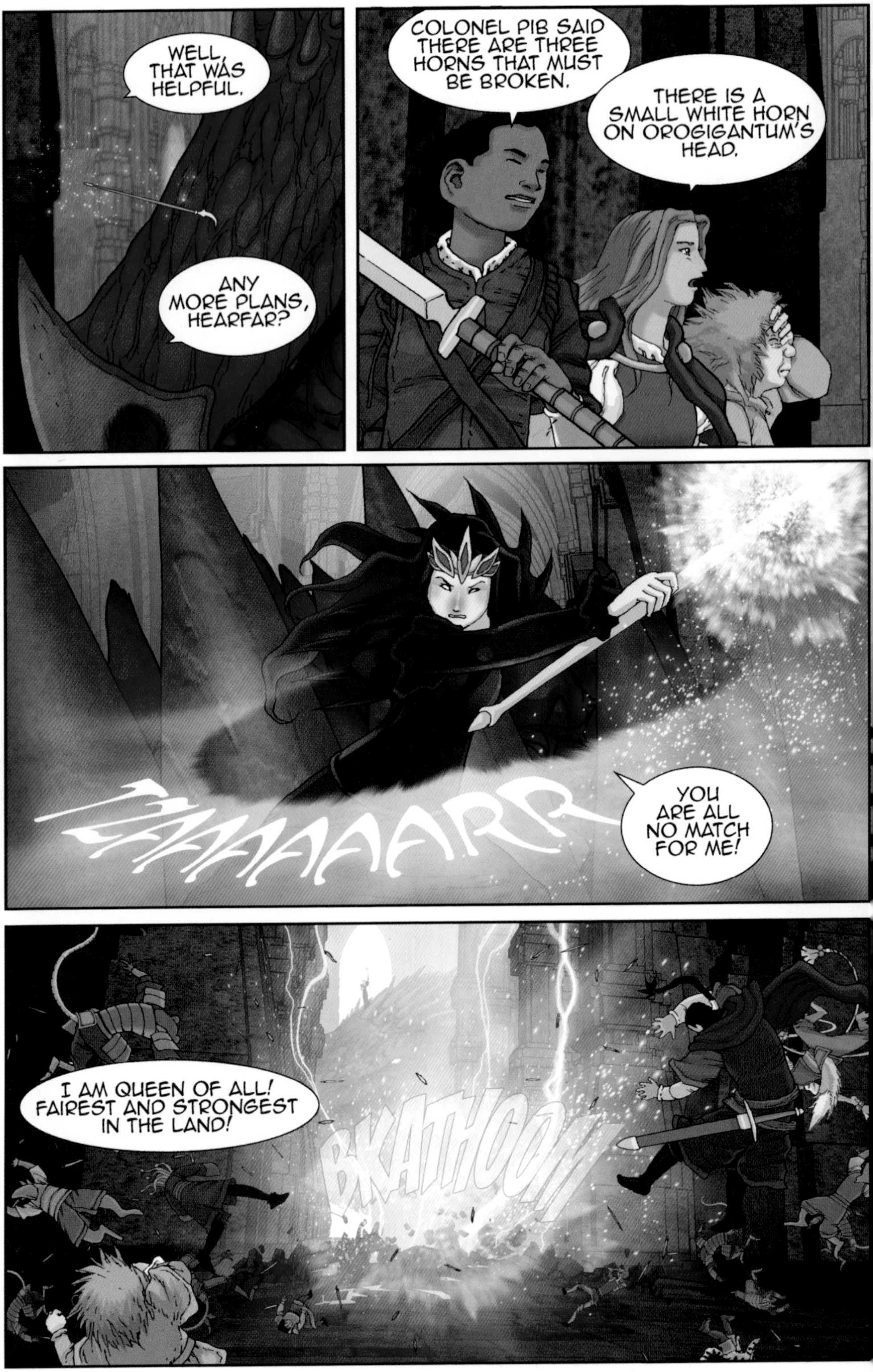
WELL, THAT WAS HELPFUL.
ANY MORE PLANS, HEARFAR?
COLONEL PIB SAID THERE ARE THREE HORNS THAT MUST BE BROKEN.
THERE IS A SMALL WHITE HORN ON OROGIGANTUM'S HEAD.
AAAAAARR
YOU ARE ALL NO MATCH FOR ME!
I AM QUEEN OF ALL! FAIREST AND STRONGEST IN THE LAND!
BKATHOOM!

WE'LL SEE ABOUT THAT!

?!

!

SWOOOO-

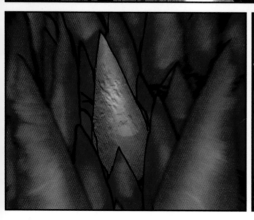

KRAK

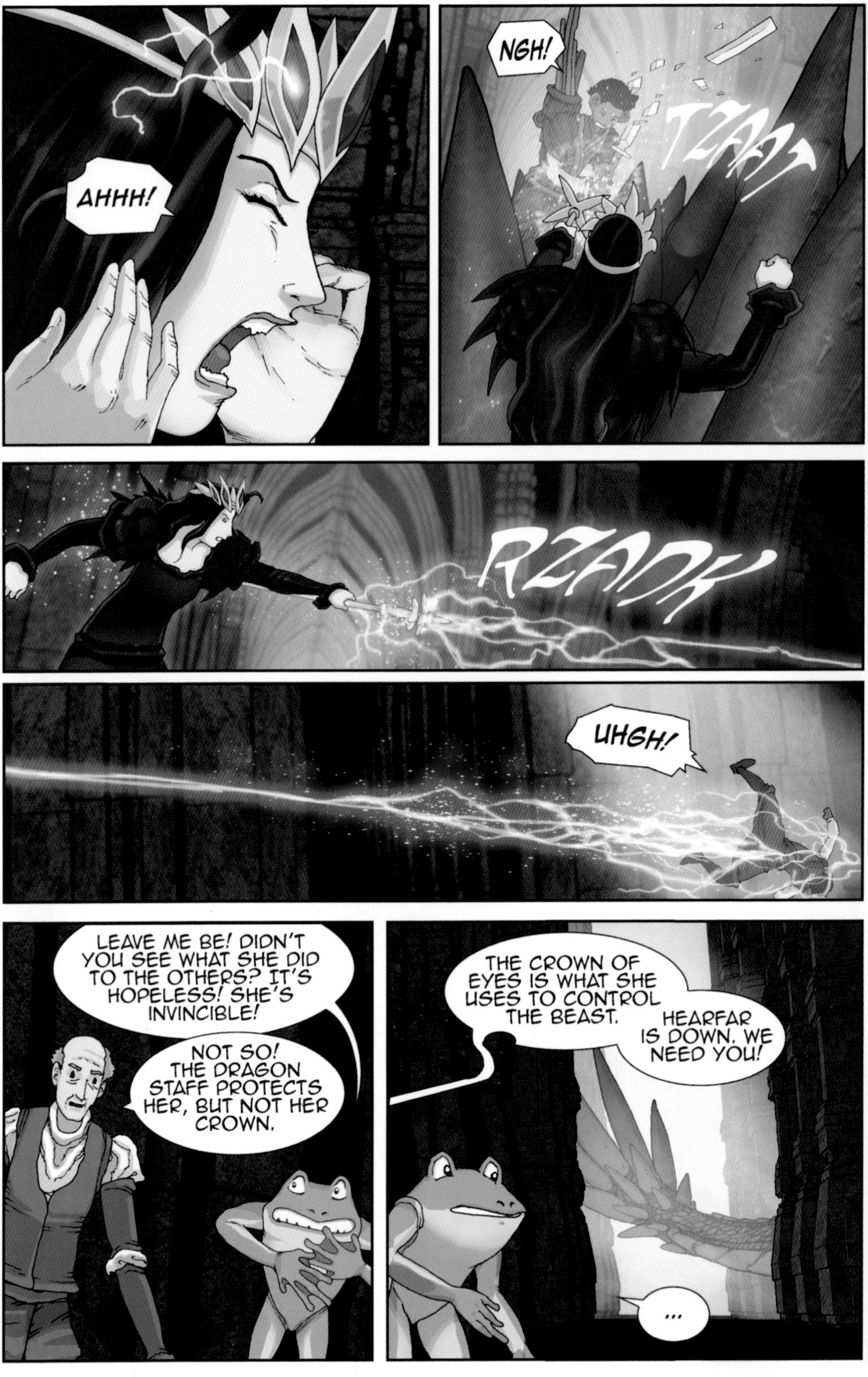
AHHH!
NGH!
TZAAT
RZADK
UHGH!
LEAVE ME BE! DIDN'T YOU SEE WHAT SHE DID TO THE OTHERS? IT'S HOPELESS! SHE'S INVINCIBLE!
NOT SO! THE DRAGON STAFF PROTECTS HER, BUT NOT HER CROWN.
THE CROWN OF EYES IS WHAT SHE USES TO CONTROL THE BEAST.
HEARFAR IS DOWN. WE NEED YOU!
...

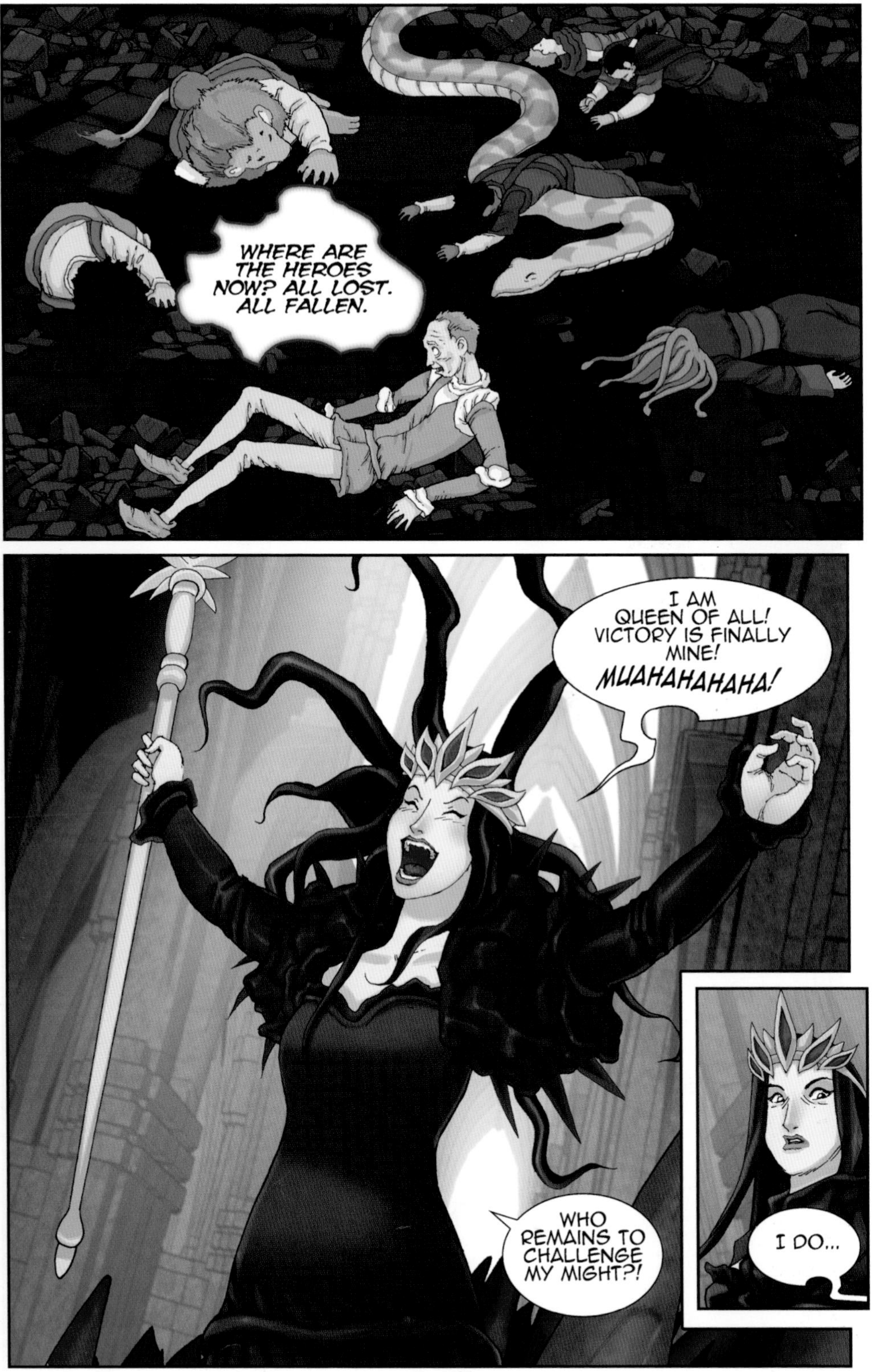
WHERE ARE THE HEROES NOW? ALL LOST. ALL FALLEN.
I AM QUEEN OF ALL! VICTORY IS FINALLY MINE! MUAHAHAHAHA!
WHO REMAINS TO CHALLENGE MY MIGHT?!
I DO...

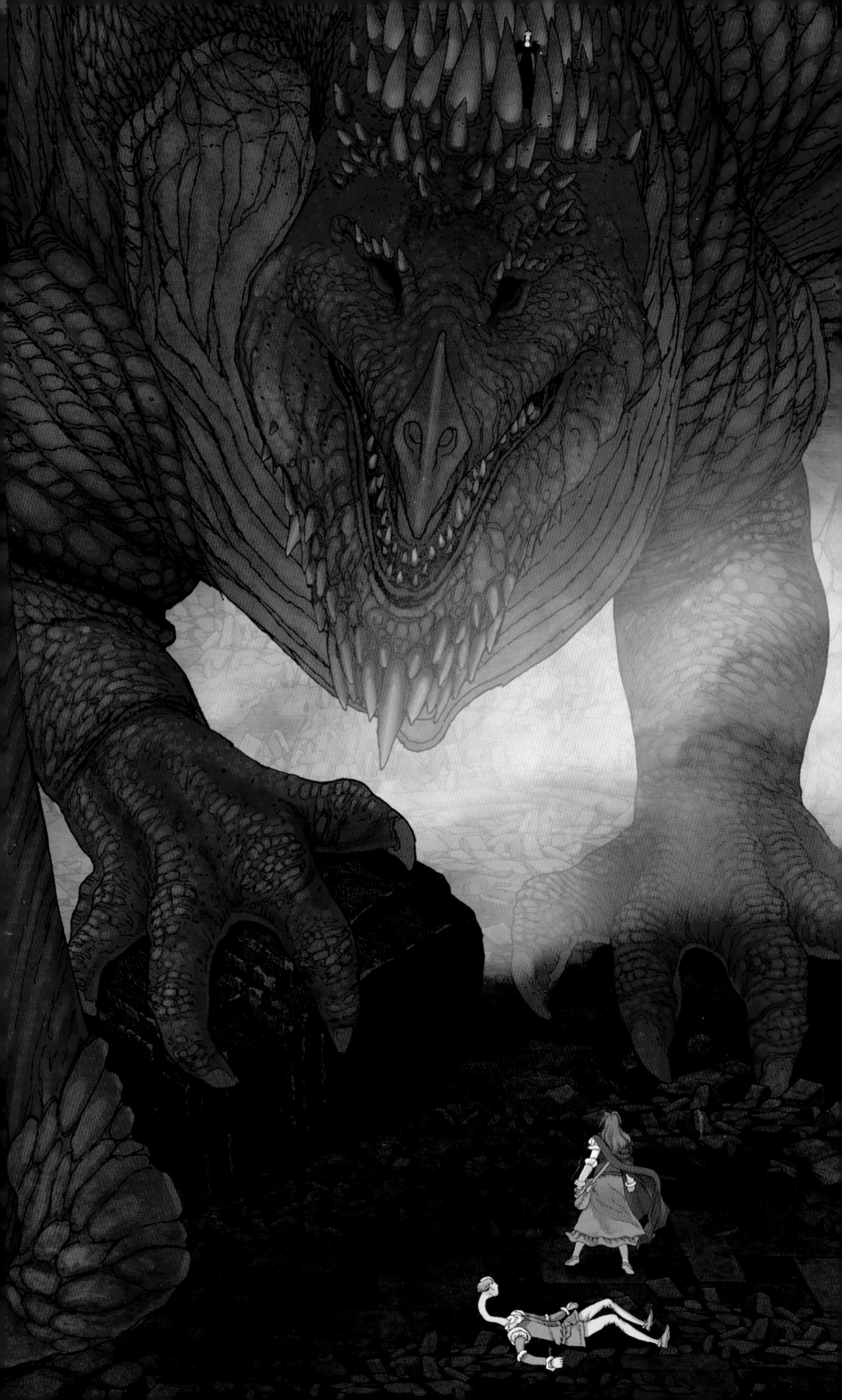

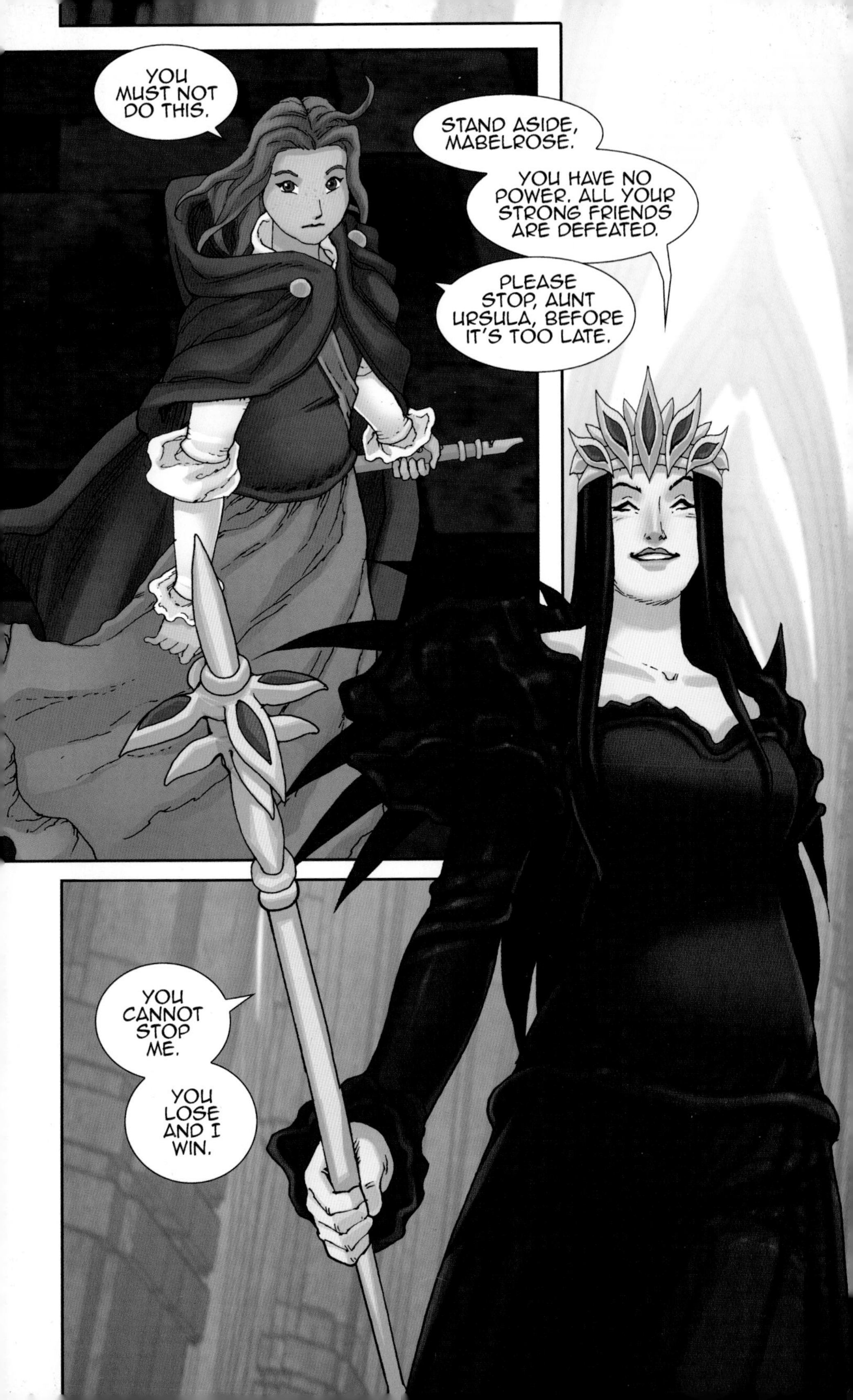
YOU MUST NOT DO THIS.
STAND ASIDE, MABELROSE.
YOU HAVE NO POWER. ALL YOUR STRONG FRIENDS ARE DEFEATED.
PLEASE STOP, AUNT URSULA, BEFORE IT'S TOO LATE.
YOU CANNOT STOP ME.
YOU LOSE AND I WIN.

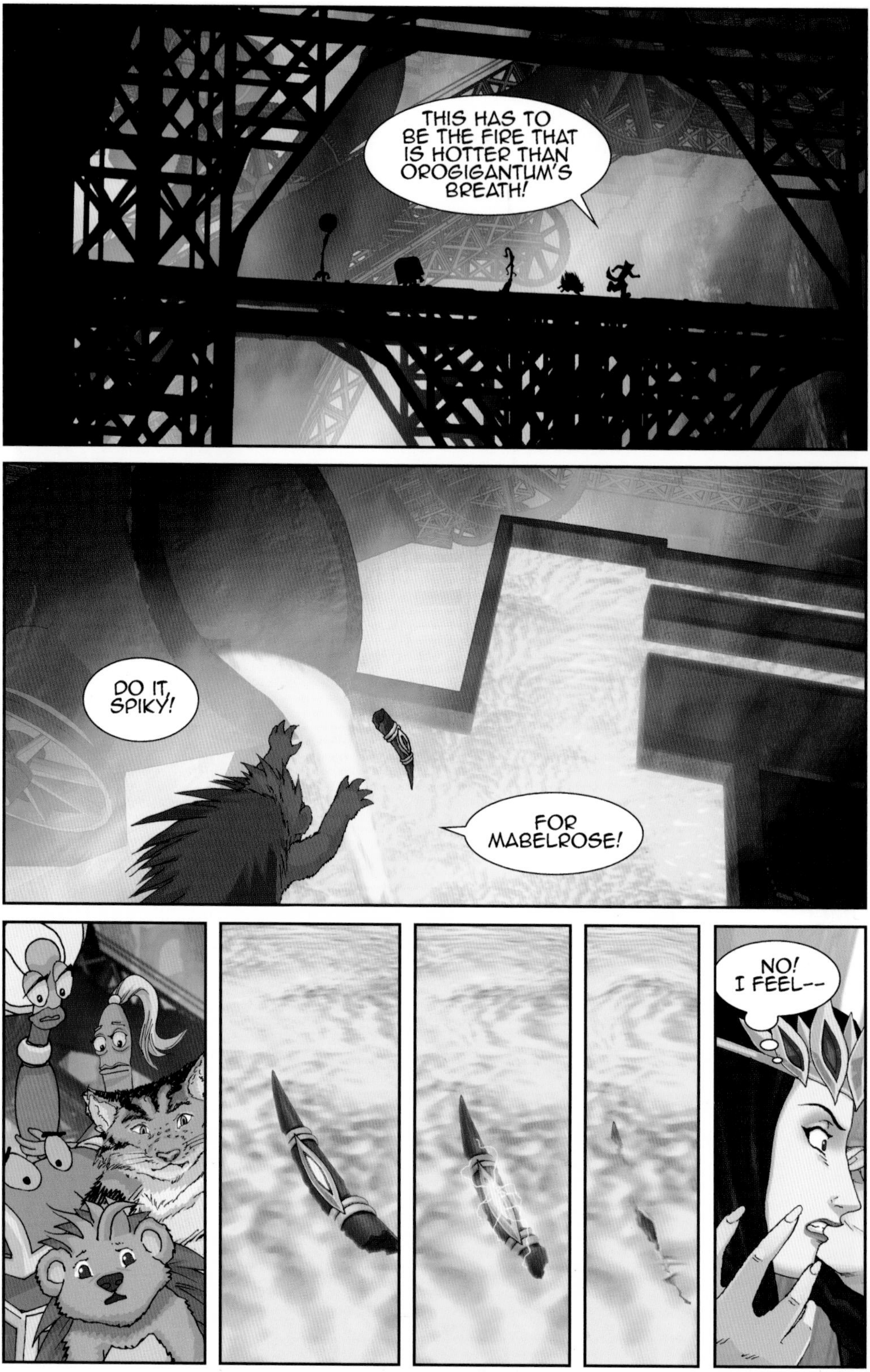
THIS HAS TO BE THE FIRE THAT IS HOTTER THAN OROGIGANTUM'S BREATH!
DO IT, SPIKY!
FOR MABELROSE!
NO! I FEEL--

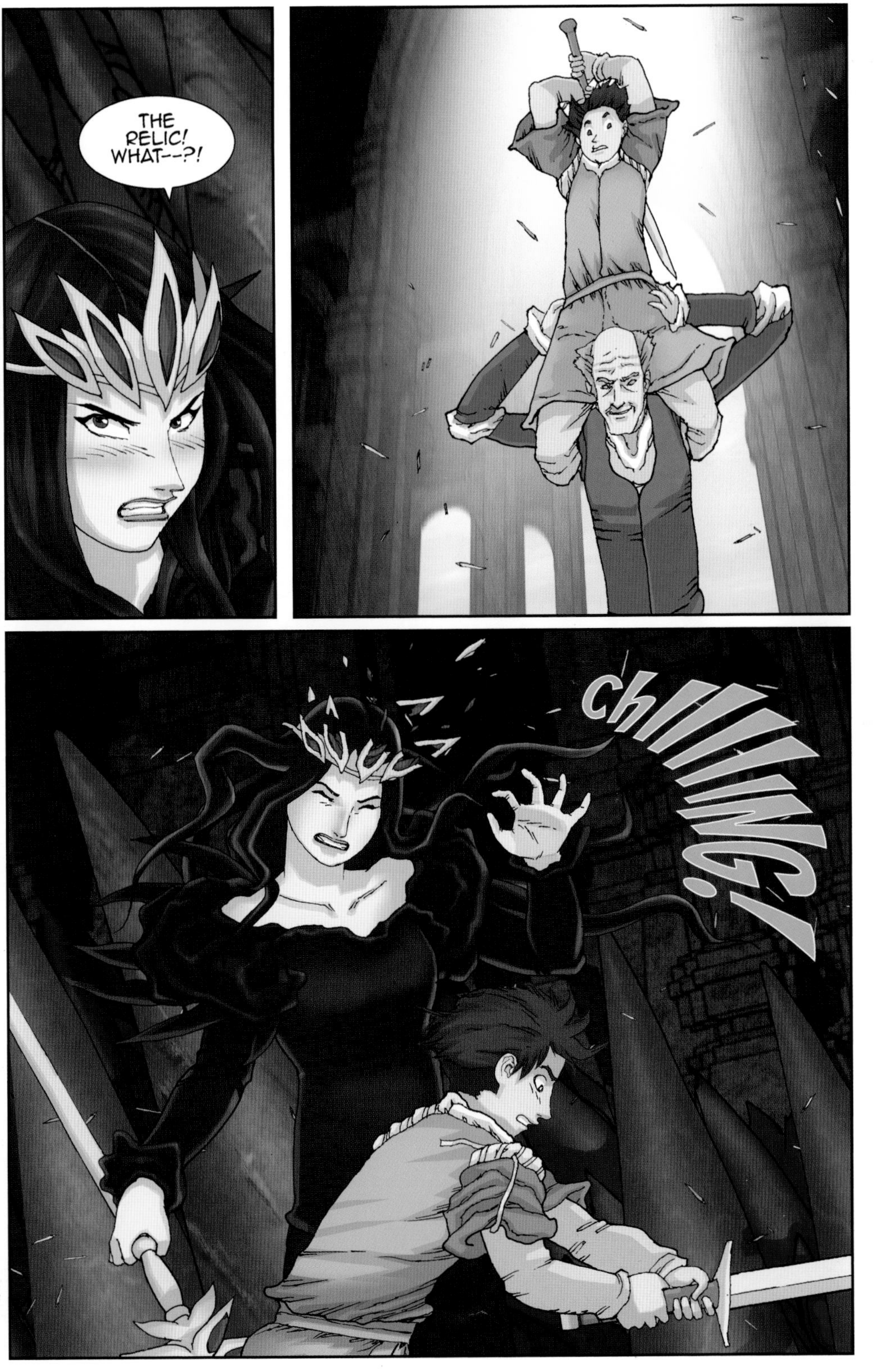
THE RELIC! WHAT--?!
chIIIIING!

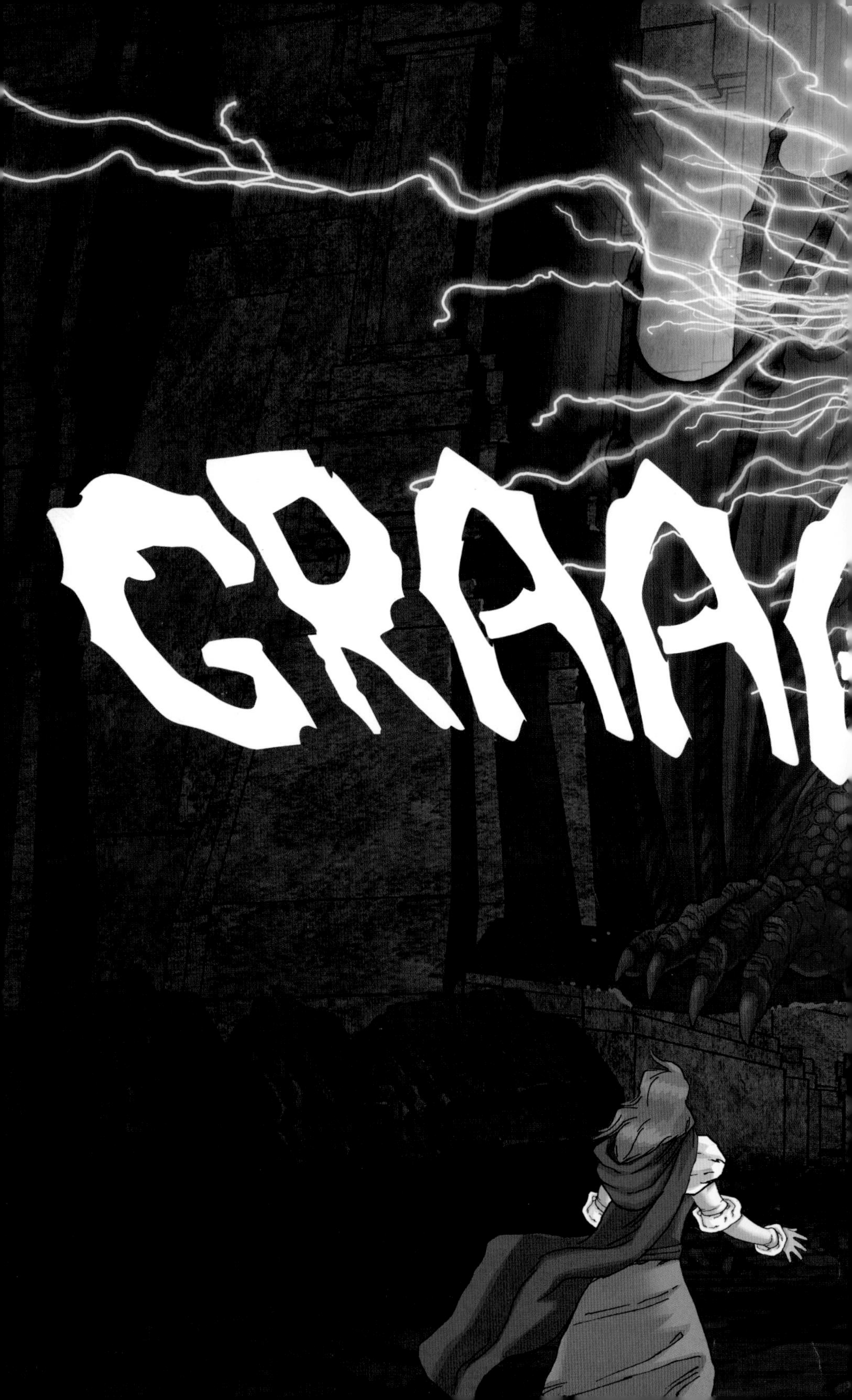
GRAAA

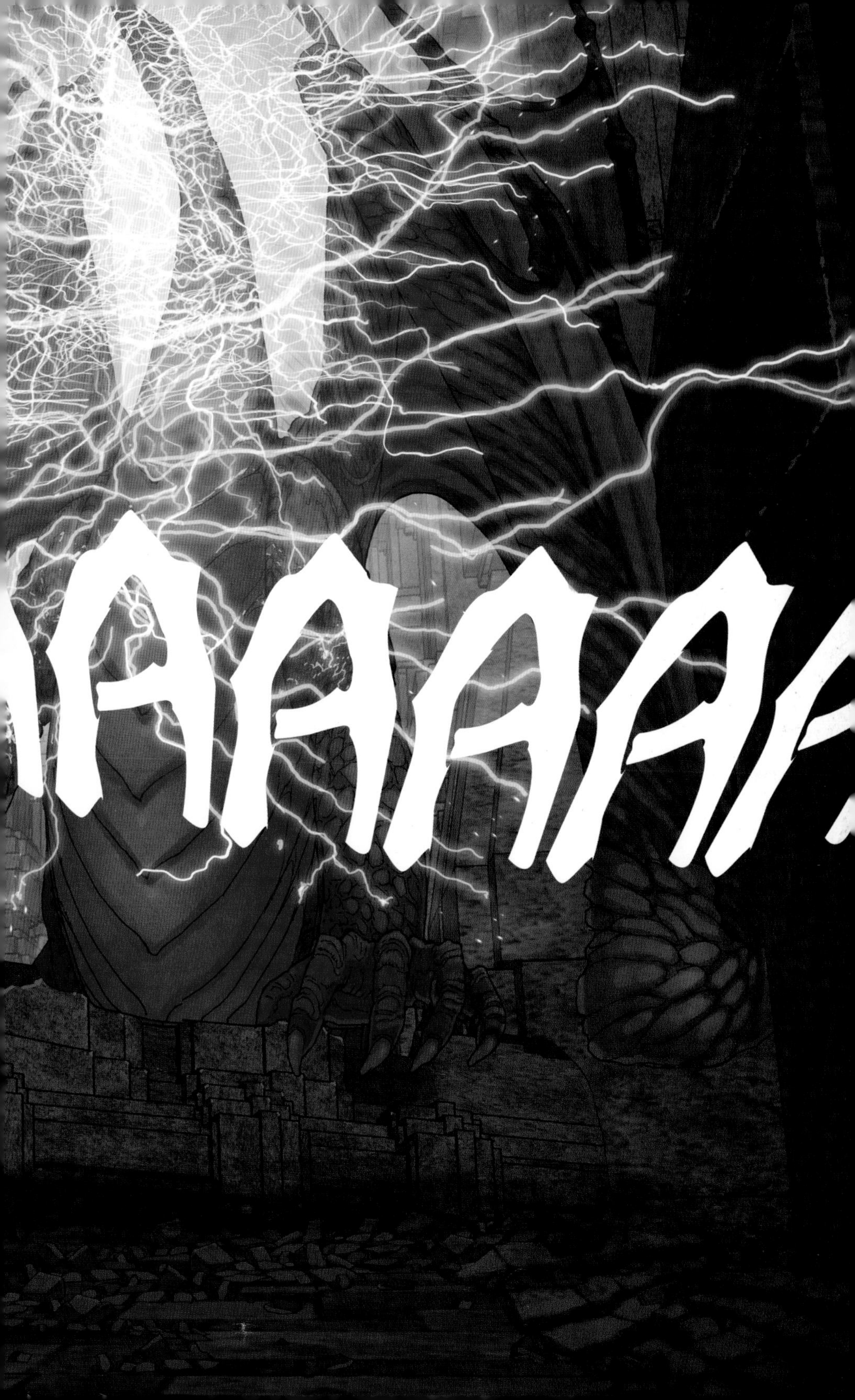
AAAAAA

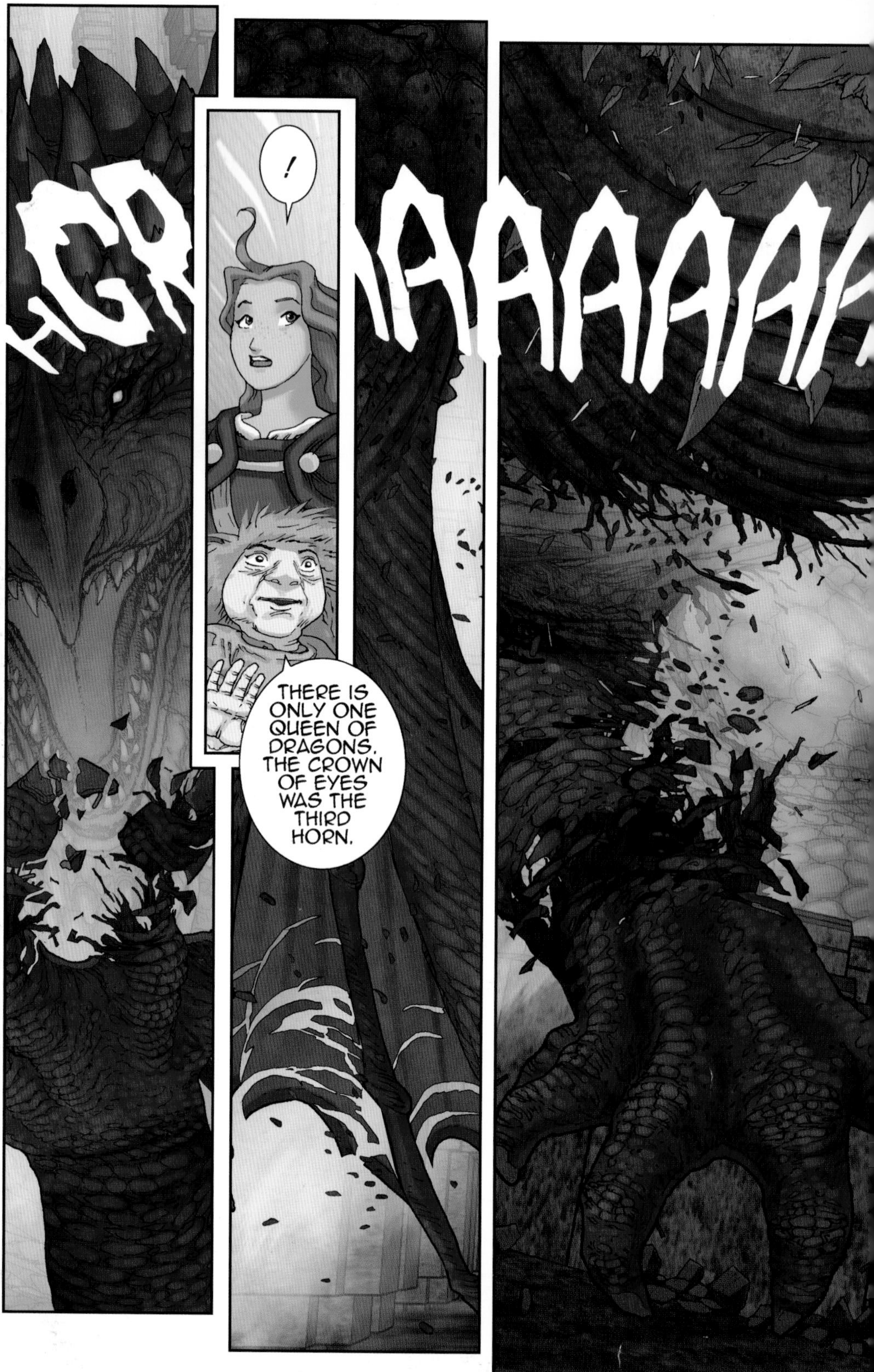
HGRAAAAAAAA
!
THERE IS ONLY ONE QUEEN OF DRAGONS. THE CROWN OF EYES WAS THE THIRD HORN.

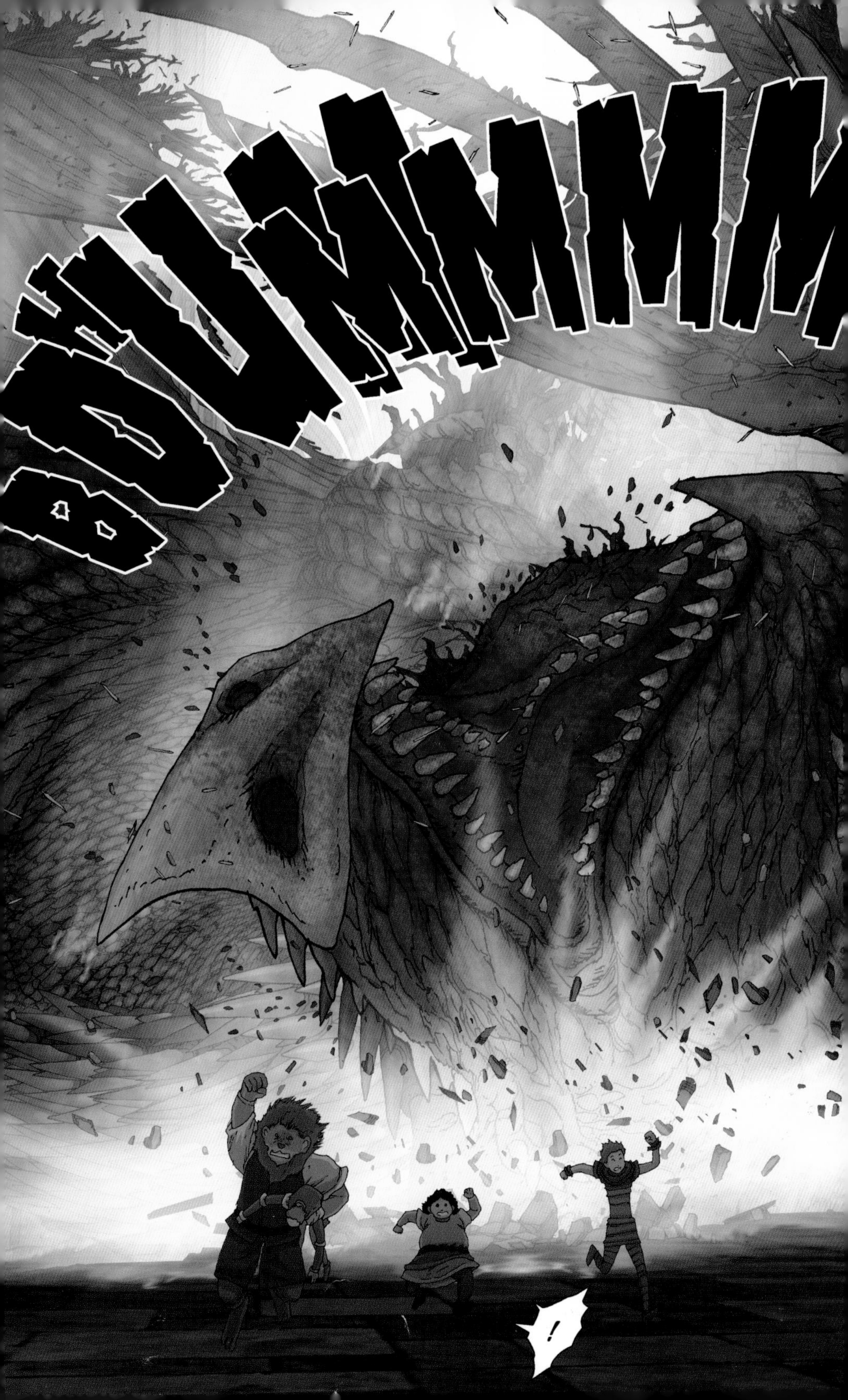
BOOMMMMMMM
!

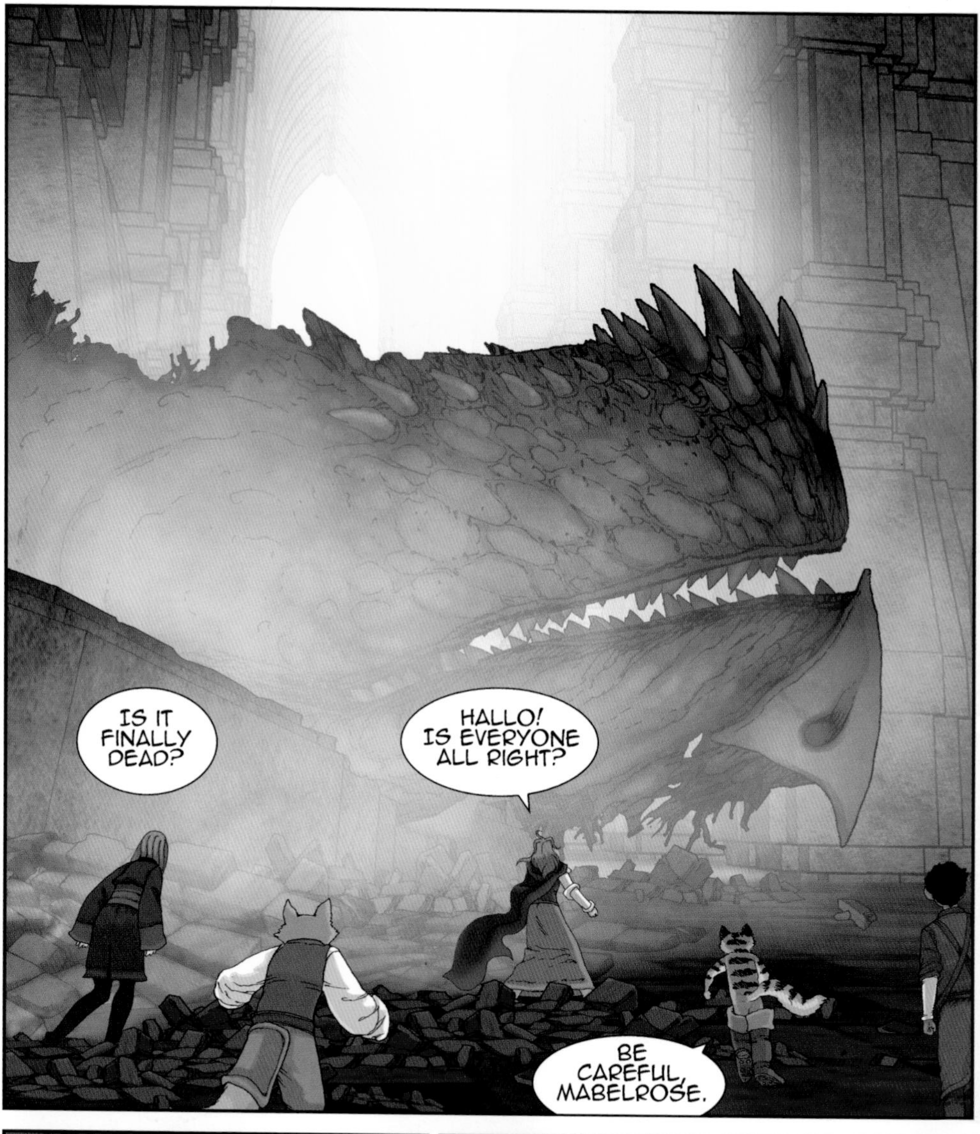
IS IT FINALLY DEAD?
HALLO! IS EVERYONE ALL RIGHT?
BE CAREFUL, MABELROSE.

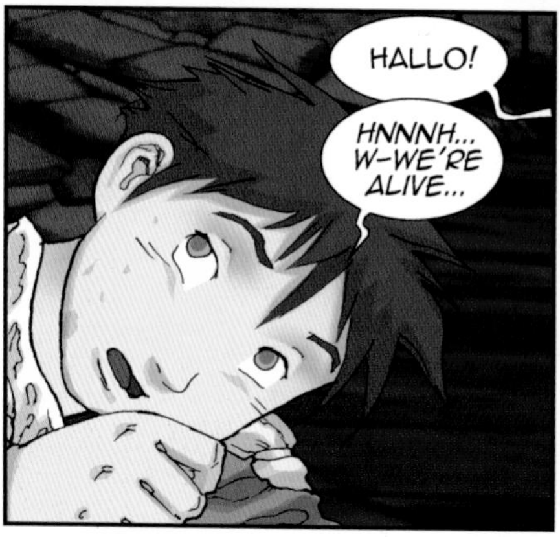
HALLO!
HNNNH... W-WE'RE ALIVE...

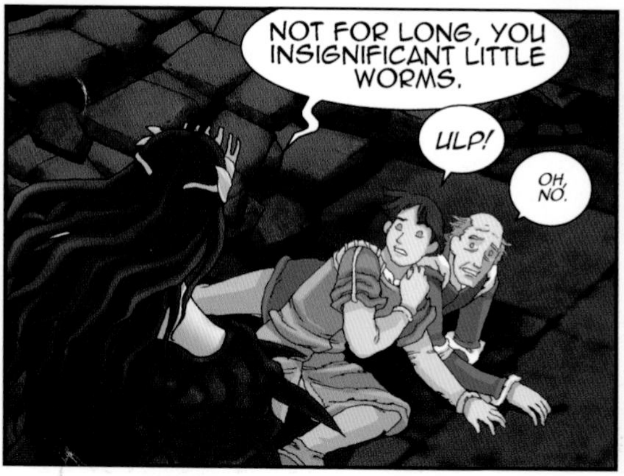
NOT FOR LONG, YOU INSIGNIFICANT LITTLE WORMS.
ULP!
OH, NO.

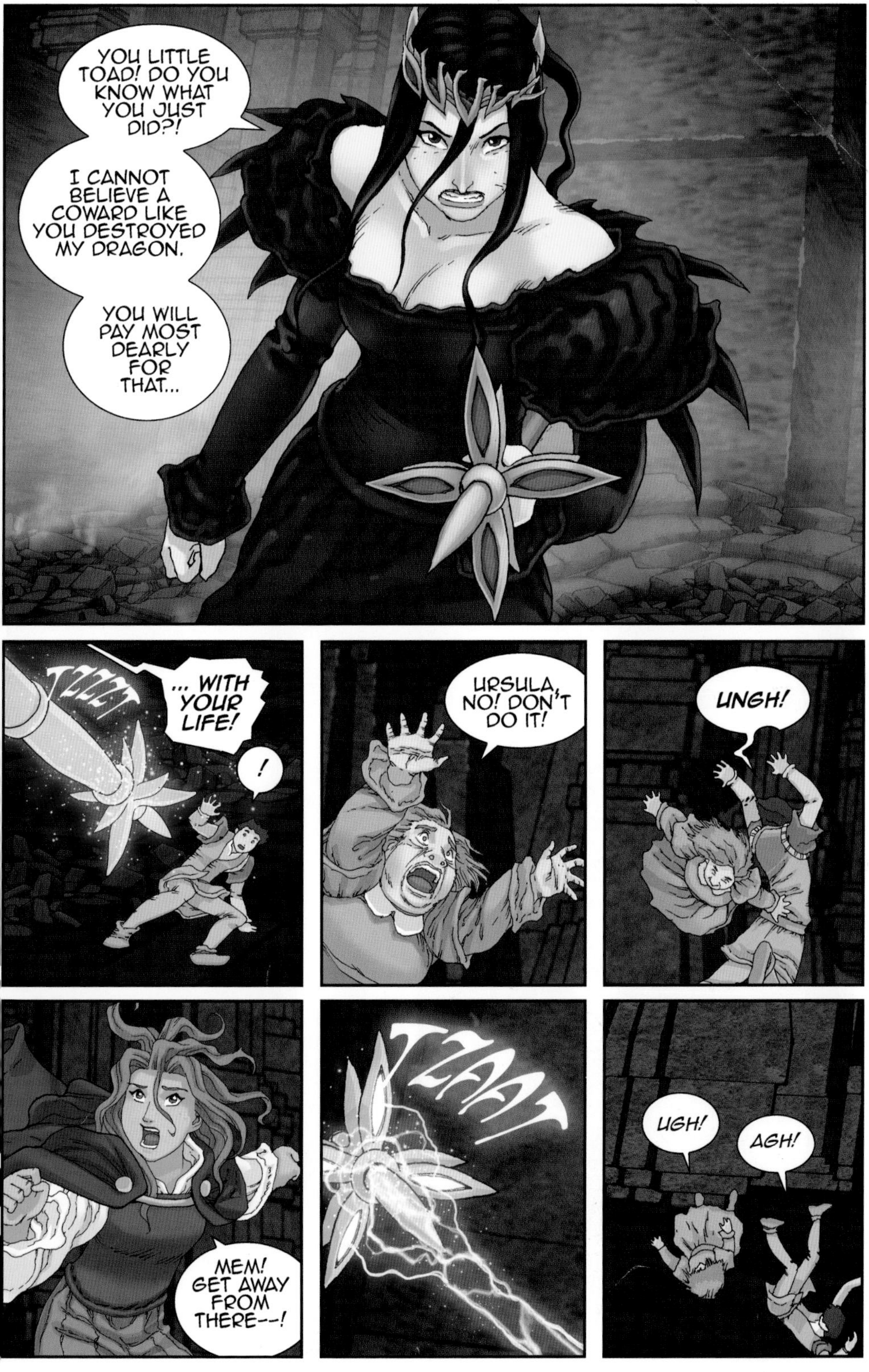
YOU LITTLE TOAD! DO YOU KNOW WHAT YOU JUST DID?!
I CANNOT BELIEVE A COWARD LIKE YOU DESTROYED MY DRAGON.
YOU WILL PAY MOST DEARLY FOR THAT...
TZZZT
... WITH YOUR LIFE!
!
URSULA, NO! DON'T DO IT!
UNGH!
MEM! GET AWAY FROM THERE--!
TZAAT
UGH!
AGH!

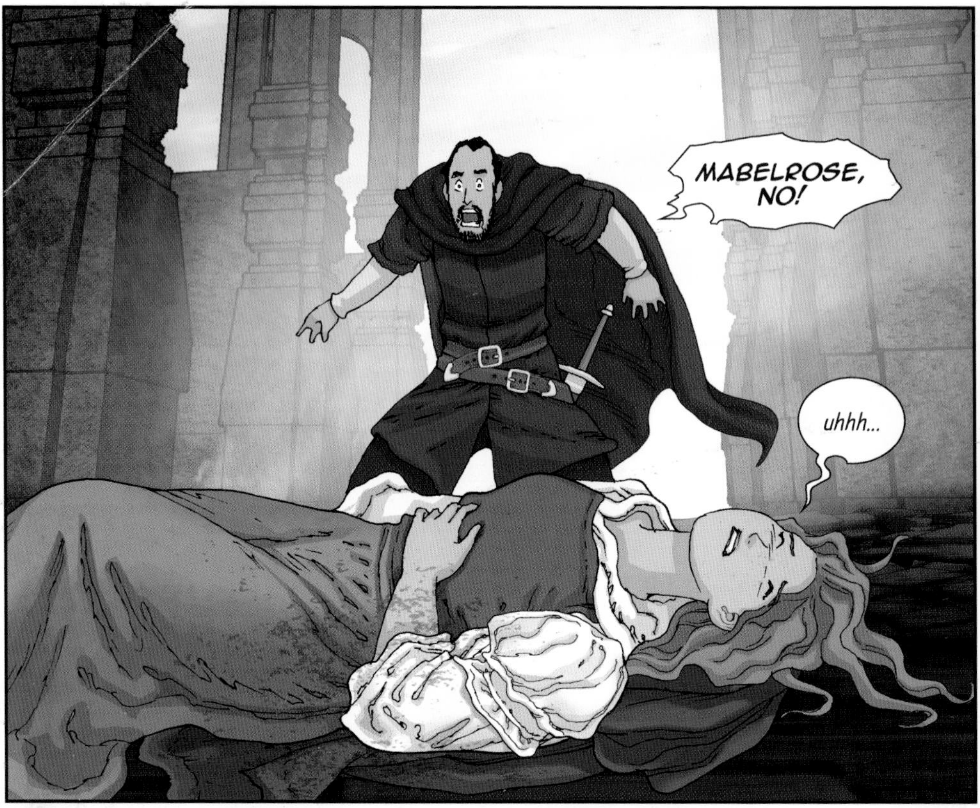
MABELROSE, NO!
uhhh...

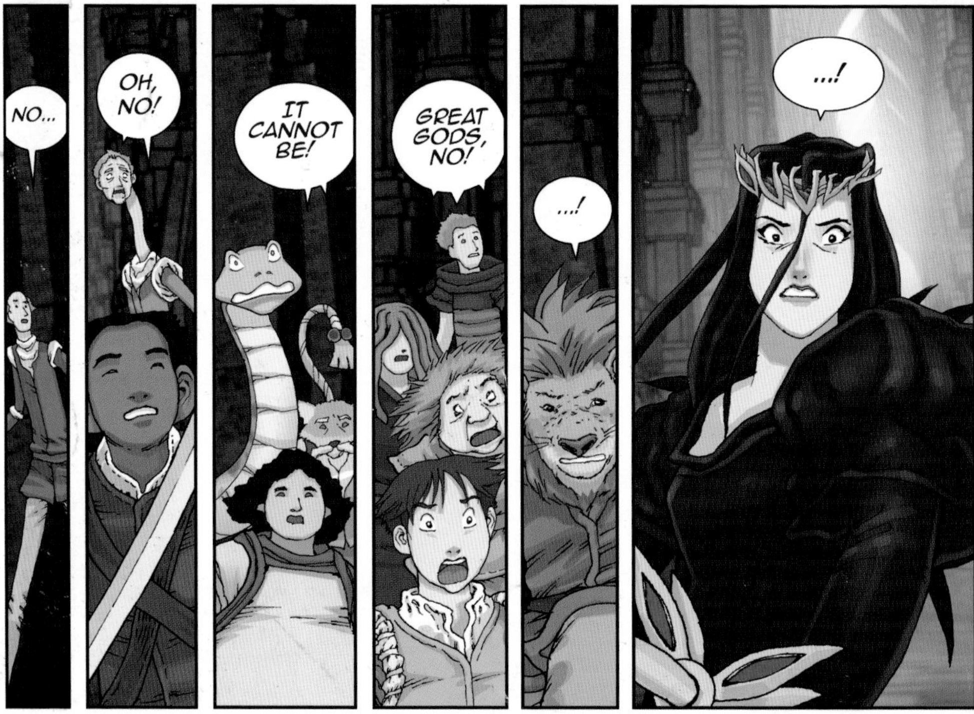
NO...
OH, NO!
IT CANNOT BE!
GREAT GODS, NO!
...!
...!

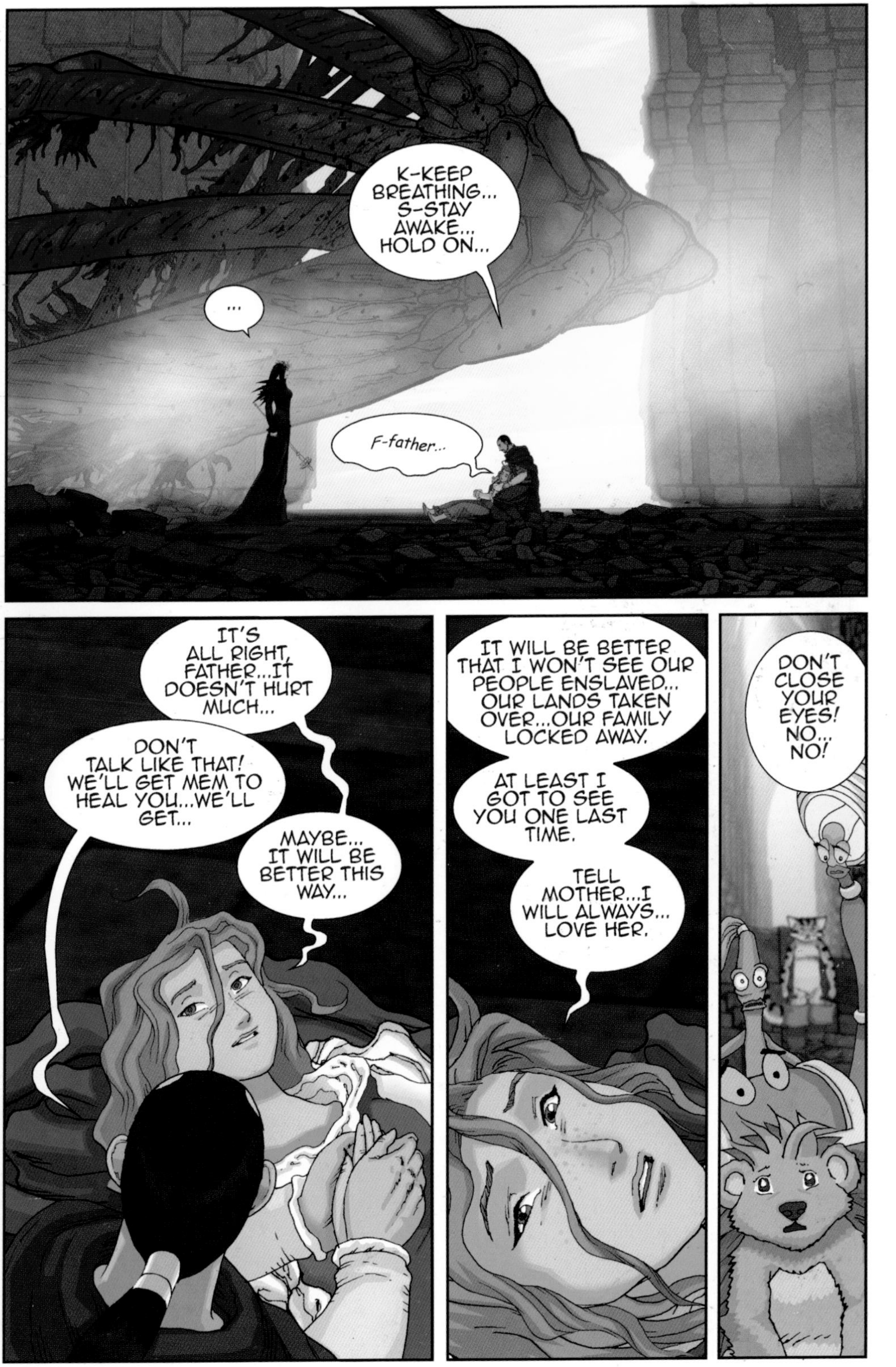
K-KEEP BREATHING... S-STAY AWAKE... HOLD ON...
...
F-father...
IT'S ALL RIGHT, FATHER...IT DOESN'T HURT MUCH...
DON'T TALK LIKE THAT! WE'LL GET MEM TO HEAL YOU...WE'LL GET...
MAYBE... IT WILL BE BETTER THIS WAY...
IT WILL BE BETTER THAT I WON'T SEE OUR PEOPLE ENSLAVED... OUR LANDS TAKEN OVER...OUR FAMILY LOCKED AWAY.
AT LEAST I GOT TO SEE YOU ONE LAST TIME.
TELL MOTHER...I WILL ALWAYS... LOVE HER.
DON'T CLOSE YOUR EYES! NO... NO!

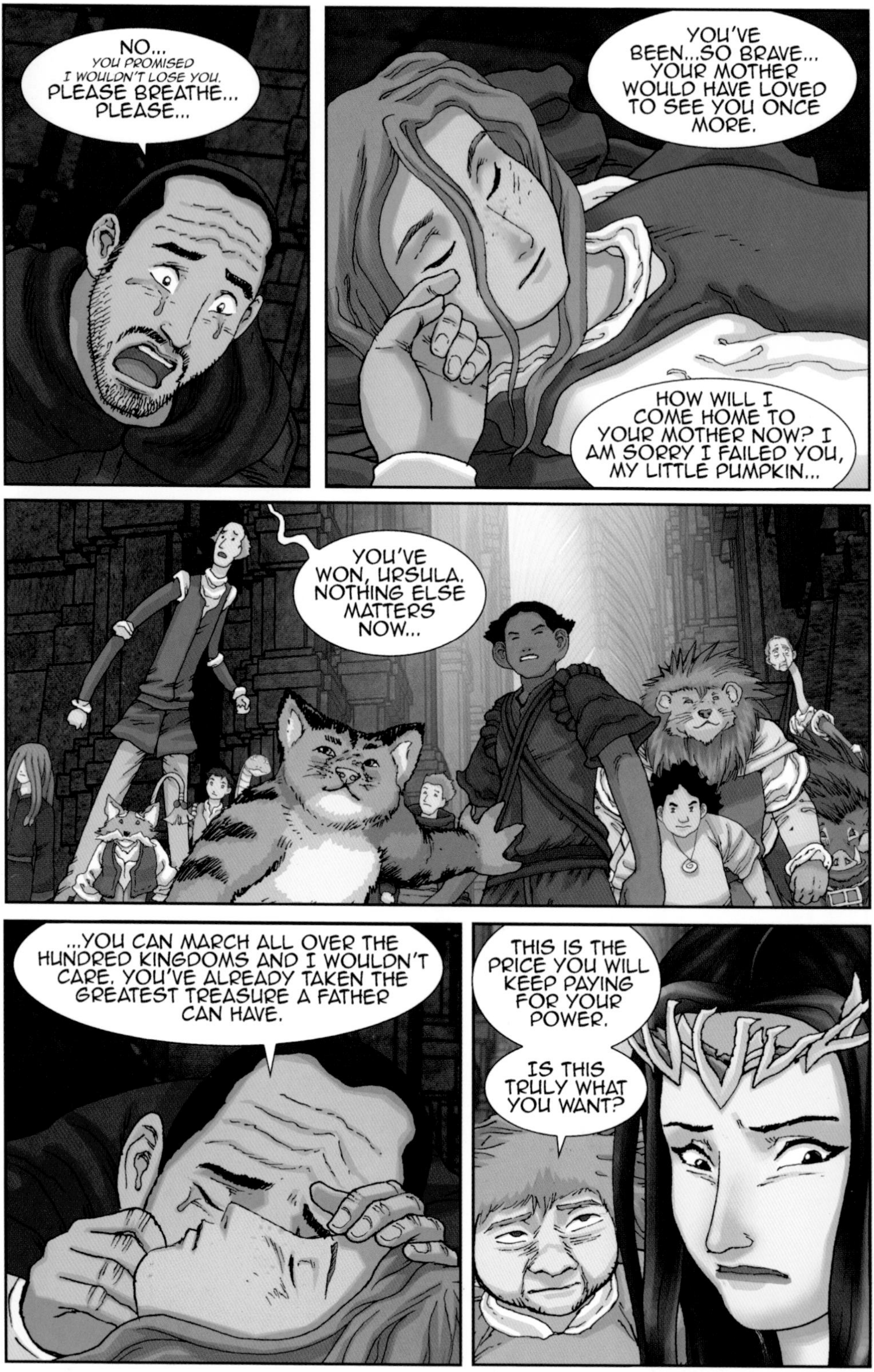
NO... YOU PROMISED I WOULDN'T LOSE YOU. PLEASE BREATHE... PLEASE...
YOU'VE BEEN...SO BRAVE... YOUR MOTHER WOULD HAVE LOVED TO SEE YOU ONCE MORE.
HOW WILL I COME HOME TO YOUR MOTHER NOW? I AM SORRY I FAILED YOU, MY LITTLE PUMPKIN...
YOU'VE WON, URSULA. NOTHING ELSE MATTERS NOW...
...YOU CAN MARCH ALL OVER THE HUNDRED KINGDOMS AND I WOULDN'T CARE. YOU'VE ALREADY TAKEN THE GREATEST TREASURE A FATHER CAN HAVE.
THIS IS THE PRICE YOU WILL KEEP PAYING FOR YOUR POWER.
IS THIS TRULY WHAT YOU WANT?

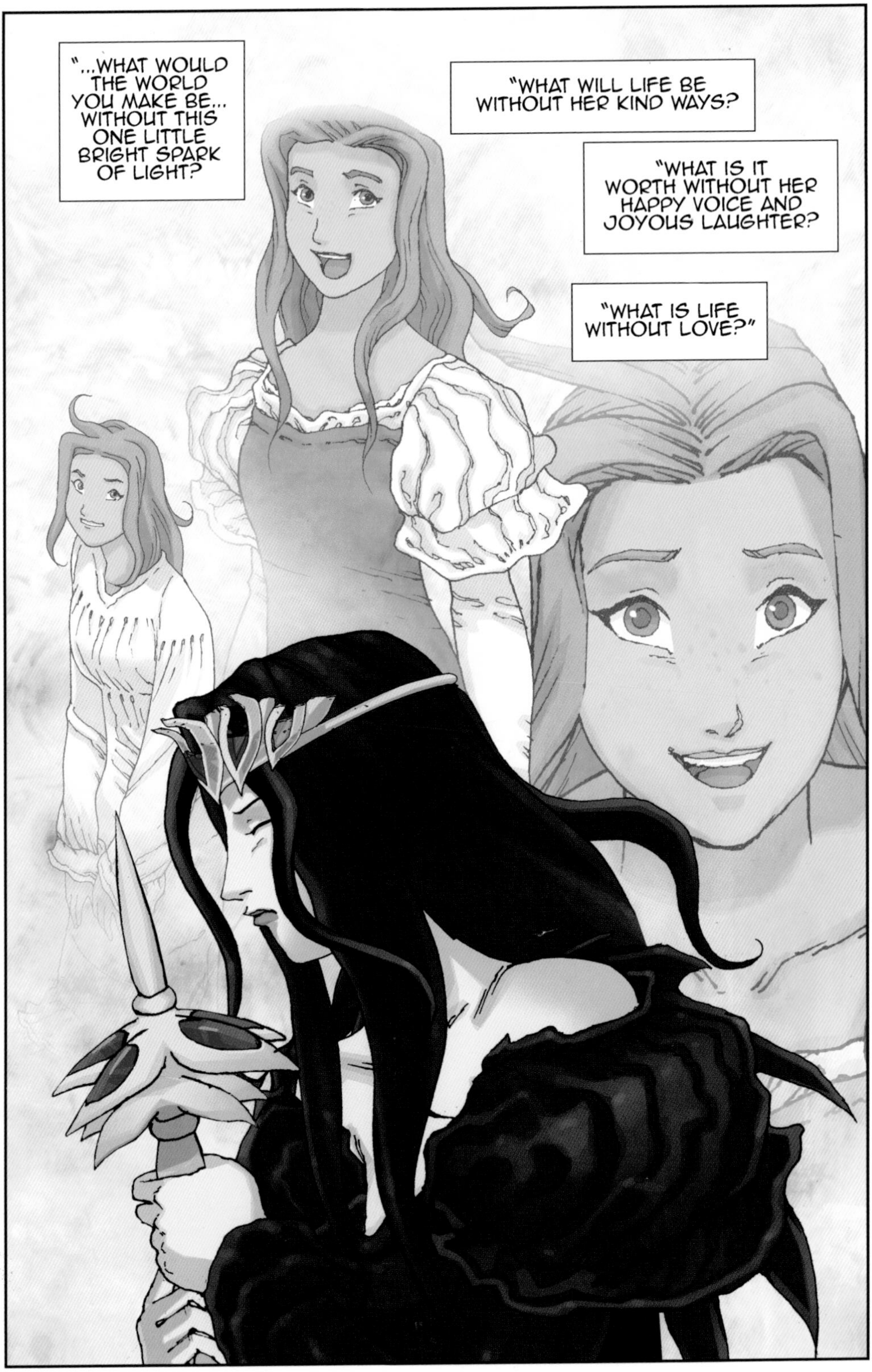
"...WHAT WOULD THE WORLD YOU MAKE BE... WITHOUT THIS ONE LITTLE BRIGHT SPARK OF LIGHT?
"WHAT WILL LIFE BE WITHOUT HER KIND WAYS?
"WHAT IS IT WORTH WITHOUT HER HAPPY VOICE AND JOYOUS LAUGHTER?
"WHAT IS LIFE WITHOUT LOVE?"

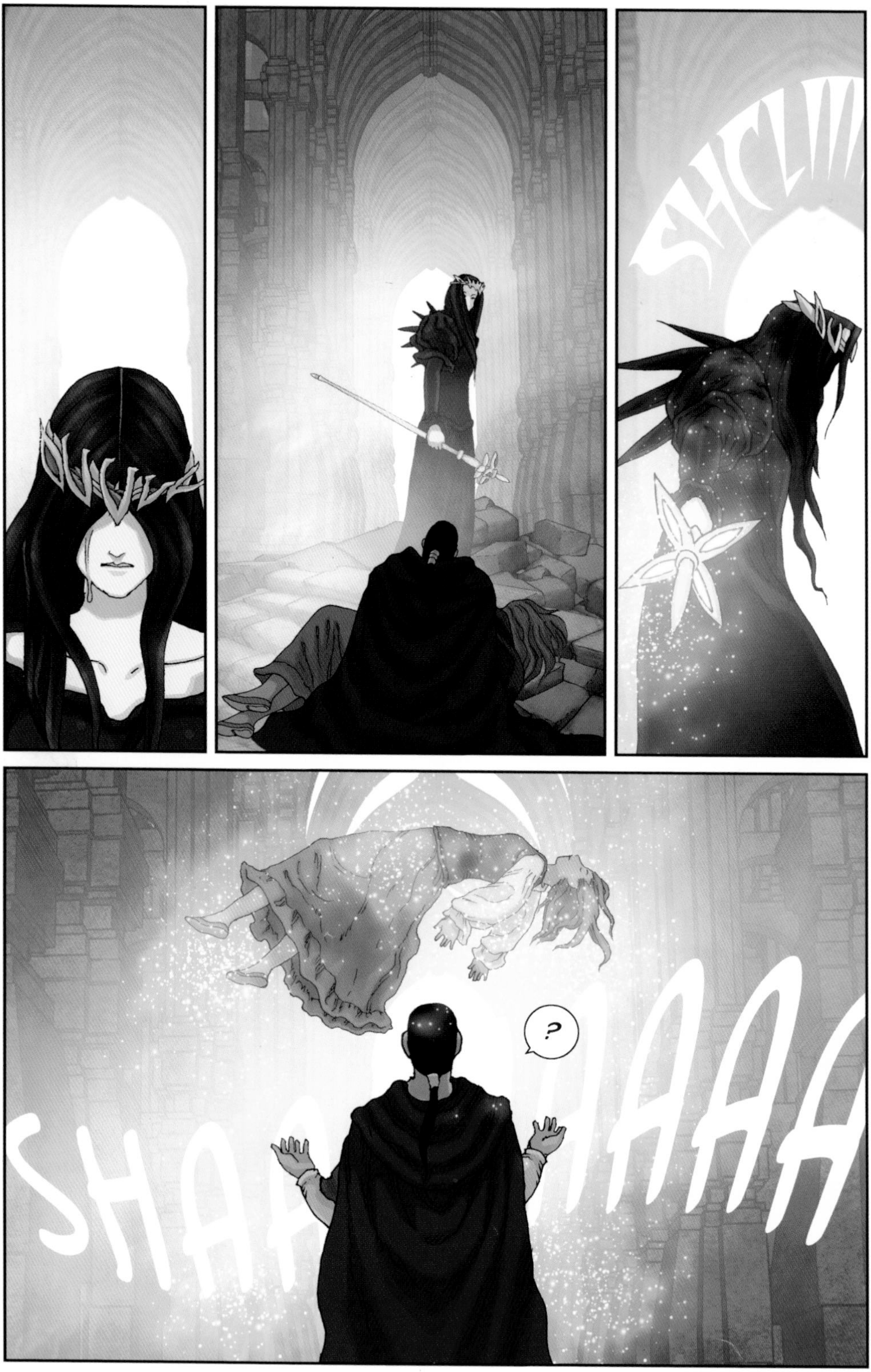
?

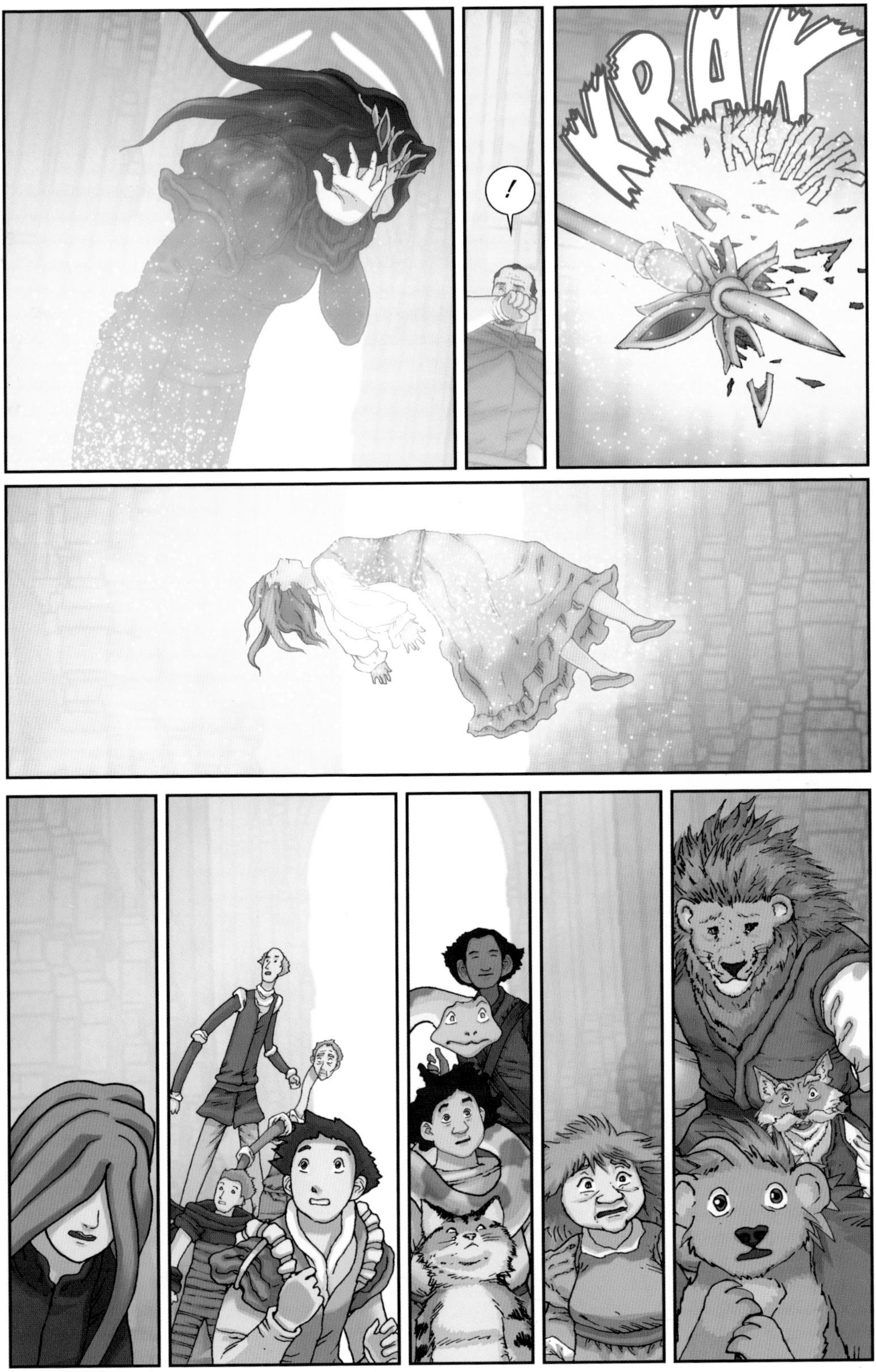
!
KRAK
KLINK

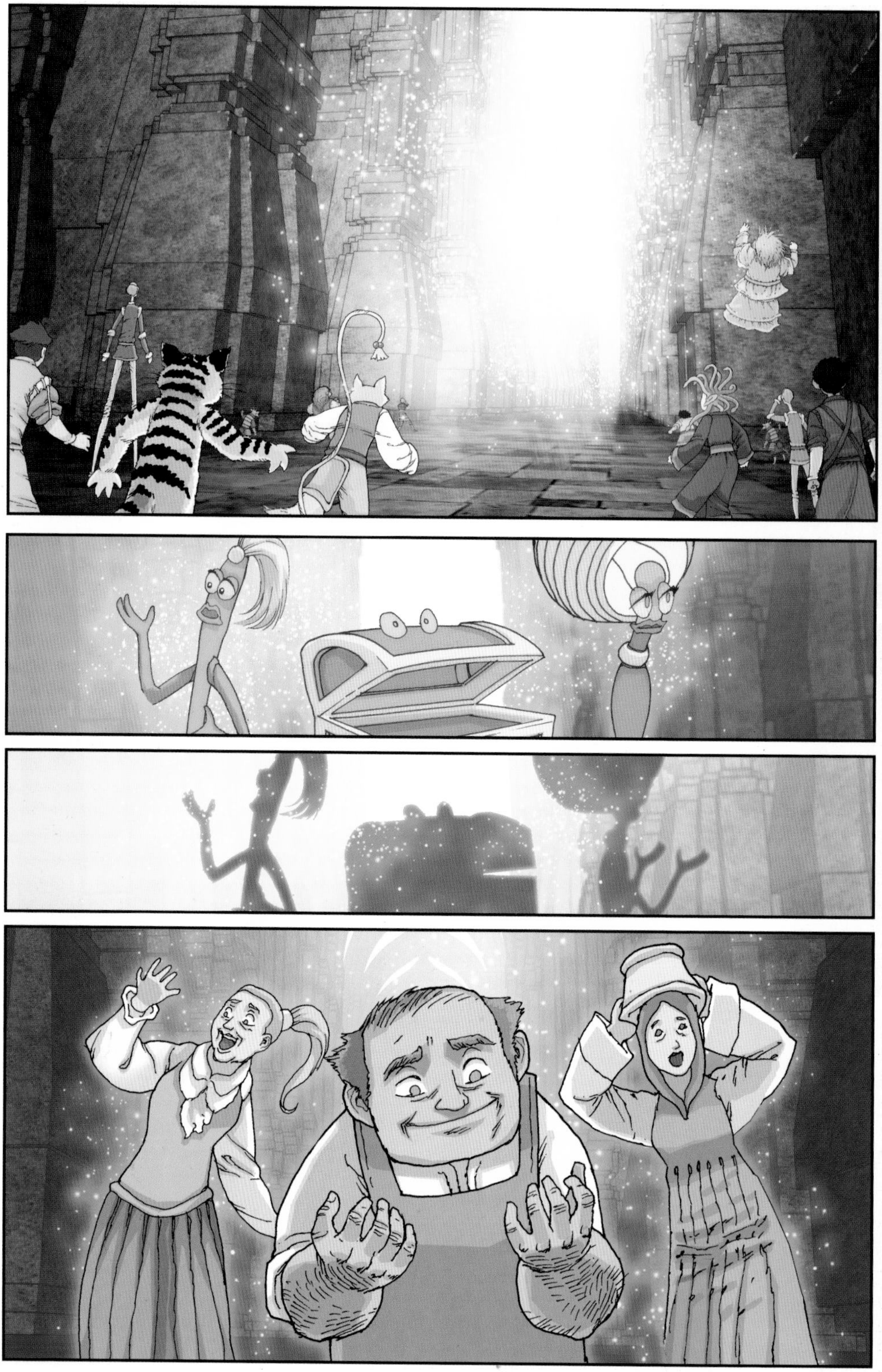

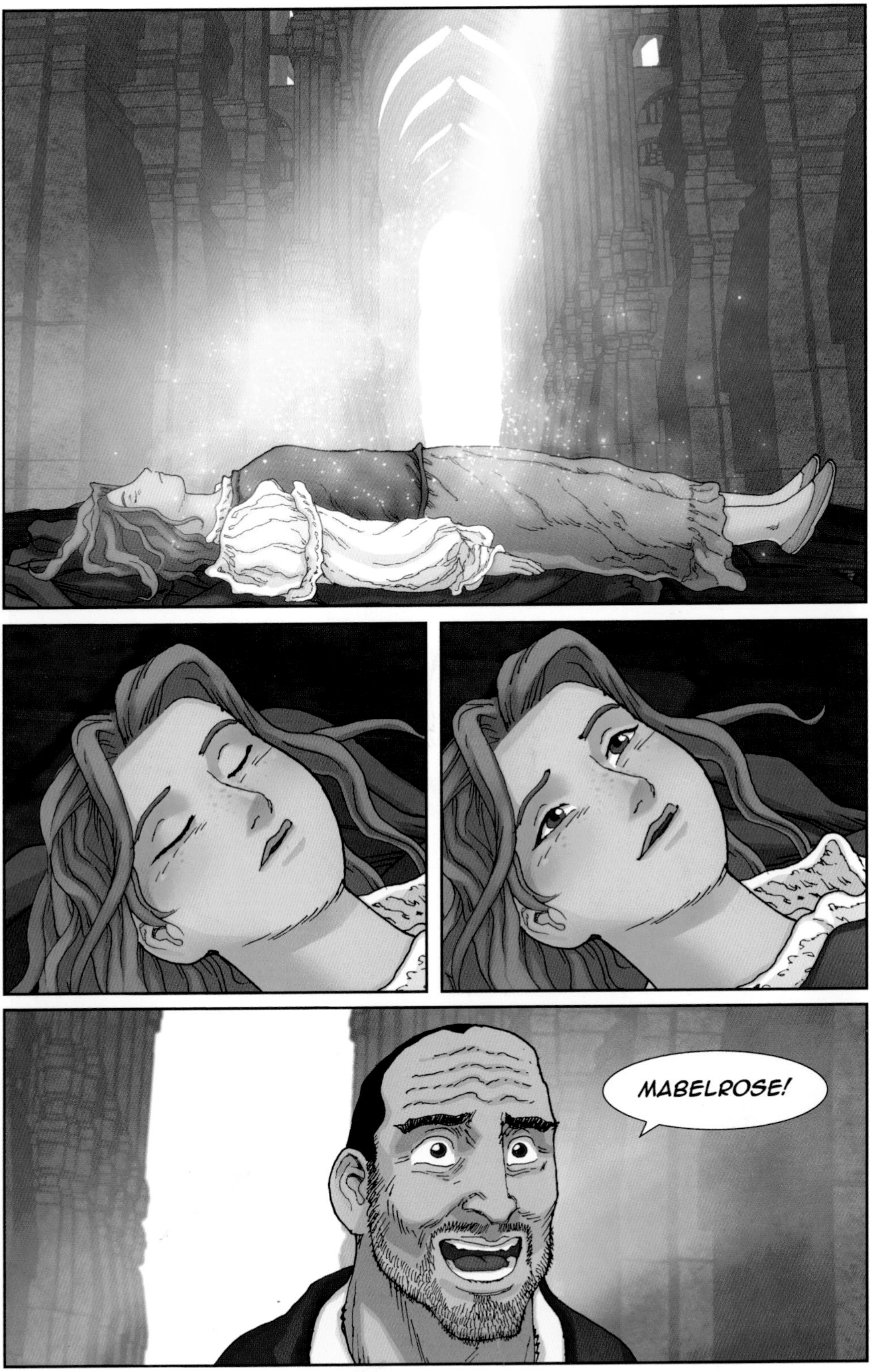
MABELROSE!

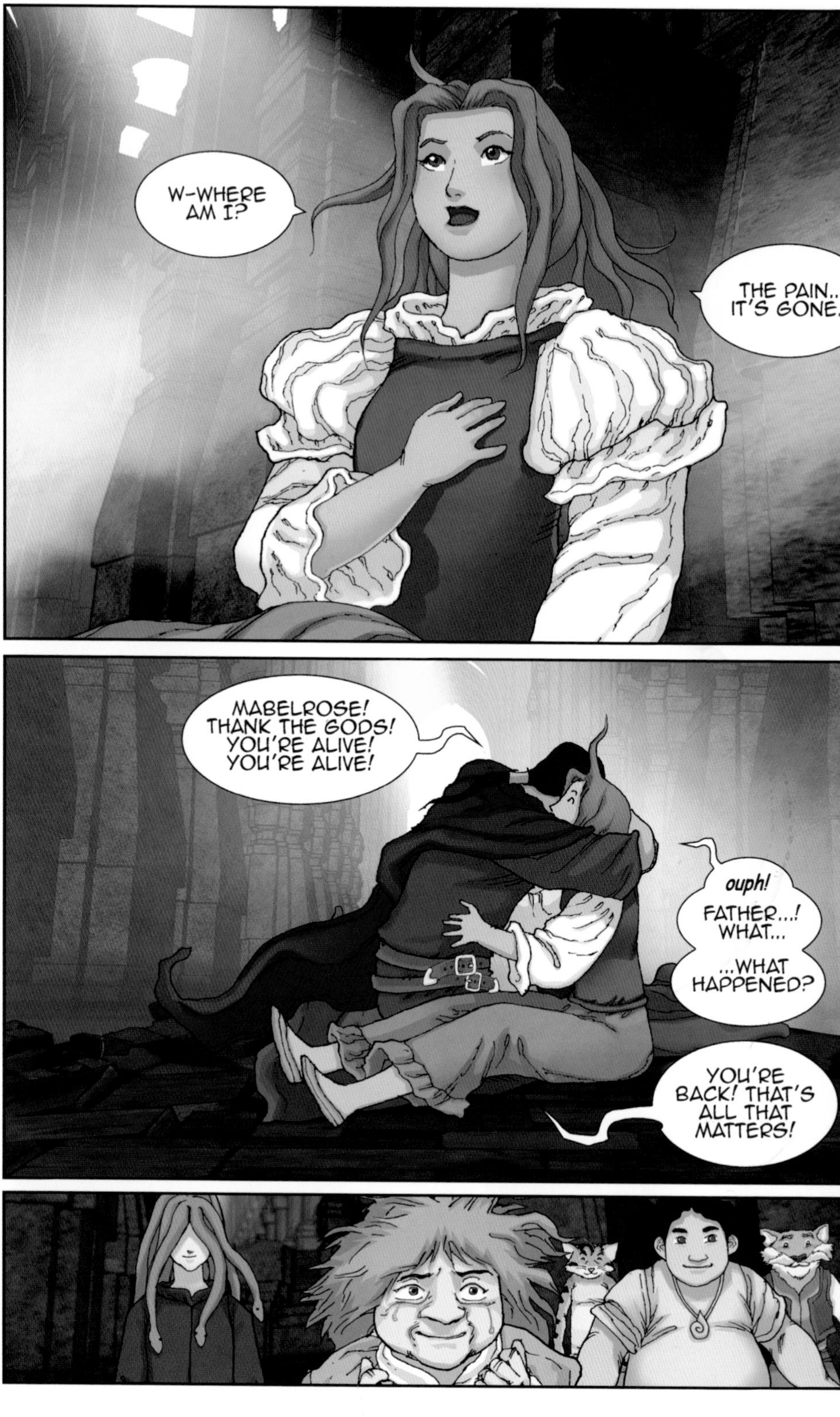
W-WHERE AM I?
THE PAIN... IT'S GONE...
MABELROSE! THANK THE GODS! YOU'RE ALIVE! YOU'RE ALIVE!
ouph!
FATHER...! WHAT...
...WHAT HAPPENED?
YOU'RE BACK! THAT'S ALL THAT MATTERS!

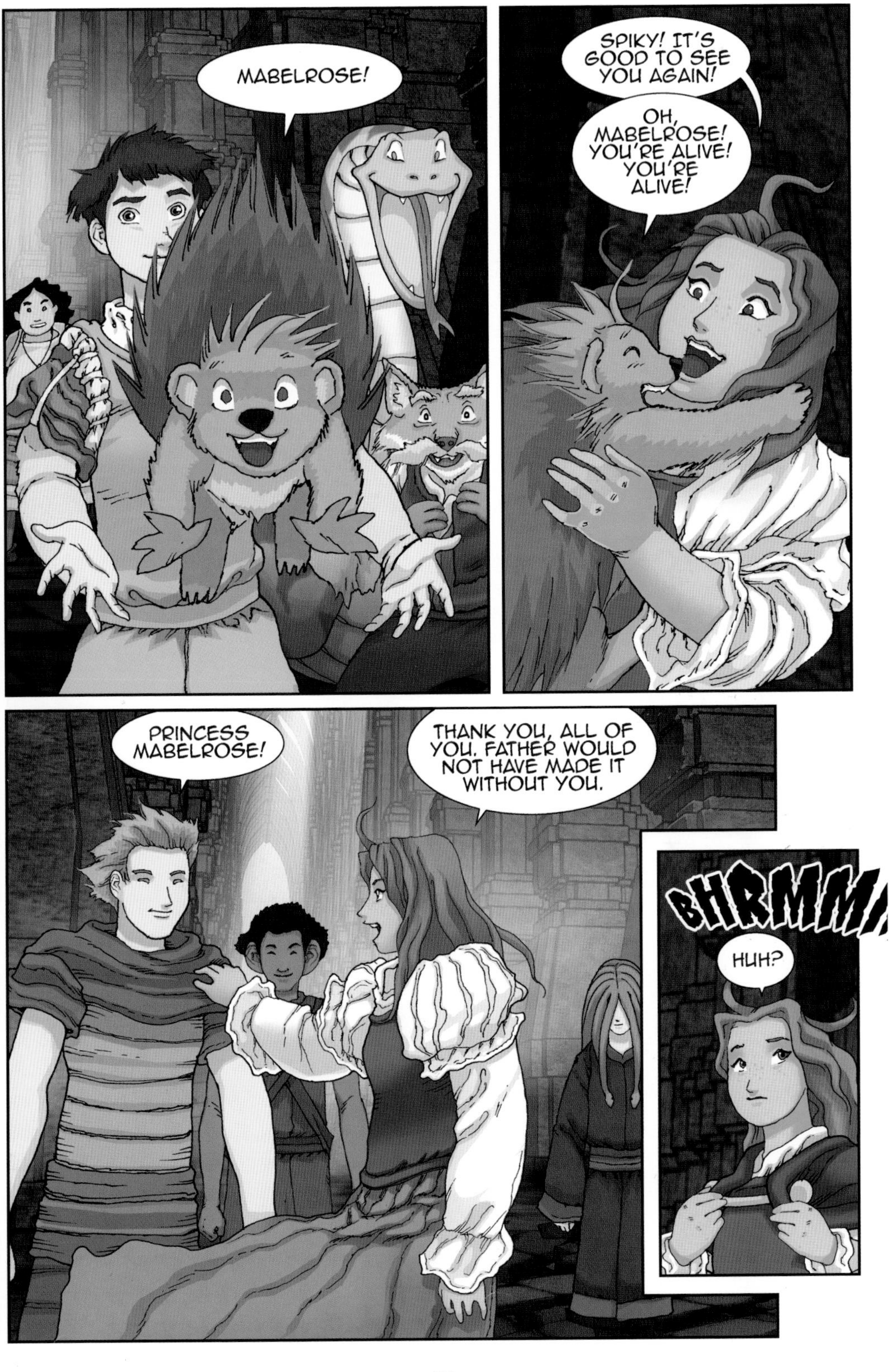
MABELROSE!
SPIKY! IT'S GOOD TO SEE YOU AGAIN!
OH, MABELROSE! YOU'RE ALIVE! YOU'RE ALIVE!
PRINCESS MABELROSE!
THANK YOU, ALL OF YOU. FATHER WOULD NOT HAVE MADE IT WITHOUT YOU.
BHRMMM
HUH?

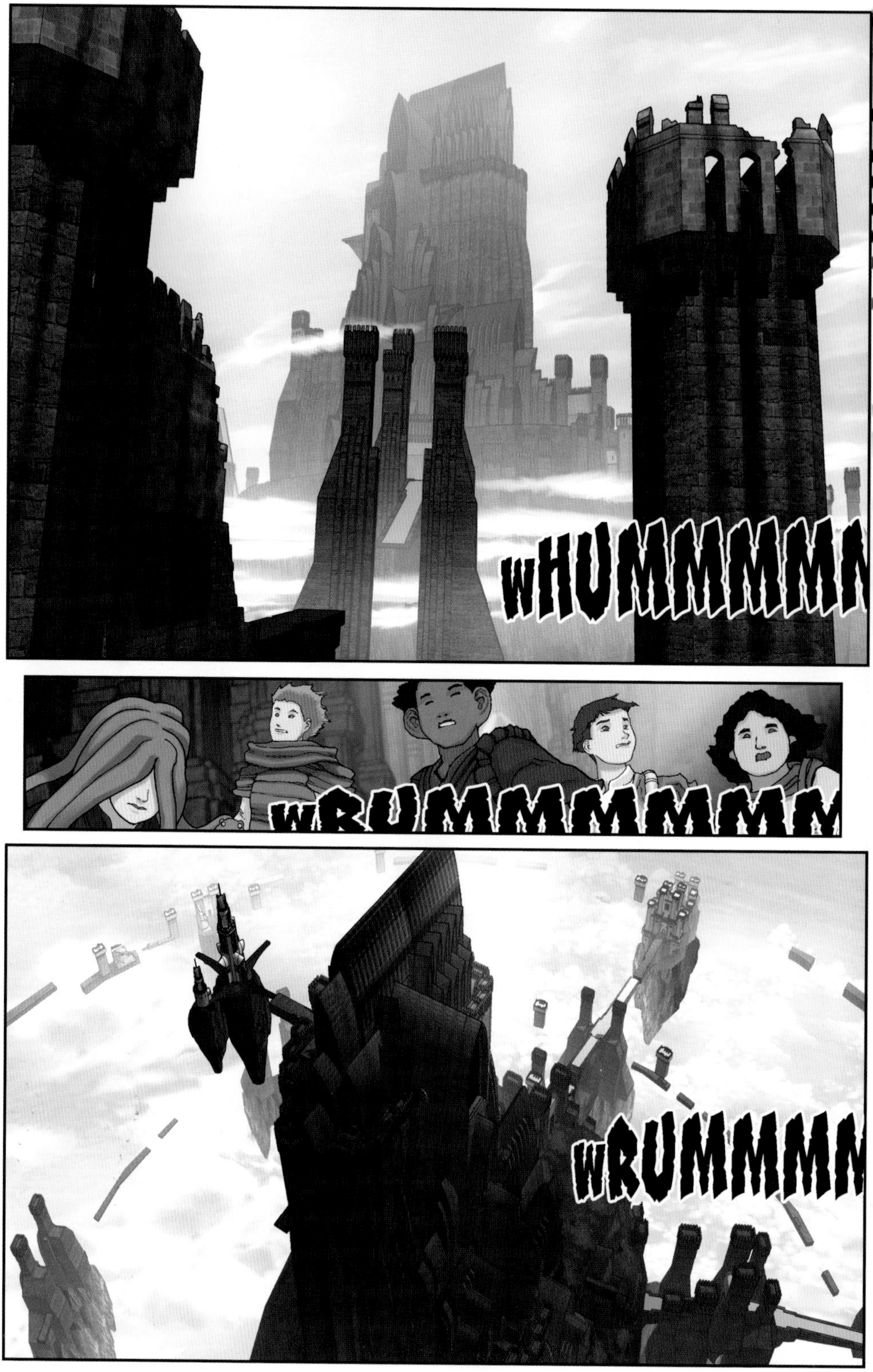
wHUMMMMM
wRUMMMMMMM
wRUMMMM

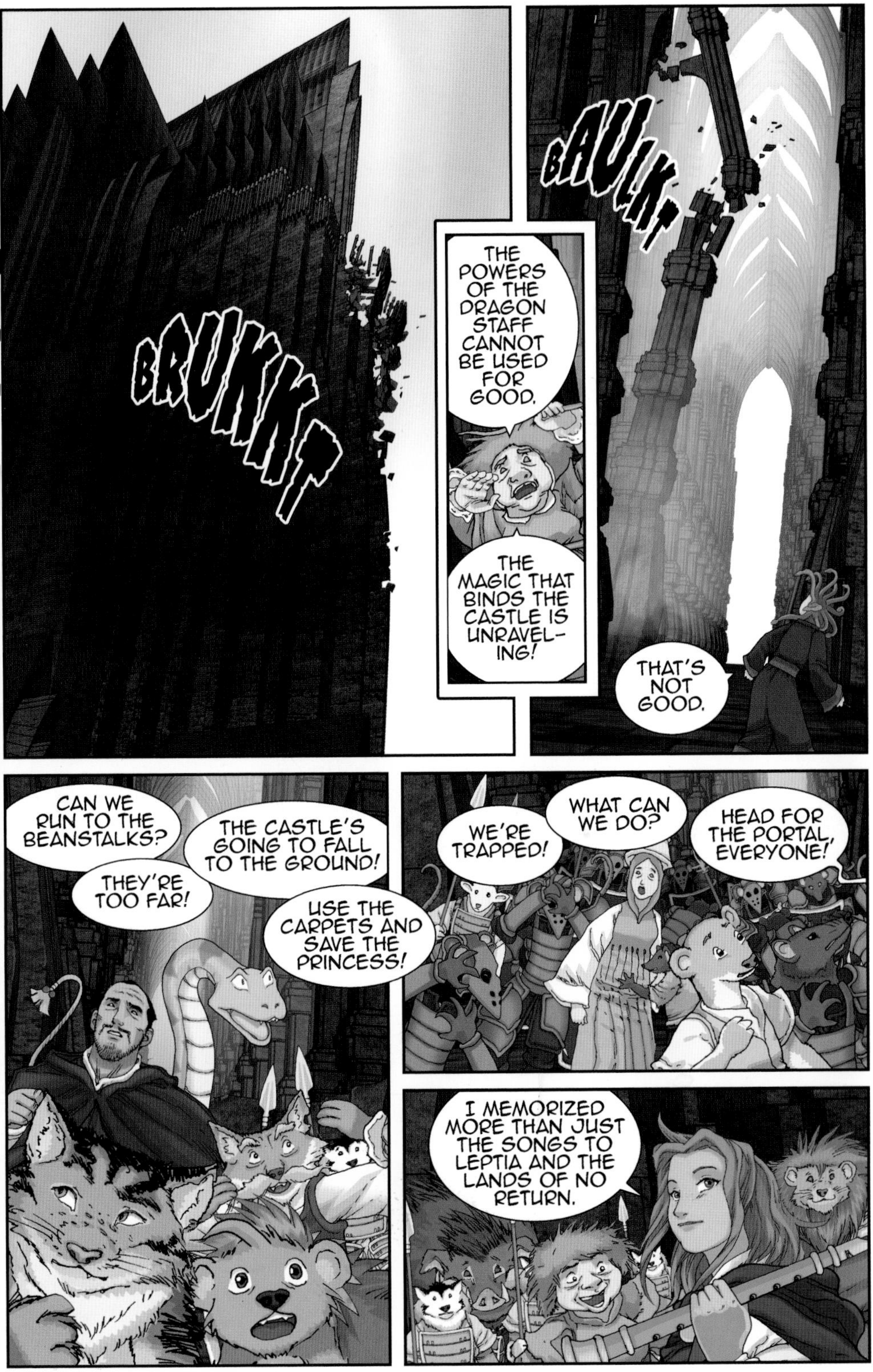
BRUKKT
BAULKT
THE POWERS OF THE DRAGON STAFF CANNOT BE USED FOR GOOD.
THE MAGIC THAT BINDS THE CASTLE IS UNRAVEL-ING!
THAT'S NOT GOOD.
CAN WE RUN TO THE BEANSTALKS?
THE CASTLE'S GOING TO FALL TO THE GROUND!
THEY'RE TOO FAR!
USE THE CARPETS AND SAVE THE PRINCESS!
WE'RE TRAPPED!
WHAT CAN WE DO?
HEAD FOR THE PORTAL, EVERYONE!
I MEMORIZED MORE THAN JUST THE SONGS TO LEPTIA AND THE LANDS OF NO RETURN.

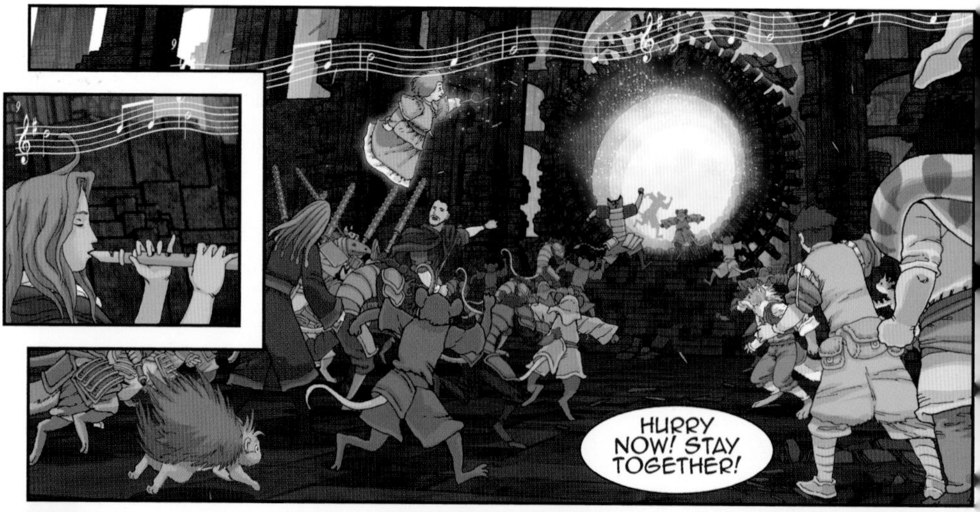
HURRY NOW! STAY TOGETHER!

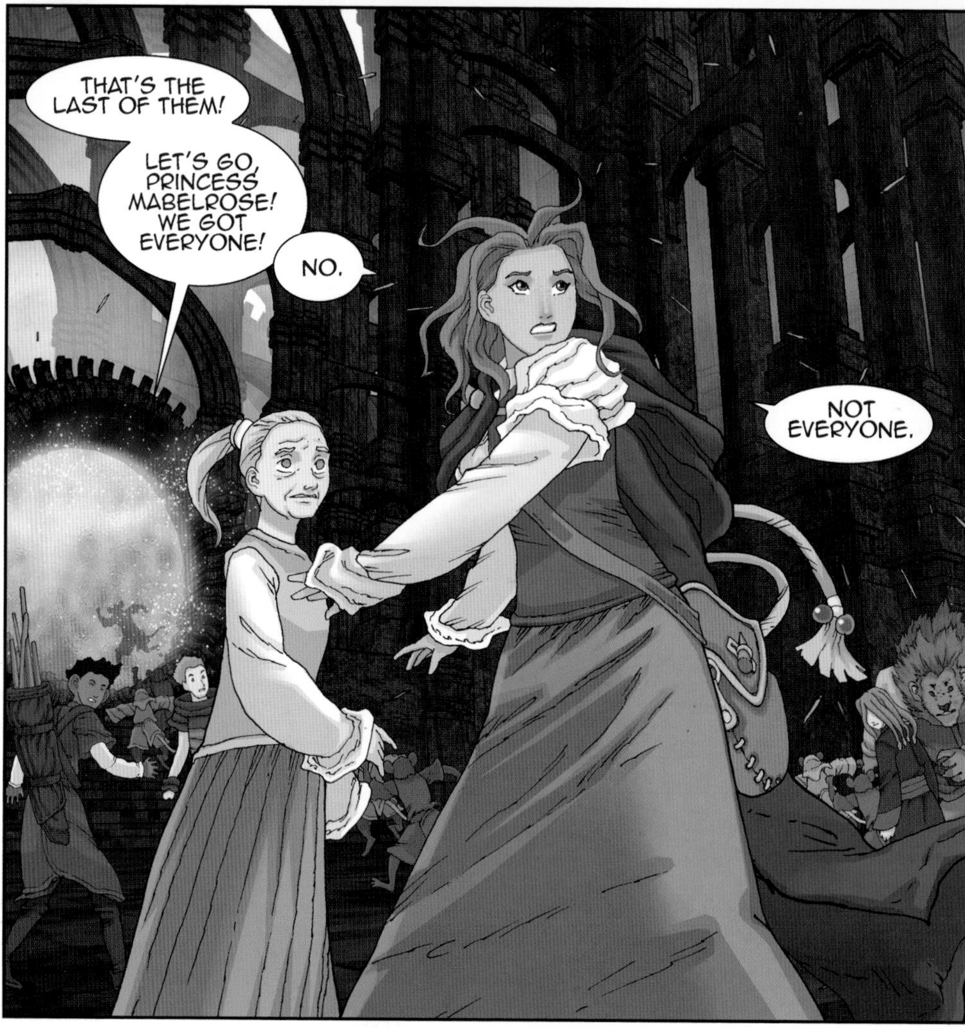
THAT'S THE LAST OF THEM!
LET'S GO, PRINCESS MABELROSE! WE GOT EVERYONE!
NO.
NOT EVERYONE.

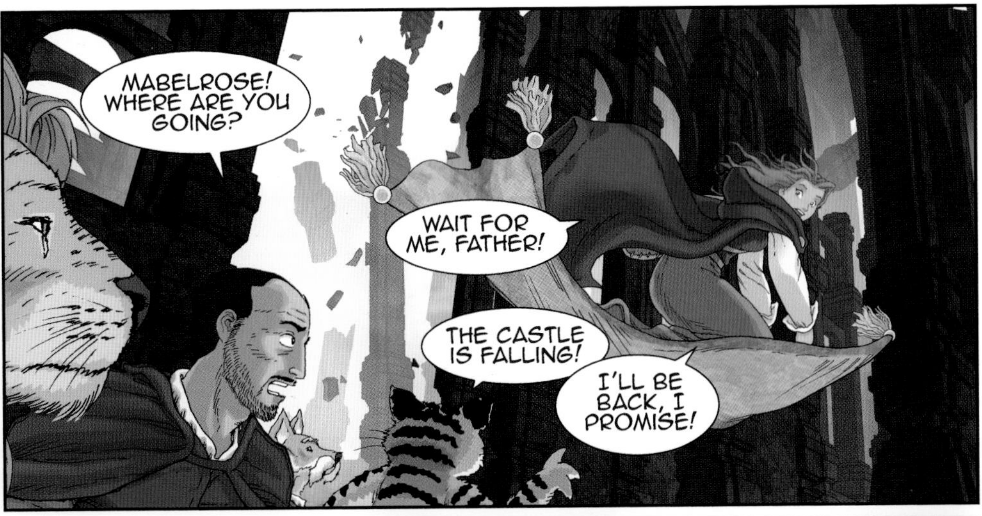
MABELROSE! WHERE ARE YOU GOING?
WAIT FOR ME, FATHER!
THE CASTLE IS FALLING!
I'LL BE BACK, I PROMISE!

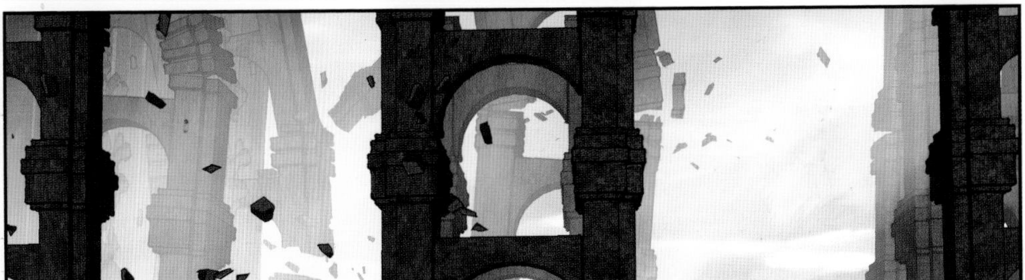

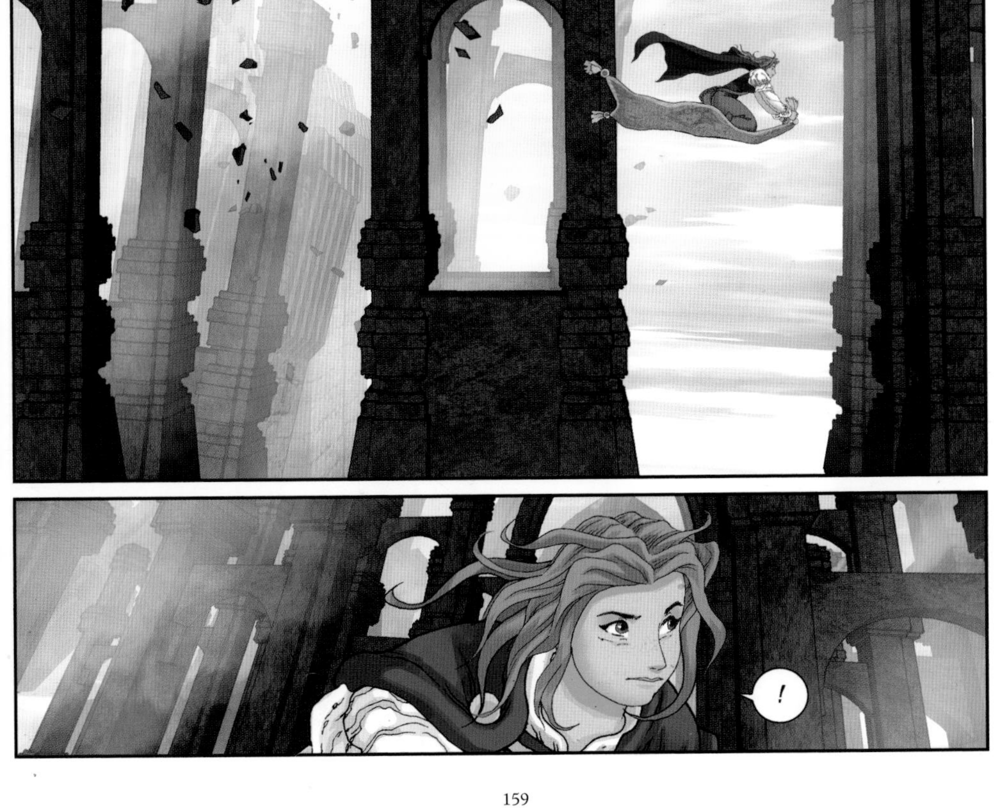
!

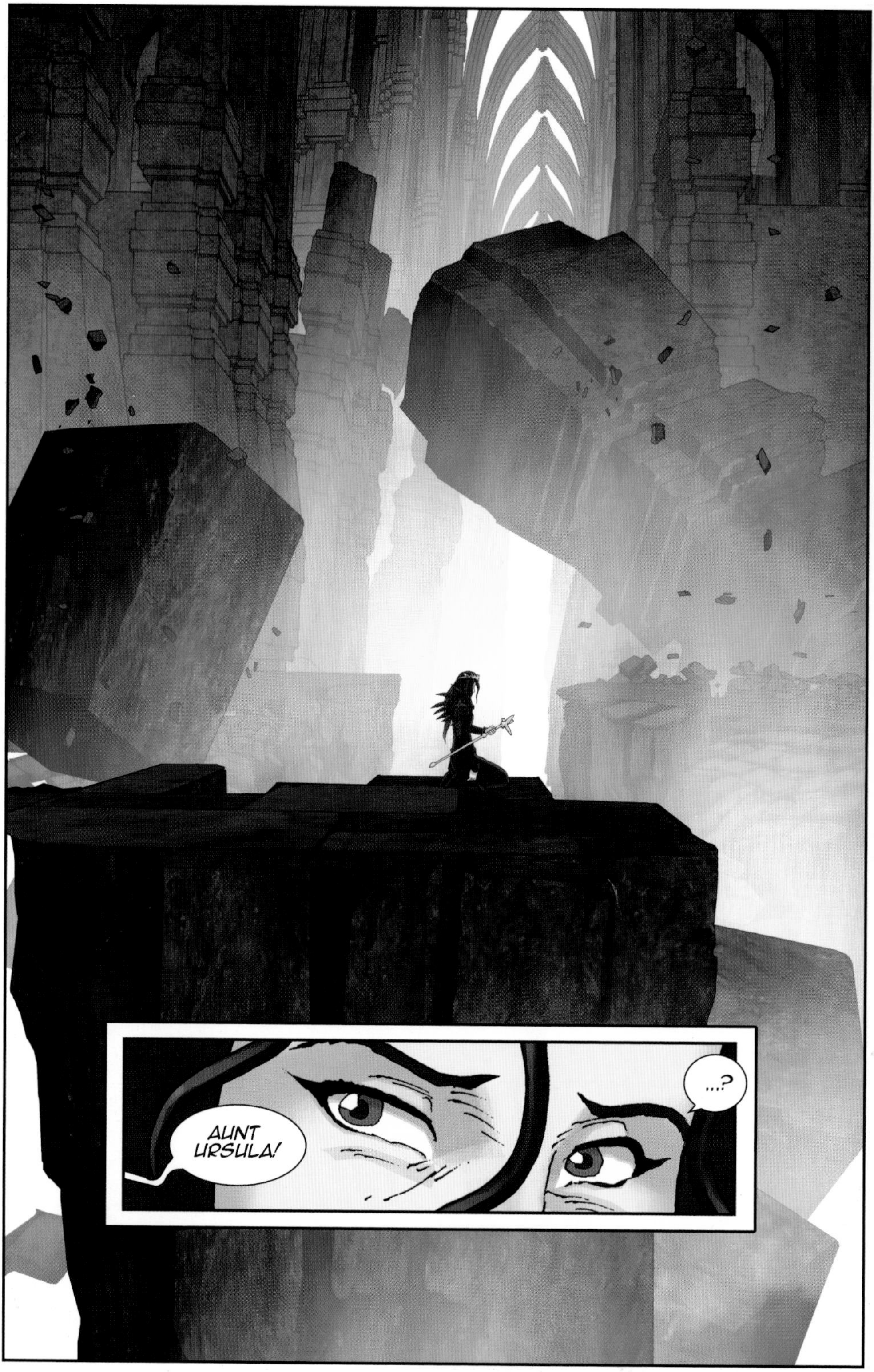
AUNT URSULA!
...?

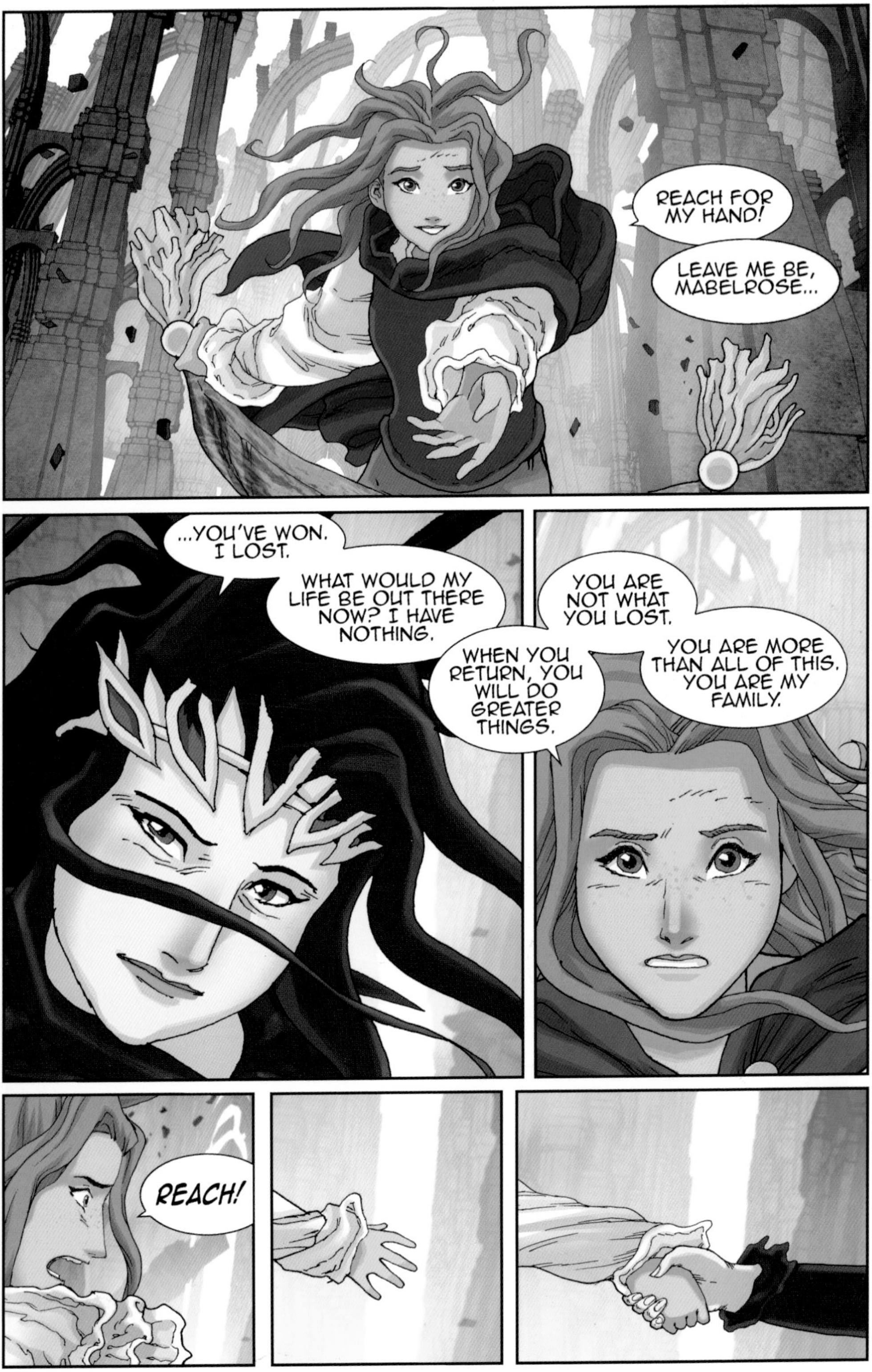
REACH FOR MY HAND!
LEAVE ME BE, MABELROSE...
...YOU'VE WON. I LOST.
WHAT WOULD MY LIFE BE OUT THERE NOW? I HAVE NOTHING.
YOU ARE NOT WHAT YOU LOST.
YOU ARE MORE THAN ALL OF THIS. YOU ARE MY FAMILY.
WHEN YOU RETURN, YOU WILL DO GREATER THINGS.
REACH!

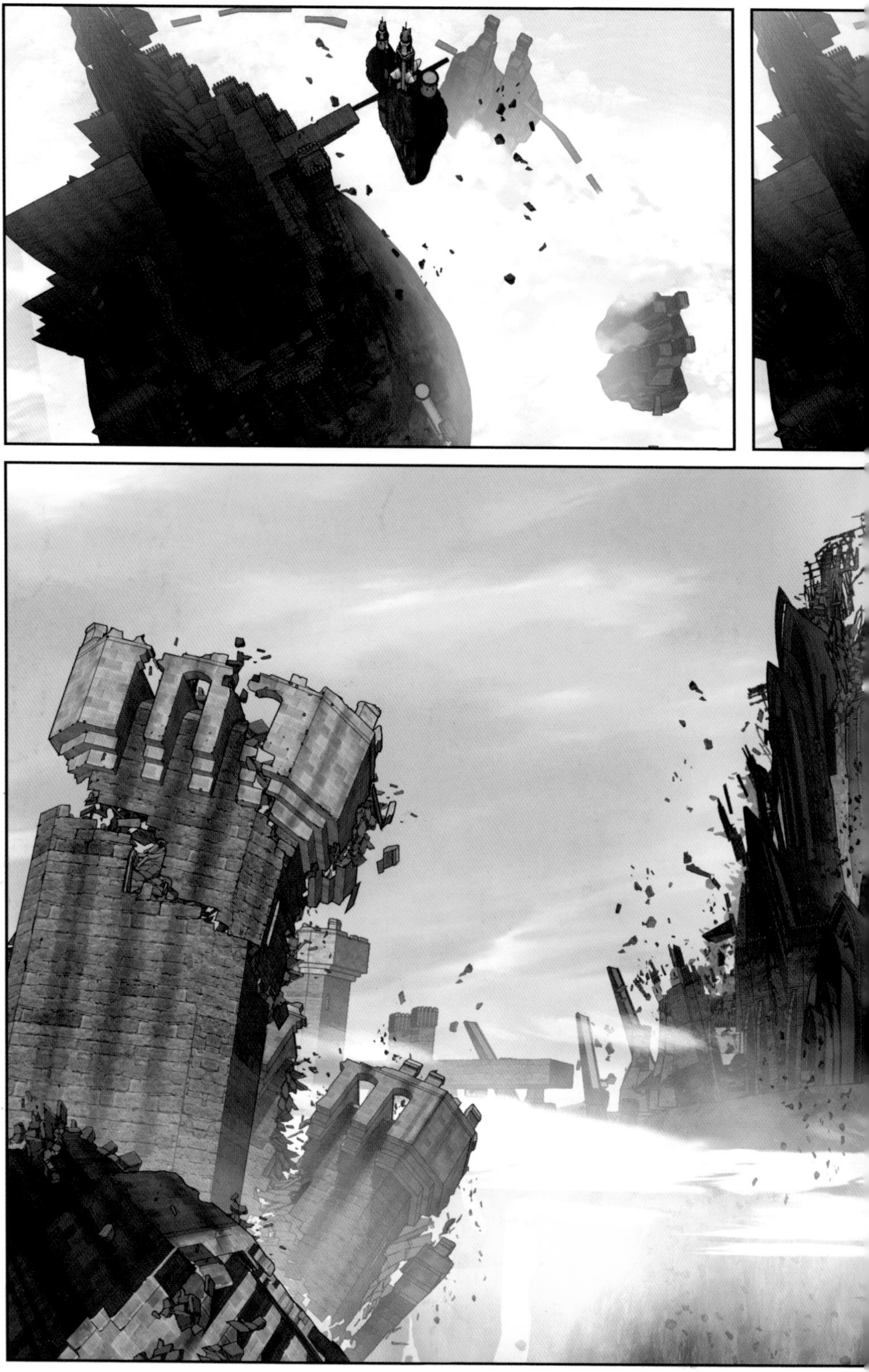

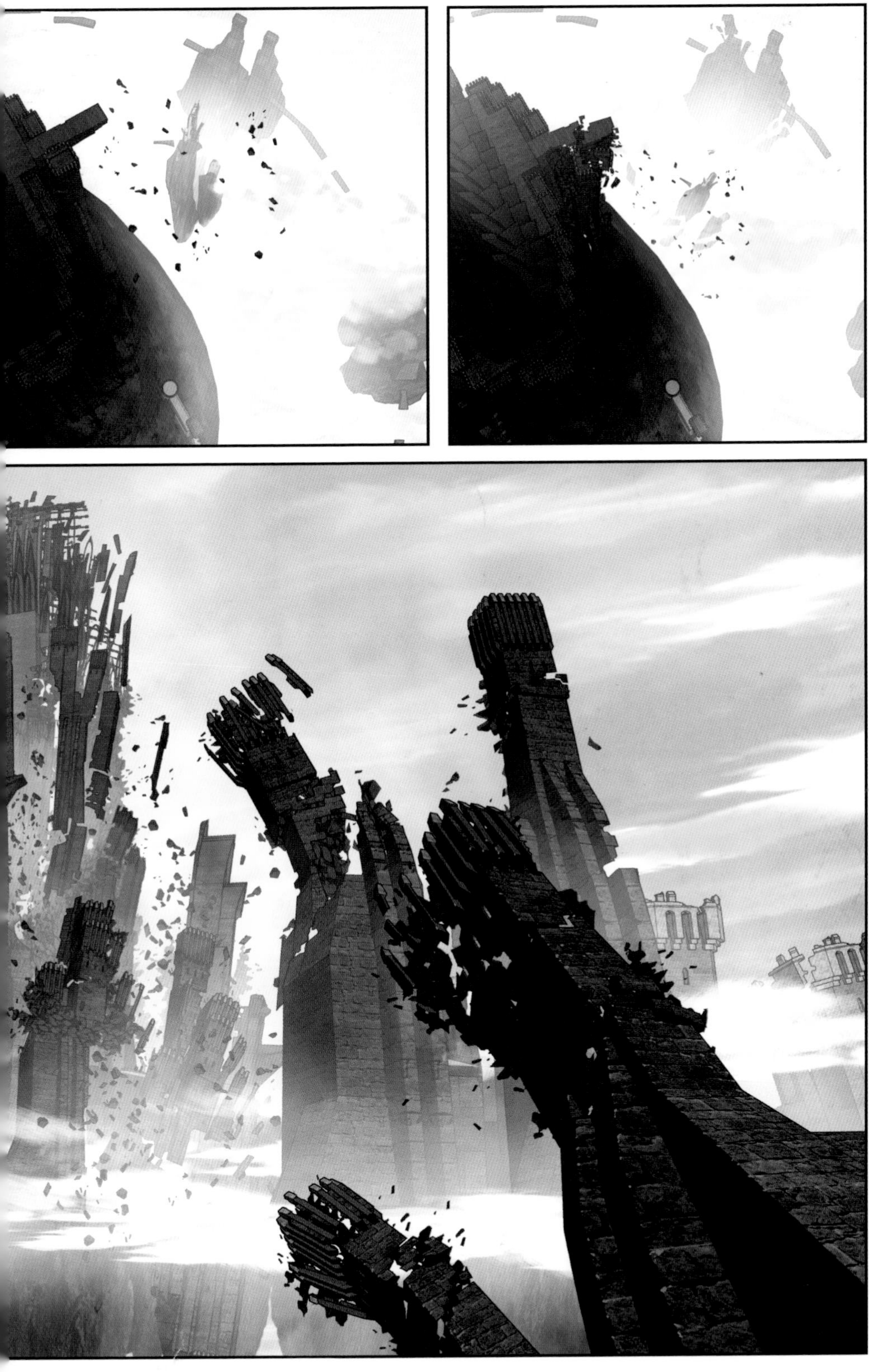

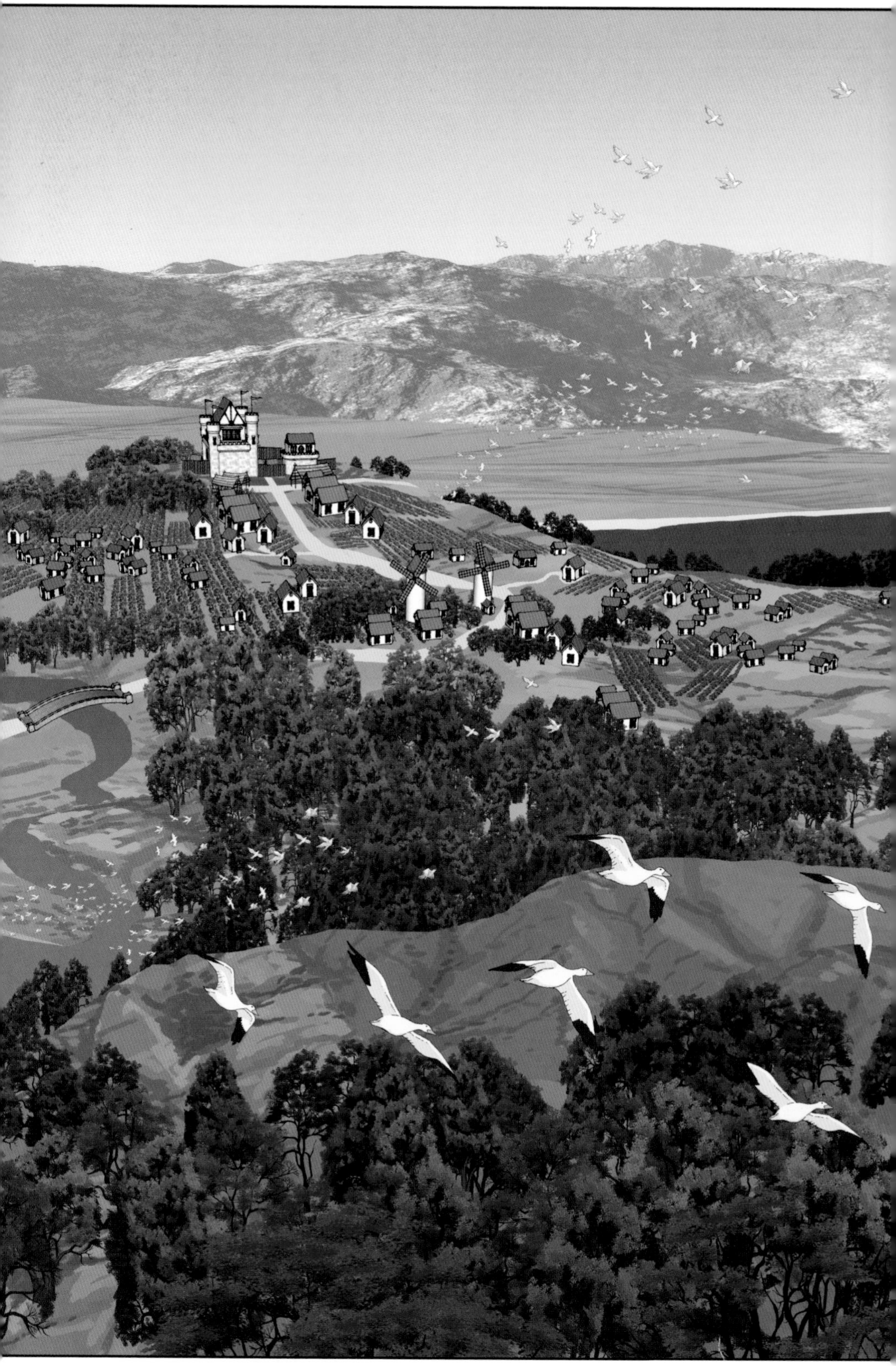

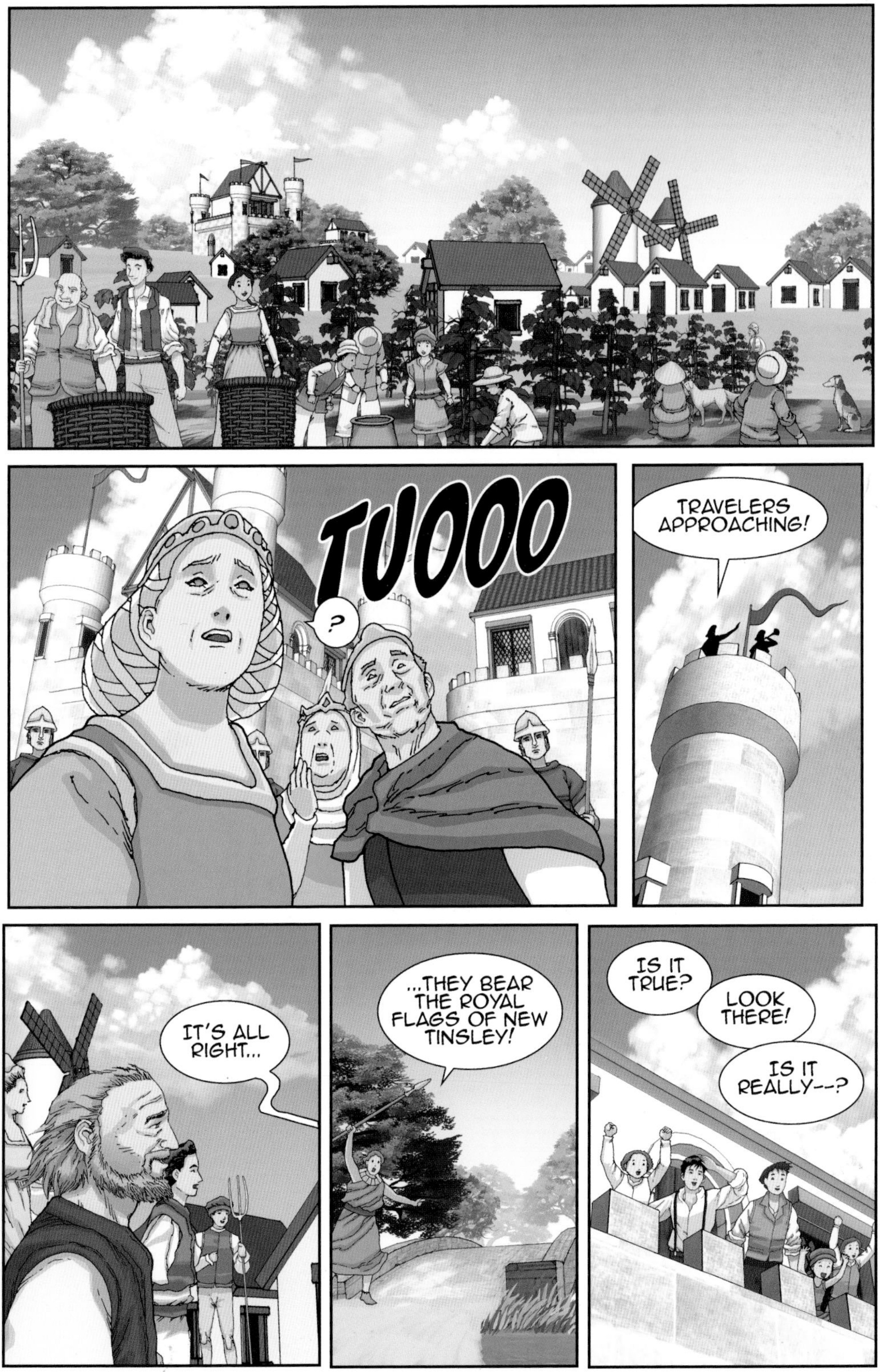
TUOOO
?
TRAVELERS APPROACHING!
IT'S ALL RIGHT...
...THEY BEAR THE ROYAL FLAGS OF NEW TINSLEY!
IS IT TRUE?
LOOK THERE!
IS IT REALLY--?

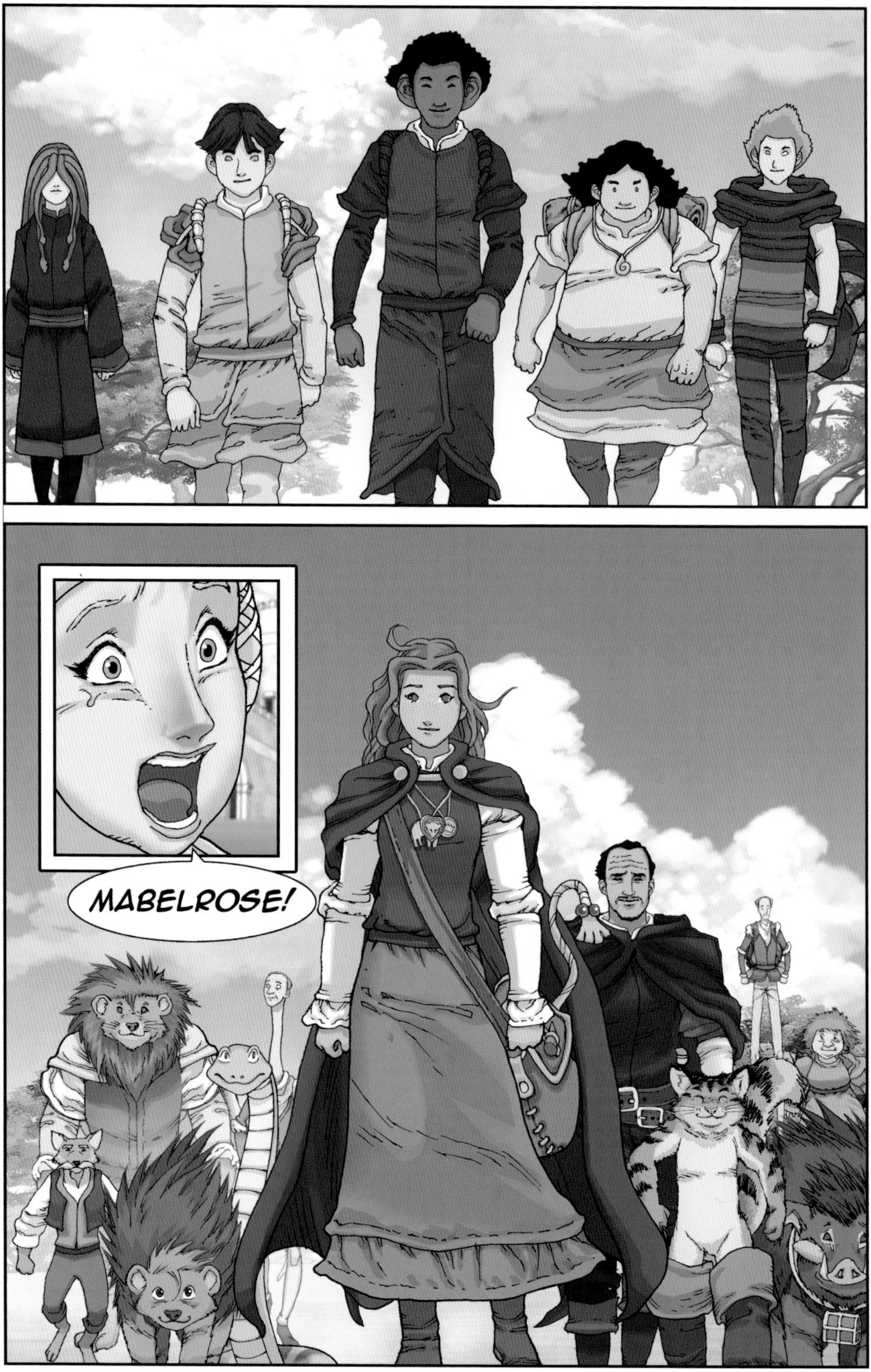
MABELROSE!

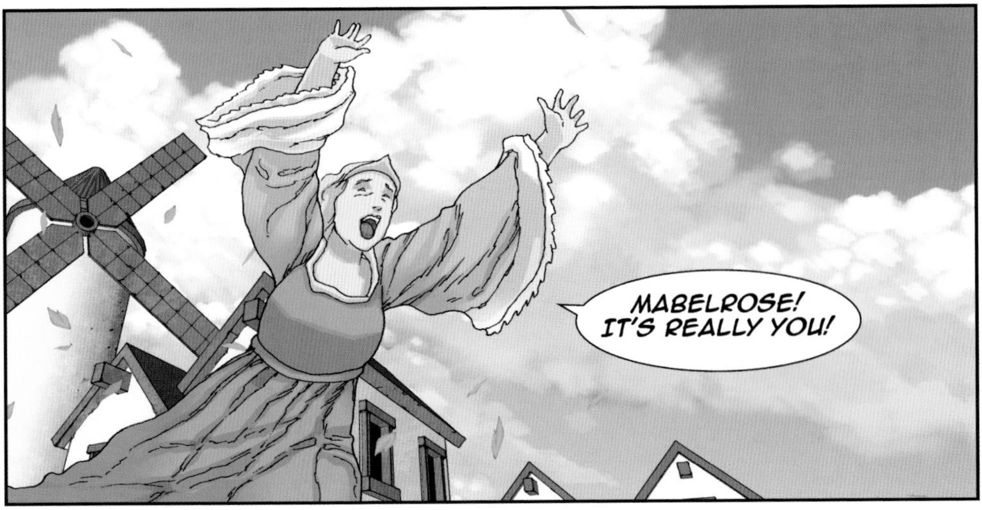
MABELROSE!
IT'S REALLY YOU!

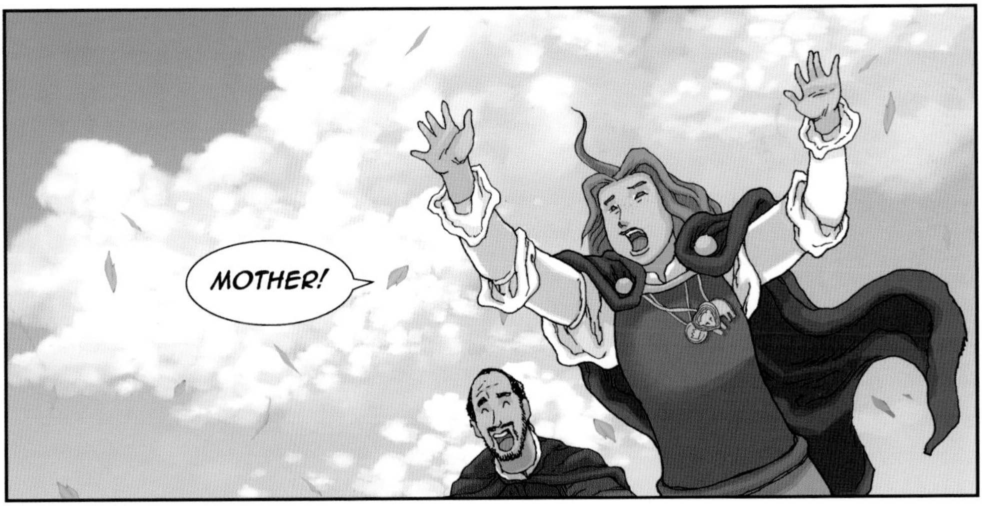
MOTHER!

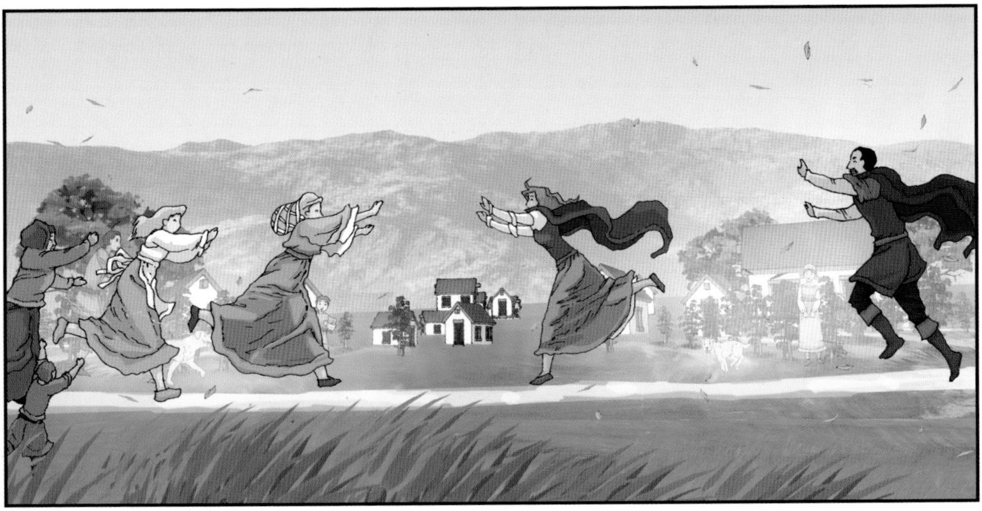

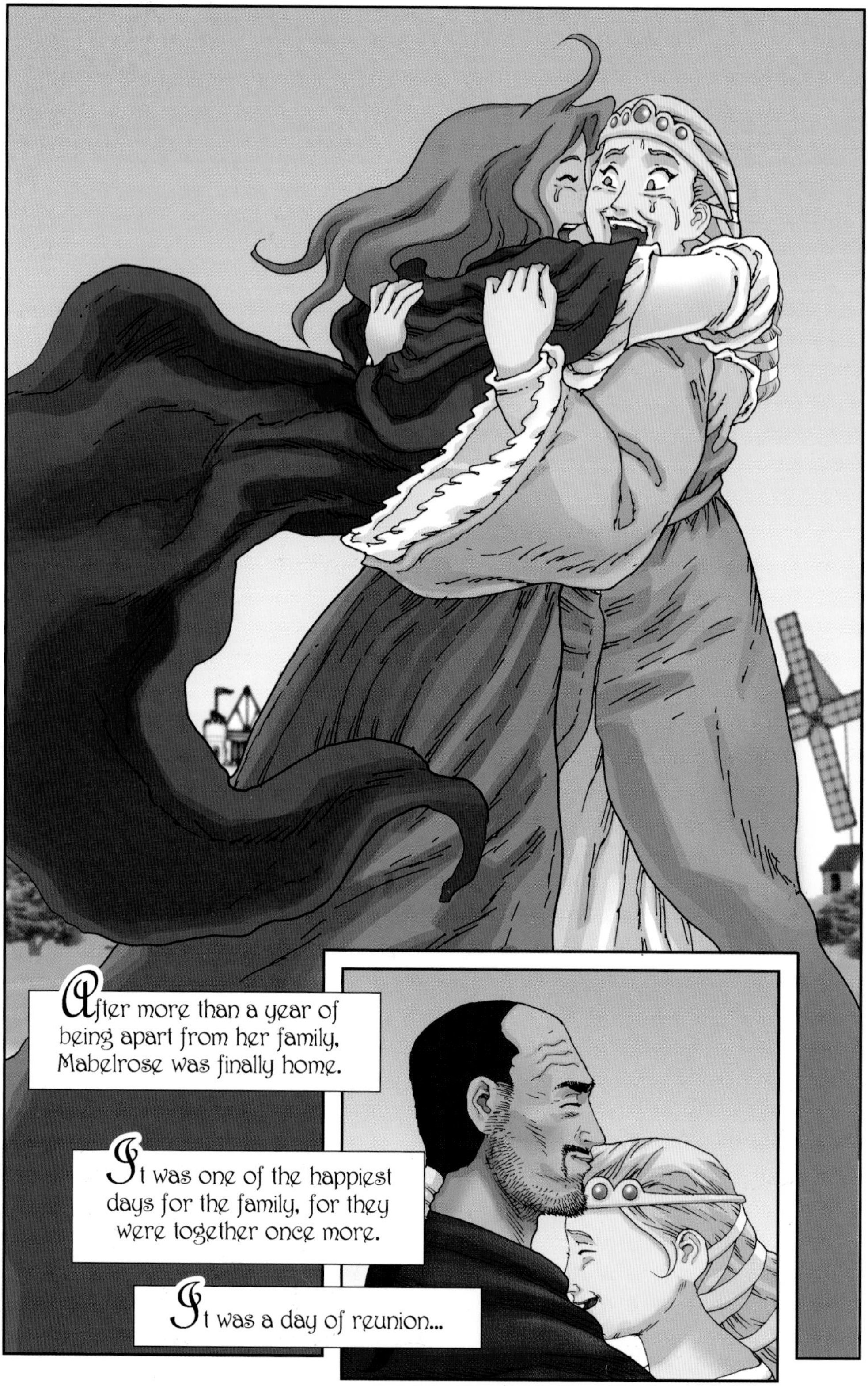
After more than a year of being apart from her family, Mabelrose was finally home.
It was one of the happiest days for the family, for they were together once more.
It was a day of reunion...

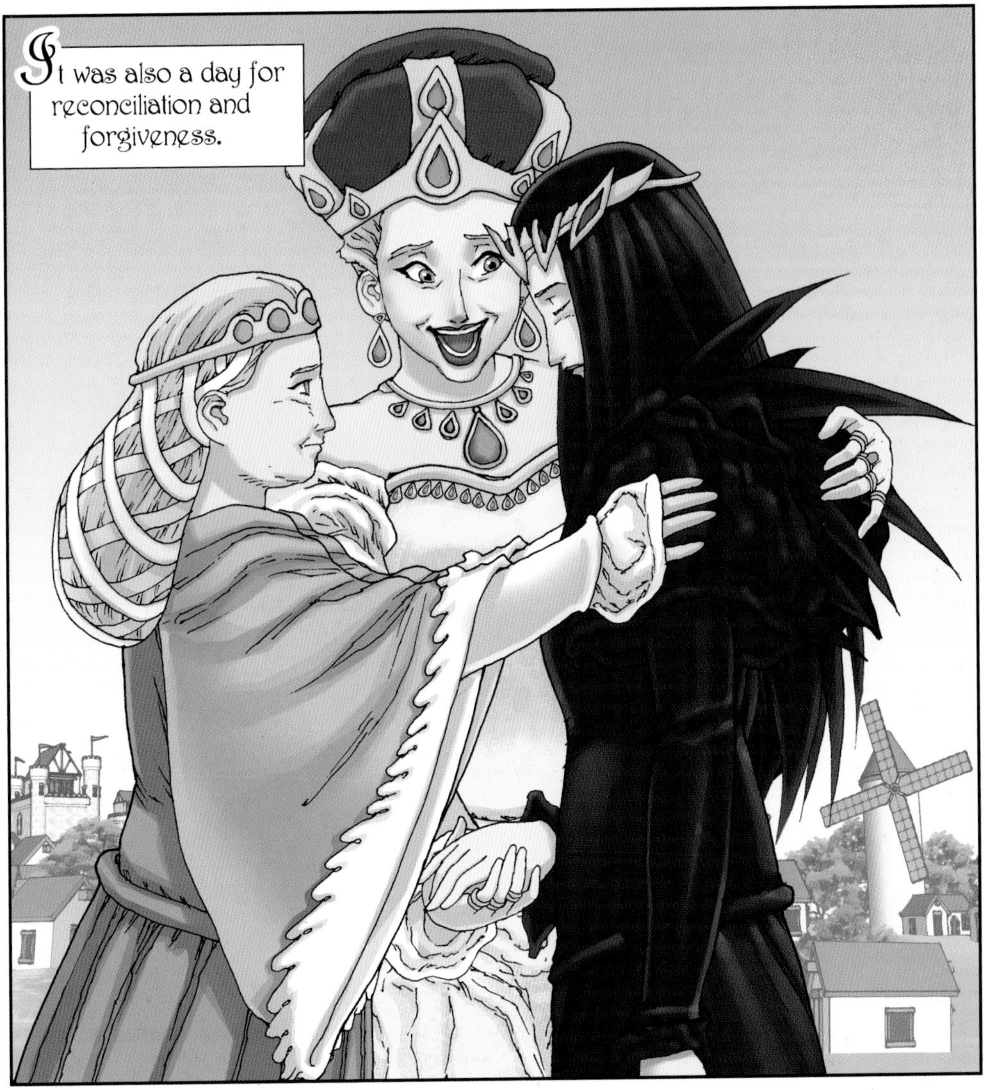
It was also a day for reconciliation and forgiveness.

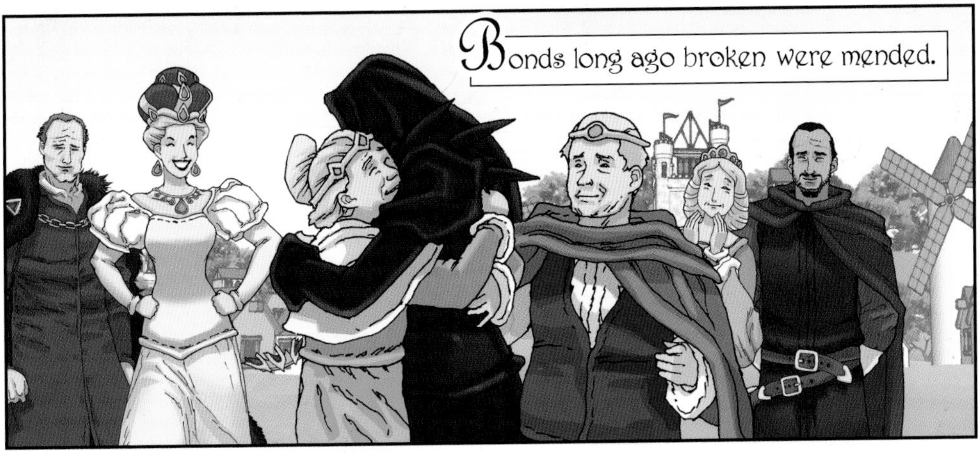
Bonds long ago broken were mended.

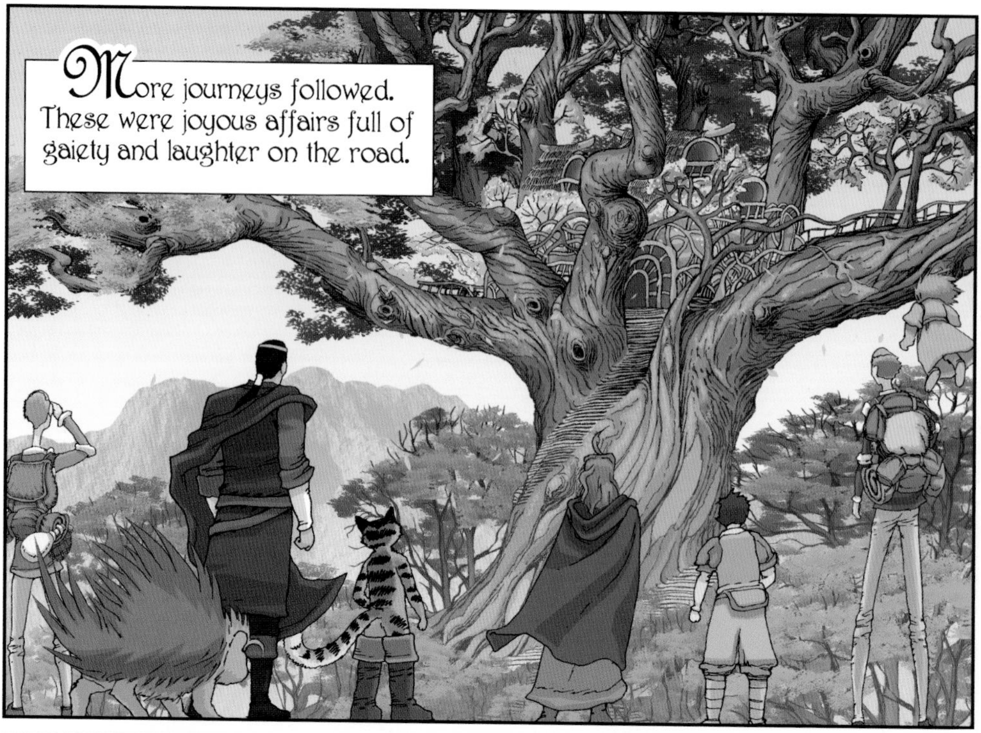
More journeys followed. These were joyous affairs full of gaiety and laughter on the road.

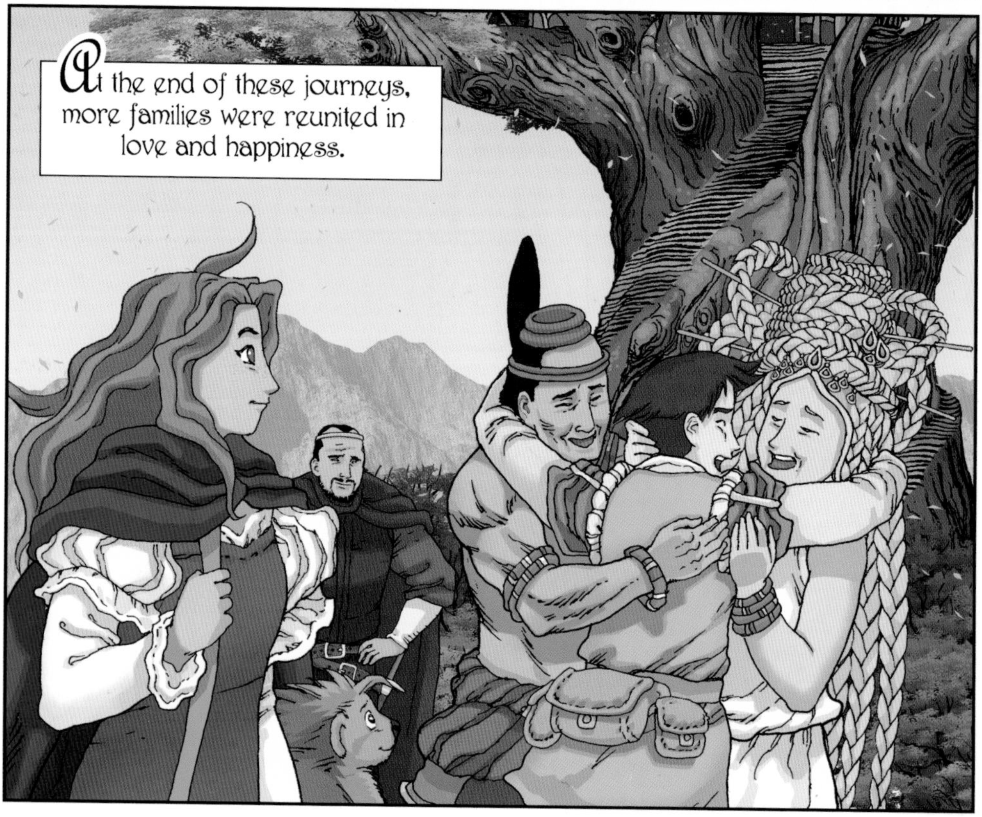
At the end of these journeys, more families were reunited in love and happiness.

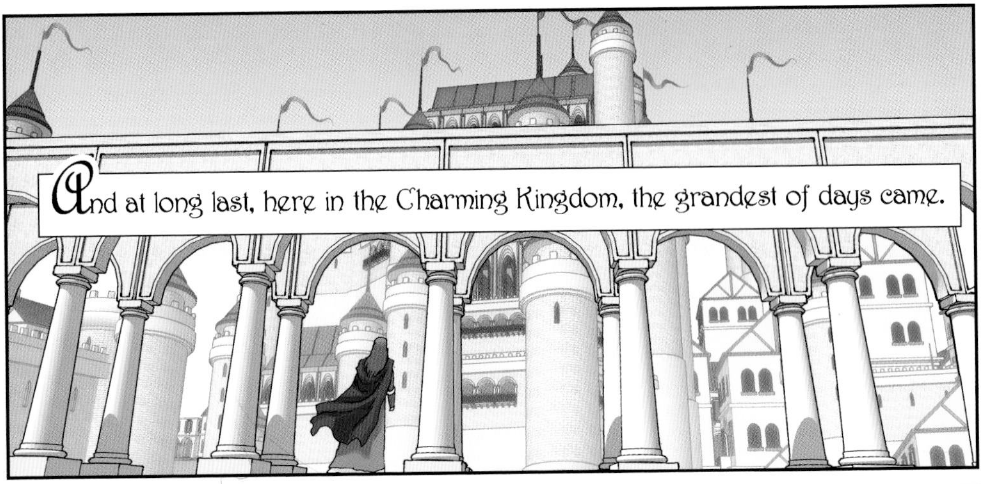
And at long last, here in the Charming Kingdom, the grandest of days came.

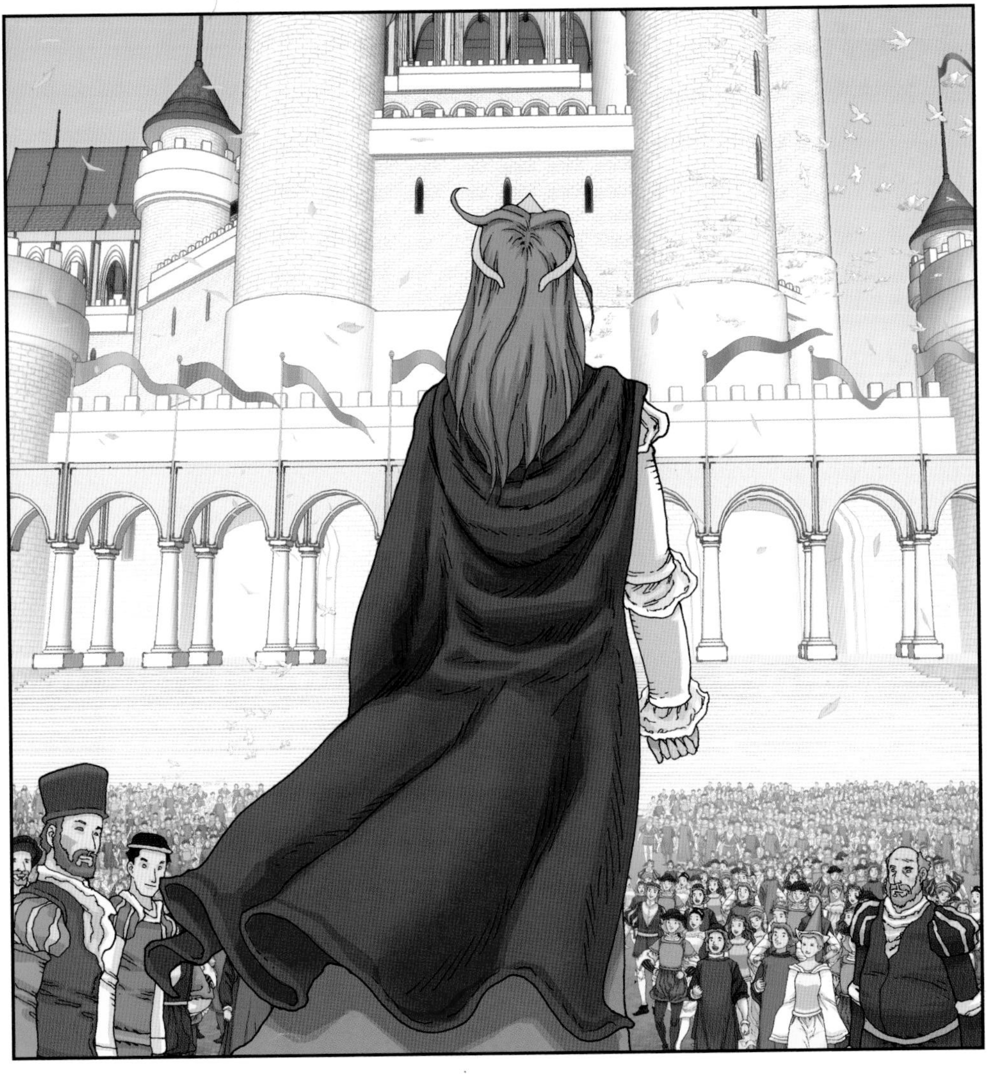

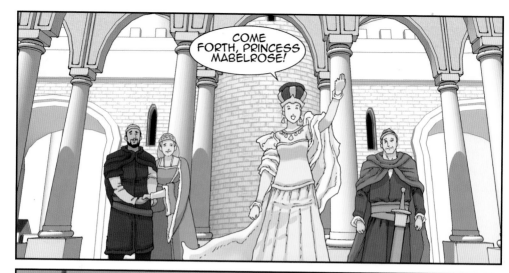

COME FORTH, PRINCESS MABELROSE!

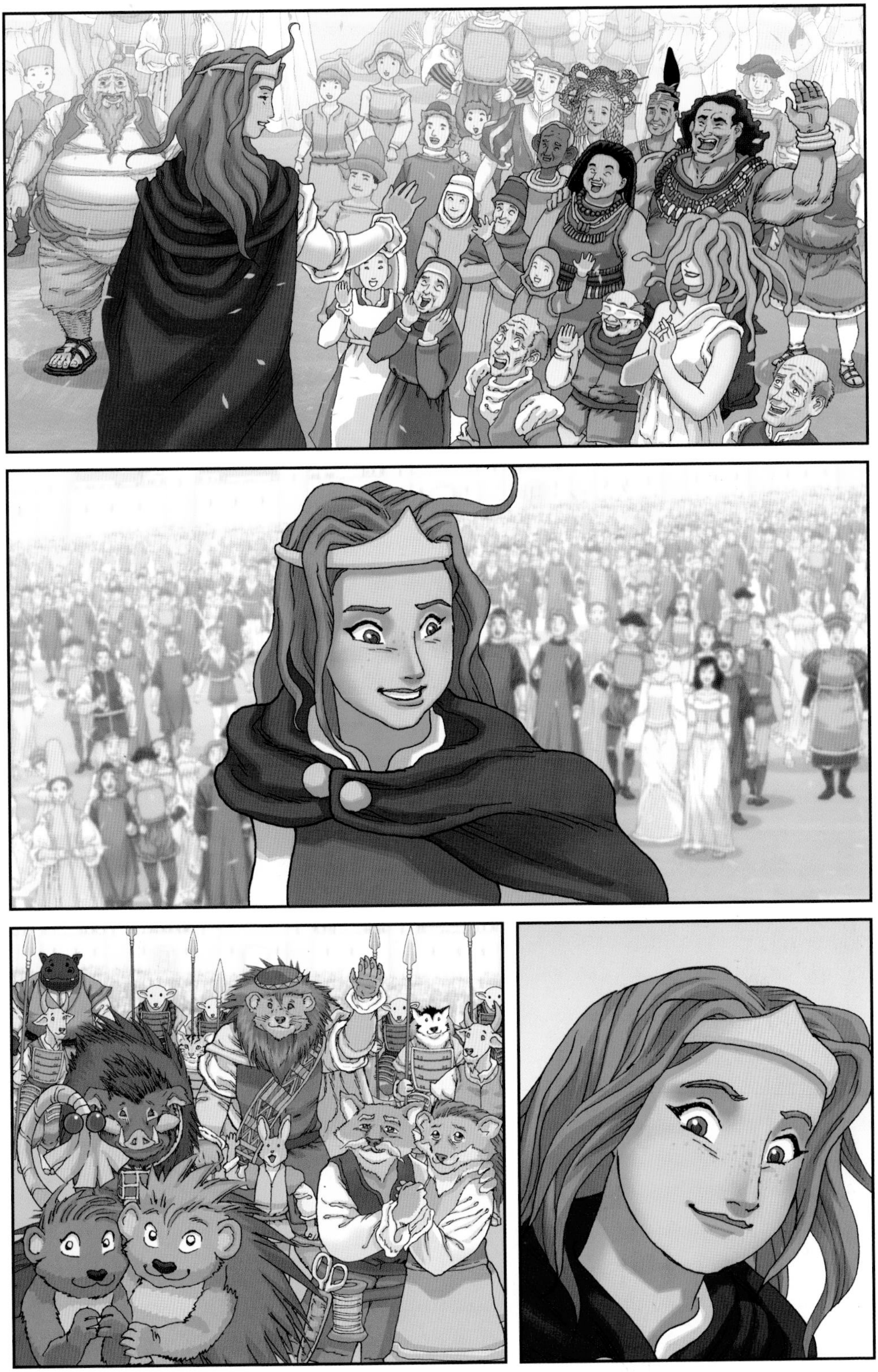

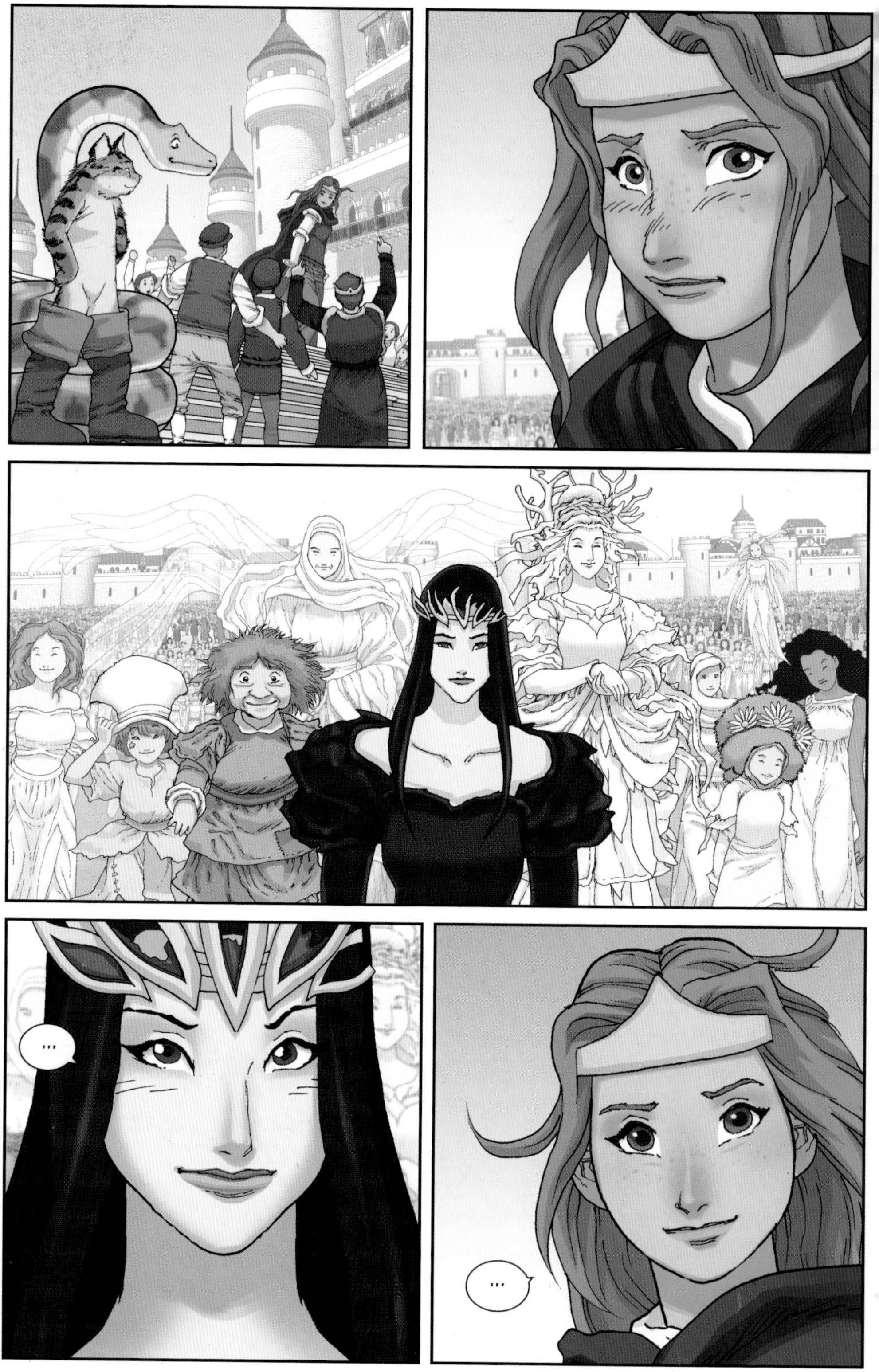
...
...

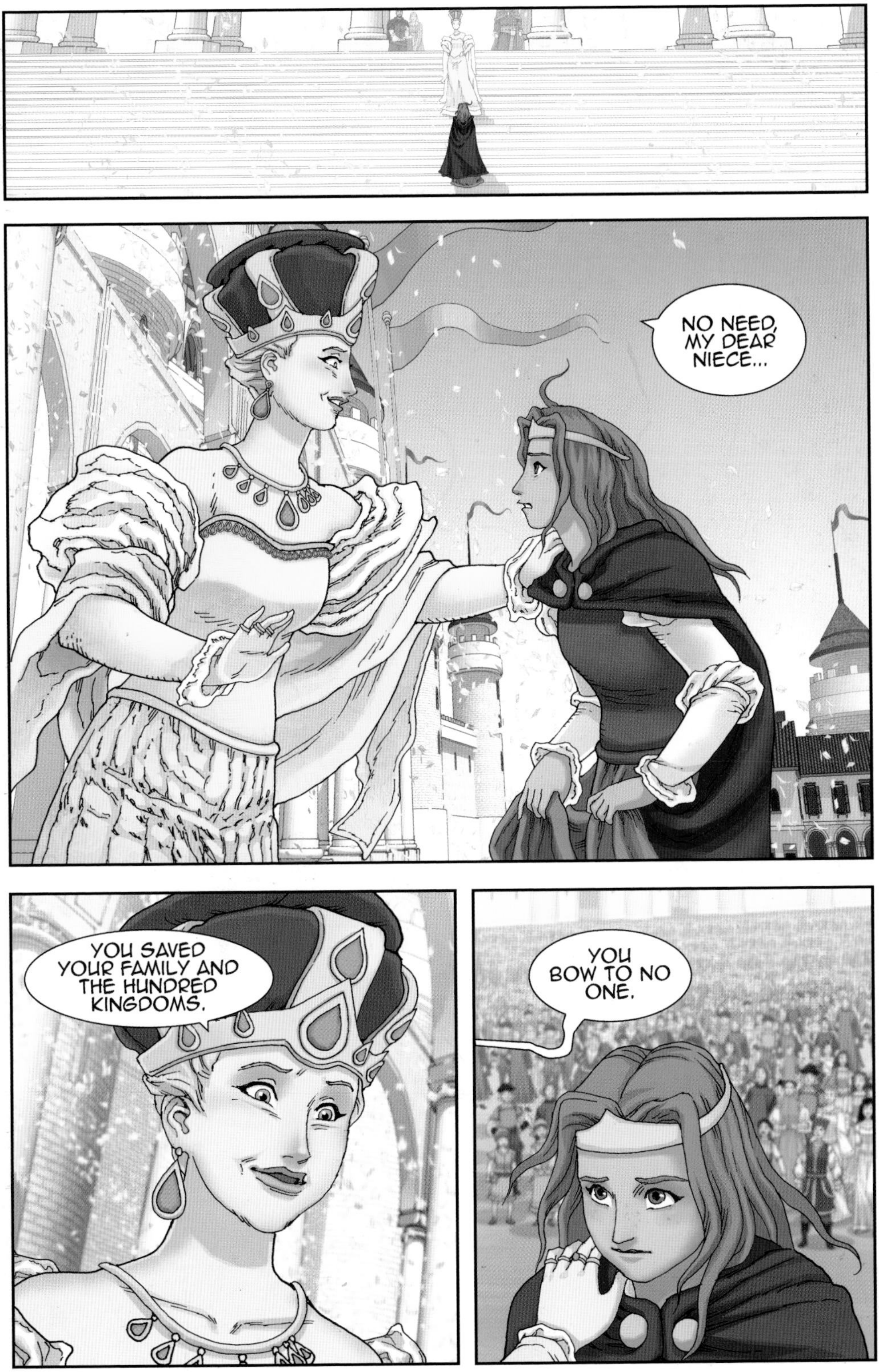
NO NEED, MY DEAR NIECE...
YOU SAVED YOUR FAMILY AND THE HUNDRED KINGDOMS.
YOU BOW TO NO ONE.

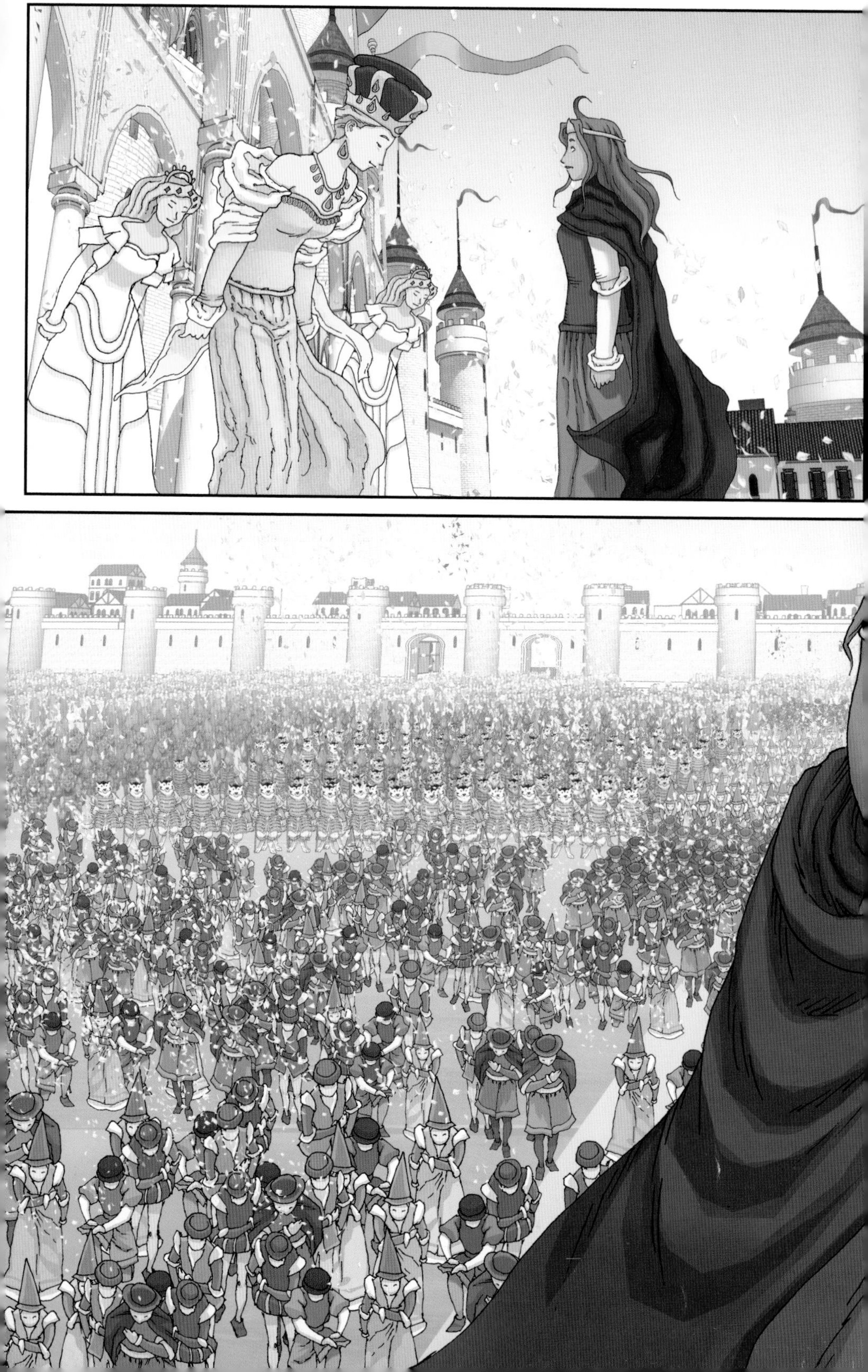

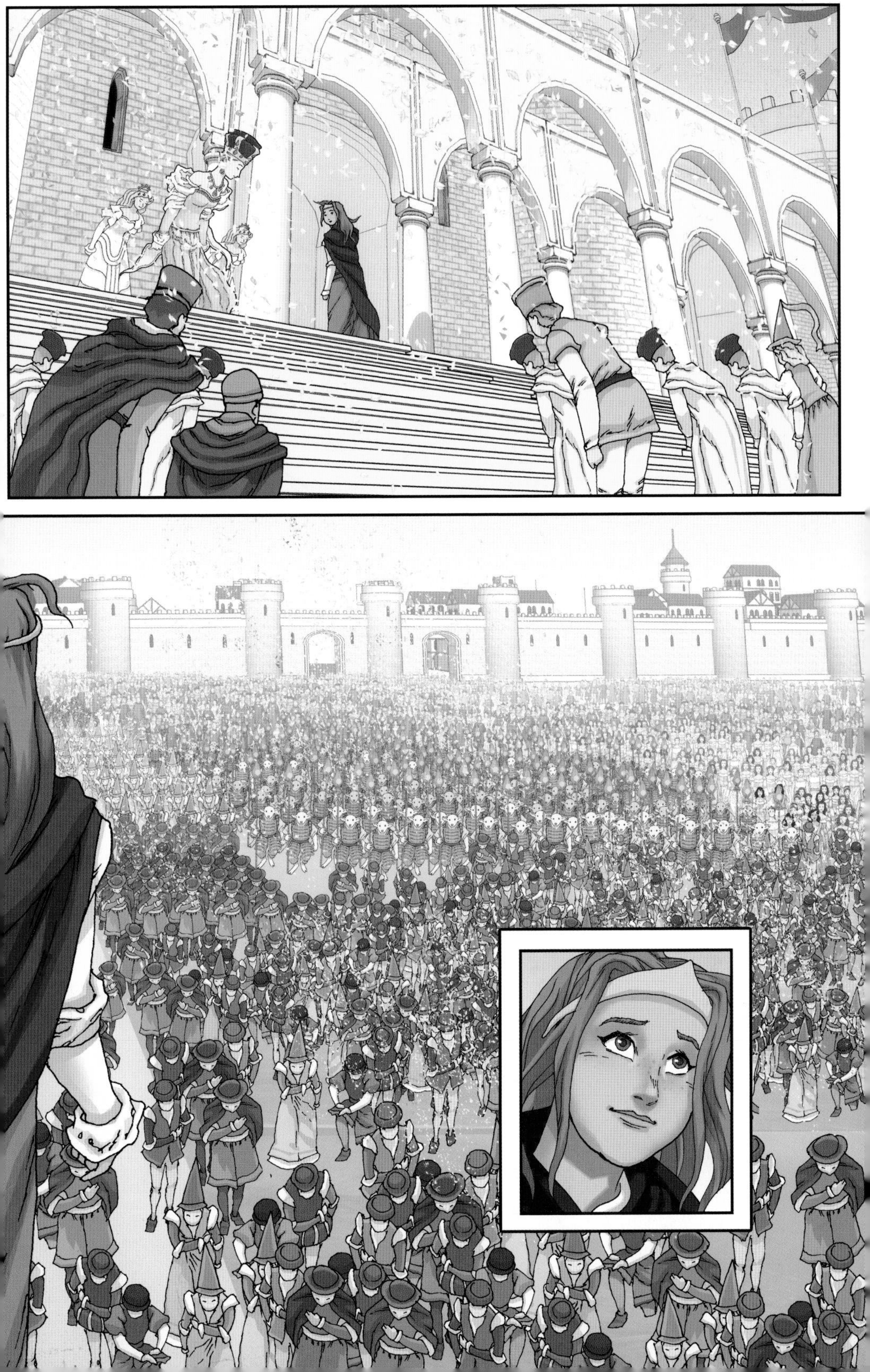

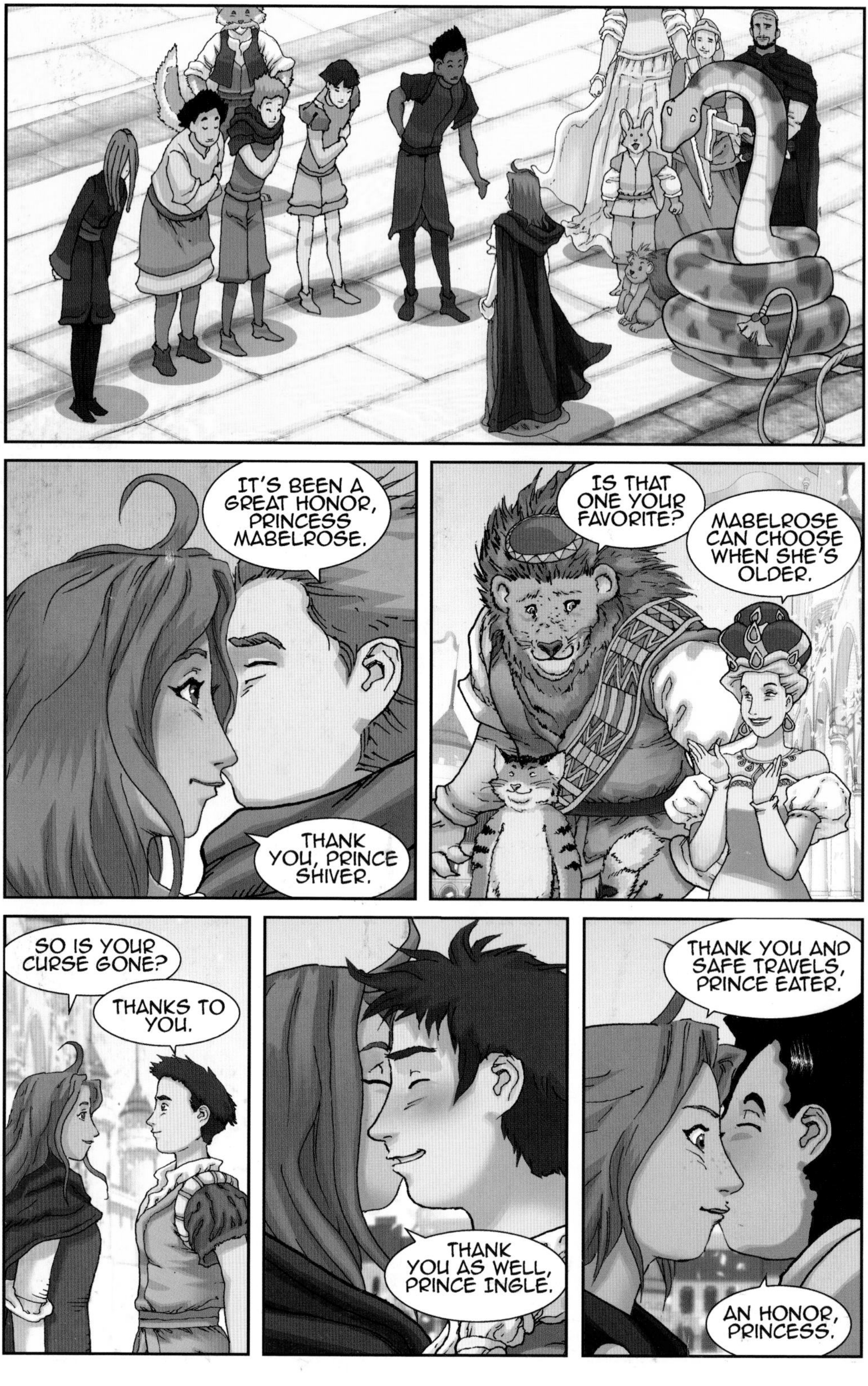

IT'S BEEN A GREAT HONOR, PRINCESS MABELROSE.
THANK YOU, PRINCE SHIVER.
IS THAT ONE YOUR FAVORITE?
MABELROSE CAN CHOOSE WHEN SHE'S OLDER.
SO IS YOUR CURSE GONE?
THANKS TO YOU.
THANK YOU AS WELL, PRINCE INGLE.
THANK YOU AND SAFE TRAVELS, PRINCE EATER.
AN HONOR, PRINCESS.

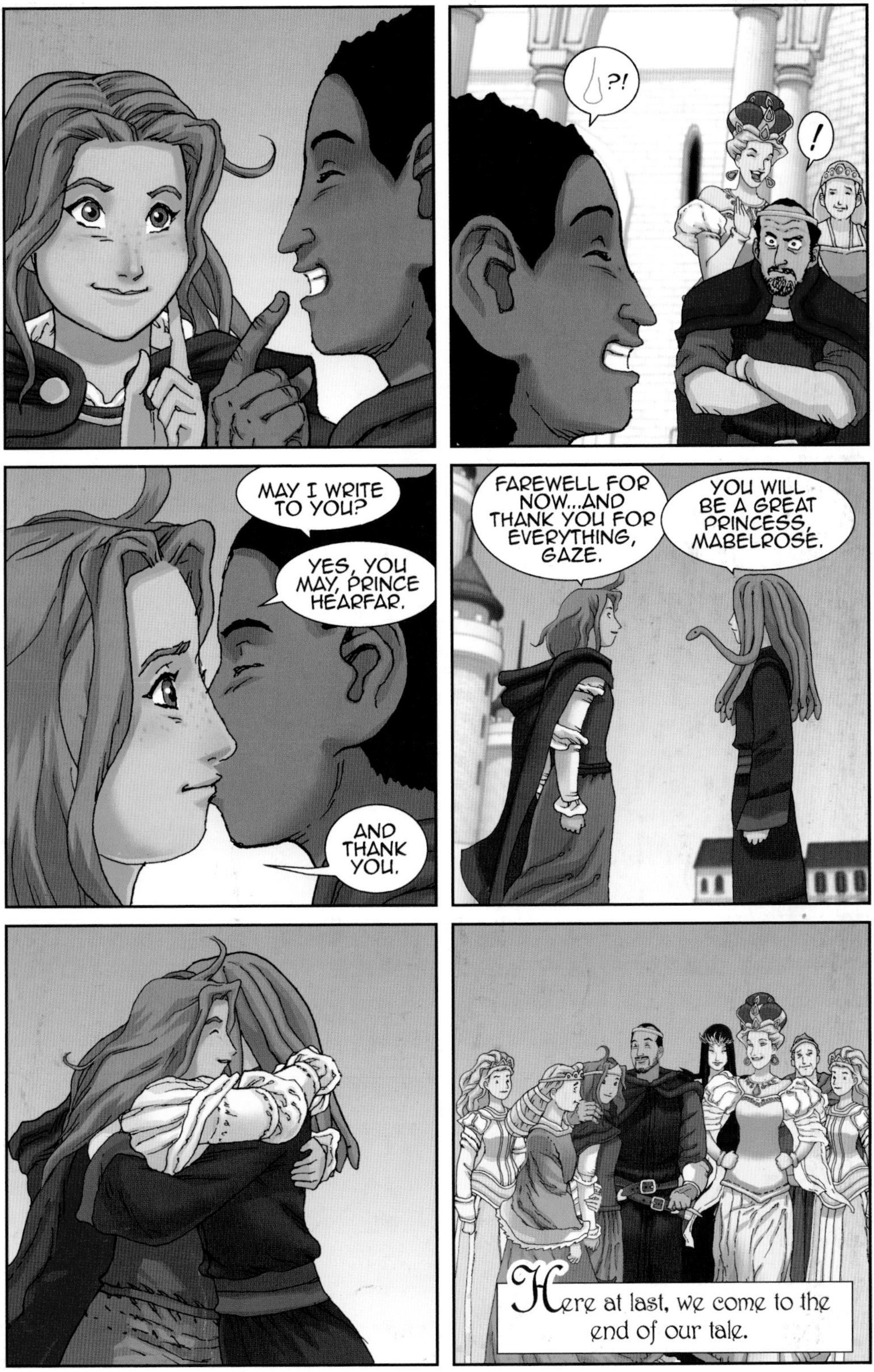
?!
!
MAY I WRITE TO YOU?
YES, YOU MAY, PRINCE HEARFAR.
AND THANK YOU.
FAREWELL FOR NOW...AND THANK YOU FOR EVERYTHING, GAZE.
YOU WILL BE A GREAT PRINCESS, MABELROSE.
Here at last, we come to the end of our tale.

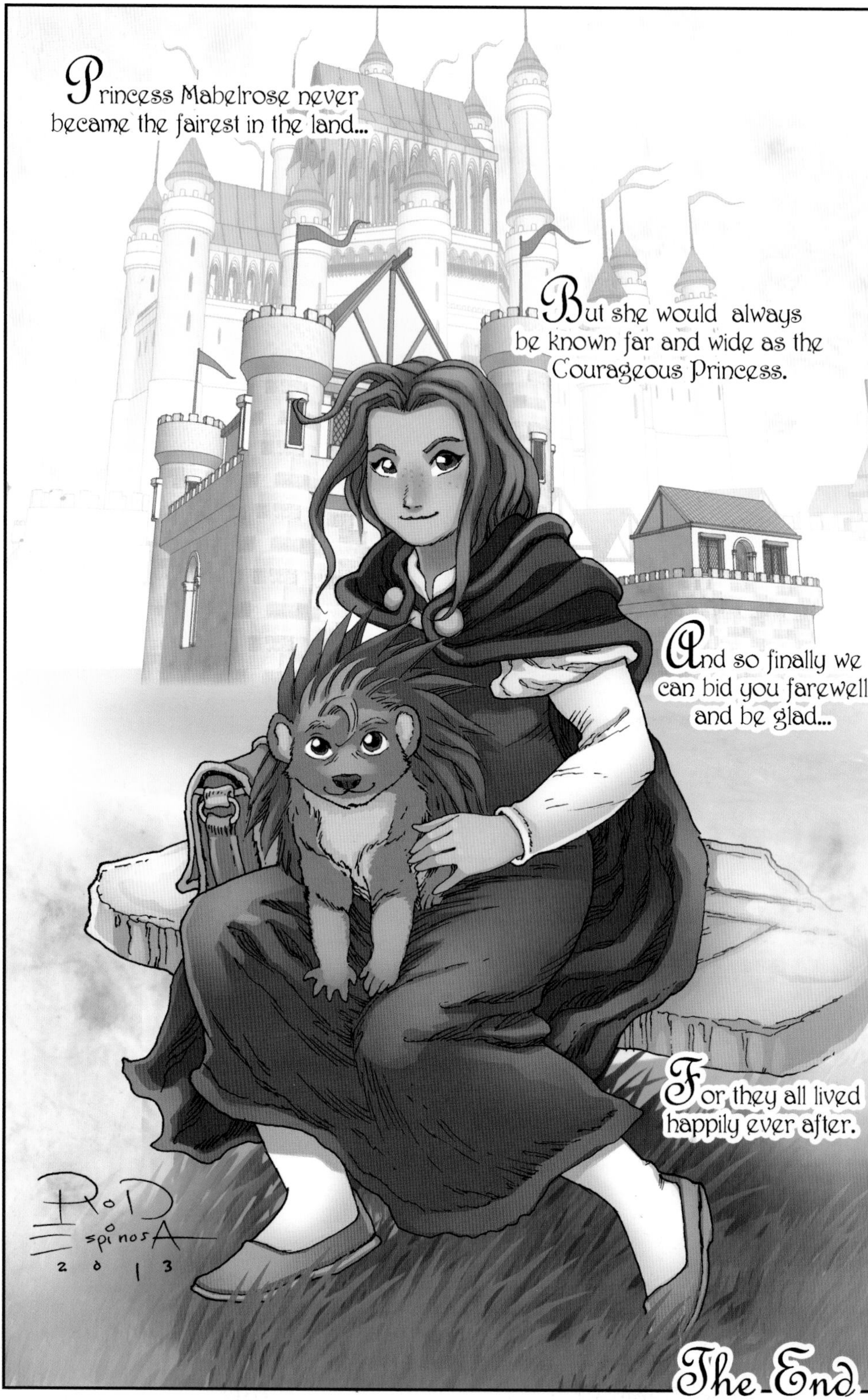
Princess Mabelrose never became the fairest in the land...
But she would always be known far and wide as the Courageous Princess.
And so finally we can bid you farewell and be glad...
For they all lived happily ever after.
Rod Espinosa 2013
The End

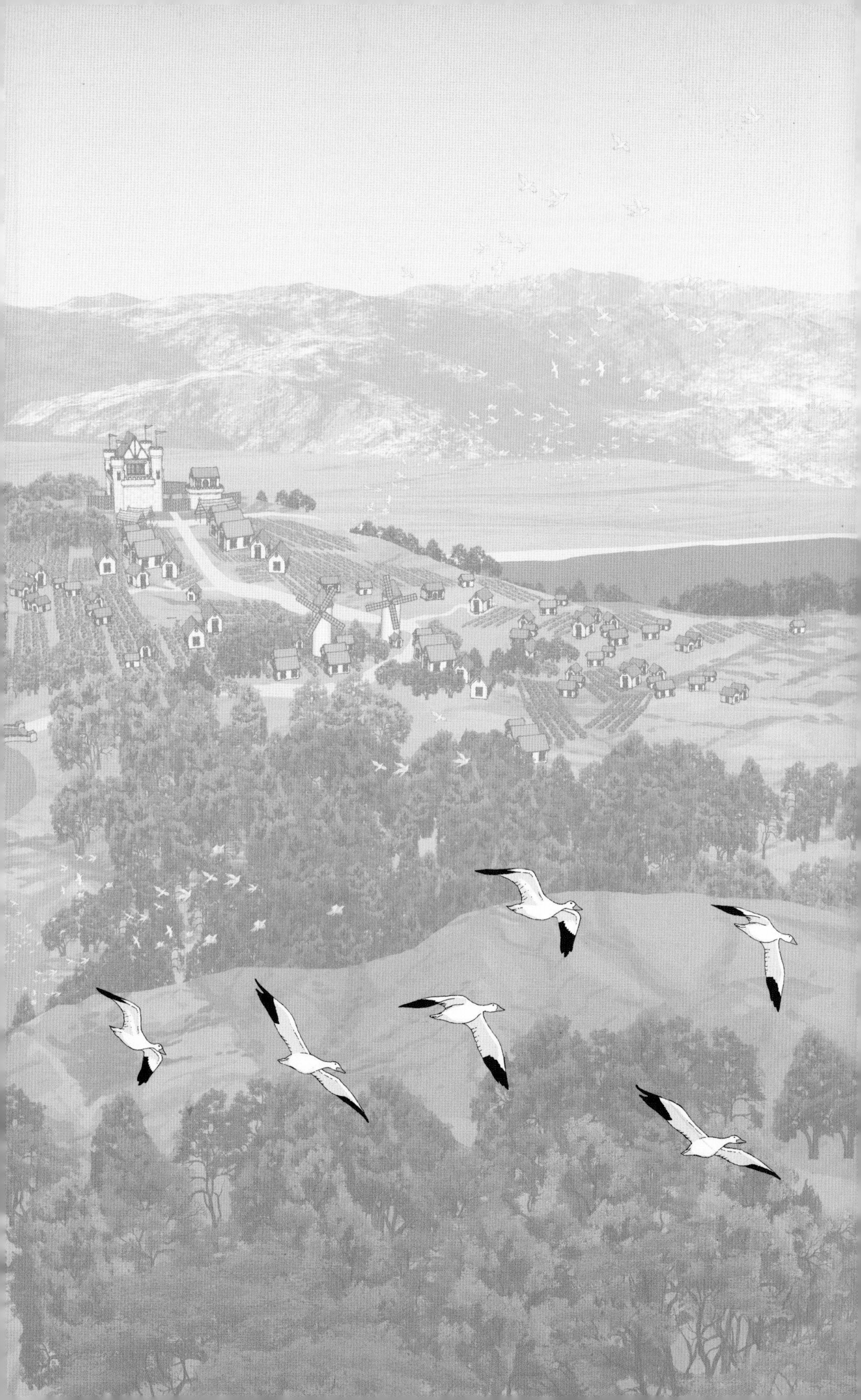

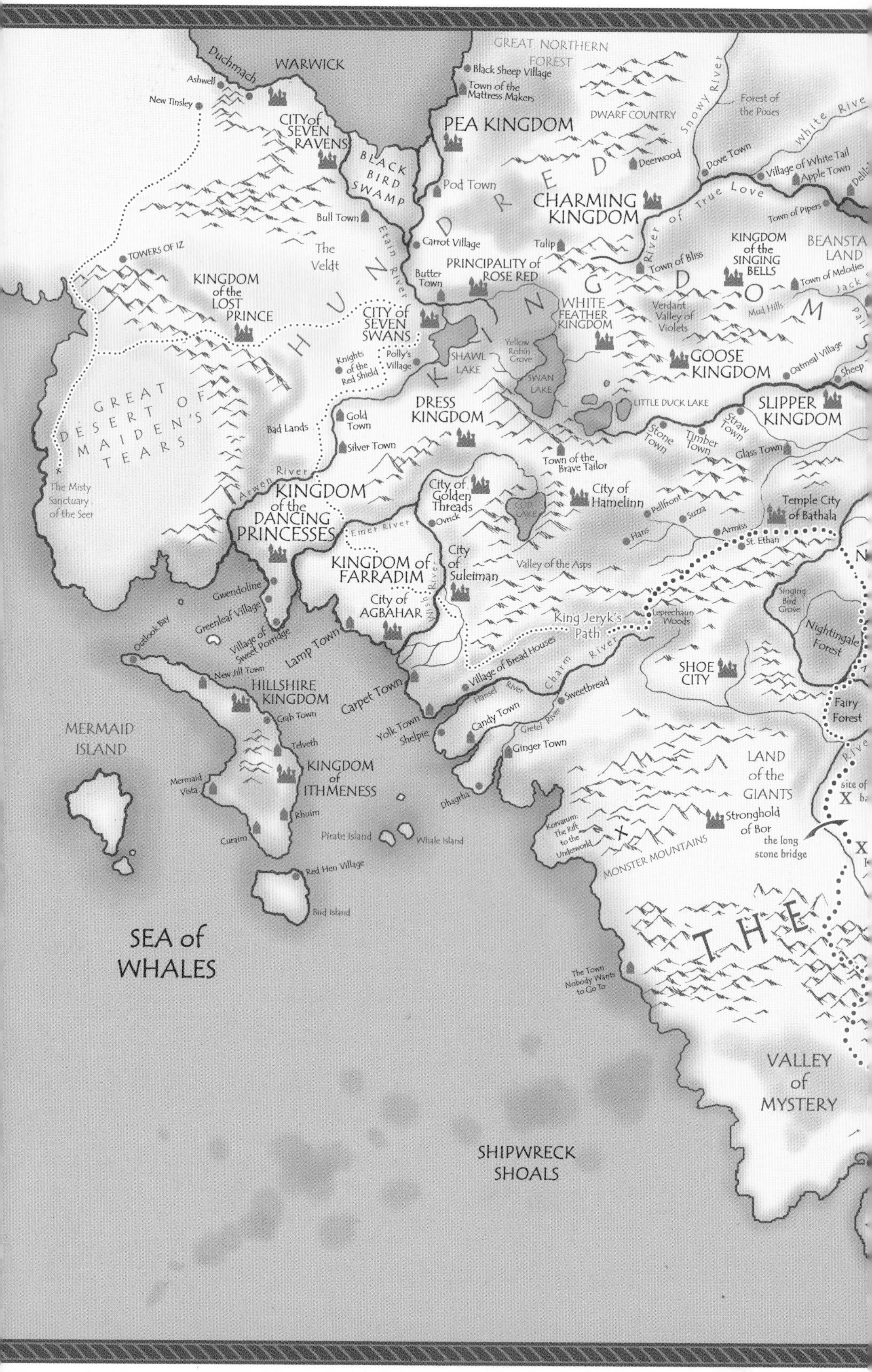
GREAT NORTHERN FOREST
WARWICK
Duchmach
Ashwell
New Tinsley
Black Sheep Village
Town of the Mattress Makers
Snowy River
Forest of the Pixies
White River
DWARF COUNTRY
CITY of SEVEN RAVENS
PEA KINGDOM
BLACK BIRD SWAMP
Deerwood
Dove Town
Village of White Tail
Apple Town
Pod Town
River of True Love
CHARMING KINGDOM
Town of Pipers
Bull Town
Etain River
Carrot Village
Tulip
KINGDOM of the SINGING BELLS
The Veldt
TOWERS OF IZ
PRINCIPALITY of ROSE RED
Town of Bliss
Butter Town
KINGDOM of the LOST PRINCE
WHITE FEATHER KINGDOM
Verdant Valley of Violets
Mud Hills
Town of Melodies
CITY of SEVEN SWANS
Yellow Robin Grove
SHAWL LAKE
SWAN LAKE
Knights of the Red Shield
Polly's Village
GOOSE KINGDOM
Oatmeal Village
GREAT DESERT OF MAIDEN'S TEARS
DRESS KINGDOM
LITTLE DUCK LAKE
SLIPPER KINGDOM
Gold Town
Bad Lands
Silver Town
Stone Town
Timber Town
Straw Town
Glass Town
Town of the Brave Tailor
The Misty Sanctuary of the Seer
Arwen River
KINGDOM of the DANCING PRINCESSES
City of Golden Threads
COD LAKE
City of Hamelinn
Pellfront
Temple City of Bathala
Ovrick
Suzza
Emer River
Hans
Armiss
St. Ethan
KINGDOM of FARRADIM
City of Suleiman
Valley of the Asps
Wish River
Singing Bird Grove
Gwendoline
City of AGBAHAR
Greenleaf Village
Outlook Bay
Village of Sweet Porridge
Lamp Town
King Jeryk's Path
Leprechaun Woods
Nightingale Forest
Village of Bread Houses
Charm River
New Jill Town
HILLSHIRE KINGDOM
Carpet Town
SHOE CITY
Hansel River
Sweetbread
Fairy Forest
Crab Town
Candy Town
Gretel River
Yolk Town
Shelpie
Ginger Town
MERMAID ISLAND
Telveth
KINGDOM of ITHMENESS
LAND of the GIANTS
Mermaid Vista
Dhagrha
Rhuim
Stronghold of Bor
Korvarum: The Rift to the Underworld
Curaim
Pirate Island
Whale Island
the long stone bridge
MONSTER MOUNTAINS
Red Hen Village
Bird Island
SEA of WHALES
THE
The Town Nobody Wants to Go To
VALLEY of MYSTERY
SHIPWRECK SHOALS

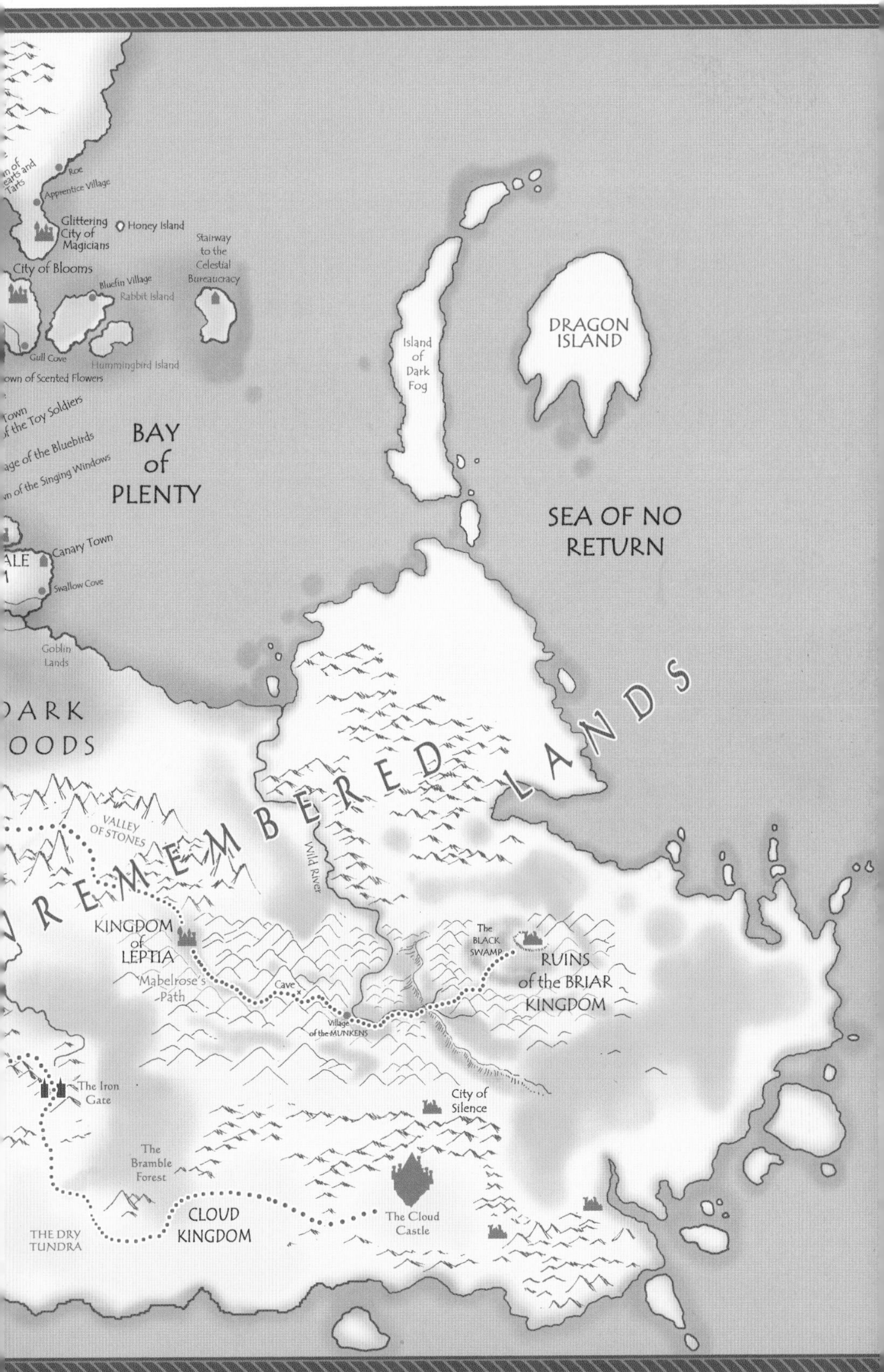
Roe
Apprentice Village
Glittering City of Magicians
Honey Island
Stairway to the Celestial Bureaucracy
City of Blooms
Bluefin Village
Rabbit Island
Gull Cove
Hummingbird Island
Island of Dark Fog
DRAGON ISLAND
BAY of PLENTY
SEA OF NO RETURN
Canary Town
Swallow Cove
Goblin Lands
REMEMBERED LANDS
VALLEY OF STONES
Wild River
KINGDOM of LEPTIA
Mabelrose's Path
Cave
Village of the MUNKENS
The BLACK SWAMP
RUINS of the BRIAR KINGDOM
The Iron Gate
City of Silence
The Bramble Forest
CLOUD KINGDOM
The Cloud Castle
THE DRY TUNDRA

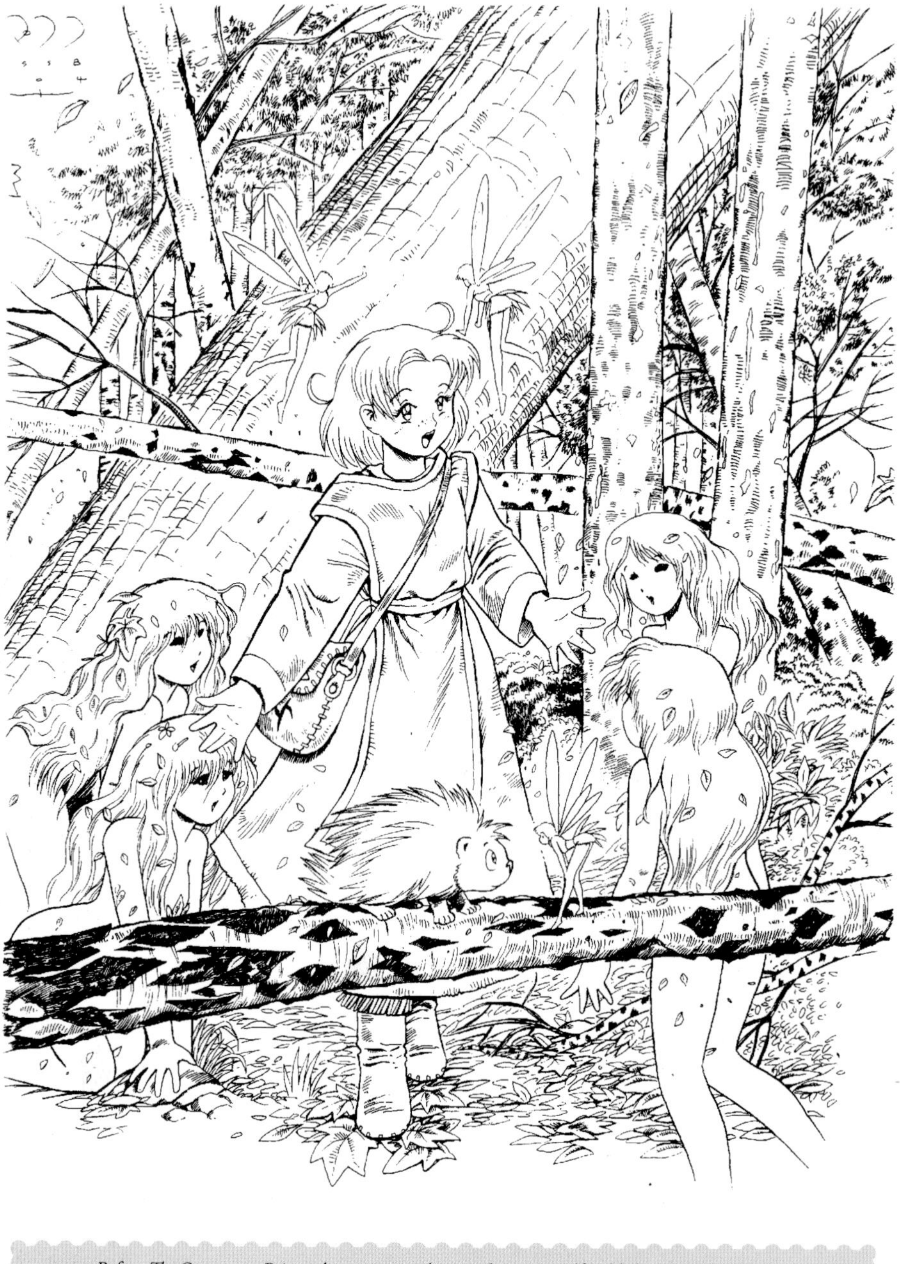

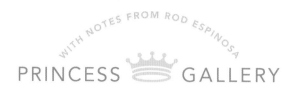

Before *The Courageous Princess* became a graphic novel, it was a self-published prose book with spot illustrations. This was one of the illustrations, where Mabelrose encounters some kindly fairies. Generally harmless, they wanted her to stay in their grove forever as their friend.

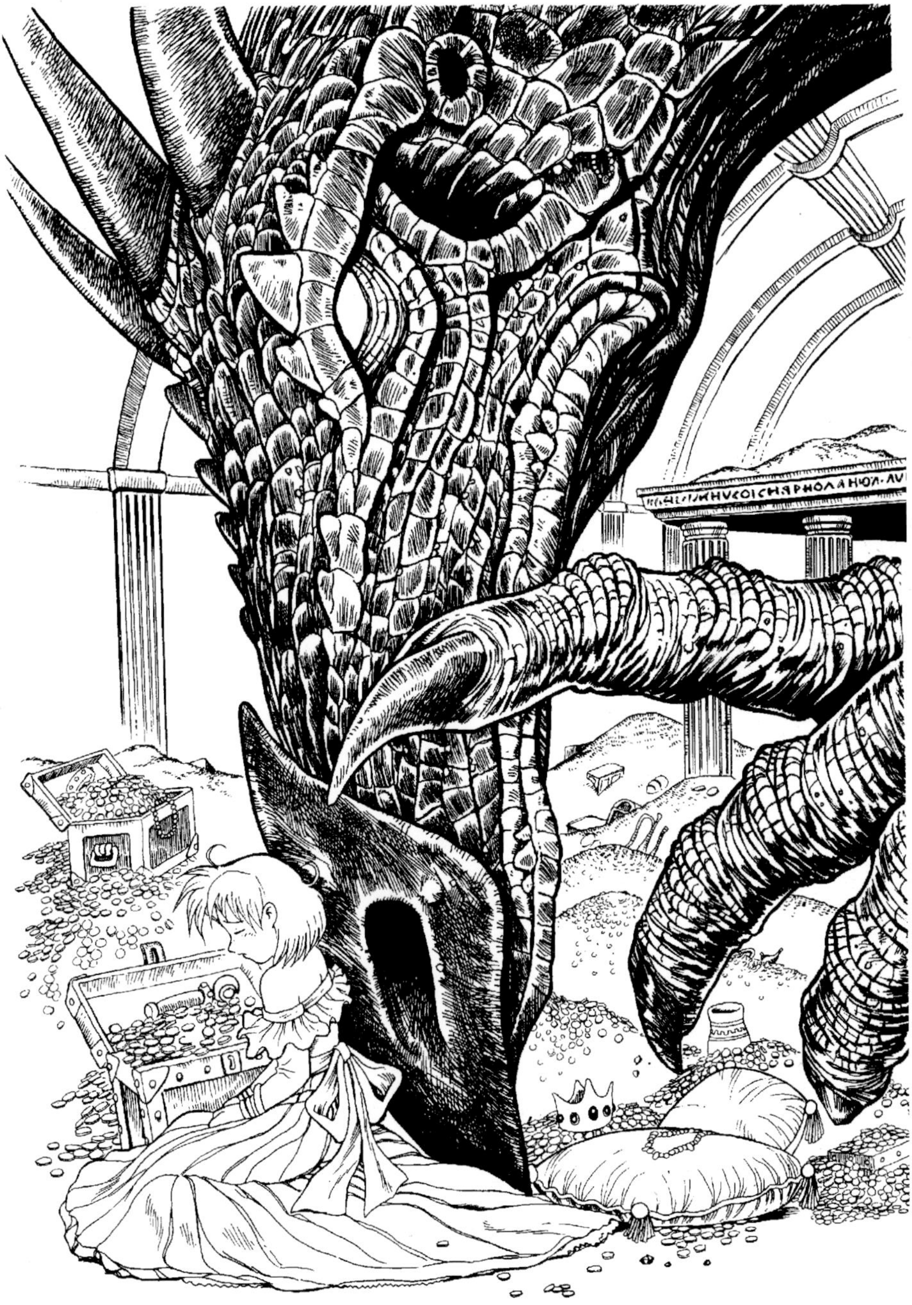

Some of the prose book's illustrations were adapted to the graphic novel. This particular drawing was cut from the graphic novel for scripting reasons. There wasn't a proper place to put it in the sequences within the dragon's castle.

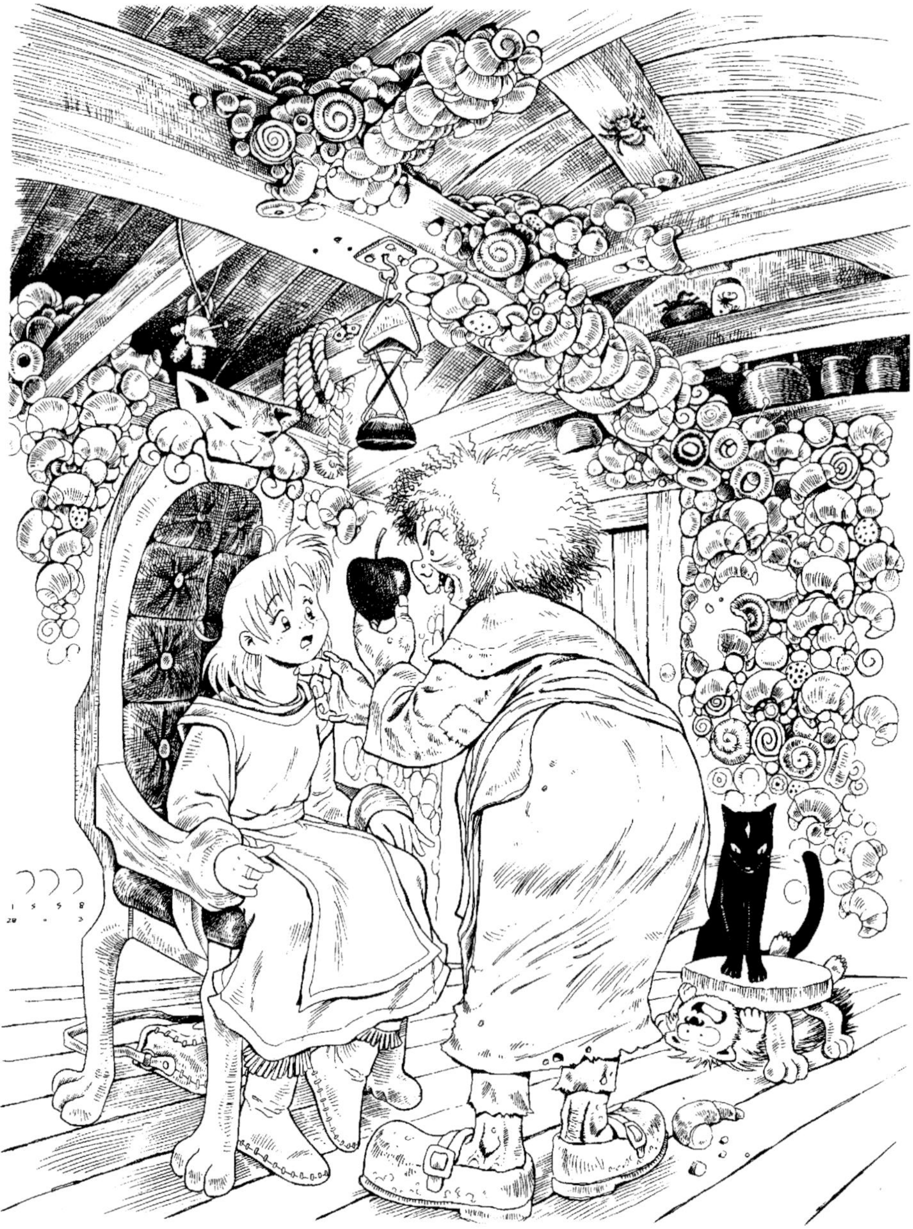

Another of the illustrations from the prose book is this scene with a witch in a gingerbread house. Mabelrose encountered her as she escaped the kingdom of Leptia. In the graphic novels, the witch was reimagined as Mem, who is a more conflicted and interesting character. The grasping chair was moved to the Lord Commander's tower, where Mabelrose is able to free herself the same way she did in the original story—by stomping on the chair's foot.

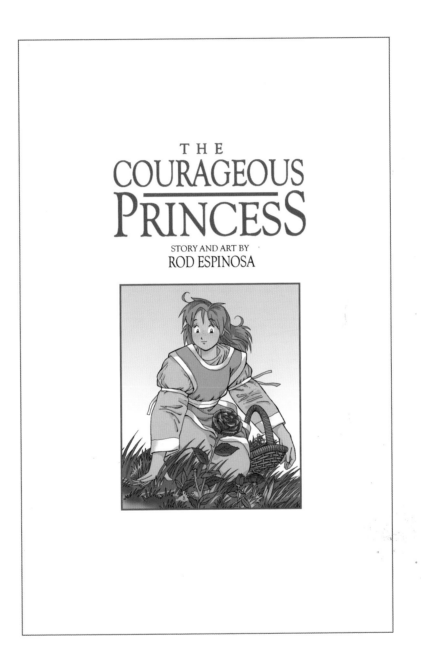

THE
COURAGEOUS
PRINCESS

STORY AND ART BY
ROD ESPINOSA

The Courageous Princess Volume 1 was first released in three separate chapters. This was the first chapter's cover.

THE
COURAGEOUS
PRINCESS
THE QUEST FOR HOME

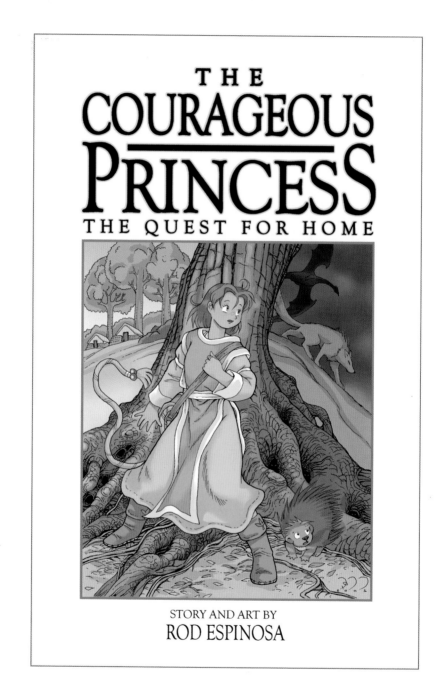

STORY AND ART BY
ROD ESPINOSA

The second chapter's cover. The large wolf that tracks Mabelrose for the dragon, shown on this cover, was inspired by a similar animal villain in the 1984 film *The NeverEnding Story*.

THE
COURAGEOUS
PRINCESS
THE KINGDOM OF LEPTIA

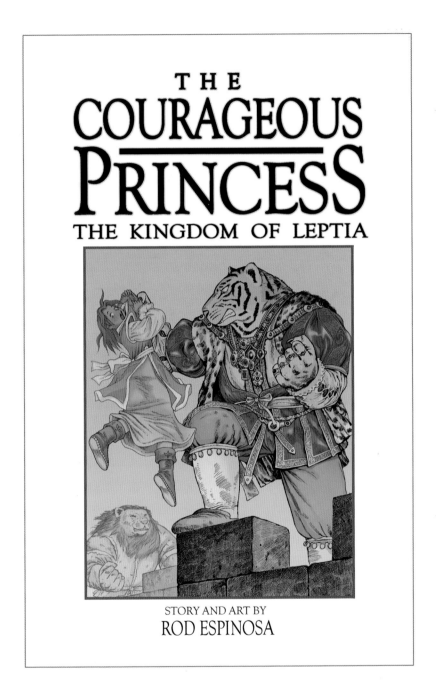

STORY AND BY
ROD ESPINOSA

This is the third chapter's cover (and my favorite). Incidentally, this cover was also a repurposed spot illustration from the original prose book. Anthropomorphic characters are a favorite story element of mine, going back to Walt Disney's 1973 animated feature film *Robin Hood*.

MASTERPIECE EDITION

THE
COURAGEOUS
PRINCESS

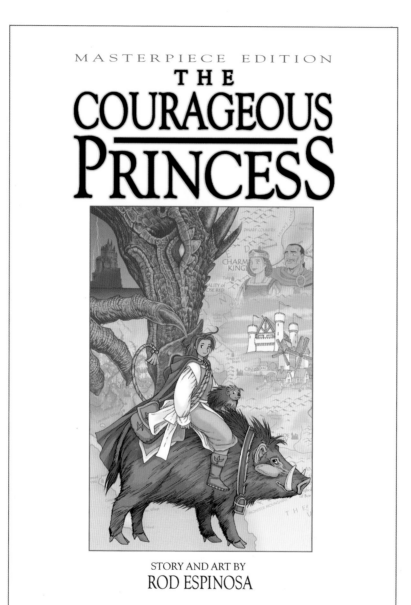

STORY AND ART BY
ROD ESPINOSA

The cover for the first collection of *The Courageous Princess*, published by Antarctic Press.

*B*orn in the Philippines and now residing in Texas, Rod Espinosa is the author and/or illustrator of more than forty-five comics and graphic novels for children and young adults. His wide range of work has covered everything from biographies of American historical figures, to graphic-novel adaptations of the works of William Shakespeare, Charles Dickens, and Lewis Carroll; from benefit books for the World Health Organization and the relief efforts for Typhoon Haiyan, to science fiction and fairy tales.

Rod's works have won him a number of nominations and awards from around the world:

2000 — Ignatz Awards for Promising New Talent and Outstanding Artist for *The Courageous Princess*

2002 — Eisner Award nomination for Best Title for Younger Readers for *The Courageous Princess*

2006 — Max and Moritz Prize nomination for Best Comic for Children for *Neotopia*

2008 — Winner of an international competition to be the artist for *Luís Figo and the World Tuberculosis Cup*, an educational comic book sponsored by the Stop TB Partnership and the World Health Organization

OTHER BOOKS BY

ROD ESPINOSA

THE
COURAGEOUS
PRINCESS
BEYOND THE HUNDRED KINGDOMS
ROD ESPINOSA

THE
COURAGEOUS
PRINCESS
THE UNREMEMBERED LANDS
ROD ESPINOSA

THE
COURAGEOUS
PRINCESS
THE DRAGON QUEEN
ROD ESPINOSA

THE COURAGEOUS PRINCESS
VOLUME 1: BEYOND THE HUNDRED KINGDOMS
THIRD EDITION

Once upon a time, a greedy dragon kidnapped a beloved princess . . . but if you think she just waited around for some charming price to rescue her, then you're in for a surprise! Princess Mabelrose may not be the fairest of the land, but she has enough brains and bravery to fend for herself in a fantasy world of danger and adventure!

ISBN 978-1-61655-722-5 / $19.99

THE COURAGEOUS PRINCESS
VOLUME 2: THE UNREMEMBERED LANDS

ISBN 978-1-61655-723-2 / $19.99

THE COURAGEOUS PRINCESS
VOLUME 3: THE DRAGON QUEEN

ISBN 978-1-61655-724-9/ $19.99

Lewis Carroll's
Alice in Wonderland
Adapted and Illustrated by Rod Espinosa

Charles Dickens's
A CHRISTMAS CAROL

ALICE IN WONDERLAND

ISBN 978-1-61655-046-2 / $19.99

A CHRISTMAS CAROL: THE NIGHT THAT CHANGED THE LIFE OF ELIZA SCROOGE

ISBN 978-1-59582-991-7 / $19.99

DARK HORSE BOOKS

DarkHorse.com

AVAILABLE AT YOUR LOCAL COMICS SHOP OR BOOKSTORE | TO FIND A COMICS SHOP IN YOUR AREA, CALL 1-888-266-4226
For more information or to order direct: **On the web:** DarkHorse.com. **E-mail:** mailorder@darkhorse.com. **Phone:** 1-800-862-0052 Mon.–Fri. 9 AM to 5 PM Pacific Time.

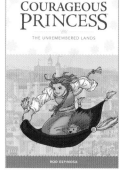

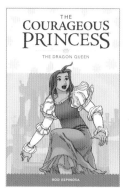

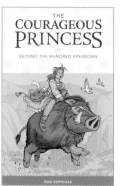